Together for Christmas

Carol Rivers, whose family comes from the Isle of Dogs, East London, now lives in Dorset. Visit www.carolrivers.com and follow her on Facebook and Twitter @carol_rivers

Also by Carol Rivers

Lizzie of Langley Street
Bella of Bow Street
Lily of Love Lane
Eve of the Isle
East End Angel
In the Bleak Midwinter
East End Jubilee (*previously* Rose of Ruby Street)
A Sister's Shame
Cockney Orphan (*previously* Connie of Kettle Street)
A Wartime Christmas

Together for Christmas

CAROL RIVERS

SIMON & SCHUSTER

London · New York · Sydney · Toronto · New Delhi

A CBS COMPANY

First published in Great Britain by Simon & Schuster UK Ltd, 2014
This paperback edition published 2014
A CBS COMPANY

1 3 5 7 9 10 8 6 4 2

Simon & Schuster UK Ltd
1st Floor
222 Gray's Inn Road
London WC1X 8HB

www.simonandschuster.co.uk

Simon & Schuster Australia, Sydney
Simon & Schuster India, New Delhi

A CIP catalogue record for this book is available from the British Library

Paperback ISBN: 978-1-47116-877-2
EBOOK ISBN: 978-1-47113-131-8

Typeset by Hewer Text UK Ltd, Edinburgh
Printed and bound in Great Britain by CPI Group (UK) Ltd, Croydon CR0 4YY

For the Fallen

Acknowledgements

This year, 2014, has been a great year for me. I would like to acknowledge the reviewers and readers who have kindly recorded the book's journey on Amazon, Twitter, Facebook, blogs and websites of all shapes and sizes. I hope you know by now how much I appreciate your feedback.

This is my first year working with my skilled and supportive editor, Jo Dickinson, and inspirational agent, Judith Murdoch. It has been wonderful! Thank you. I am more than grateful to all the guys and gals at Simon & Schuster, who make everything flow so seamlessly en route to publication.

Prologue

August 1914

Flora Shine smiled at her watery double shimmering on the surface of the Serpentine in London's Hyde Park. But all too soon her reflection disappeared, lost in the ripples that spread towards the excited revellers on the far bank.

'Just look at them silly chaps!' exclaimed Hilda Jones, Flora's best friend. 'You'd think Britain had won the conflict already from the way they're carrying on. And it was only four days ago the prime minister announced we are at war!'

'And now Mr Asquith's calling for our boys to volunteer,' said Flora. She was not for war at all, though watching the rejoicing crowds today it seemed that the rest of the country disagreed with her.

Hilda nodded, causing her brown curls to bounce on her leg-of-mutton sleeves. 'Just listen to 'em, boasting they'll teach the kaiser a lesson he'll never forget.'

'The kaiser should have accepted Britain's help after Franz Ferdinand and his wife were assassinated,' Flora said knowledgeably. 'Instead, he took offence and in no time at all, the Austrians declared war on Serbia.'

'I don't even know where Serbia is,' said Hilda.

'Serbia is near Russia and the Russians are on Serbia's side,' Flora began to explain. 'France, who is Russia's ally, was forced to join in. And Germany stuck with the Austrians, declaring war on Russia and France. So if you look on a map—'

'Politics befuddle me brain,' Hilda interrupted. 'But I don't mind the sight of a nicely turned-out uniform.'

Unperturbed by her friend's disinterest, Flora stretched out on the soft green grass, arranging her long skirt modestly over her ankles. 'A dirty-brown colour and rough material doesn't appeal to me in the least.'

'Bet you wouldn't mind an admiring wink from a handsome young soldier, though?' Unlike her friend, Hilda tugged up her skirt to reveal an enticing three inches of ankle above her laced boot. 'Neither of us have sweethearts, do we? What's to stop us from finding two nice fellows from the army?'

'No,' Flora swiftly replied. 'A soldier might be wounded or killed.'

'But just think,' said Hilda, a mischievous twinkle in her big brown eyes, 'since you're a nurse you could cure him. That is, if he didn't end up stone-cold dead before you could lay your hands on him.'

Flora frowned at her friend's mockery. 'War is a solemn matter, Hilda. And anyway, I'm not a qualified nurse.' Her sunny blue eyes widened under her fringe of strawberry lashes. 'I'm just a doctor's assistant.'

'Don't seem to matter to your Dr Tapper, does it?' said Hilda. 'He calls you nurse and insists you wear that posh blue uniform.'

'Only because the patients expect it,' said Flora, feeling a little hurt. 'Dr Tapper says the sick and desperate need to see signs of medical authority. Not, of course, that I have any,' she added hurriedly.

'Hark at you!' Hilda spluttered, looking astonished. 'If I was one of your patients, I'd cut me tongue out before I'd dare answer you back.'

Flora chuckled and snatched Hilda's parasol. She gently poked Hilda in the side with it.

'Ouch! You see?' said Hilda. 'You're a real sergeant major when you want to be.' She squirmed away from the parasol as the tears of laughter slipped down her pink cheeks.

'And you're no shrinking violet yourself, Hilda Jones.' Flora chuckled. 'You're never lost for a word or two, especially when poor Mrs Bell asks for your help.'

Hilda stopped laughing and lifted her dimpled chin. 'It's not my job to slave in the kitchen. Mrs Bell seems to forget she has Aggie for the scullery and she piles all her work on muggins here. As a matter of fact, I'm thinking of changing me job. I'll never amount to much if I stay there.'

'You could do worse, much worse,' warned Flora.

'I'm sure I could do much *better*,' Hilda argued. 'After all, it's two years now since we left the orphanage. Time for a change, I'm sure.'

'But you were in raptures when Sister Patricia found you the position. It was like going to heaven, you said.'

'It's more like purgatory now,' muttered Hilda with a scowl. 'I'm at the beck and call of down-and-outs and drunks. Even the smell of the soup makes me feel sick. And then, after wearing meself out on the ungrateful rabble, I'm expected to have her ladyship's private rooms all spic and span for her visits. Sometimes, you know, I'm quite dizzy with fatigue.'

'You're doing God's work,' Flora replied kindly. 'There's no better calling in life, according to the Sally Army.'

'Well, I'm no Salvationist!' Hilda burst out. 'I'd never wear one of them funny bonnets for a start.' Her ample bust heaved indignantly under her blouse. 'Imagine banging a tambourine all day. I wouldn't be caught dead going into taverns to beg for alms. Charity might be God's work, but it ain't mine.'

Flora shook her head disapprovingly. 'I've never known anyone so particular as you, Hilda. 'Specially as we're orphans and lucky to have jobs. You could have ended up in the workhouse if it hadn't been for the nuns of St Boniface.'

At this comment, Hilda recoiled. 'The workhouse? Never!' She wrinkled her proud little nose. 'Mother would never have let such a thing happen. She'd have taken me off to a better life if she hadn't been killed by that perishing steam from the orphanage laundry.'

'It was a job, after all.' Flora didn't remind Hilda that the nuns had practically saved Rose Jones from a life on the streets. She knew that would upset her friend.

Hilda scowled at the young men who were now throwing their hats, ties and shirts into the Serpentine. 'Men can lark about and show off. But we women can't act like idiots and strip down to our knickers. We'd get arrested in the blink of an eye. That is, if the bluebottles could run fast enough to catch us!'

Once again, they were smiling.

'Hilda, you don't sound like the God-fearing young lady the nuns raised you to be.'

'I could never be as holy as you, dear girl. In fact, now I come to think of it, these days, you're the very image of Sister Patricia herself. All chin and long nose under that silly white wimple.'

Flora ignored the face that Hilda pulled. 'Sister Patricia was strict but she was kind. We were taught that being humble is what God wants of us.'

Hilda snorted loudly. 'Answer me this then. Why ain't the king humble if it's what God wants?'

'Perhaps he is,' Flora replied uncertainly.

'Don't be daft. He don't come to the East End and put right all the slums. He don't shake your hand or ask how you are. I reckon we was taught to be humble to keep us in our place. God is on the side of the well-to-do. Just like the king is.'

'That's an awful thing to say, Hilda.'

'Do you think so? It seems sense to me.'

Flora considered Hilda's outburst; it was quite a revelation. 'I didn't know you felt like that about God. Or even the king.'

'I didn't know meself until I said it.' A long moment passed before Hilda added, 'You being humble an' all is why the nuns gave you the good job, and sent me into service.'

Flora allowed a shocked breath to escape. 'Is that what you really think, Hilda? That the nuns favoured me above you? Well, you're quite wrong there. I was sent to Dr Tapper because I'd assisted the nuns in the convent infirmary and had some experience with the sick. That was the only reason. And as for being humble, it's what we were taught. You should be grateful we had an education. And a good one at that.'

Hilda turned away, mumbling to herself.

'You could have worked in the infirmary too, if you'd volunteered.' Flora felt it was unfair of Hilda to think she was hard done by. 'The sick children liked your sunny smile when you visited them. Even though it was only once or twice,' she added cautiously.

But Hilda only shuddered. 'I ain't got a strong stomach.'

Flora smiled. Hilda *was* squeamish. She had been known to faint at the briefest sight of blood.

'I didn't even like looking at the cross in chapel,' Hilda admitted with a rueful grin. 'I hated seeing a dead body. It felt like we was worshipping death, not life.'

'Hilda!' Flora was hearing things from Hilda she'd never heard before. 'What's come over you? Why are you talking this way? Weren't we happy at the orphanage? You, me and Will – just the three of us, as close together as a real family could be?'

Hilda plucked a few shiny blades of grass and leaned forward to scatter them on the water. 'We were close – are close,' she agreed, though with a reluctance that Flora couldn't fail to miss. 'You and Will are family to me. But it's just – just that . . .'

'What?' Flora urged, confused.

'Oh, I don't know!' Hilda threw up her hands. 'Perhaps it's all this talk of war. But you see, I don't want to end up being a skivvy like Mum. I want . . .' She hesitated, the words trembling on her full lips. 'I want bracelets and rings that sparkle like boiled sweets in the sunshine. Like Lady Hailing wears on her white neck and slim wrists. I want shoes that are real leather with bows and frills. Ones that ain't worn and scuffed at the heel. I want a soft bed to lie in and a bedroom far away from the old biddy next door who snores and farts all night.'

'Mrs Bell would have a fit if she could hear you,' Flora said, disapprovingly.

'Well, it's true.'

Flora couldn't understand these complaints. Was the change in her friend's character to do with becoming fifteen in April, just four months before Flora's own fifteenth birthday in August? Or was it, as Hilda suggested, the turmoil of the nation that was turning them all a little barmy on this sunny August day?

'Just look at those idiots!' Hilda pointed to the young men, who were now boasting to some young women. The girls scurried away, giggling behind their gloved hands. 'They're happy, wouldn't you say? Really happy. They're about to leave their boring old jobs for a new life.'

'Yes, but an unknown one.'

For a while they sat in silence. Then Hilda snatched up her straw hat and planted it on her head. 'Well, I'm bored. How much longer must we wait for Will? It's past one o'clock. Why can't he arrive on time for once?'

Flora searched the crowds for Will's tall, gangling figure. He looked like a lost puppy with his shaggy golden hair and big blue eyes peeping out from under his curls, Flora thought with amusement. Who would think that Will Boniface was a foundling and hadn't even got a name of his own, just as she hadn't. The nuns had chosen their names, even their birthdays, which were taken from the day they had been found outside the convent. Will was older by two years than herself and Hilda. But despite the age gap, he had somehow attached himself to them.

'Let's wait just a few minutes longer,' she said, and ignored Hilda's protesting frown.

'I had to nearly twist Mrs Bell's arm to let me come today,' Hilda muttered. 'She complained she'd have to do all the chores, as Aggie is in the family way again.'

'Aggie is blessed, then, to have such a kind sponsor as Lady Hailing.'

Hilda drew herself upright. 'Well, Lady Hailing is a do-gooder, ain't she? One of them "slummers" that the newspapers write about, what give their fortunes to the poor. But I've decided I want to work for real gentry.'

'Lady Hailing *is* real gentry,' Flora said in surprise.

Hilda pursed her lips and folded her arms across her chest, just as she always had as a little girl when in one of her stubborn moods. Flora reflected on their life at St Boniface's Orphanage in the heart of the East End. It had been hard. But though it was a thousand times better than the workhouse, Hilda hadn't always appreciated it. Flora saw Hilda in her mind's eye, a sprat of a girl, barely eight. She had been allowed by the nuns to live with her mother, Rose, in the laundry outhouse. Flora could still remember Hilda's grief after Rose's death. Poor Hilda, a proud little girl who refused to think of herself as just another waif and stray added to the nuns' long list of dependants.

'Oh, where is that naughty boy?' demanded Hilda. 'You don't think he's stood us up for a girl, do you?'

'Will wouldn't do that.'

'He's seventeen in December. Quite old enough for courting.' Hilda jumped to her feet and dragged Flora up with her. 'Come on, let's stretch our legs.'

'Will's too thoughtful to stand us up.' Flora placed her own straw hat on her head and tucked her golden ringlets behind her ears. 'Besides, Will would need a very special girl, someone kind and loyal, who would look after him.'

'Like us, you mean?' Hilda laughed.

'We'd need to investigate her,' Flora agreed with a giggle. 'Size her up. Put her to the test and see that she came up to our standards.'

'Which are high – in Will's case,' Hilda agreed, as she slipped her hand over Flora's arm. Swinging her parasol, she glanced across the lake. Some of the young men had jumped into the water.

'Our Will is a well-mannered boy, not like them, the tearaways.' Hilda giggled as the swimmers called out and waved. 'Oh, you'll be lucky, m'dears, we've got high standards!' Hilda called back, then, turning to Flora, she whispered, 'The cheek of it! Thinking we'd look twice at drowned rats like them. Oh, watch out!' Hilda pulled Flora back with a jolt as a pony and trap sped towards them on the path a few feet away. Flora gazed up into the florid, moustached face of the driver who quite openly winked at her.

'The old devil!' Hilda said angrily as the trap passed. 'He wouldn't dare to do that if we was real ladies. Did you see his backside, bulging out of his breeches like cream from a Lyons scone?'

They burst into laughter again and were still giggling when a group of women approached them. Flora stared at their big floppy hats and bands across their chests. They were handing out pieces of paper.

'Join our movement, why don't you?' one young woman asked them. 'Read this and it will tell you all about the National Union of Women's Suffrage. If it were up to women, there would be no wars.'

'Yes, but would you get us all arrested instead?' Flora asked. She'd heard of the force-feeding the Suffragettes had suffered in prison. She didn't hold with the angry crowds of screaming women either, or the protests that caused riots in the streets. There had been many casualties that Flora had read of in the newspapers.

The woman smiled. 'Don't you want to have the right to vote, my dear?'

'I don't know enough about politics,' responded Flora. The nuns had taught them never to cause trouble in society and always obey rules and regulations.

'If we're successful, you'll have a say in how we run the country. We'll have equal rights with men.' The crowd of elegant, upper-class ladies began to move on, waving their papers and flags.

'I wouldn't mind joining the Suffragette cause,' Hilda admitted. 'But these women are the posh lot from up West. You've got to be a lady to join them.'

Flora looked sternly at her friend. 'Hilda, you're every bit as good as any of them.'

Hilda stopped and gazed down at her scraped-leather boots. 'If I was dressed nice and didn't drop me aitches I might pass muster.'

'Flora! Hilda!'

They both turned to see a slender young man hurrying across the park. His curly blond hair flopped over his blue eyes. His smile was eager.

'Will, it's so very good to see you.' Flora embraced him, quickly stepping aside for Hilda to kiss his cheek.

'You're late,' Hilda scolded. She took one of Will's arms and Flora took his other. 'But we forgive you.'

'A baker's life is a temperamental one, girls, as I've told you before.' Will's deep blue eyes twinkled in his extremely pasty face. 'If the bread bakes limp or the bagels go square, the apprentice is brought back by the scruff of his neck and stood over the boiling ovens again.'

'I've never seen a square bagel,' said Hilda sceptically.

'And as for limp bread – well, whoever bakes limp bread should be prosecuted!' Flora grinned as Will assumed a hurt expression.

'There's no sympathy likely from these quarters, I can tell,' complained Will, but all the same, Flora felt his elbow squeeze tight over her arm as they began to stroll along.

'We'll forgive you for making us wait,' Hilda decided, 'just as long as you buy us an ice cream.'

'I'll buy you two,' Will replied keenly. 'Or three, if you like.'

Both girls stopped still. Flora's jaw dropped and she said, 'Have you come into money?'

'No, but I've worked my socks off in those stifling kitchens. Can't you see the bags of exhaustion under my eyes?'

'Rubbish! Your skin is as soft as a baby's!' exclaimed Hilda, unsympathetically. She thrust her hand through Will's shining cap of hair. As they spun away, teasing each other, Flora sat on a nearby bench to watch their playful larks. They scrambled like children around the tall plane trees and over the green grass, just as they had in the orphanage yard. But their only space then had been a barren quarter-acre of patchy grass, kicked muddy in winter and sand-dry in summer. Over their playground had loomed the convent of St Boniface. Its many bleak windows and draughty passages wound like a maze through the building's vast interior. Unlike Hilda, Flora had always been comforted by the sight of the rows of shiny wooden benches and fingers of chalk attached by string to squares of slate in the freezing-cold classrooms. She had been grateful for the chance to better herself. The sweet scent of incense creeping in clouds from the chapel had sent Flora eagerly to Mass, whilst Hilda had done her best to escape it. Flora sighed, lost in thought. The scenes of their childhood were as clear in her mind today as they were all those years ago.

'Well, so much for our ice creams!' Hilda gasped as she plonked herself down beside Flora. 'Will's deserted us in favour of those rebels over there.'

'What can he want with them?' Flora watched curiously as Will joined the revellers.

'Guess,' said Hilda, her cheeks flushed.

'I can't think.' Flora shrugged, her frown deepening.

'Our Will is to be a soldier!'

'A soldier? Is this a tease?'

'No.' Hilda's dark eyes were quite serious. 'Isn't it marvellous?'

'I shouldn't say so at all.' Flora shook her head, thinking Hilda must have got things wrong.

'Don't be stuffy. Soldiering will make a man of him.'

'But why does he want to be a soldier?'

'Same reason as all those other fellows,' Hilda said simply. 'Will is no exception.'

'But, but . . .' began Flora, '. . . he's just a boy.'

'You agreed yourself he was old enough to court a girl.'

'That's different,' Flora objected. 'Will's too – too *sensitive* – to fight.'

'But he's after adventure. And who can blame him?'

Flora's heart sank as she listened to her friend. They couldn't let Will go to war. 'Hilda, we must stop him.'

'How can we? And why should we?'

'Will could do very well if he keeps his job.'

'Like I would, if I stuck at Hailing House, you mean?' Hilda pouted, kicking her heels. 'Is that your advice to us both?'

Before Flora could reply, Will ran up. His pale cheeks for once were pink. 'Those chaps are volunteers for Kitchener,' he told them as he sat beside Flora. 'I'm joining them later for a rally at Buckingham Palace.'

'But you can't,' Flora said before she could stop herself. She grabbed his arm. 'Will, don't do it!'

He laughed, looking puzzled. Taking her small hands in his, he squeezed them. 'Flora, what's up?'

'You can't be recruited, Will. You must stay home.'

'But it's my duty,' he told her patiently. 'Britain must protect her little brother Belgium from Germany's marauding armies.'

'Not you,' said Flora desperately. 'You'll soon be a baker.'

At this, he laughed, throwing back his head as his curls flopped over one eye. 'I don't want to be a baker. I never have. And now I've the chance to escape it.'

'But to enlist, you must be eighteen!'

'Who is going to check on an orphanage boy?'

Flora, holding Will's slender hands tightly, looked at Hilda. 'Hilda, how can we stop him?'

But Hilda, gazing into Will's amused eyes, replied unhelpfully, 'If I was a boy, I'd volunteer too.'

'Outvoted,' Will said, drawing Flora to him and kissing her cheek. 'But thank you for caring, dearest.'

'How can you even think of shooting someone? Or worse, them shooting you?' Flora shuddered.

'It won't come to that,' Will assured her. 'The lads are certain the conflict will be over by Christmas.'

'What time is your rally?' asked Hilda. 'I'd still like that ice cream.'

Will, laughing, jumped up, took their wrists and pulled them to their feet. 'Come along then, girls. Ice creams it is. The recruitment office can wait.'

Flora allowed herself to be marched along, she in the middle now, with Hilda and Will on either arm. She wanted to join with their happy chatter, but she simply couldn't. The young man beside her would soon be wearing a fighting uniform and Hilda's restless spirit refused to be caged for long. Flora loved her friends dearly. Will and Hilda were the only family she had ever known. A brother and sister that she cherished as if they were her own blood. She didn't want things to change.

Chapter One

Nine months later

'Come now, Mr Pollard, rest easy and allow me to treat your wound.'

Flora held her breath as Dr Tapper gently persuaded the stricken man's shoulders back onto the examination couch. She heard their patient's half sob in response as he lay there. His emaciated body under the dirty cloth of his cheap suit was shaking with fear.

'Good man. Now bear with me while I see what's to be done.' Dr Tapper glanced at Flora who stood in readiness to help. 'His boot first, nurse, if you please.'

Flora had no difficulty in removing the battered boot that hid a filthy sock beneath. But at the putrid stench of infection coming from his exposed leg, she had to steady herself. After Flora eased the rough and bloodstained cloth to his knee, her eyes fell on the wound. Though she had assisted the doctor ever since leaving the orphanage three years ago, this was the worst sight she had ever witnessed.

She heard the doctor's indrawn breath and saw his grey head of hair shake almost imperceptibly. 'Why didn't you return to me sooner?' the doctor asked, as Flora took the sterilized scissors from the metal trolley and handed them to her employer. As the sodden bandages caked with pus and blood fell away, Flora found herself unable to distinguish what had once been a human leg from a mass of diseased flesh.

'I was afraid you'd chop off me leg,' said the man with a choke, trying to hide the pain that had turned his gaunt face a marble-grey.

'The decision isn't for me to make,' the doctor answered. 'Now, hold still. I shall have my nurse clean your wound the best she can. Meanwhile, I'll find you something to ease the pain.'

The man caught the doctor's arm. 'I'm no use to me family with only one leg, Dr Tapper.'

'You're even less use to them dead,' the doctor said gravely, nodding to Flora, who stood ready to repair what she could of the result of the terrible infection. 'But we won't discuss it further until I have made a thorough examination.'

Flora knew that the man would almost certainly lose his leg. When she had been present at his first visit two months ago, the doctor had judged there was some hope to save the limb. The wound had been treated at the field hospital. But, like many who were injured at the front lines carved across Europe's battlefields, many cases proved hopeless.

In just a few minutes, Dr Tapper returned with the pain-relieving Jamaican balm that was derived from arrowroot, a pap that Flora herself had helped him to prepare that morning. After she had cleansed the wound, she took the boiled application from the bowl in the doctor's hands and laid it carefully on the weeping sores that were eating down to the bone of the man's limb.

'Thank you, nurse.' Dr Tapper placed his hand on Stephen Pollard's shoulder. 'Is your wife here today?'

The man nodded, his agony causing him to writhe uncomfortably beneath the doctor's grasp.

'Nurse, will you please inform Mrs Pollard that my intention is to refer her husband to the infirmary.'

'No! No!' protested the distraught patient. 'They'll rob me of my leg for sure!'

Dr Tapper was silent. After washing her hands in the china bowl, Flora left for the waiting room. Here, every seat was taken. Despite it being late on Saturday morning, twenty or more bodies filled the small space, making it clear to Flora that the handful of wooden chairs she had arranged on the bare boards were insufficient for their needs.

Flora looked with pity at the babies wrapped in their dirt-ridden shawls, the runny-nosed, shabbily dressed toddlers who whimpered at their mothers' feet, the older patients full of the ague and vapours, together with disabled veterans of Europe's devastating war. Three younger men leaned against the peeling walls, supported by crutches and crudely made walking aids. Every face turned to her expectantly. One woman rose to her feet. Flora beckoned her.

'It's all right for some,' an older lady shouted after them. 'I've been sitting here for over an hour. All I want is something for me rheumatics.'

'Think yourself lucky!' wheezed an elderly man who occupied the chair beside her. 'I'll be dead before I'm seen, at this rate.'

Flora led the way to the small room adjoining the doctor's that she used to sterilize the equipment on a burner and help the doctor prepare his prescriptions. It was also a place she used to comfort the patients.

The smell of carbolic and herbal remedies was strong as Flora entered the tiny space. Here, Flora kept rows of bottles on the shelves in neat order; they were the doctor's armoury against disease. Smelling salts for fits of the vapours, poultices made from hot water and mustard, Sloan's Liniment for the agues, camphorated and eucalyptus oils for congestion of the lungs, arrowroot to alleviate nausea, Fuller's Earth for stings, burns and sores, and compounds of mercury and chloride that were used in emergencies to treat the bowels. There was laudanum too, and opium, for the more serious and sometimes terminal cases. She kept these under lock and key in the cabinet on the wall. On the bench below and in the cupboards were dressings and saline solutions, bandages, lints and sterilized equipment ready for use. Flora often worked at the big porcelain sink with its single tap. She kept it spotless.

'What's happening, nurse?' The young woman sat down on the only wooden chair. Flora knew Mrs Pollard was in her twenties but looked twice her age. Haggard and frail, she was old before her time.

'Your husband's wound is infected. He will have to go to the infirmary.'

'But how will we manage?' Tears came to Mrs Pollard's eyes. 'We've got four nippers and an infant. The few pennies Stephen earns are all that we have and—' She began to cough. It was a deep, racking cough that caused her to bend over and hang her head as she tried to smother the pitiful choking. Flora gave her a clean rag and the woman pressed it to her mouth. A stain glowed bright red on the white cloth.

'How long have you been sick, Mrs Pollard?' Flora took the blood-spattered cloth and threw it in the pail.

'It's only a cough.' Mrs Pollard gazed up at the shelves. 'Give me something from one of them glass bottles, won't you? Some wintergreen. Or maybe a bit of embrocation for me chest.'

'I'll ask the doctor.' Flora knew that none of the remedies on the shelf could help this young woman.

Just then the doctor walked in and heard for himself the sickly sounds the woman was making. Flora looked into his eyes. His gaze went to the cloth in the pail and he gently put his hand on Mrs Pollard's shoulder. 'The ambulance has been sent for,' he said quietly. 'Your husband must go to the infirmary.'

'No!' shrieked Mrs Pollard. She gazed tearfully up at the doctor. 'Please don't send him away.'

'I'm sorry,' Dr Tapper replied firmly. 'Now, let us see about you. How long have you been coughing like this?'

Flora left them alone and went to the waiting room. She did her best to calm the doctor's anxious patients. But she couldn't help thinking of Mrs Pollard. There was little doubt in her mind that the young woman had tuberculosis: a cruel and highly infectious disease of the lungs.

Woken by a banging on the front door, Flora left the warmth of her bed and pulled on her dressing gown. As she hurried to the sitting room she fastened back her long, tangled locks that had been kept orderly under her white cap for the working week. Flora blinked at the strong daylight streaming in through the drapes. The embers of last night's fire still glowed in the hearth and had kept the basement, which Flora and Dr Tapper always called the airey, warm.

Flora pulled back the heavy bolt and opened the door to find Hilda standing there. 'Goodness, Hilda, what are you doing here at this time of the morning?'

'Let me in, I've some terrible news.' Hilda flung herself from the basement step into Flora's sitting room. 'It's the *Lusitania*. She's been sunk.'

'But that's impossible,' replied Flora. 'Not a great liner like the *Lusitania*.'

'She was torpedoed by the Germans yesterday. Just off the Irish coast. Over a thousand passengers are missing.' With her brown curls flying around her face and her jacket unbelted at the waist, Hilda was breathless.

'Sit down.' Flora indicated the chair by the fire, with its plump cherry-red cushion. 'I'll open the curtains.'

'I can't stay long. I've got to get back to the house.' Hilda flopped down on the chair. 'Mrs Bell just told me. She heard it from her ladyship's maid. One of Lady Hailing's friends, a wife of a high-ranking government official, was on board and is unaccounted for, along with her staff.'

Light filled the room, and Flora sat down. 'What a terrible catastrophe!'

'Yes, and it's gentry who'll suffer the most losses. It's only them with money who can afford passage with the Cunard Steamship Company.'

'Does this mean all Britain's ships are at risk now?'

'Dunno. But you can't deny that this changes everything.' Hilda swallowed hurriedly. 'More men will be drafted to the Front, leaving their jobs to the women. It's already been written in the newspapers that female workers are twice as good as the men. I reckon I'd do all right for meself in a factory.'

'You'd hate it, I'm sure.'

Hilda rolled her brown eyes. 'No more than I hate the house. Anyway, what I've come to tell you is, I'm giving in me notice today. The *Lusitania* sinking is a sign.'

'But you can't, Hilda. It's a good job you've got.'

'I told you, it ain't. Mrs Bell gives me all Aggie's jobs. Aggie is worn out with her kids and husband to look after. The mistress calls on me for help in the soup kitchen, and with all me other jobs, I'm going down the very same road as Mum. She was at the nuns' beck and call. Stuck in the laundry, washing her life away in those great big tubs. Well, I won't be treated the same. I won't!'

Flora looked at her friend with sympathy, but knew things could be much worse. 'You have a roof over your head. Many girls would be envious of your position.'

'It's all right for you to say, living here at Tap House.' Hilda got up and began to pace round the comfortable room. With puzzled eyes, Flora watched her friend treading slowly over the wooden duckboards and stroking her fingers across the chintz covers that Flora had made for the fireside chairs. 'You've made it so pretty, so homely. Three rooms all to yourself, even a little kitchen and scullery. I'd be very happy to live here.'

'Hilda, you have very pleasant quarters at the house.'

'I'm glad you think so,' Hilda replied sourly. 'A room in the attic not big enough to swing a cat.'

'Compared to our dormitory at the orphanage—' Flora began.

'You're right,' Hilda interrupted. 'I came from one prison and now I live in another.'

Flora smiled. 'Hilda, such drama!'

'Added to my imprisonment,' Hilda continued sulkily,

'Mrs Bell insists I finish Aggie's silver polishing today. Which means that we can't meet this afternoon.'

Flora decided to cheer up her friend. 'In that case, I'll come over to you. Mrs Bell will let me help you with the silver, I'm sure.'

Hilda rushed to the chair and clapped her hands together. 'I hoped you'd say that. Seeing as you're a favourite of Mrs Bell, she'll bake a cake – oh, how good it is to have a friend like you!'

'Hilda, please think again about leaving.'

'But I might miss me chance. What with the *Lusitania* and all—'

'There's no rush, I'm sure.'

Hilda sank down on the cushions and yawned.

'I'll make us some tea.' Flora hurried out to the kitchen. She knew how impulsive Hilda was. If only she could persuade her to change her mind.

Hilda was asleep in the chair when Flora brought in the tea tray. Flora poured the tea and shook Hilda's shoulder. 'Drink this before you go.'

Hilda gulped down her tea. She blinked at Flora. 'Have you heard from Will?'

'Not since he joined his regiment in January.' They both glanced up at the photograph that Will had sent them. It stood proudly on Flora's mantel.

'He looks very handsome in uniform,' said Hilda.

Flora instantly thought about Will fighting, and shook her head to rid it of the image. 'Hilda, please don't give up your job.'

Hilda rolled her dark eyes.

'Promise me, won't you?' Flora hoped Hilda would soon realize how lucky she was to have such a comfortable life at Hailing House.

'All right,' Hilda said eventually. 'I promise.'

Flora smiled. Though when Hilda left, she didn't bother to hug Flora goodbye.

Chapter Two

Flora sat in the kitchen of Hailing House, enjoying the afternoon tea that Mrs Bell had generously served up. The fruit cake was still warm from baking in the black-leaded range. 'Oh, this is heaven,' said Flora as she swallowed, closing her eyes for a brief second.

'You're welcome, dear. I've not seen the silver shining so bright in a long time. It was very obliging of you to help Hilda.' Flora saw Mrs Bell eye Hilda suspiciously.

'I like coming here,' Flora replied with a smile.

'And don't you look a picture!' The cook patted Flora's arm.

Flora glanced down at the clothes that she had worn for Mass that morning. It was a pleasant change to be out of her uniform. This checked brown wool suit was her favourite, with its broderie-anglaise collar and ankle-length skirt. Her curls were tucked above her collar, under the brim of her brown felt hat. Mrs Bell had given her a very large apron to wear for the silver cleaning, an apron so large that Flora had looped the belt twice round her waist. The suit was old, bought second-hand from a market stall and needed no special protection after years of hard wear; but she wore the apron anyway.

'As slim as a reed,' continued Mrs Bell, approvingly. 'A figure that I envy.' Mrs Bell gestured to her own full bosom and wide, matronly hips hidden under her apron and grey skirt. 'As for me, I'm cursed to be as round as a barrel. Forced to test the food I serve, the pounds and ounces just pile on.' Self-consciously, she touched her white cook's cap, under which her grey hair was pulled back in a bun. 'Still, I'll happily suffer for a deserving cause like the poor and needy of this island.'

Flora smiled but Hilda looked put out. 'Forced!' she repeated, gawping at the generous wedge of cake on the cook's own plate.

'None of your cheek, my girl,' Mrs Bell scolded. 'My goodness, I don't know how I put up with you.'

'Because if it wasn't for me, this place would be brought to its knees,' Hilda argued. 'Aggie's about as much use as a lamp without a wick.'

'She does what she can,' said Mrs Bell patiently. 'She's a trier.'

'Blimey, is that what you call her?' Hilda answered rudely. 'Aggie certainly tries it on, that much I agree with.'

'Don't you let her ladyship hear you speaking in such a fashion.' Mrs Bell's voice was sharp. 'She's fond of Aggie, as I am. Aggie has a big family to care for and a husband not always in work.'

'I was very sorry to hear the news of the *Lusitania* sinking,' Flora said, quickly changing the subject. 'And that Lady Hailing's acquaintance was on board.'

Mrs Bell glanced at Hilda, who kept her eyes down. 'Yes, it's a tragedy,' agreed Mrs Bell as she poured the tea. 'Though we don't know the outcome yet. The chauffeur who told me came last night to collect her ladyship's things. We won't be graced with a visit for a while. Lady Hailing will be in mourning, I should think, for her friend on that ill-fated ship.'

'Wouldn't catch me on a boat, anyway,' sniffed Hilda. 'Can't swim.'

Mrs Bell ignored this and turned to Flora. 'Remember the HMS *Titanic*? The unsinkable liner that went down after hitting an iceberg several years past? So many good folk perished in the icy seas. Gentry and servants alike.'

'Leaving their big country houses without servants,' Hilda said slyly.

Mrs Bell waved a wooden spoon in Hilda's direction. 'Oh, so we're back to that kind of talk, are we? Well, hints and threats are water off a duck's back to me, Hilda.'

'You'd put me in chains if you could,' Hilda mumbled under her breath.

'What nonsense!' Mrs Bell exclaimed. 'It's your own character that's against you, Hilda. Believing you're too high and mighty for your position here. And letting your feelings show on your face. You had pretty, innocent looks when you first came to us. And now in their place, all I can see is grasping and wanting.'

At this, Hilda tore off her apron and cap and threw them on the kitchen table. With a toss of her brown curls, she stalked out of the kitchen.

'Oh, dear! Oh, dear me!' Mrs Bell sank down on a chair. Taking a hanky from her pocket she wiped a tear from her eye. 'Her ladyship has told Hilda she can leave.'

'What? When?' Flora sat up.

'I suppose Hilda's hints were listened to.'

'Hilda didn't tell me.'

Mrs Bell looked at Flora with a soft smile. 'Nor me, dear. I suppose she thought we'd try to talk her out of it.'

Flora felt very sad. Only this morning, Hilda had promised not leave Hailing House. 'Where is it that Hilda wants to go?' Flora asked with a heavy heart.

Mrs Bell drew her hands together and pleated her plump fingers. 'To the estate of Lord William Calvey, the fourth Earl of Talbott, in Surrey. The earl fought in the Boer Wars and was an acclaimed hero. But sadly, his first wife, Lady Amelia, died in childbirth. The infant grew up without a mother's love, and was governed by his aunt, Lord William's younger sister, Lady Bertha. He's said to be – well, no other words for it, a devilish rake and as unlike his heroic father as a son could be!'

'But why would Lady Hailing let Hilda go there?'

Mrs Bell sat back with a long sigh. 'Hilda is to go on loan. Supposedly, only till the men come home from war to take up their jobs again. The Calveys' housekeeper, Mrs Burns, is understaffed, you see. All the big houses in England are having to help each other out.' Mrs Bell shook her head worriedly. 'Still, Hilda could have refused. But when consulted on the matter, she agreed without hesitation, the silly wench. All smiles and pretty nods, she was, and yet playing a tight-lipped game with me ever since. As though she don't trust me. That's what pains me the most.'

'Hilda don't mean it, Mrs Bell.'

Mrs Bell nodded. 'I've said enough. I shouldn't have spoken me mind. But I've experience behind me that the girl doesn't have. I've worked for Lady Hailing since I left school at twelve, was a between-stairs maid at the Hailings' country seat, working seventeen hours a day, seven days a week. I scrubbed till me fingers bled so I know the hard work the lowers have to contend with. I ended up carting and carrying for the whole household. But I worked me way up, till they made me the cook. It was only five years ago, when my legs started to trouble me, that Lady Hailing suggested I move here. In all that time, Flora, I saw many a young woman fall victim to vanity. A gentleman might praise her, tell her she was pretty as a picture, and before you knew it, the maidservant got herself into trouble. She'd be dismissed by the housekeeper and sent away without the lady of the house even knowing it. Of course, the girls would always say it was through no fault of their own, and sometimes it wasn't. They were the poor wenches I felt sorry for.'

'But why do you think this might happen to Hilda?' asked Flora.

A little quiver spun around the cook's lips. 'Hilda's very impressionable.'

'But Mrs Bell, this is 1915!'

'I can see you don't believe me.' The cook's back straightened. 'But why put temptation in Hilda's way? Who will be there to keep an eye on her?'

'You have been very good to her,' Flora agreed, 'but even Hilda has to grow up.'

'Yes, perhaps I'm just a silly old woman, fearing the worst.' The cook nodded slowly. 'Go and tell Hilda I shan't breathe a word more on the subject. For better or worse, the die is cast.'

After finishing her tea, Flora made her way up the back stairs of the servants' quarters. Pausing at one of the high windows, she gazed out through its dirty panes. Before her was spread the Isle of Dogs. The island, a horseshoe of land that jutted out into the River Thames, was the very heart of the East End. The blue sky above it was cloudless. A few tugs and small boats bobbed on the river's calm surface. The dome of Greenwich Observatory sparkled in the sunshine. Her gaze drifted downriver to the Pool of London; she sighed with pleasure. She and Hilda were living in one of the most famous ports in the entire world!

But as Flora continued along the passage, she began to feel troubled. What would Mrs Bell do without Hilda for company? The house only came to life when Lady Hailing made her visits. But was it fair to try to persuade a girl of sixteen to stay in this rambling old house, with no younger staff?

As Flora reached the last flight of stairs, a cobweb touched her face. She had never noticed before how dark it was up here, or how musty the air smelled. The carpet on the landing had worn away to shreds. The banister wobbled as she grasped it.

Flora knocked on Hilda's door and was not really surprised when it flew open and Hilda fell into her arms, sobbing.

Flora sat beside Hilda on the rickety bed. The room was very cold. The two windows which overlooked the winding roads of the island were grey with soot and grime. A pair of faded curtains hung limply at their paint-peeling frames. Suddenly Flora saw Hilda's quarters in a very different light.

'You're about to scold me for being rude, aren't you?' Hilda said resentfully.

'Mrs Bell has been a good friend.'

Hilda blinked tearfully. 'I'll bet she gave you an earful. About what terrors are certain to befall a wayward girl like me.' She picked at the frayed seams of the faded floral bedcover, then wiped her red eyes with a hanky. 'I know I promised you I wouldn't leave, but how I wish I could!'

'Then you must go, Hilda.'

'What?' Hilda's tears dried immediately. 'You'd let me go?'

'It's not up to me to keep you.'

'I won't regret leaving here, Flora, I won't. It's not as if I'm leaving on the sly, or even giving me notice in. It was Lady Hailing herself who gave me the offer.'

'Yes, Mrs Bell told me.'

'And you ain't cross?'

'I only want what's best for you. And so does Mrs Bell. But you must follow your own path.'

'Do you mean that?'

'Yes, of course.'

Flora gazed around the room. A cold draught whistled up at her feet from the cracks in the floorboards. Even in May there was no warmth in the attic. The ceiling, like the passage, held trails of cobwebs that clung to the crumbling plaster. Even the little study, once lit by a gas lamp, was cloaked in darkness. Had it always been so dingy, Flora wondered? Perhaps it was all for the best that Hilda left.

'Oh, Flora, Adelphi Hall is in Surrey, and it is beautiful,' Hilda began, her eyes shining. 'I looked the earl's name up in a library book and found a picture. The house is very big with white pillars at the front and dozens of sparkling windows above. Oh, what a dream it looks!'

'Did the book tell you about the earl?'

'No, only that he fought in the African wars.'

'What about the rest of the family?'

Hilda nodded. 'The mistress of the house is Lady Bertha Forsythe. If only I can become her maid!'

'Hasn't she got one already?'

'She's probably old and stuffy,' Hilda said with a shrug. 'It's fair to say, don't you think? I'm young and have an eye for fashion. Given the chance, I'd be a real asset to

Lady Bertha's boudoir. All I have to do is make myself known to her.'

'Do you think you have a chance?'

Hilda looked surprised. Tossing back her ringlets, she nodded. 'I've read books and magazines. I know much more than you think.'

'Will we still be friends?' Flora asked quietly.

Hilda threw her arms around her. 'Fancy asking that. You'll visit me, of course, perhaps in spring when it's warmer. The perfect time of year.'

'Surrey is a long way away.'

'Not as far as Scotland or Wales.'

Flora smiled. Hilda always had an answer.

'Oh, Flora, I knew I could count on you.'

'When will you go?'

Hilda shrugged. 'I'm to have an interview first.'

'I hope you'll be happy.'

'Do you mean that?'

Flora nodded. 'Of course I do.' She smiled. 'But you'll have to watch your Ps and Qs.'

'And I won't drop me haitches neither.' Hilda started to laugh.

Suddenly, the room seemed brighter as they sat on the bed, laughing. Hilda, thought Flora, was happy at last.

Chapter Three

It was Monday morning two weeks later when a letter arrived from Will. Flora recognized his large, looping handwriting and was about to open the envelope when a shadow passed over the window. A man carrying a small child in his arms came down the airey's steps. Flora pushed the envelope into her uniform pocket and opened the door.

'Me name's Riggs and this is me little girl, Polly. Please, nurse, help me. She's ill.'

Flora looked at the child. She was lying with her head against her father's chest. Her eyes were closed and it was clear that she was struggling to breathe. 'Come along,' she said, quickly closing the door to the airey behind her.

Flora hurried up the basement steps to the surgery door and let them in with the key that she kept strung on her belt. The ground floor of Tap House smelled of carbolic and the sharp tang of Friars' Balsam.

Flora was surprised that the doctor had not yet come down from his rooms above. It was his habit to speak with his daily help, Mrs Carver, and make his way down to the surgery on the stroke of eight.

Flora glanced at the longcase clock standing at the foot of the wide staircase. Its ornate hands showed that it was already ten minutes past the hour. After asking Mr Riggs to sit with Polly in the waiting room, she hurried up the stairs. There was never much light reflected from the tall, heavily draped windows on the landing; Flora always found the air rather stuffy. The doctor's door was at the end of a long passage. On the wall hung portraits of Dr Tapper's relatives. The painting that Flora liked best was of the doctor's only child, Wilfred. He sat together with his mother, Edith, whose hand rested on his shoulder. Had she lived to see Wilfred go into the military, Flora decided, she would have been very proud of her son.

Flora knocked softly on the doctor's door. She expected to see Mrs Carver's, thin, smiling face. But when the door opened, it was not Mrs Carver, but the doctor himself. With some surprise, Flora saw that the doctor – who always wore a black frock-coat – was not yet fully dressed. He stood in just his stiff-collared shirt, waistcoat and trousers. His silver fob watch had not yet been pinned in place. His lined face regarded her blankly, as if he was wondering why she was standing there.

'Good morning, Dr Tapper. Is everything all right?'

'Oh, Flora . . .' He nodded, frowning slightly.

Flora waited for the sounds of Mrs Carver moving about. But she heard none.

'Has Mrs Carver arrived yet?' asked Flora.

'Yes, but I've sent her home,' Dr Tapper muttered without further explanation. 'Have we patients downstairs?'

'Yes, I've asked Mr Riggs to wait. His little girl looks very ill.'

'I'll come immediately.'

Flora knew the doctor tried very hard not to keep his patients waiting. She watched him reach for his jacket. Without further ado, he led the way downstairs.

'I can't rouse my Polly,' Mr Riggs said, as they walked into the waiting room. 'She won't wake up.'

'Follow me,' Dr Tapper said calmly. 'Bring her to my room.'

After the child had been laid on the examination couch, Flora watched Dr Tapper peel away the collar of her dirty, torn coat to reveal an even filthier garment beneath. Her skin was covered in an unsightly rash. Dr Tapper lifted her eyelids, which showed nothing but two white orbs and closed quickly together again.

'How long has she been like this?' the doctor asked as he examined the swollen glands of her neck.

'Dunno,' replied the father. 'I came home this morning and found her like it. I work nights, see, and with the missus gorn last year, I have to leave the kids to look after 'emselves. Polly here's the eldest at eleven. She ain't been her old self for a while.'

Flora saw that Polly had turned a ghastly bluish colour. The doctor took a wooden tube from his Gladstone bag, which he kept packed and ready for night-time emergencies, and put it to her chest. He rested his ear on the other end, and his face looked grave. Quickly, he pulled a small brown bottle from the bag. Lifting Polly's head, he placed the smelling salts under her nose.

To Flora's dismay, there was no response. Polly's head fell back and her small mouth, which had at first been trying to suck in air, went slack.

The doctor attempted to rouse her, but Flora knew it was too late. The little girl's life had slipped slowly away before their very eyes.

That afternoon, Flora and Dr Tapper were riding in the doctor's open trap pulled by his elderly grey pony. The death of the little girl had put everything else from Flora's mind but now Flora had a little time to think about the mysterious events earlier that morning. She had never known the doctor to be late for his surgery. Added to this was his early-morning dismissal of Mrs Carver. Flora wondered if there had been a disagreement between them.

'You know what to look out for, Flora,' the doctor called to her as the trap bounced along. 'Swollen glands or a sickly cough and skin infections. When I examined Mr Riggs, I found nothing but fleas and malnourishment. Pray God that it's the same for his other children.'

Flora tried to hide her shudder. What would they find at Mr Riggs' riverside hovel? The buildings in the road he lived in were derelict. It was a dockside terrace that often flooded at high tide, and the crumbling structures were condemned. Flora knew the doctor had to examine Polly's sisters and brothers. If any of them showed signs of diphtheria – the deadly, infectious disease from which the doctor confirmed Polly had perished – they must be sent to the isolation hospital. There had been an outbreak of diphtheria two years ago. The quick march of the disease had taken many of their patients' lives.

'Here we are.' The doctor reined in the pony and climbed down from the cab. Flora followed. They looked up at what had once been a waterside cottage. Now its mossy green stonework had collapsed. The windows were boarded. Mr Riggs opened the front door, which was a rotting piece of wood with no handle. His eyes were red-rimmed, his face full of grief.

Flora tried not to breathe in the overpowering smell of damp and decay. She trod carefully over the duck-boards, careful to avoid the muddy puddles creeping over them.

There were just two rooms left in the broken, almost roofless building. The staircase had vanished. Above them were worm-eaten rafters. Flora saw what must be the kitchen and scullery to the left – dark spaces, with a filthy stove. To the right was a large room, bereft of furniture. Two mattresses, stained by water, lay on the duckboards. Four children – two boys and two girls, all younger than Polly – were huddled in a group. They were dressed in what were little more than rags, and barefoot. Flora's heart went out to them.

'I would like some clean water, boiled on the stove,'

the doctor told Mr Riggs. 'My nurse will wash the children.'

'Ain't got no coke to light the stove,' Mr Riggs said with a shrug.

'Then we'll have to make do with cold.'

Flora always had strong disinfectant to hand. Naptha was used liberally for all forms of disease. Taking her apron from her bag, she tied it around her waist. Since the water was drawn from the pump in the yard, she carried in a full pail for each of the children, adding a little of the disinfectant. The children screamed and kicked as she cleaned them. Flora tried to comfort them with her soft voice, but their cries were too loud. There were no towels to dry them with, so she used a blanket from the trap. The doctor found the children to be like Mr Riggs: under-nourished and infested with lice.

'I'm very sorry about your sister,' the doctor said to them when the miserable task was over. 'Please try to wash yourselves each day. Learn to keep yourselves clean.' He turned to their father. 'Have you no help?'

'Nah. Who'd help us?' Mr Riggs' eyes filled with tears. 'My Polly was the one who looked after 'em.'

'Do the children go to school?'

'They get sent 'ome again. The stink's too much for the other kids.'

The doctor frowned. 'Something must be done about this.'

'You ain't gonna take 'em away, are yer?' Mr Riggs scratched his unshaven face.

'How can you continue to live under these circumstances?' Dr Tapper indicated the filthy mattresses and cockroaches on the walls. 'You must allow me to help you.'

'I don't want 'em sent off.'

'But you don't want your children to suffer the same fate as Polly.'

The man began to weep. Flora saw Dr Tapper take some coins from his pocket. He pressed them in Mr Riggs' dirty hand. 'Buy some food for your family. An officer of the law will call on you tomorrow.'

Flora watched as the children clung to their father. All of them had runny noses and dirty faces. They scratched at the lice running over them. It was a miracle, Flora thought, that none of them showed signs of diphtheria, living as they did in this squalor with no heat or fresh water. The disease thrived in such insanitary conditions.

'What will happen to them?' Flora asked as she and the doctor climbed back into the trap.

'I shall have to report the case,' Dr Tapper told her as he picked up the reins. 'Better the workhouse than a slow death in that miserable slum.'

Flora thought how lucky she had been. Her fate might have been the same. Flora didn't know who her parents were or if they had been as poor and unfortunate as Mr Riggs and his family. But she had been taken to the safety of the convent. Flora would always be grateful to her unknown parents for the precious gift of her life.

'Come, come, my dear, don't look so down. Their fortunes will improve.'

'And Mr Riggs, what of him?'

'What indeed,' the doctor said, sighing.

Flora knew the grieving father's fortunes would be unpredictable, just like the many hundreds of men who were destitute. She looked at the kindly doctor. The brim of his black felt hat, damp with rain, hid his eyes and the thoughts reflected in them. He tickled the whip lightly over the pony's back to encourage a faster speed. He had given money from his own pocket to help the family – Flora had seen this happen many times before. He cared for his patients beyond the call of duty.

'Pull your cape round you,' he told her as they clattered through the wet streets. 'We don't want you going down with a cold.'

Flora smiled. He was, to her, the father she had never had. Wilfred must be a very proud son. Flora's thoughts went back to the children they had just left. If only Hilda could have seen Mr Riggs and his family. She would have thought herself very lucky to be living in such a fine place as Hailing House.

Chapter Four

Flora sat alone in her small room after cleaning it, and herself, thoroughly. She was glad they had reached the end of this exhausting day; the undertakers had been called to perform their duties and Polly's death reported to the authorities. The only light was from the gas lamp, spreading over the scrubbed surfaces.

Flora sighed, trying to find the strength to stand up. When she and Dr Tapper had returned from their visit to Mr Riggs and his family, there had been patients waiting. Among them were more wounded men from the Western Front. Some had obvious physical injuries, but others were suffering mentally. She had seen one man weeping, unable to stop the shivering and shaking that racked his whole body. Another soldier had been brought in by his elderly mother. He had lost the power of speech, his face twisted by a grimace, as though he was haunted by the harrowing memories he must carry with him.

'Flora?'

She jumped to her feet, surprised to see the doctor standing there.

'You must go now, it's past eight o'clock.'

Flora tried to smile, pushing her straying blonde locks under her white cap. It was an effort even to part her lips.

'I shall be on time in the morning,' he told her. 'Unfortunately, I had some rather bad news today.' He shook his head slowly, loosening the untidy thatch of grey hair, so that a lock fell across his forehead. 'I sent Mrs Carver home, since a letter came . . . a letter that needed my full attention.' The doctor looked sadly into Flora's concerned face. 'I'm afraid Wilfred is reported missing in action.'

Flora took a sharp breath. 'But when . . .? How?'

'I know nothing more,' the doctor replied, his voice rough with emotion. 'But I pray for better news to come.'

Flora swallowed. A stone seemed to lodge where her heart should be.

The doctor touched her shoulder. 'You have done very well today, Flora. Now, off you go and get some rest. I'll turn out the lights.'

As she left, Flora thought about Wilfred. Dr Tapper was so proud of his son. At twenty-five, Wilfred was an officer with the British Expeditionary Force. Dr Tapper had told her that Wilfred had joined up at the outbreak of war. He had sailed to France last September. Flora thought back to the day, a month before Wilfred had left England, when she had met Hilda and Will in Hyde Park. To the young men on the banks of the Serpentine who were eager to answer Lord Kitchener's call to arms. Their assumption, like Will's, was that the war would be over by Christmas. But Christmas had come and gone and the war continued. Thousands had been slaughtered on the battlefields. Many of those young volunteers would never come home again.

Closing the heavy surgery door behind her, Flora remembered Will's letter. There had been no time to read it today. Whatever news Will had written was welcome. Up until the date on the envelope, Will had been alive and able to write to her.

Flora settled herself by the unlit fire in the airey and drew out the single sheet of paper, which was addressed to both her and Hilda and dated simply 'March'. Flora wondered why there had been a delay in posting. But Will's news was better than expected, as, at the time of writing, he had still been in England. This both surprised and delighted her. The longer Will remained in England, the safer he would be. The reason was, she now discovered, that he had fallen sick.

'The inoculations had a very bad effect on me,' he complained.

> At first, the doctors thought I might be suffering from the measles or some other infectious pox. They at once quarantined me. Dreadful red, itchy spots brought me very low. There was no hope of joining the London Regiment who enjoyed exercises on Hackney Marsh. But the rashes wore off eventually, though leaving me quite deflated and confined to the medical hut. It was

an agony to get myself going again, especially as the roughness of the uniform irritated my skin. I'm determined though. I'll be ready for our next inspection in two days' time. A friend is posting this letter in the village for me as I am still unable to leave camp. How are things with you and Hilda? Is there anything exciting going on? Life is very dull here at Hemsley Camp. But word is, we're bound for France soon. I can't wait to join our boys. Take care of yourselves and write when you have time. God bless you both. Your soldier, (in waiting), Will.

Flora sank back in the fireside chair where a cup of tea had gone cold at her side. Without a fire, the room held no warmth at all. She shivered, aching for the warmth of her bed. Will, at least, was safe. But for how long would that state of affairs last? Flora had always believed he wasn't at all robust. Though tall, he was extremely thin. And such a pallor under the baker's flour! To think that a boy as gentle as Will would soon be fighting to kill with a gun or bayonet.

Falling asleep that night was impossible. First, she saw Will, exposed to the elements in the mud-soaked trenches that the returning troops had described to her. Then her mind went to Polly and her last, brief gasps for breath as she lay on the couch. Then to Mr Riggs, grieving and desperate for his four remaining children. Lastly, she thought of the doctor himself. Of the moment he had told her about Wilfred. A warm tear slid slowly from

Flora's eye. He had spent his life in service to other people, yet those closest to him had been cruelly taken away.

Flora sniffed back her tears. 'Oh, Jesus, calm my fears, increase my trust and help me to aid those less better off than me,' she whispered, recalling the words Sister Patricia had taught them. She took comfort in the fact her prayers had helped her through so far. If she was to be of any use to Dr Tapper, she had to believe her faith would help them in the many testing weeks and months to come.

It wasn't until the first Saturday in June that Flora next saw Hilda. They had decided to go to the market together on their afternoon off. For the occasion, Flora had worn her only really good day dress. The colour was a soft pigeon-breast grey and buttoned through from top to bottom. Together with a grey velvet-trimmed hat, they had been her first purchases after she'd left the orphanage and started work. Although Dr Tapper allowed her to live in the airey rent-free, he also gave her a wage of twelve guineas a year. At first, she had felt very well-off. She had never had any money before. But, as the days and weeks passed, she discovered that money spent in the big wide world disappeared very quickly. After paying the gas, coal and food bills, there wasn't much left over. She'd had to buy clothes; she only had what she stood up in on the day she left the orphanage. Boots and shoes were needed too. The market became the source of all her purchases.

Flora was surprised to see Hilda wearing new clothes: a bright green hat with an ostrich feather, together with a smart belted jacket worn over a brown skirt.

'You look very nice,' Flora said as they met at the top of the street.

'Well, if I'm going to be a lady's maid, I've got to practice at being a lady meself,' said Hilda, swaying her hips and making Flora giggle. 'I had to borrow a shilling off Mrs Bell to buy it.'

'Are you short again?' Flora knew Hilda was hopeless with money. Mrs Bell always helped Hilda out.

'When I get my new job, I'll be in the pink.'

'Do housemaids earn much?' Flora asked, doubtfully.

'I told you before, I won't be a housemaid for long. I'm going to be a lady's maid.'

'Well, I must say, you look the part.'

Hilda beamed. 'How do you get your fringe to curl so prettily?'

Flora blushed at the unexpected compliment. She touched her hair. She was grateful for its natural curl. Wetting her fringe and rolling it around her finger as it dried brought effective results. 'Oh, it doesn't take a moment.'

'I'm saddled with a cow's lick,' Hilda complained. 'Me fringe parts in the middle and sits on my forehead like a blooming great moustache.'

Soon they were laughing and Flora knew Hilda was happy. It was at times like this that Flora knew she would miss Hilda a lot if she went away. They loved walking through the market together. Flora often bought fruit and vegetables and occasionally fish. Cox Street market served all the nearby island hamlets: Millwall, Cubitt Town, Blackwall and even Poplar. Flora found all the traders very friendly. There was more than enough choice of goods. From bric-a-brac and second-hand furniture to jewellery and clothes, fresh meat, fish and costermonger stalls. Flora's favourite was the tea and coffee stall. The trader sold hot and cold beverages, sweets, biscuits and toffee apples. She also liked the barrow boys offering roast chestnuts, shrimps, cockles and muscles when in season. Sometimes she called in to the little shops running the length of the market on both sides. Flora noticed their trade hadn't suffered in the first year of war. Grocers, butchers, bakers and food shops were always busy. The stewed eels, tripe and onion and pease pudding café sold the favourite dishes of the day. The smells wafting out of the door were tantalizing. And on Saturday, you had to push your way through the crowds to enter them.

'Well, what's all your news?' asked Hilda as they joined the hustle and bustle.

'We've had a letter from Will,' Flora said and she opened the clasp of her small bag.

'Let's sit down and read it together,' Hilda said excitedly. 'I'm thirsty, are you?' They looked over to the refreshment stall.

Flora bought two ginger beers and they sat on the wooden benches. Hilda sipped daintily from her enamel mug, her little finger turned out, a new practice that Flora hadn't noticed before.

'Inoculations? What are they?' asked Hilda, with a frown, as she read Will's letter.

'Our troops have to be protected against some diseases they could catch in a foreign country.'

'Poor Will,' Hilda said as she read on. 'He wants so much to be a soldier.'

'If only he didn't!'

Hilda rolled her eyes. 'Flora, he *wants* to fight for his country. For goodness' sake, he's old enough to know his own mind.'

Flora thought, but didn't say, that Will was far too young to know his own mind, just as Hilda was. But she knew it would start Hilda complaining that Flora didn't understand either of them. And so she kept silent.

'Dear Will,' sighed Hilda, returning the letter to Flora. 'I can't wait until he comes home to tell us about his adventures.'

'Hilda, it's no fun fighting a war.'

'But what's the point in worrying? It won't bring him home any sooner.'

Flora nodded. 'No, it won't.'

Hilda smiled at Flora's approval. She straightened the cloth of each gloved finger, her eyes twinkling. 'I've something else to tell you.' She looked about to burst. 'I'm invited to Adelphi Hall in August, to be interviewed by Mrs Burns, the housekeeper.'

Flora looked surprised. 'So soon?'

Hilda gave a little sigh. 'Imagine, me going to the grand mansion itself! Oh, what will I wear? What will look best? Should I do me hair different? Shall I look older, as if I know me onions? Or—'

'Just be yourself.'

'But this is my big chance, Flora. I've got to look the part.'

'Just like you do today.'

Hilda touched her hat lightly. 'Do you think green is right for such an occasion? And is my feather a bit overdone?'

Flora knew Hilda was flying into her imagination as usual, forgetting the practical arrangements. 'How are you going to travel there?' she asked.

Hilda looked startled. 'I hadn't thought. Why?'

'Can you afford the train?'

Hilda shook her head and her ringlets danced on her shoulders. 'Don't know. How much will it be?'

'It's expensive to travel by train.'

'I've never been on a train before.' Hilda looked nervous.

Flora hadn't either, but she knew it wouldn't be cheap. 'What day are you going on?'

'I've to write back and confirm a Sunday. Mrs Burns hasn't got time in the week. Oh, Flora, would you come with me?'

Just then there were yells and shouts behind them. They turned to see a commotion at the bric-a-brac stall. Several people were yelling at the owner, an older man wearing a black felt hat and glasses. He was hurriedly trying to clear his stock away as the crowd pushed and pulled at the stall. Flora saw one man reach out and take hold of the stallholder's jacket. He began to shake him, and as they struggled, another man swept the shelves clean with his arm. Pieces of china and cutlery, books, trinkets and other items scattered over the cobbles. Flora gasped as everyone rushed forward to help themselves.

'You dirty German!' a woman shrieked. 'Get out of England, back to your own country.'

Before very long, the stall was demolished. The owner fell to his knees, cowering, trying to ward off the blows until a policeman arrived and the poor man was removed from harm's way.

'Fancy a German trying to sell in an English market!' a lady exclaimed as she walked by, talking to another woman. 'The blighters sink our boats and murder the passengers, and still expect Britain will give them a living.'

'How do you know he was German?' Flora asked, causing the woman to stop abruptly.

'He's called Old Fritz, ain't he?' the woman snapped back. 'And his accent is enough to give him away.'

'But he's run that stall for years,' Flora said in a shocked voice.

'He won't no more,' the woman replied angrily. 'Haven't you heard? The coppers are interning all wot they call "suspect aliens". After the *Lusitania*, you won't see no foreigners selling their ill-gotten gains round 'ere.'

'If you ask me,' said the other woman, poking a finger towards Flora, 'the bluebottles are late off the mark as usual. They should have rounded the buggers up after that Zeppelin flew over at the end of May. It's said people were killed by it and others injured. You'd soon change your tune, dearie, if one of them flew over here.'

As the two women walked on, Flora looked back at the broken stall. Two young boys were kicking the remains and shouting out curses. She felt very upset and was surprised when Hilda said beside her, 'She's right, you know. That big airship was terrifying. Not that I saw it meself, but Mrs Bell said a friend of hers did and she ain't felt safe since.'

Flora hadn't witnessed the arrival of the German Zeppelin but she had seen the searchlights in the sky and heard the crackle of British guns. Combined with the sinking of the *Lusitania* and the heavy losses of troops in France, the public's anti-German feeling was strengthening. 'But Fritz is a nice old man,' Flora protested, 'always courteous and wouldn't do anyone harm.'

'Don't change the fact he's German.'

'He still didn't deserve to be beaten up.'

'Oh, forget him,' advised Hilda, dismissively. 'He only had a few bumps and bruises.'

Flora looked back as they walked on. She saw one of the boys trying to light the tarpaulin with a match. Another stallholder rushed up and cuffed him round the ear, shouting that they didn't want a fire at the market. Flora noticed that none of the other traders had come to

Fritz's aid. It was very sad to see people turn on one another like that.

'So will you come with me to Adelphi?' Hilda pleaded again. She took Flora by the arms, her face very serious. 'I'll pay you back, every penny.'

'We'll see,' Flora answered. Somehow Hilda made it impossible to refuse.

'Oh, thank you!' said Hilda joyfully. She threw her arms around Flora.

Flora smiled. Hilda could always get round her. One way or another.

Chapter Five

It was early on Sunday morning, August 1st, and Flora's sixteenth birthday. She didn't expect to be celebrating it in the back of a cart. But Dr Tapper had made the suggestion of hiring Albert the farrier when she told him about Hilda's invitation.

'The trains are expensive,' he warned. 'Our farrier runs a carrying service for the Kent hopping season. I'm sure you'd have a comfortable enough ride at a reasonable cost.'

Later that day, Flora had gone to Albert's yard, where the doctor's pony was stabled. She had shown Albert the address that Hilda had given her. Flora was delighted when she managed to persuade him to be hired for just a shilling. She paid him in advance so he couldn't change his mind.

Flora glanced at Hilda, who was wearing her green hat and feather. She looked very smart with her dark hair drawn up under its rim and the tailored grey suit moulded perfectly to her generous curves. Flora had decided to wear a tan-coloured ankle-length skirt and cream buttoned blouse with leg-of-mutton sleeves. She had pinned her hair back in a knot, suitable for a formal occasion such as this.

Albert had provided them with cushioned benches to sit on. The ride was bumpy, and with plenty of fresh air. He had offered to pull the canvas top over the cart to shield them from the elements, but as there was very little breeze, they had decided to use their parasols instead. Flora tilted hers as they passed over Tower Bridge. She could see ferries and tugs of all shapes and sizes moored along the river. Bigger craft, too, though they were not as colourful as the old ships. Here in the city, the waterborne traffic seemed to glide along. The wake of each vessel barely caused a ripple. Flora was pleased that it was Sunday. They didn't have to breathe in the smoke of the chemical-belching factories.

'We'll tell Albert to leave us at the gates of Adelphi,' Hilda decided as they left the bridge and began their journey through the streets of the South Bank. 'Imagine us, walking up the grand driveway. Just like I saw in the library book.'

'But we're not grand visitors, Hilda.'

'I ain't being caught in a farrier's cart!' Hilda exclaimed and sat quietly, frowning. Then, adjusting her parasol, she gasped. 'Look over there, by the omnibus. It's one of them new-fangled motorized vehicles without a roof. Oh, Flora, I wish I was riding in one of them!'

Flora stared at the gleaming black motor car. The lady passenger was dressed in cream lace and a wide-brimmed hat. The man drove in a stately manner and Flora and Hilda watched admiringly, although, when a small explosion came from the vehicle's rear, they burst into laughter.

'At least a cart don't make bangs to blow out your eardrums,' Flora said ruefully. 'And we hired Albert at a bargain price.'

'I'll pay you back, I promise,' Hilda answered, latching her gloved hand over Flora's arm. 'Soon as I get my wages. I'll take you out somewhere special. Promise.'

Flora smiled. She would be rich if she had a penny for all of Hilda's broken promises.

By twelve o'clock, the sun was still shining and their journey was almost over. Flora had never imagined that birds could sing so sweetly; the green, leafy trees were full of wings and warbles and she'd seen squirrels and a fox too. Albert had rarely used the long, curling whip over the horse's back. Instead, they had jogged slowly along the winding lanes and narrow roads, through the hills and dales of the countryside. Hilda had fallen asleep, but Flora was wide awake. There was so much to see. She hadn't been outside of London before. Here the animals roamed freely in the fields and the little villages looked like the ones in picture books. Thatch-roofed cottages dotted the roadside. Flowers and shrubs grew everywhere. The gardens were full of colour, light and shade. The country air made her head reel.

'I hope Albert knows the way,' Hilda mumbled sleepily, waking after the cart went over a bump.

'Of course he does. This countryside is very beautiful.'

'Yes, but there's no people. It must be very lonely.'

Flora looked at her friend. 'Are you having second thoughts?'

Hilda tossed her head. 'No, course not.'

The cart rattled along and into a wood. The path was full of overhanging bushes and the smell changed to a musty, damp odour. Flora tried to peer through the undergrowth, but she couldn't: it was too thick.

'Are you sure we're going the right way?' Hilda shouted up to Albert.

'It's what it says on this 'ere bit of paper,' Albert yelled back.

For the next ten minutes, they were both very quiet until Albert stopped the cart at a crossroads. Flora and Hilda stood up to look over his shoulders. On the far side of the road was a pair of very imposing iron gates. To the right was a small cottage. It wasn't as pretty as those in the villages, but it had a certain charm.

'That's it,' said Albert, nodding. 'That's your Adelphi Hall.'

Flora looked at Hilda. Her mouth was open. 'It can't be,' Hilda objected. 'The place in the books is much bigger.'

'Don't mean the gatehouse,' said Albert with a laugh. 'We have to drive through them big gates.' He urged the horse across the road, and a stooping, elderly man came out from the cottage. He exchanged a few words with Albert, opened the gates at a very slow pace, and stood watching as they passed through.

'Poor fellow,' shouted Albert over his shoulder. 'Told me he's been brought out of retirement as some of the male staff have joined Kitchener.'

Hilda looked anxiously at Flora. 'Do you think there will be any nice-looking young men left at Adelphi?'

'Or any young men at all,' said Flora with devilment.

'They can't *all* have gone to war,' said Hilda unhappily.

'You said yourself that the women were filling the men's posts.'

Hilda looked annoyed. 'Yes, but not all of them.'

Flora was still smiling as Albert brought the cart to a halt. He nodded to the wooden sign in the middle of the path. 'Tradesmen, servants and haulage to the left,' he called. 'You two girls ain't royalty, are you?' He chuckled.

'Maybe not, but I want to walk up to the house,' Hilda insisted.

'The drive is for gentry, not the likes of us,' Albert replied. 'Now I can see a few potholes in the road. You'd better hang on to the sides.'

Flora glanced quickly at Hilda as the cart bumped along. Hilda was chewing her lower lip and the look on her face told Flora that things weren't quite as she had expected them to be. The cart bumped so violently that Flora could hear her own teeth rattling. The woods around them were full of dense thickets. The blue sky disappeared from view and Hilda's face grew even darker.

It was not long before the sun shone again and the woods were behind them. Flora took a sharp breath at the landscape now revealed. Green fields and parkland curved into a graceful arc around a large mansion. The four marble columns that Hilda had described from the library book gleamed brightly. The winding pathway that Hilda had wanted to walk down curled out of the woods and down to the house. The gravel surface swept up to a large fountain in front of splendid doors. Four floors and gabled attics rose above them. Flora lost count of the chimneys. She was dazzled by the many tall windows.

'Adelphi Hall is beautiful,' Hilda said the moment she saw the house. 'Better even than Buckingham Palace.'

Flora smiled. She had to agree that in its own way Adelphi Hall had a particular majesty. Her gaze settled on the lush hedges and manicured gardens surrounding the house; she thought how sweet the air smelled. In the distance, she could see white dots in the fields. These must be sheep, she decided, though they looked unmoving as large black crows soared above them.

A motorized vehicle chugged slowly up the drive and paused outside the house. 'Look, a motor car, just like

Lady Hailing's,' Hilda cried. 'Oh, Albert, stop the cart, will you? I want to remember all this when I get back to London.'

Albert drew the cart to a halt. The two girls sprang to their feet, craning their necks to watch the visitor climb out.

'It's a gentleman,' Flora said as she caught a brief glance of a tall, striking-looking figure being greeted by a servant. 'But I can't see very much more.'

'I wonder if it's Lord Guy,' said Hilda excitedly.

'Who's Lord Guy?'

'He's the son of Lord William.'

Flora thought about what Mrs Bell had said about Lord Guy. She wondered if Hilda had taken much note.

'The earl himself is rarely seen by anyone,' Hilda continued, 'but it's Lord Guy and his aunt Bertha, Lord William's sister, who run the house, together with Lady Bertha's husband, James Forsythe.'

'You seem to be well up on all this,' Flora said in surprise.

Hilda grinned. 'I told you, I've read books and magazines.'

'I hope you've not got any daft ideas.'

'I shall be rubbing shoulders with gentry,' Hilda boasted.

'As a servant, you won't mix with the family.'

'As Lady Bertha's maid, I will.' Hilda straightened her spine and proudly lifted her chin. 'Just think, I'll not have to wear a pinafore, nor will I share a room with any of the lower servants.'

'Better get cracking, miss,' Albert said impatiently.

Flora feared that Hilda was allowing her imagination to run away with her. Hilda had been trained as a housemaid and never experienced working in a country house. The rules would be very different. And she was expecting to rise quickly through the ranks of the servants, but Flora wondered if Hilda's dream was even a possibility.

Albert urged the horse on. A smaller lane took them to the side of the house and through another wooded area. Flora noted as they emerged from the trees again that the gardens and lawns were as immaculate as at the front. Here and there were beds of flowers, all tended to perfection. A Grecian statue of a half-clothed woman was the first of many decorating the gardens. When they came to a set of stone arches, beyond which there were stables and outhouses, Flora glimpsed a line of high walls and vines growing thickly over them. All the paths were swept clear of weeds and had borders of small plants that looked recently added to the well-tended earth.

The courtyard was very busy with stable hands. Some youths were cleaning and brushing the cobbles. Others were grooming the horses which were tethered outside the many boxes. Several younger boys in dirty breeches and heavy boots used spades to fill their barrows.

Albert stopped the cart and climbed down. 'I'm off to the find water and a nosebag for the horse,' he told them as he helped them from the cart. 'Looks like the kitchens might be over there, through the garden beyond to the back of the house.'

Flora and Hilda nodded in silence. Flora knew Hilda was nervous. Her face was pale and her brown eyes full of apprehension. They made their way together along the path and Flora heard Hilda's gasp as the magnificent building rose above them.

'It's so big,' said Hilda. 'I wonder who cleans all them windows?'

Flora was thinking the same. She hoped it wouldn't be Hilda's job.

They passed several ornamental ponds and nodded to an older man who was trimming the hedges with shears. A smaller paved courtyard led up to the back door. Two women stood talking. The younger, who wore a pinafore and mob cap, hurried into the house. The remaining woman was in her fifties, Flora guessed, and her tall, erect posture, her black garb and silk apron trimmed with black beads, indicated her high rank. Her white collar was ruffled around her neck and a ring of keys hung at her waist.

'Do you think it's Mrs Burns?' whispered Hilda nervously. 'Oh, Flora, do I look all right? Will she like me?'

Flora smiled. 'Course she will.'

'I feel sick with nerves.'

'No, you don't.' Hilda squeezed her friend's hand. 'You'll make a fine impression.'

But Flora felt her heart sink a little. The face beneath the white lace cap showed little welcome. A tight mouth and unsmiling eyes gave nothing away as she clasped her hands in front of her and narrowed her gaze at their approach.

Chapter Six

'You must be Jones,' the housekeeper said to Hilda.

'Hilda Jones,' replied Hilda breathlessly.

'We refer to lowers by their surnames. You may call me Mrs Burns.'

'Thank you,' Hilda said, adding quickly, 'Mrs Burns.'

'And this?' The housekeeper frowned at Flora.

'I'm Flora Shine, Hilda's travelling companion,' answered Flora, as Hilda seemed all of a fluster.

Mrs Burns looked them up and down. 'We follow the rule of invitation here. Myself and Mr Leighton, the butler, must be consulted first. But, since you've had some way to travel, you'd better come in.'

'Thank you, Mrs Burns,' Hilda said again.

Mrs Burns led them inside the house. 'You've arrived at a busy time. Mrs Harris is just cooking the staff meal. I usually conduct interviews in the morning,' she said over her shoulder, 'but you're fortunate that I can see you as most of the family are away.'

Despite the cool welcome, Flora was impressed by the busy kitchen, with staff darting here and there.

Trays were held high over people's heads and uniformed footmen shooed maids out of their way. Flora stared around the large room full of shining pots, pans and freshly washed cutlery. Flora saw the cook, a small woman with very red cheeks, busy at the stoves. Around her worked the kitchen staff, carrying and fetching the dishes.

'This is Mrs Harris.' Mrs Burns said, nodding to the cook.

Mrs Harris gave them a quick glance but said nothing.

'Follow me.' Mrs Burns led them through the kitchen and into a passage. They flattened themselves against the wall as a footman rushed past. He was carrying a tray of glasses and a decanter. Dressed in a black coat with brass buttons and starched shirt front, the good-looking young man smiled.

They were on their way again, hurrying after Mrs Burns. At the end of the passage, an older man in a black-tailed suit stepped into their path. Flora noted his immaculate appearance.

'Mr Leighton, this is Jones,' Mrs Burns announced. 'Lady Hailing's recommendation.'

Flora watched Hilda almost curtsey. She knew her friend was trying to make a good impression.

'And the other?' the butler asked in a gruff voice.

'Her companion for the day.'

'An unfortunate time to arrive,' Mr Leighton muttered.

'Yes,' agreed Mrs Burns. 'But allowances must be made for the length of the journey.'

Mr Leighton curled his hand over the two inches of greying hair on his head. 'Perhaps, Mrs Burns, you might like to use my rooms, as we are so busy. I'm to be upstairs for Lord William in just a few minutes.'

'Thank you, Mr Leighton.' The housekeeper turned to Hilda. 'Follow me.' Then, as if remembering Flora, she added, 'You'll wait in Mr Leighton's office.'

Flora was about to thank her – or the butler, she didn't know whom – when a commotion came from behind them. Flora turned to see a young maid on her knees and recognized her as the girl she'd seen outside with Mrs Burns. Her apron and the floor were covered in what looked like soup.

Mr Leighton strode towards her. Flora could hear the angry tone of his voice as the maid tried to clean up the mess. Flora felt sorry for her. She must have bumped into the footman who'd been rushing down the passage with a soup tureen.

'You clumsy girl,' called Mrs Burns, and Hilda met Flora's glance. Her friend gave a stifled giggle. But Flora didn't think there was anything amusing about the maid's predicament.

Once more, they were flying down the passage. The dark wood surrounding them and lack of light made the downstairs rooms very gloomy. But at least here, thought Flora, the rooms were cooler, being away from the intense heat of the kitchens.

'Here,' said Mrs Burns as they entered a room. There was a highly polished desk in front of Flora, with a high back and thick ledgers neatly balanced in a row. The big chair beside it had spindles forming a pattern from the seat to the headrest. Beside it was a small table at which a simple wooden chair stood. Flora decided it was here she must sit.

'Jones?' Mrs Burns crooked a long, bony finger at Hilda. Picking up her skirts in an effort to catch up with the housekeeper, Hilda almost tripped over. Receiving a glare from the older woman, the two figures disappeared from sight.

In silence, Flora sat on the smaller chair and looked around her. The dark wood felt oppressive; though the fire was made up in the hearth, it wasn't lit. Two un-cushioned leather armchairs stood to either side of it. A number of black-framed photographs were mounted on the walls. Just below the ceiling there was a long wooden rack with a row of labelled metal bells.

Flora began to feel thirsty. They had gone all morning without a drink. Breakfast, a crust of bread and cheese eaten in the cart, had been hours ago.

How different this was to Mrs Bell's cosy kitchen, Flora thought with dismay. She looked at the door that Hilda had gone through. It remained firmly shut and so Flora sat back, trying to ignore the loud rumbling of her tummy.

''Ello, miss.' The maid who'd had the accident with the soup stood before Flora, carrying a tray full of silver pots. 'You been waiting all this time?'

'I was told to sit here by Mrs Burns while she interviews my friend, Hilda.'

'Oh, is she the new girl? The one we was told was coming from London?'

Flora nodded. 'Hilda's in – or was in – service to Lady Hailing.' To Flora, the little maid looked no more than a child. She was scrawny, and her head looked too big for her small body. Her cap was pulled down over her straggly brown hair, wisps of which burst out over her pale face. Her apron still bore the stains of the soup. 'Did you hurt yourself when you fell?' Flora asked kindly.

'Nah. Gets knocked about regular, but it don't worry me. Mrs Harris belts me with a wooden spoon when she's a mind to. But I don't care. I'm from the workhouse, see. Anyfink's better than that.'

Flora smiled. 'I'm Flora.' She stretched out her hand.

The maid giggled. She put her small, damp hand in Flora's. 'I'm Gracie, the scullery maid. I should be Smith, but everyone just yells Gracie. Dunno why. You coming to work here an' all?'

'No, I just travelled up with Hilda. She's my best friend, you see.'

'I'd like a best friend meself,' Gracie said brightly. 'I ain't never 'ad one. It's everyone for themselves in the work'ouse.'

'I'm sure you'll like Hilda,' Flora assured her. 'Hadn't you better put those pots down? They look very heavy.'

Gracie gave a little chuckle. 'I'm taking 'em to Mr Leighton's pantry. All the silver's cleaned there by the footman. James is the one wot ran over me.'

'You took a hard fall.'

'Never mind. I ain't crippled, am I?' She glanced at a closed door on the other side of the room. 'Come wiv me, if you like.'

'What about Mrs Burns and Mr Leighton?'

'We won't be long.'

Reluctantly, Flora followed Gracie. She hoped the butler wouldn't appear suddenly. Or Mrs Burns cut short her interview with Hilda.

'This is Mr Leighton's dining room and pantry,' Gracie explained as they entered a room fitted with a long table, with six or so chairs on either side. Gracie placed the tray on the table. There were cupboards and drawers to the rear and a low sink and draining board next to a small annexe. Gracie set the tray down by a tall cupboard. 'The silver's washed and polished here, and over there is the safe where all the valuables is kept. It's only Mr Leighton wot has the key.' Gracie indicated another door fitted with a large brass lock. 'Down there's the cellar. Great big blooming place it is, with booze of all sorts. Spirits, ales, sherries and ports, cases of the best champagne and wines from all over the world. Mr Leighton's in charge of that an' all.'

'I think we'd better go back.' Flora felt uneasy, as if she was snooping.

Gracie smiled secretively, her pale, thin face almost lost

under her cap. 'Don't worry, they won't know we've been 'ere.'

Flora followed Gracie back to the office, her heart thumping, and quickly sat down on her chair.

Gracie stared at her. 'Bet you're gasping, ain't you?'

Flora nodded. 'I am a little.'

'I'll see if I can get yer a cuppa.'

'Oh, don't trouble yourself.'

Gracie winked. 'I'll tell Mrs 'Aarris you're a breath off fainting.'

'Oh, no, don't!' Flora called, but Gracie scurried off. Flora hoped Gracie wouldn't get them into trouble. Flora didn't want to create a poor impression for Hilda's sake.

The minutes ticked by, and Flora's eye was caught by the many photographs on the walls. As neither Gracie nor Mr Leighton had returned, she got up to look at them. One was dated January 1912 and this made Flora smile. She recognized Mrs Burns and Mr Leighton immediately, with their sombre expressions and backs stiff as brooms. They were the only two members of the large group of staff who were seated.

'That one was taken three years ago, just after I started,' said a small, squeaky voice behind Flora. Gracie put a cup of tea on the table. 'I was just eleven.'

'So you're only fourteen now?'

Gracie nodded. 'Mr Leighton didn't want me in it, but Mr Flowers slipped me in when 'e wasn't looking.'

'Who's Mr Flowers?' Flora asked curiously.

'That's 'im there.' Gracie pointed to a tall young man with a pleasant, friendly expression. ''E was 'ead footman. Everso nice 'e was. But 'e volunteered. Same as . . .' She drew her rough red finger along the row of men. '. . . Mr Sherwood who was the chauffeur and Mr Frith – 'im there, with the moustache and gun, the gamekeeper. They all went to war in the 'eat of the moment, thinking they'd be back by Christmas last year.' Gracie hesitated, gesturing to the footman Flora had seen in the kitchen. 'Lucas took Mr Flowers' place. Reckons 'e's got a bad back and couldn't do any marchin'. James and John, these two, are brothers and footmen. Chosen special by Lady Bertha, as they're tall and good-looking. And there's Maxwell, of course, Lord Guy's valet. Says he's got dropped arches and flat feet and wouldn't be no good at marchin'. Then there's Turner, see, but 'e's too old to volunteer, and Lord William couldn't do without 'is valet. Dunno what'll happen if the government takes all our young men. That's why Mrs Burns wanted your 'Ilda. In case we're caught short.'

'And the women will do all the men's jobs?' Flora asked.

'We'll all muck in. Mr Leighton has taken on girls from the village.' Gracie scuffed the back of her hand across her nose. 'But they ain't very respectful, not like us wot live 'ere.' Gracie returned her attention to the photograph. 'This 'ere is Violet, Lady Bertha's maid. She's in Italy with the family at their summer 'ouse.'

'How long has she been Lady Bertha's maid?'

'Dunno. Mrs Bell said she started as a housemaid and worked her way up.'

Flora thought of Hilda as she studied Violet, who according to the photograph was a smartly dressed woman in her thirties. She had an air of confidence about her as she stood with her hands clasped together.

Gracie shuffled along to a large black-framed photograph at the end of the row. ''Ere's Mr Leighton's pride and joy. The only photograph we've got of the earl and his family. Course, I ain't ever seen the earl, Lord William. Not with me own eyes. Mrs 'Arris told me something 'appened to 'im to make 'im go a bit barmy after his wife died. But 'e looks a fine gent in 'is uniform, don't he? And that's his sister Lady Bertha and 'er 'usband, Mr James Forsythe.' Gracie's dark eyes, ringed by purple smudges, narrowed as she indicated another young man. Once again, her voice dropped to a whisper. 'That's Lord Guy, the earl's son and heir. 'Andsome, ain't 'e? Yer'd never believe the mischief he's reputed to get up to.'

Again, Flora thought of what Mrs Bell had said. 'Why isn't he at war?' asked Flora curiously.

'They say 'e's not right upstairs.' Gracie tapped her forehead. 'Something to do with when 'e was born and the cord bein' round 'is neck.'

'That sounds like an old wives' tale.'

'Well, his poor mother died pushing him through, didn't she? Lady Amelia was young and beautiful. She was a great loss to the old lord, who they say never grew close to the child that killed 'er.'

Just then the door creaked behind them. Flora saw Gracie start.

'What are you doing here, Gracie?' the butler demanded.

'Nothin', sir, nothin' at all.'

'Gracie brought me tea,' Flora volunteered, aware that Gracie seemed to be shrinking down into her boots. 'It was a long journey from London.'

Mr Leighton scowled at the scullery maid. 'You'd better get back to your duties. And for goodness' sake, don't drop anything else today.'

Flora saw Gracie scoot off. The butler looked at Flora, then at the photographs on the wall. Squaring his shoulders, he demanded, 'Is there anything you wish to know?'

Flora blushed. 'No, nothing, thank you.'

'In that case, you had better drink your tea. After which, I daresay you'd like to take some fresh air. The kitchen gardens provide adequate shelter from the elements.'

Averting her eyes, Flora returned to her seat. She lifted the cup and sipped from it, aware of the butler's burning gaze. She realized she had been told to leave.

Mr Leighton swept out of the room. Flora gave a deep sigh of relief. Would Hilda be happy here? Though her best friend complained about her life at Hailing House, Flora thought that things were likely to be very much harder here at Adelphi Hall.

* * *

Hilda was speechless. She was standing inside the entrance hall of the house she had been dreaming about ever since she first saw its picture in the library book. But all her dreams had been surpassed. The vaulted ceilings above her were higher than the convent's chapel. A wide, carpeted staircase led up to the interior rooms. She gazed in awe at the mahogany balustrades, the gilt-framed paintings on the walls, mostly of military men, and the dazzling treasures in their glass cases. Mrs Burns indicated a shield above the entrance doors.

'The Talbott coat-of-arms,' she said in a proud voice.

Hilda stared at the shield. On the left was carved a red dragon, breathing fire. On the right, a golden lion curled at the feet of a knight who wore silver armour. Around his lance was plaited strands of gold and red.

'As you know, the family are away, except Lord William,' said Mrs Burns, as they stood on the creamy waxed flagstones. 'I'm at liberty to show you some of the rooms and the duties you will be expected to perform in their upkeep. Think yourself lucky. Lowers are not usually given this honour. But since you come with a recommendation from Lady Hailing . . .'

Hilda blushed. She felt as though she had already been singled out for special attention. Did Mrs Burns see in her something that had always been overlooked at Hailing House? Hilda didn't much care for the housekeeper, but what did it matter, when she was soon to be part of all this?

'Every room in this house has a discreetly placed communicating door to the servants' stairs. We serve the family twenty-four hours a day, and quite often it is necessary in the middle of the night. Mr Leighton and the footmen are free to come and go according to their duties. You are not. Maids are never to be seen by the family. You go about your duties when the rooms are unoccupied. Should you by chance, or mistake, meet your employer, you give way immediately, lowering your eyes, making yourself invisible. Is that understood?'

'Yes, Mrs Burns.' Hilda thought of the informal practices she had been accustomed to at Hailing House. Lady Hailing always acknowledged her and Aggie, should they meet. She often asked them how they were and gave them a friendly smile. But, thought Hilda proudly, this was a proper aristocratic mansion and run on quite different lines, the rules of which she was sure she would soon get used to.

'Furthermore, there is to be no fraternizing with the opposite sex. No gambling, smoking or abusive language. You are to be punctual, clean and polite. There is no admittance to visitors, friends or relations without my knowledge and approval as I have already warned you. You will bring your own clothes: two uniform dresses, two working pinafores, a black dress, a white cap and apron. A cap must be worn at all times, under penalty of dismissal for not doing so. A black bonnet is required for Sunday service.' Mrs Burns narrowed her eyes disapprovingly at Hilda's green hat and feather. 'No colours are to be attempted. Hair to be drawn back, braided and pinned securely.'

Hilda nodded vigorously. She would do anything to live here in this wonderful house. She would make herself new uniform and a black dress in no time at all. As for the black bonnet and going to church, Hilda gave a slight shudder. She hadn't been to Mass since she left the orphanage, except at Christmas with Flora and Mrs Bell and Aggie.

'Underwear and footwear,' continued Mrs Burns, glancing down at Hilda's rather worn brown boots. 'Lisle stockings, black of course, and boots polished daily, twice if necessary. Laced stays, cotton vests, petticoats and bloomers.'

Hilda thought that she would have to go to the market to buy herself some of these things. Most of her underclothes were darned to within in an inch of their lives. She had only recently made one petticoat out of two, since the cotton had frayed so badly. As for her bloomers . . .

The housekeeper drew herself up, her flat chest rising. 'Now, your wage. As an under housemaid, for the time being, you'll earn twenty pounds in the year.'

Hilda smiled. Although this was three pounds short of her current wage, Mrs Burns had added those tantalising words, 'for the time being'. This must mean there was hope she might become a permanent member of staff. Hilda vowed silently that she would try to keep on the good side of Mrs Burns. Already Hilda could feel the house drawing her in. She imagined herself as Lady Bertha's personal maid. She knew it was possible if she really tried.

Mrs Burns was moving on. Hilda hurried to follow. At the top of the staircase, on the first landing, Hilda's heart leaped. A life-sized painting hung before her of a dark-headed young man, perhaps the most handsome she had ever seen. He posed for the artist, a gun and a dog at his side. His glimmering dark eyes fixed her. Hilda heard her own gasp. Shod in sturdy brown boots, leather gaiters and tweed jacket, he looked every inch the huntsman. The matching breeches and knee-length stockings, which Hilda had rarely, if ever, seen before, added to his slightly arrogant stance. The artist had caught the rich, black texture of his hair, and his aloof, sensual gaze and broad shoulders. Hilda took her breath once more. She couldn't tear her eyes away.

'Lord Guy Calvey,' announced Mrs Burns, as though she was addressing an audience. 'Son of Lord William, the fourth Earl of Talbott.'

All Hilda could do was stare. Lord Guy's presence seemed to fill the wide landing, the next set of stairs, the spacious, opulent and magnificent rooms around them, indeed the whole of Adelphi Hall. She had never felt as if a painting was alive before. There was any number of works of art at Hailing House, hung in the private rooms. She dusted their frames every day. But none of them had an effect on her like this.

'Come along, there's no time to waste,' scolded Mrs Burns, frowning at Hilda's hesitation. 'There are the state rooms to visit yet, where we shall examine the duties you will be expected to perform at six a.m. sharp, before the household wakes. The saloon, the dining, drawing and smoking rooms, and the library.' She nodded to a room to her left. Through gold-gilded double doors Hilda could see shelf upon shelf of exquisitely bound books. An ornate black marble clock stood on a slim oblong table, flanked by delicate vases and pottery. The highly polished floor was covered by a large oriental rug. Hilda had never seen such opulence. 'And above us, forty bedrooms and Lord William's suites to be catered for,' ended Mrs Burns sharply.

Hilda was trying to concentrate. She found it almost impossible. Her gaze was being drawn back to those dark, bewitching eyes in the painting. They called to her, just like Adelphi Hall had called to her the moment she had seen it.

Chapter Seven

Flora jumped. She had fallen asleep on the garden bench. She looked around her. There were dragonflies and damselflies soaring over the water of a lily pond. Its centrepiece was a mossy urn from which flowed a stream of water. An arbour of pink roses, holly bushes and fruit trees grew by the greenhouses. A gardener and several young boys were working in one, tending the flowers and vegetables grown under the glass roof. It was a peaceful scene, and Flora thought how much more she was enjoying her visit now that she had left Mr Leighton's office.

Her thoughts went back to the dark, unwelcoming butler's quarters. However, she had liked the interesting photographs on the walls. Lord William had looked very distinguished, despite Gracie's comments of him being slightly barmy. His thick, dark hair was streaked with grey and he wore his military uniform with pride. His bearing was upright and dignified. Not so his son, Lord Guy, who stood almost casually in a fashionable tailored suit and offered an impatient, arrogant expression to the camera. A mane of black hair, the ends of which touched his collar, surrounded his somewhat surly face. What had Gracie meant when she'd whispered those words about mischief? Flora wondered. The likeness between Lady Bertha and her nephew was remarkable. Her thick black hair was swept up to the back of her head and it was pinned at the side with a jewelled comb; her dark eyes fixed the camera with a disdainful expression. It was clear, Flora thought, that Lord William's sister had a taste for expensive silks and the latest style in corsetry! As for her husband, James Forsythe, he was quite the dandy. A foppish looking man, with a long, thin nose in an equally thin face.

'Flora, at last, I've found you!' Flora came swiftly back to the present as Hilda rushed up. There were two bright spots of red on her cheeks. She sat down beside Flora and pulled off her hat. 'I won't be wearing this cheap thing any more.'

'Why not?' asked Flora.

'The colour is common. Mrs Burns thought so, I'm sure.'

'But you've only just bought it.'

'Yes, but at the market where everything is second-hand. I'll have to smarten meself up a bit.' Flora listened to Hilda's breathless account of her interview with Mrs Burns. 'My old grey working dress won't do either. I'll have to buy quality material and make new dresses. I need underwear and boots too.'

'But can you afford all this?'

'I don't know,' Hilda said worriedly.

Flora thought of her savings in the china teapot at home. 'I could help with a pound or two, perhaps.'

'It won't be long before I can pay you back.'

'What did Mrs Burns show you?'

'I can't begin to describe the house,' Hilda replied with a far-away look in her eyes. 'There were silk-covered walls and beautiful furniture I ain't ever seen the likes of before. Sofas as big as boats, mirrors that shone so bright you have to squint to look into them, and the finest silver and porcelain just about everywhere I looked. Mrs Burns showed me the music room first. It had a great piano in the middle and all the walls, even the ceiling, was painted with scenes of the olden days.' Hilda tried to catch her breath. 'The dining room had a polished table I couldn't hardly see the end of and as for the bedrooms, well, me mind went into a spin! There's over forty and even more in the attics. There's beds I didn't even know existed, with big lumpy covers and posts to hold up their great tasselled tops. They've even got curtains round them.' Hilda giggled. 'I suppose curtains are hung there to stop anyone disturbing the magic moments!'

Flora smiled. 'Did you see your room?'

'There wasn't time. But I'm sure it'll be nice.'

'The house sounds very big, with plenty to clean.'

Hilda ignored this and rushed on. 'We didn't even go up to the top floor where Lord William's rooms are. No one's allowed up there expect Mr Leighton and the footmen and Turner, Lord William's valet.'

'Did Mrs Burns explain your duties?'

Hilda looked vague. 'Yes, but I wasn't really listening.'

'Why not?'

'I was thinking of the painting of Lord Guy at the top of the staircase. Oh, I couldn't believe me eyes, Flora. I've never seen any man so handsome.'

'It was only a painting.' Flora recalled the photograph in Mr Leighton's office. Quite the opposite of Hilda, she thought Lord Guy had an unpleasantly spoiled expression.

'The painting is a good likeness, so Mrs Burns said,' Hilda said with a tilt of her chin. 'Anyway, I'll tell you the rest on our way home.' Hilda looked back at the house. 'Though I don't want to leave.'

'When do you start?'

'Dunno. But soon,' Hilda said, her brown eyes shining, 'just before the family return from abroad.'

Flora looked for a long while at her friend. 'Are you sure it's what you want, Hilda?'

'Why do you keep asking me that?'

'Because country life will be very different to London.'

Hilda's gaze went longingly back to the house. 'I've never belonged anywhere before. Not since Mum died. I know I'll belong here.'

'Remember, you'll be under Mrs Burns' eye.' Flora stood up.

'I know, but I think she favours me,' Hilda said as she rose to her feet. 'I can make meself a life here, Flora. A proper one. Somewhere I know I'm appreciated.'

'I hope that's true.'

They linked arms to walk through the kitchen garden towards the stables. 'I'll be a lady's maid before long. In no time at all, I'll have everything I always wanted.'

'I hope so.'

'I'll miss you and Will. But you can come to visit me. Of course, I have to ask Mrs Burns first.'

Flora nodded a little sadly. She would be parted from Hilda, her very best friend, her sister. But if this was what Hilda wanted, then Flora hoped she would find happiness here at Adelphi Hall. A happiness she believed she hadn't been able to find before.

As they walked into the courtyard, Albert stood waiting. Flora's spirits lifted at the sight of him. Unlike Hilda, Flora loved her life on the city's island and couldn't wait to get home.

Albert pulled the canvas sheet across the cart, then helped them aboard. 'We're not likely to be back afore nightfall,' he warned. 'You'd better wrap yourselves up warm in them blankets. Didn't reckon on waiting for yer this long.'

'I'm sorry,' Flora said. 'Mrs Burns showed Hilda round the house.'

'It's a big 'un, an' all,' agreed Albert, gathering the reins in his hands. 'Did you get the job?' he asked Hilda.

'Yes. Of course,' Hilda replied primly.

'Well, at least you'll not starve here,' Albert replied with a toothless grin. 'Not if the food is anything like the tasty pie I was given to eat, washed down with a mug of ale.'

Flora thought that Albert was lucky to have been shown such hospitality. If it wasn't for Gracie she wouldn't even have had a cup of tea.

As the cart rumbled out of the courtyard, Hilda sighed. With two fingers she lifted the corner of the blanket. 'What a dirty rag this is.'

Flora laughed. 'You're not living at Adelphi yet.'

'I can't afford to catch fleas.' Hilda pushed the blanket on the floor.

'Did Mrs Harris give you anything to eat or drink?'

'Yes, a slice of caraway cake and a cup of tea.'

'That was nice,' said Flora. 'Did she ask you any questions?'

'No, she's not nosey like Mrs Bell.'

'You don't really know her yet.'

Hilda gave Flora a quick glance. 'Who did you talk to?'

'Mr Leighton and Gracie, the scullery maid. The one who the footman bumped into in the passage. Gracie showed me inside the butler's quarters. To his dining room and pantry where the silver is polished. There was a cellar downstairs, but we didn't go down there.'

'A butler is the most important member of all the staff,' Hilda said in a reproving tone. 'He wouldn't have liked you going into his rooms.'

'We weren't there long.'

Hilda was silent, then burst out, 'Well, what did you think of them?'

'Mr Leighton's rooms?' Flora shrugged. 'They were quite dark and gloomy. But I liked the photographs on the wall. Some were of the servants and one was of the family.'

Hilda sat upright. 'So you saw Lord Guy?'

'Yes.'

'Isn't he handsome?'

'Some would say so.'

'Who else did you see?'

'The earl, Lord William. He looked very distinguished in his military regalia. Lady Bertha looked very fashionable. As for her husband, James Forsythe, he didn't strike me as much at all.'

'Did you know that a lady's maid accompanies her mistress when she goes abroad?' Hilda said eagerly. 'I might see Italy one day. Or travel on a steam train to some other country house. I hear there are special trains that carry the entire family, their personal belongings and staff, together with their automobiles.'

Flora giggled. 'I can't keep up with your wealth of knowledge.'

Hilda laughed too. Then, turning to Flora, she murmured, 'I haven't forgotten it's your birthday today.'

Flora looked surprised. 'So it is. I'd almost forgotten it myself. But it don't feel any different to be sixteen.'

'I'll take you up to Lyons for tea one day.'

'I'll remember that.'

As the cart jogged along, Hilda fell asleep, her hatless head on Flora's shoulder. Flora's thoughts tumbled through her mind in time with the clattering wheels of the cart. She had hoped to persuade Hilda to go to St Edmund's with her and celebrate Mass today. But Hilda would have gone reluctantly, if at all. Instead, they had enjoyed a look into a very different world. Hilda had been impressed by Adelphi Hall. It was fair to say, Flora reflected, that her friend now had only one thing on her mind: to move from Hailing House as quickly as she could.

But in the light of what Flora had seen today, she was certain that Mrs Burns would demand much more of Hilda than Mrs Bell ever had. It hadn't occurred to Hilda, it seemed, that like all would-be lady's maids, she would have to work her way up the ranks, as Mrs Bell had once warned her.

Chapter Eight

It was the beginning of September and Flora was listening to the patients. They were talking excitedly about the recent attack by a German Zeppelin.

'Did you see the airship?' asked one elderly man who had just left the doctor's room.

'It dropped a bomb near Westferry Road, where I live,' an expectant mother confirmed. 'I nearly went into labour right there and then.'

'Which way did it go?' someone else asked.

'Flew over the river to Greenwich.'

'Bermondsey and Rotherhithe was hit,' another man informed them. 'Then it had the cheek to go back and cross the city.'

'The cost of the damage it done will be down to us,' a tall lady, nursing a bandaged foot, added. 'As if the war's not costing us enough already.'

Flora had been woken by a thump in the night, but she had been too tired to investigate. The day before had been very busy. It hadn't been until a quarter to nine in the evening that she and the doctor had ended their exhausting day.

'Now you see 'em, now you don't,' the first man complained. 'It's inhuman, that's what it is. You can't get yer revenge on something as high up as those damned balloons.'

'The newspapers say our aeroplanes can't fly high enough to catch 'em,' the lady with the bad foot protested. 'What is the government going to do about it? That's what I'd like to know.'

Just as Flora was about to interrupt the complaints, she heard a woman's screams outside.

'Is that the airships back again?' someone yelled. Everyone began to panic.

Flora hurried to open the door and as she pulled the handle, a man rushed in at her, pushing her out of the way. Flora fell back, momentarily stunned. An older woman followed him breathlessly. Her coat was half-on over her nightdress and her grey hair tied in plaits.

'Mrs Howe, what's the matter?' Flora asked the widow, a patient of Dr Tapper's. 'Is it the Zeppelin coming again?'

'No, nurse, it's my boy, Tom. He's home just a week from the Front. A bullet's gone through his hand, but it's his mind what's injured. He's like a trapped animal. Can't sleep because of his nightmares, won't eat. And last night when the Zeppelin flew over, he went crazy. The noise of the bomb sent him running down the road, shrieking. And because it's so dark in the blackouts, I couldn't catch him. If it wasn't for my neighbour persuading him back, I dread to think what would have happened.'

Flora hurried after the young man who had run into her small room. When she arrived there, he was cowering in the recess by the sink. His eyes blinked rapidly. 'Tom?' she asked softly.

'You see, nurse,' Mrs Howe whispered at Flora's shoulder. 'I'm at me wit's end.'

Flora moved an inch closer to the trembling soldier. 'Tom, let me help you.'

He shook his head, trying to curl himself into the wall. His skin was ashen under his pale hair. His eyes must once have been a very light blue, like her own, she guessed. But now they looked colourless. The bones of his shoulders under his cheap jacket stood out like sticks. One hand was folded against his chest, wrapped in a dirty bandage.

'What am I going to do?' Mrs Howe clutched Flora's arm. Like her son, she was thin and lean-featured, but a deep despair filled her eyes. 'He was caught up in a German bombardment that left him half crazy. It took them over two months to get him home from France after they'd patched up his hand. You won't let him run off again, will you?'

Flora smiled at the distressed soldier. 'Tom, you're safe now.'

'B . . . bombs,' he gasped, trying to shrink away.

'There are no bombs now,' she told him, and took a beaker from the shelf and filled it with water. 'Drink this, it will help.'

With shaking hands he took it and gulped greedily. At that moment, the doctor walked in. Flora saw the fear in

Tom's eyes, but the doctor's voice was soft and enquiring as he addressed his patient.

'Hello, Tom. Do you remember me? I brought you into this world, young man.'

'That's right, Tom,' Mrs Howe agreed. 'This is Dr Tapper.'

'Come into my room,' the doctor urged in a gentle manner. 'Nurse will bring you along as soon as you feel comfortable.' Taking Mrs Howe's arm, the doctor steered the anxious woman out of the door.

Flora knew the doctor was giving Tom time to compose himself. She managed to take the beaker from his clenched hand. 'I'll pour you some more in the doctor's room,' she told him. 'Are you feeling better?'

Tom gave her a wary nod, his pale eyes blinking rapidly.

'You can tell Dr Tapper what's upsetting you,' Flora said softly. 'Then he'll give you something to help.'

'They ain't taking me back,' Tom mumbled. 'No more bombs.'

'No, Tom. No more bombs. You're home now, and safe.' She held out her hand. 'Come with me.'

The distressed soldier allowed Flora to guide him slowly to the hall. She felt him pull back when the row of faces turned towards him from the waiting room. But this time, there were no protests from the assembled. Instead looks of sympathy and compassion filled their faces. The sight of the wretched victims of war was becoming all too common in the streets of the East End.

'Yer'll be all right, son,' a man called. 'You've been in hell, but now you're free of it.'

If only that were true, Flora thought as she helped Tom towards the doctor's room. The battlefields were a living hell for all those who fought so valiantly on the killing fields. But the suffering did not end when they returned home.

If the Zeppelin had caused Tom Howe to believe he was back in the trenches of France, Flora was to discover a more distressing threat to the soldiers' lives. The doctor had given Tom a mild sedative for his mental agitation and suggested that with time and his mother's care and understanding, the effects of shell shock would disappear. But early the next morning, when Flora was presented with Eric Soames who was barely able to stumble into the waiting room, her heart sank.

Unlike Tom, this soldier was not in a state of terror. Rather, he had the apathy and yellow pallor of a sick old man. His face was scarred and ugly. At only twenty years of age, with barely nine months of service behind him, he hardly had the strength to walk.

'Can't breathe, doc,' Eric said, coughing. He lowered himself into the chair, even this small movement seeming to sap all his energy. His scarred cheeks and forehead were a deep red with tiny veins showing tightly over the thin skin.

Dr Tapper asked Flora to help him remove the young soldier's coat. It proved difficult, as any exertion caused

Eric to become distressed. When finally his shirt buttons were open, Dr Tapper examined the thin skin drawn over the young man's chest with his earpiece.

'How long have you been sick?' Dr Tapper asked.

'Since April.' Eric's chest rose and fell with difficulty as he spoke. 'Me and my mate was caught in a gas attack.'

'Gas?' repeated the doctor.

Eric nodded. 'Fritz's new weapon of war.'

The doctor's face darkened. 'But I heard it was the French and Algerian troops who suffered that monstrous onslaught.'

'It was, doctor,' agreed Eric, wheezily. 'We was ordered to scout up to where our lines met the French. I wish to God now I'd disobeyed that order and run in the opposite direction. When me and Reg got up there, the troops that survived the gunfire were making a dash towards us. And that was when we first saw it. A bloody great yellow-green cloud, hanging in the air, like a bank of fog. We thought it was fog too and just stopped to stare at it wondering why the French was bottling out.' Eric cleared his throat and the sweat broke out on his face. 'Then we started coughing—' As if the memory was too painful to voice, he hid his scarred face in his hands.

'Water, please, nurse,' Dr Tapper said, nodding to the pitcher on the side.

Flora poured a full tumbler and put it to his lips. As he sipped, Eric's sad eyes met hers. 'The French stood no chance. They was falling around us as the breeze brought this terrible stink. It made your throat tickle at first, then your eyes started to smart. I tried to cover me face with a rag, but it weren't no use. This coughing started and has never left. All we could do was run, like our allies. Through the bodies and the dead horses and the screaming wounded. My face felt as though it was burning.' He stopped again and his shoulders shook as he heaved and threw back his head to breathe air. 'Something must have been on the rag as my skin peeled off under it. They did their best back at our lines, but I was in so much pain with me face, they took me to the base hospital.' He gave a hoarse gasp. 'Dunno what went on after that. They put me out and I was thankful they did.'

'I can give you something to help,' the doctor said, patting his shoulder.

'Am I gonna die, doc?'

'I'd like you to see another physician. Could you get to the East London Hospital? I have a colleague there who is more experienced than I in these matters.'

Eric looked into the doctor's face. 'I've a wife and two kids. I'd like to see the youngsters grow up.'

'We'll make every effort to see that happens,' the doctor said with a nod.

After their patient had left with a letter from the doctor to the hospital physician, Flora saw the doctor slowly close his written notes. He looked up at her. 'A sad case, Flora. Very sad indeed. What was on the rag we shall never know. Surgeons are beginning to discover new ways of skin reconstruction. But I fear his lungs are collapsing.'

Flora thought of Will, of his innocent, gentle eyes and mop of blond hair flopping over his forehead. Had he experienced this new menace of gas poisoning? She loved her friend so dearly, as she loved Hilda. He had become her little brother and she his protector. But how could she help him now?

'We must press on,' said Dr Tapper, rising to his feet. 'And do what good we can in this perilous time.'

Flora knew he was hiding his fear for Wilfred, as she was for Will. The son the doctor treasured, whose fate remained unknown, may have been exposed to the same dreadful weapon as Eric.

'My plans have changed,' announced Hilda, on a bright September Saturday as the two girls met in their usual spot at the market.

'You've decided *not* to leave Hailing House!' Flora wanted to jump and clap her hands for joy.

'No, silly. Of course I haven't changed my mind.' Hilda pouted.

'Sorry.' Flora sighed. For a moment, she had thought Hilda had come to her senses.

'You said you were happy for me.'

'I am.' Flora hoped she'd be forgiven her fib. 'But as the time grows close, I know how much I'll miss you.'

At this, Hilda's face softened. 'I'll miss you, too. But think of what we'll have to tell each other when we meet.' Hilda pushed her towards the tea stall. 'Let's have lemonade. I've some very good news.'

Flora bought the two drinks from the tea stall. They sat on the bench under the tarpaulin to enjoy them, hearing the rattle of the wind in the canvas folds.

'Lady Hailing came to the house last week,' Hilda began in a confidential tone. 'She brought her two daughters, not much older than us. Oh, you should have seen them, Flora. So nicely dressed, I could have wept!'

Flora smiled. 'I hope you didn't.'

'Course not. But me, er, my head spun when I saw their pretty frocks and shoes. Not boots, mind, but lovely pale leather shoes with pointed toes and buckles. And . . .' Hilda tilted up her chin and waved her gloved hand, one finger drawing a circle as if she was royalty. 'Lady Hailing said, "Girls, this is Hilda, who will be leaving us soon." Can you believe it, Flora? I was speechless and couldn't breathe a word in reply.'

'That's not like you.'

'I know.'

'So what happened?'

Hilda sat erect, saying in a high voice, '"Annabelle and Felicity, what have you to tell 'Ilda?"'

Flora giggled. 'You just dropped an haitch.'

'I nearly dropped down dead an' all when I heard what came next.'

'What was that?' Flora loved to watch Hilda acting the part.

'"'Ilda, would you take it as an insult if we offered you these clothes? We've outgrown them and wondered if you'd like them."' Hilda rolled her dark eyes and placed her hand on her heart. 'Oh, Flora, I couldn't believe my ears. I couldn't catch me breath and thought I was about to faint!'

'But you managed not to in the end?' Flora smirked.

Hilda pushed Flora's arm. They burst into laughter. 'The girls even said they hoped I was coming back to Hailing House after the war, but, if I wasn't, I was bound to do well at Adelphi. I think it was the best day of my life, second to going to Surrey.'

Flora put down her mug of lemonade. 'Are you sure you want to leave the family?'

There was longing in Hilda's voice when she replied. 'I want to be like them, Flora. But I know I can't. And never will be. So the next best thing is being a lady's maid, ain't it? I've got to go somewhere with prospects.'

Flora gazed into her friend's deep brown eyes. 'You're a lady to me.'

Hilda smiled. 'I'll look like a lady in me, er, my new clothes. Mrs Bell is helping me to alter the ones that need changing. Not that there's much to do. Quality counts, and even if a dress is too big or too small, I reckon it don't matter. Lady Bertha will see that I'm not a cheap-skate when it comes to me fashion sense.'

Flora smiled with her friend. It seemed everything was working out all right for Hilda after all.

Chapter Nine

Flora had never seen such lovely clothes. 'Hilda, this is beautiful,' she said as she touched the pink dress folded on Hilda's bed. The dress was striped, with a cotton bodice and tapered skirt. The long sleeves and pleated cuffs were very fashionable.

'That dress was Annabelle's,' said Hilda. 'She's a year younger than me, but taller.' Hilda went to the wardrobe and drew out another dress. Flora saw that this one had purple embroidery around the collar and hem. 'It's real silk, Flora, touch it.'

Flora was almost afraid to touch the delicate, slippery material. 'Hilda, this must have been very expensive.'

'I know. I've never worn silk before.'

'I've only ever seen silk in shop windows.'

'There's more, too.' Hilda took out a beige linen suit with a tailored jacket and ankle-length skirt. Inside the skirt was a dark-brown lining that matched the brown velvet trims on the collar and cuffs. 'This will be just right for autumn. I've decided to wear it when I go to Surrey. Mrs Burns won't be able to look down her nose at me ever again.'

Flora watched breathlessly as Hilda showed her more of the outfits: a day dress of pale green cotton, and several more suits, all of which had gloves and scarves to match. On the bare floorboards beside the bed were leather shoes, six pairs in all. 'One or two pairs are a little large, but I'll stuff the toes with paper which always works a treat.' Hilda kicked off her old boots and slipped on a pair of black buckled pumps. 'What do you think?'

'They'll go very well with the suit.'

'I tried everything on last night. Mrs Bell, who's very good with a needle, says she'll make all the alterations next week.' Hilda gave a deep sigh. 'Though in return she expects me to listen to her long stories of how she's worked for Lady Hailing since she was twelve and how she's scrubbed till her fingers bled. You'll be pleased to know I listened patiently. And for once, I even got a good word out of her. She said as long as I kept me feet on the ground and didn't let all this go to my head, I might do very well in me new job.'

'I told you before, Mrs Bell only wants what's best for you. She looks on you as a daughter, as she's never had a family of her own.'

'I know. She's not really even a "Mrs".'

'Cooks are always called "Mrs this or that".'

'I'll be just "Jones", but when I'm Lady Bertha's maid, I'll have Mrs Burns call me "Miss Jones".'

Flora could never see that happening, but didn't say so.

'Why don't you try this hat?' Hilda picked up a pretty blue cloche. 'Ain't it pretty? Blue is your colour. It matches the colour of your eyes.' Hilda placed it on Flora's blonde curls. 'Look in the mirror.'

Flora looked into the mirror that was nailed to the wardrobe door. The hat looked lovely, but her other drab clothes didn't. The hat showed up her brown-checked wool suit for what it really was: old and unfashionable. Her shoes were bulging at the sides where they had been worn out by their previous owner, and her stockings were snagged. She tried not to look disappointed in herself.

'And to go with the hat, there's this.' Hilda lifted a blue tailored suit with a calf-length skirt and fitted sleeves. She placed it against Flora's slender form. 'There you are, don't you look the part? I wish I could wear blue, but it doesn't do me justice. You'll have something nice to wear on Sundays now.'

'I couldn't accept this, Hilda.'

'Why not?'

'Because they were given to you.'

'But this suit won't fit at all. I tried it on and even with my stays laced tight, I can't do the jacket buttons up.'

'No, it's just not right.' Flora took off the hat. 'I'm sorry, Hilda, but I'm sure Mrs Bell could make it fit.'

'I want to give you something. And now's my chance. After all, I said I'd take you up West for tea for your birthday and I haven't.'

'There's still time.' Flora lay the suit and hat on the bed.

'I'm afraid there's not,' Hilda said quietly.

Flora turned to stare at her friend. 'What do you mean?'

'The family are coming back from abroad early. Mrs Burns wrote to say she wants me to start next month, just two weeks away.'

Flora felt sad, though she knew she should be happy for Hilda. She was soon to lose Hilda; her best friend and sister was leaving London and the only life they had ever known.

'I've already asked Albert if he'll take me in the cart,' Hilda said shyly. 'He's agreed on a shilling like before.'

Flora was trying not to shed any tears. 'You'll write the moment you get there, won't you?'

'I've told you, I will. There's no one else I can boast to.'

'And not just a few sentences with bad spelling mistakes.'

Hilda giggled. 'Yes, Sister Patricia.'

Flora smiled. 'You won't think much of my news as you don't like to hear about the walking wounded.'

They looked at each other and laughed. Flora scooped a tear from her eye, as did Hilda. They knew each other well, as sisters and good friends should. But it was hard to say goodbye. However, Flora couldn't blame Hilda for leaving. Even Mrs Bell had come to that conclusion. Her friend was exchanging one life for another. A life that seemed to have all that Hilda had ever dreamed of.

Chapter Ten

The day arrived when Hilda was to leave. It was a misty Sunday morning in October and the sound of Albert's cart on the cobbles caused Flora to hurriedly put on her coat. There would only be a few minutes to say their last goodbyes. Before leaving the airey, she picked up the parcels of crusty bread and thickly spread dripping that she had made for Hilda and Albert's breakfast.

Outside, the air was heavy with the scents of the island: spices and oils and confectionaries from the factories; tarry ropes and musty timbers and smoke-belching chimneys. All this was mixed with the falling leaves from the trees and the dust and dirt of the streets, together with the waste and flotsam from the water traffic. On smelling the scents, Flora knew she was home. She marvelled at Hilda's courage to leave what was safe and familiar.

'Mornin',' Albert called, lowering the reins. His weather-beaten face and long straggly hair were shielded by his cloth cap and the collar of his greatcoat. 'Good enough weather for travelling, ain't it? No rain, and that's what counts.' He clucked through his teeth as the horse tossed his head. 'Steady, boy. We'll not be stopping for long.'

From out of the back of the cart climbed Hilda. She wore one of her new outfits – the beige linen suit and tailored jacket with brown velvet trims. Over her hair, she wore a small felt hat that discreetly hid her abundance of youthful curls.

'Hilda, you look very grown-up.'

'I'm all fingers and thumbs this morning. I could hardly dress meself. Do you know I've three bags full of clothes? And another of shoes and hats. I can't imagine I'll need them all, but I can't bear to leave any behind.'

'Have you got your new uniform?' Flora asked, wondering if Hilda really had made all her dresses.

'Mrs Bell helped me.'

'And enough underwear?'

'All that, too.' Hilda paused. 'There were a few tears from Mrs Bell and Aggie before I left.'

'I'll go and visit them soon.'

Hilda smiled. 'They'll like that.'

Flora handed Hilda the parcel. 'You might get hungry on the journey.' Then she reached into her pocket and brought out a small black book. 'This is for you, too.'

'Your catechism?' Hilda asked as she turned the pages.

'To remind you of who you are. A good Catholic girl.'

'I lost mine when I left the orphanage.' Hilda went red.

Flora knew that Hilda had probably thrown it away. 'You won't lose this one, will you?'

'No. Course not.'

Flora smiled. 'You'd better not keep Albert waiting.'

Hilda caught hold of her. 'I'll miss my big sister,' she said, shakily.

Flora kissed her friend's cheek. 'God bless, dearest.'

Hilda climbed back under the canvas and Albert shook the reins.

'Take care of yourself. Remember to say your prayers,' Flora called as the cart moved off.

Hilda stuck out her head. 'Light a candle for me at church!'

As the sound of the horse's hooves faded away, Flora shivered. She felt very alone. Her dear friend had always been part of her life. Now, Hilda was travelling far away. Her new home was not even within walking distance or a bus ride. At the earliest opportunity, Flora decided, she was going to St Edmund's, the parish church at Millwall, and would do as Hilda had asked. The nuns had taught them that if they lit a candle to accompany their prayers to heaven, their requests would be granted. Flora had always lit candles for the poor, sick children in the convent infirmary. When some of them had died and she'd helped the nuns to lay out their often emaciated and crippled bodies, she imagined their souls rising up from their earthly forms and, helped by their guardian angels, being borne away to heaven's gates, free of suffering and shining brightly like stars. Of course, no one knew if this was true, not even the nuns. But Flora believed that such innocent little souls were welcomed to heaven by their creator, in the light of the candles. She never felt sad, but happy that they were finally out of all pain and misery. Flora still believed in the power of prayer and a burning candle. Hilda insisted that prayers and religious practice were not for her. But Flora believed that Hilda was not at all the lost soul she pretended to be.

The very next Sunday, Flora decided to visit Sister Patricia at the orphanage. Instead of going to St Edmund's, she would go to Mass in the chapel. It had been three years since she and Hilda had left St Boniface's. Had there been many changes in that time? she wondered. She would ask Sister Patricia to offer prayers for Will and Hilda. The nun had taken on a motherly role with all of them, even though Hilda, having strong memories of her own mother – unlike Flora and Will who knew nothing of their parentage – had always insisted that no one could take Rose's place. But it was also Sister Patricia who had given Rose the job in the laundry when she was destitute, and taken Hilda in when Rose had died.

When Flora set off, a cold October breeze blew in her face and whistled round her ears. She had wrapped up warmly in a coat and scarf, though she knew a brisk walk would soon make her cheeks burn. The streets of the East End were deserted at such an early hour. If she'd made her journey during the week, she could have caught the number fifty-seven bus. But on Sundays, transport was scarce. The convent was on the far side of Victoria Park.

The streets slowly came to life as she hurried along. She nodded to the early-morning churchgoers who made their way to worship, dodging the horse-drawn traffic as it began to fill the roads. Flora preferred the weekday hustle and bustle of trade: the many port workers with regular jobs who arrived by bicycle or on foot at the dock gates; the less fortunate stevedores waiting at the dock gates for casual work; and labourers, shore gangs, bargemen and lightermen making their way towards the river. But this morning the hooters from the boats on the river were silent. Only the hungry gulls screamed, their cries interwoven with church bells. The small shops were all closed and shuttered. A few young children played hopscotch or cat-o'-nine-tails. The grimy, noisy environment of the docks was at peace this morning and Flora hoped she would find help and inspiration from the place that, from her earliest memory, had been her only home.

When the docks were behind her and she eventually arrived at the park, she stopped still. She hadn't come this way for three years. The tall trees had lost their green leaves. She remembered the day of her and Hilda's first communion when they were nine years old. After the long morning service and a modest breakfast in the refectory, the nuns had given her and Hilda and Will permission to walk to the park. They had played under these very trees. Will had fallen over. She and Hilda had washed the grazes on his hands and knees with water from the pump. The injuries had hurt, but Will had refused to cry. He hadn't wanted to spoil their communion day. Flora saw his pale face in her mind, his curls bouncing across his forehead, his lips buttoned tightly against the pain. She sighed at the precious memory.

Hurrying on, Flora took the next turn to her left. This was the road that led to St Boniface's Convent and Orphanage. All the identical houses in the road were in good repair, unlike the slums of the island. Their windows and doors were clean. The roofs all possessed slates and sturdy chimneys. The railings outside were painted a shiny black.

Flora looked for the tall bell tower of the convent. She walked on a little and the convent appeared. Soon she was standing in front of the red-brick building with its three storeys and stained-glass chapel window. Her heart raced. The memories began to tumble back.

Flora pushed open the heavy iron gate. Slowly she crossed the yard that she and Hilda and Will had played in so many times. At the big double doors, one of which still bore the old brass crucifix, she paused, her heart racing.

Flora hadn't recognized the nun who let her in. She sat alone in the convent visitors' room in front of a polished round table. There was a large painting on one wall of St Boniface with his hand raised in a blessing. He wore a cloak of gold and his bare head was encircled with a ring of light. The small room smelled of polish and incense, a mixture that was familiar to Flora even though she had never been in this room before. But then, she had never been a visitor before.

There was a large open book on the dresser, its gold-leafed pages open and a quill standing in a pot of ink beside it. The tall, thick, creamy white candles on either side were unlit. She couldn't help thinking of Hilda's sensitive stomach as she gazed at the crucifix hanging on the white wall opposite. The blood dripping from Christ's wounds would have made Hilda feel faint.

As Flora sat on the hard chair, she thought of the times she had worshipped in the chapel. The older orphans had been allowed to attend Mass before school began. She remembered how hungry they were after the night's fast as they sat in the pews. Flora smiled as she recalled the sound of the empty tummies that rumbled during the service. The breakfast that followed in the dining hall was only unbuttered bread and sugarless porridge. But none of them had ever left a crumb!

Though the chapel's mitre-shaped wooden doors were closed as she and the nun had passed, Flora had been relieved to see that the alabaster holy water font outside was full. The nuns always filled it before Mass.

Flora began to recite in her mind the words of the hymn all the orphans loved most: 'Immaculate Mary! Our hearts are on fire.' She could hear their sweet voices, and the power of the words of the chorus: 'Ave, ave, ave Maria!'

The door opened and Flora came back to the moment. Would Sister Patricia still look the same? Tall and thin, she had kind grey eyes and the part of her face that was exposed under her wimple was also very thin. Hilda had joked about their teacher's long nose, especially as sometimes in winter a drip would slide from it. But Flora always thought Sister Patricia looked like an angel. Her age was hard to place. Her skin was so pale it looked transparent. Her movements were graceful. She didn't smile much, but when she did, Flora thought her smile made her look beautiful.

There was a time when Flora had wanted to be a nun too. But working in the infirmary with all the sick children had soon made her think she would prefer to be a nurse. Not that either one of these options would have been open to an orphan like her. Most girls were sent at thirteen to factories or into service. It was only Sister Patricia's letter of recommendation to Dr Tapper that had given Flora the start in life that she was so grateful for.

'Good morning,' a nun said, entering the small room. 'God's blessing on you.'

Flora jumped to her feet. Mother Superior, unlike Sister Patricia, looked old and wrinkled; she was a tall, bent figure who only appeared when there was High Mass, a crisis or a celebration. As far as Flora knew, a visit to the convent from an ex-orphanage girl was none of these.

'Good morning, Mother.' Flora knew that this reply was expected of her.

Mother Superior kept her hands folded under the black linen of her habit. She squinted through the thick lenses of her spectacles. 'Flora Shine, is that you?'

'Yes, Mother.' Flora felt happy to be recognized, although at the same time she was a little alarmed. Hundreds of girls had passed through the orphanage doors. Unlike Hilda, she had managed not to draw much attention.

'How long has it been since you left us?'

'Three years, Mother.'

'So what has brought you here today, my child?'

Flora hesitated. 'To ask for permission to attend Mass in the chapel. And to ask the Blessed Virgin for something . . . something special. And . . . and also, I hoped to see Sister Patricia.' Flora felt nervous as she watched the nun make her way silently to the table. Very slowly she folded her long skirts around her and sat down. 'Please join me.'

Flora did so. Her heart was beating very fast.

'There have been changes since you left,' the nun told her. She stared at Flora through her thick lenses. 'Sister Patricia has returned to our Motherhouse in France. She left before the outbreak of war.'

'France?' Flora repeated in surprise.

'It was deemed that a period of spiritual refreshment was needed.'

'Will she come back?' Flora asked.

The nun hesitated, seeming to choose her words carefully. 'We must pray that Sister Patricia, and indeed the entire Motherhouse, is safe in God's hands. As we all know, France is a country participating in war.'

Flora knew the church frowned on war. As children they had been taught to pray for peace and forgiveness in the world.

'What was it you wished to pray for at Mass?' the nun asked.

'I wanted to pray for my friends, Hilda and Will.'

The nun nodded slowly. 'I remember them.'

Again Flora was surprised.

'You may be interested to know that I supported your teacher's decision to send you to Dr Tapper. You worked well in the infirmary and we felt you deserved the opportunity.'

'Thank you, Mother.'

The nun gave a slight smile. 'Dr Tapper is very pleased with you.'

Flora looked up. 'He is?'

'We ask our benefactors to keep in touch and are always interested to hear of the souls who have left our care.'

Flora felt a warm glow at the thought that the doctor approved of her.

'The baker that Will worked for has told us he volunteered to fight. Pray God he will keep safe.' The nun made the sign of the cross over her chest. 'But we have not been informed of Hilda's progress.'

Flora lowered her eyes. It would seem ungrateful to say that Hilda had been unhappy at Hailing House.

Mother Superior's hands disappeared into her black sleeves again. 'Things are not as we hoped for Hilda? Life in service is a disappointment to her?'

'Oh, no,' Flora said at once. 'She was happy at Hailing House. It was just that – well, she had a chance to do better.'

Mother Superior blinked. 'I should think it very unlikely that a position in Lady Hailing's service could be bettered.'

Flora looked into the nun's small eyes hidden behind the thick lenses. 'It was Lady Hailing who suggested that Hilda move. Or rather, loaned her out, because of staff shortages due to the war.'

'So all was done with the approval of her employer?' clarified Mother Superior, raising an eyebrow.

Flora nodded. She hoped that nothing more was asked about Hilda. She had already told another small fib about Hilda being happy at Hailing House.

'We shall be glad to have your company at Mass,' the nun decided after a few moments.

Flora sighed softly. She was very pleased that this awkward conversation was over. But, as she was about to stand, the nun reached out. 'Please stay seated a while longer.' She went to the dresser and opened a drawer.

'This is yours, my child,' the nun said, handing a neatly folded cloth to Flora.

Flora took the soft wool in her hands. 'Mine?' said Flora, frowning.

'You were wrapped in it as an infant. It has been in the drawer ever since.'

Flora stared at the fragile weave, seeing as she opened it that the wool was a shawl. 'This belongs to me?'

The nun nodded silently.

'But why . . . how—'

'If you wish to know more, you will have to speak to Sister Patricia.'

'But she isn't here.' Flora stared at the shawl.

'As you well know, no orphan is allowed more than the other. Any personal items are kept until the young person is considered responsible enough to take them. You are now turned sixteen, Flora. The shawl is yours to do with as you wish.'

Flora curled her fingers around the soft, lacy shawl that was beginning to yellow with age. There was a 'W' and an 'S' embroidered in one corner.

'Whose are these initials? Could they be my mother's?'

'I'm afraid I can't tell you. I was not here at that time.'

Flora couldn't take her eyes from the shawl. She had never had anything from her past before. This shawl had been wrapped around her as a baby. Someone had loved her. Was it from her mother? Could Sister Patricia tell her?

In the chapel, Flora sat at the back on one of the highly polished pews. The nuns all bowed their heads in worship.

Pencil-slim candles lit up the chapel in a creamy glow. The smell of incense drifted out from the sacristy.

When the priest walked slowly to the altar dressed in his long white robe, the nuns made the sign of the cross. The priest greeted them in Latin.

Flora closed her eyes and began to pray.

If only, dear God, the war would end soon.

Chapter Eleven

As Flora arranged the sterilised instruments on the trolley, she was thinking of the shawl. She hadn't done anything else but think of it since her visit to the orphanage on Sunday.

'Good morning, Flora.' Dr Tapper walked into the room.

'Good morning, Dr Tapper.'

'I have heard from the hospital that Eric Soames has passed away.'

Flora felt guilty. She was thinking only of herself, and now the young soldier had died.

'We must prepare ourselves for more injuries of this type if the war continues,' said the doctor as he took a seat at his desk. 'Show our first patient in, please.'

Just as the doctor had foretold, Flora observed similar symptoms in the young man who next sat down in front of the doctor's desk. His arm was in a sling and his jacket hung loose on one side.

'My regiment was able to break through the German defences and capture Loos,' Private Cecil Morris told them in a wheezy voice. 'But I saw bodies caught in the wire . . . twisted . . . bleeding. Some of the men were still alive, choking from the gas they'd swallowed. And doctor, the gas came from our own side. Blown back on the wind to fill the British troops' lungs. I tried to run from it.'

'Were there no gas masks provided?' the doctor asked.

'Most of the blokes threw them away as they thought they did more harm than good,' Cecil explained. 'We couldn't see through the fogged-up eye pieces. You didn't know who you were shooting at. Or who was shooting at you. But I managed to keep mine on somehow. Still, I reckon I must have swallowed some of that stuff as I've been short of breath ever since.'

'And the wound on your arm?' The doctor nodded to the sling.

'In the fog, I ran right into the enemy lines. A bayonet ripped into my arm. The blade didn't go through the bone, but it ain't a pretty sight, doctor.'

After removing the sling, Flora undid the dirty bandages.

'I can see no infection,' the doctor told him as he examined the injury. 'But you must keep the wound clean.' Then he took his wooden listening tube and placed it on Cecil's chest. After a few seconds, he nodded. 'You were sensible in wearing your mask, even though you couldn't see through it. I'll give you a linctus to help, but take it only when needed. Now, my good man, are you staying with your family?'

'Ain't got none,' Cecil replied. 'My old mother died when I was away. I've a bed with the Salvationists.'

Dr Tapper nodded. 'I shall want to see you again in a few days' time.'

'Us lads from the artillery were lambs to the slaughter,' the next patient, Sidney Cowper, told them, holding his shoulder. He was a young recruit of just nineteen. 'We tried to make a dash across the fields, the German machine guns opened up and mowed us down. I took a bullet in the shoulder. The next thing we knew, Fritz was on us, polishing off any life they could find. I played for dead and somehow I survived. But my shoulder still hurts like billy-o!'

Flora helped the young man to take off his jacket, shirt and vest. The wound left by the bullet's entry had been treated and stitched. But when the doctor made his examination, Sidney cried out in pain. 'When did this happen?' asked the doctor.

'More than a month or so ago,' Sidney replied. 'I was put on a merchant ship, else I'd still be 'oled up in France.'

When the doctor's examination was over, he sat at his desk. 'The nerve endings in your shoulder have been damaged.'

'What does that mean? Can't I be helped?' Sidney asked as Flora helped him to dress.

'In some cases, there's little that can be done. But perhaps in yours, it may be different. You are, after all, in the early stages of healing.'

'Can you help me, doc?'

'I can send you to a colleague who would consider your case for treatment.'

'I'd rather you do it, if yer can.'

Dr Tapper smiled. 'Your best chance is with the hospital. You may need surgery again. Or, if you are lucky, the treatment of exercise and massage will bring results.'

'I could do with a nice bit of massage, doc.' Sidney grinned.

'I'm afraid you will not find it very pleasant,' the doctor warned as he wrote on a piece of paper. 'In fact, quite the opposite.'

'What have I to lose?' Sidney said as the doctor sealed the letter in an envelope.

'Take this to the London Hospital. See it is delivered to Mr Whitham's office. Say the letter is from me and is urgent. Wait until you are told it has been handed over safely. Leave your name and address and say that you will return the next day for an answer.'

Sidney rose to his feet. 'Thank you, doctor. God bless yer.'

'You've had a rough time of it, Sidney. Godspeed.'

After Sidney had left, the doctor turned to Flora with a deep sigh. 'I have done my best, but the hospitals are under pressure. Gordon Whitham believes, as I do, that there is more to be done for certain cases than going repeatedly under the knife. Whether or not Sidney is a candidate for his busy list, I don't know.'

'Couldn't you give him the treatment?' Flora asked, just as Sidney had.

'If I were to fail, I should blame myself for not having referred the man to Gordon, who is a specialist in his field.'

Flora nodded. She wanted to say that if she had been in Sidney's shoes, she would only have wanted the doctor to treat her.

The doctor put his hand on her shoulder. 'Your faith in me is very gratifying, Flora. But I haven't attempted this method for many years.' He looked into her eyes and frowned. 'You know, you look a little tired. I insist you take this Sunday off. Even if there are knocks on your door, you must send them upstairs to me. October is almost at an end. A foggy, damp November is sure to keep us on our feet, as you well know.' He wagged a gentle finger. 'You've worked tirelessly and deserve a complete day to rest. I want you to take it.'

But Flora knew Dr Tapper would not rest. Not only did he care professionally for the sick and needy of the East End; in every soldier, he saw Wilfred and took their woes to heart. She knew he was still hoping that his dear son didn't lie in the muddy, rat-infested trenches of the battlefields. That somehow he'd escaped death, as Sidney Cowper had.

It just didn't seem fair to Flora that her kind employer might lose his only son when he devoted his life to helping so many others.

* * *

On Sunday, the weather turned cold. A fog began to settle over the rooftops as Flora made her way to Hailing House. The blanket of yellow covered everything, even the Tilley lamps of the horse-drawn vehicles.

'Fancy you being out in this pea-souper!' Mrs Bell exclaimed as she opened the back door and the fog blew in.

'Hilda asked me to visit you.' Flora stepped in to the cosy kitchen.

'Did she now?' Mrs Bell hid her rueful grin. 'Well, at least she's thinking of me, even if she can't find the strength to write.'

'I asked Dr Tapper for your embrocation.' Flora gave Mrs Bell a jar of the liniment that the doctor made up for her.

'Oh, bless you,' the cook said, gratefully. 'These cold mornings my back and legs are stiff as pennywhistles. Thank you, my love.'

Flora let Mrs Bell take her coat and hang it on the peg. After seating Flora by the warm range, the cook put the big kitchen kettle on to boil. 'We'll have a nice cup of Rosie. Matter of fact, I've a few fruit scones baking.'

Flora smiled. Mrs Bell always made her visitors feel welcome and had a never-ending supply of scones baking in the oven. She couldn't imagine Mrs Harris at Adelphi Hall being the same.

Mrs Bell took a seat beside Flora, folding her plump arms across her waist. 'I miss Hilda more than I thought, you know,' she confessed. 'Took to her like the daughter I never had, or could ever hope to have. She was an affectionate child when she arrived, and because of that, I suppose I forgot she was not my own blood.' The cook sighed. 'But she seemed to change this last year, ever since the war began. I had to bite me tongue right up to the day she left, to prevent meself from saying something that would upset her. It was no business of mine, her leaving here for pastures green. But I knew she thought I was trying to clip her wings. And maybe I shall miss her more than she'll miss me. But a girl like Hilda could easily put her trust in the wrong sort.'

'I'm sure Mrs Burns, the housekeeper, will keep an eye on her.'

'Yes, I have that thought to comfort me,' Mrs Bell agreed. 'Most housekeepers earn their stiff reputations. And from what Hilda told me about this lady, she sounds a scorcher, just as her name indicates.'

They both laughed. Mrs Bell leaned forward and dropped her voice to a whisper, as if someone might be listening. 'Tell me, now Hilda isn't here to pull a long face, what's your honest opinion of her prospects with the Calveys?'

'Hilda has high hopes,' was Flora's only reply.

'Indeed she does. But our girl assumes her good looks will get her to being a lady's maid in the blink of an eye. She don't realize she'll be worked off her feet, much more so than with Lady Hailing. It was hard enough for a housemaid in my day. But with the war and the men going away to fight it, the gentry are said to be taskmasters to their remaining staff.'

'But Hilda's young and knows what she wants.'

'She does that all right.' Mrs Bell clucked her tongue.

'Mrs Bell, I've something else to tell you.'

'About Hilda?' Mrs Bell looked hopefully at Flora.

'No, I'm afraid not. I went back to the convent where me and Hilda and Will grew up. I spoke to Mother Superior.'

Mrs Bell got up to take the scones from the oven. Flora knew she was still thinking about Hilda.

'I thought I might be able to go to Mass in the chapel and perhaps speak to our teacher, Sister Patricia. She was very good to me and Hilda.'

Mrs Bell took out a knife from the drawer and slid the sharp tip into the hot dough. When the knife came out cleanly, she nodded in satisfaction.

'But Sister Patricia is in France, at the Motherhouse,' Flora continued.

'Oh, that's a shame.' Mrs Bell took a pair of tongs from the rack and transferred the scones to a large plate.

'I hope she'll come back soon. Mother Superior gave me a shawl. She said I was wrapped in it when I was found.'

At this, Mrs Bell stopped what she was doing and looked at Flora. 'Why weren't you given this shawl before?'

'Orphans aren't allowed to have things of their own.'

'Even if it belongs to them?'

'No. It's the orphanage rule.'

A frown touched Mrs Bell's forehead. 'Was it your mother who wrapped you in it?'

'Mother Superior said Sister Patricia might know. But she's in France.'

The cook raised her eyebrows. 'The poor soul could be trapped behind enemy lines.'

'She might be.' Flora felt very worried now.

Mrs Bell frowned thoughtfully. 'What's this shawl look like?'

'There's a "W" and an "S" embroidered in one corner.'

Mrs Bell sat down and turned her full attention on Flora. 'Is this shawl moth-eaten and poor in quality?'

'Not at all. The wool is old, but still very fine.'

Mrs Bell was silent. Flora could see that she was thinking as she sliced a scone with a sharp knife. 'Well, my dear, the thing that strikes me is why was an abandoned little waif like you wrapped in such a fine shawl? You hear of orphans being found in rags and even in newspaper, but never in good shawls. Tell me, is it a clumsy hand that's attempted the embroidery?'

'The letters are sewn very carefully with gold and red silks,' Flora replied.

'If it was your mother's work, then she had great skill.'

Flora felt a warm glow. To hear someone speak about her mother was a new experience.

'The "S" may very well stand for Shine,' suggested Mrs Bell. 'And the "W" could be Winifred or Wilhelmina.'

Flora felt her heart skip a bit. 'Do you think so?'

'It's a pity this Sister Patricia's in France.'

Flora knew Mrs Bell wasn't going to say more as both of them knew that bringing the wounded troops home from the fighting was very dangerous. Some of the hospital ships had been sunk by enemy submarines. The war might take many more years to end. Meanwhile, was the Motherhouse in enemy hands and, if so, had Sister Patricia survived? All these thoughts were going round in Flora's head.

Mrs Bell patted her hand. 'Come along now, eat up your scone.'

But Flora had lost her appetite. She ate the scone slowly and quietly.

'You need to keep up your spirits.' Mrs Bell said as she cleared away their plates. 'Now, before you leave you'd better go up to Hilda's room. There's a parcel on the bed for you.'

'For me?'

'Hilda left it. You'll find everything just as it always was. Though I put a duster round her room every so often, to keep it smelling sweet. You never know . . .' The cook sniffed and went to the sink, plunging her hands into the bowl of water.

Flora reluctantly got up and let herself into the cold, dark passage. She didn't want to go up to Hilda's room.

It would be upsetting not to find her friend there. Flora went up the back stairs as usual. Her view from the landing window was only of the fog that swirled eerily over the rooftops. She wanted to run back down the stairs again. Instead, she gave a long sigh and went along the passage to Hilda's room.

Inside it, the air smelled of mothballs, which Mrs Bell must have put in the wardrobe and drawers. The faded curtains that hung at the windows had been straightened and the bed was neatly made. On the bed was the parcel.

Flora sat beside it. The last time she sat here, Hilda had been full of excitement at the thought of leaving Hailing House. Now she had gone. Flora looked around her. The room had lost its heart, as though it knew Hilda would never return.

'This is for you, Flora,' read the note on top of the parcel. 'You *must* have it. Think of me when you wear it. Yours, Hilda.'

Flora opened the parcel and took a sharp breath. It was the blue suit. Tears filled her eyes.

'Oh, Hilda, I'd rather have you than the suit,' she whispered, bringing the soft cloth against her cheek. 'But that's being selfish.'

If only Hilda knew how much she was loved by Mrs Bell and herself. But then, Flora thought in a sudden flash of understanding, as if the room itself was speaking to her, it wasn't possible to keep someone close who wanted to be free. Hilda had once had a mother. And although Rose had died, Hilda remembered a mother's love.

That's why she didn't want Mrs Bell to fuss over her. No one could ever replace Rose.

Flora thought of her shawl, safely in the drawer. She would go home and look at it once again. And try to imagine the person who had wrapped her in it.

Chapter Twelve

Hilda was still asleep in her uncomfortable bed when Gracie roughly shook her.

'It's time to get up,' the scullery maid told her.

Hilda pushed the coarse blanket away from her face. During the freezing cold night, she had burrowed down into the bedclothes, leaving only the tip of her nose to freeze. She pushed the tousled brown hair from her eyes and yawned. Sitting up, she took the cup of tea that Gracie had brought her.

'Is it morning already?' Hilda peered at the tiny girl standing at her bedside. Hilda wasn't tall herself, just five foot four, and she rarely looked down on anyone. But Gracie was several inches shorter than her, which, as Hilda blinked, brought her almost eye level to Gracie's pinched face. Hilda had noticed how red raw Gracie's hands were as she passed the cup and saucer. And even at this early hour, Gracie's white pinafore was spotted with dirt or perhaps food, which would be much to Mrs Burns' annoyance, reflected Hilda sleepily.

'It's a quarter-past five already.' Gracie gazed adoringly at Hilda and said quickly, 'I've got the kettle on. Violet and Mrs Burns' trays are ready.'

A second later and Gracie had vanished. Hilda yawned again as she climbed out of bed. It was her duty to take the housekeeper and the lady's maid, Violet, their morning tea. For this, she had to be up three quarters of an hour before her official start at six a.m. However, Hilda had soon found help in the form of the scullery maid, Gracie, who could be very annoying at times, but had been indispensible at others.

For the four weeks that Hilda had been at Adelphi Hall, Gracie had attached herself to Hilda, had almost become her shadow, watching everything she did and correcting her mistakes. But Hilda had soon found that Gracie would willingly shoulder some of the duties that Hilda didn't care for. Most importantly of all, she provided Hilda with background information on both the upstairs and downstairs worlds of Adelphi Hall. Rather humiliatingly, Hilda had found herself made to share a room with the scullery maid. The smaller servants' dormitory on the second floor of the house housed four iron bedsteads, all with very hard mattresses. Hilda had been expecting a room of her own. She had at first resented Gracie's delight in having a companion. But in exchange for Hilda's reluctant friendship, Gracie had become her willing slave. During the first week of her employ at Adelphi Hall, Hilda had collapsed into bed at night, too exhausted to even eat supper. Gracie had brought her tea and stolen biscuits from the larder, prepared her uniform for the morning and performed the sewing tasks that Mrs Burns had instructed Hilda to do.

Hilda had soon realized that Gracie was absolutely necessary to her survival here. Mrs Bell had been right. The many duties she had to perform, like the cleaning of brass, china, glass and furniture, the making of beds, the sweeping and scrubbing of floors and dusting of each visible surface, took up every moment of her day. Not to mention wrestling the dirt from the thick carpets that she had admired so much at her interview, not realizing it would be her, Hilda, who would clean them. Heaving coal into the many fireplaces and preparing the fires had only been completed with Gracie's help. Scouring the bathrooms from floor to ceiling had been Hilda's least favourite task. And without Gracie to carry the many pails of water up the servants' stairs, Hilda thought she might well have expired in the first forty-eight hours of her new life in service to the Earl of Talbott.

Still, Hilda reflected, as she washed in the freezing cold water of the bedroom's only china bowl, Gracie had proved to be her unexpected bonus. In return for her friendship, Gracie never failed to comply with Hilda's demands.

Hilda finished her washing and put on a fresh pair of knickers. After a day's labouring, a change of underclothes was most important. Next, came her chemise, tightly laced stays, flannel petticoat and, lastly, her dark-grey uniform and apron. Then, still yawning, she braided her hair rather clumsily, and tucked the braids up into her mob cap.

With her teeth chattering with cold, Hilda ran down the many steps of the servants' staircase to the kitchen. To Hilda's relief, Mrs Harris had not yet appeared. Had she been at the stove, barely a word would have been spoken before Hilda was swamped with instructions. Now that the family had returned from abroad, Mrs Harris was cooking three hot meals a day and afternoon tea and supper trays when requested. Hilda, together with two live-out housemaids from the village, was required to help clean and prepare the vegetables, together with all her other duties.

''Ere you are, 'Ilda,' said a small, squeaky voice beside her. Gracie was standing with a tray in her hands. On it was a white china cup and saucer, a sugar bowl and jug of milk. 'This is for Mrs Burns. Then you can come back for Violet's.'

'Why can't you bring Mrs Burns' tray for me?' Hilda said sulkily. 'And I'll carry up Violet's.'

'If anyone saw me, I'd be sacked.'

'But there's all those stairs to climb.'

'Mr Leighton's always about early. And so are James and John.'

Hilda grinned at the thought of the two handsome footmen. 'I wouldn't mind bumping into one of them.'

Gracie snorted. 'They ain't got the time of day for the likes of us.'

Hilda didn't like Gracie hinting that she was as lowly as a scullery maid. She took the tray begrudgingly. 'I suppose I'll have to do it.'

'If you makes it quick and gets back before Mrs 'Arris starts dolling out orders, I'll tell her you've already got going on the fires. Then the two village girls will get lumbered.' Gracie laughed strangely through her broken front teeth. 'Serve the snobby cows right.'

Hilda smiled. No one at the Hall liked the casual staff from the village. They were lazy and rude, and often left within the first few weeks, to be replaced by others who were equally rude and lazy. It was generally accepted, Hilda discovered, that they were employed under sufferance.

'It's either them dopes or no one, as Mrs Burns can't get live-in staff these days,' Gracie confided when Hilda complained about the village girls' slovenliness. Hilda herself had been given the cold shoulder by the permanent staff for the first week she'd been at Adelphi Hall. But Gracie had told her it was quite normal until she had settled in and proved her worth.

As Hilda climbed the stairs with the cold penetrating her thin uniform and making her shiver, she thought about all that happened to her since she started at Adelphi Hall on that miserable day in October. After leaving Flora in the street, doubts about what she was doing with her life had crowded in. She suddenly realized that she was on her own now. No Mrs Bell to fuss over her, no dear friend to take into her confidence. She was completely and utterly alone. The journey in Albert's covered cart had taken for ever. It was all she could do to stop herself from telling him to turn the cart round. All the excitement she'd felt as she'd dressed that morning in her fine clothes had turned to fear. Even Flora's bread-and-dripping sandwiches hadn't cheered her. By the time Albert had driven past the gatehouse and entered the long approach that was the tradesmen's entrance to the house, she had been cold, tired and very frightened.

But at the first sight of the mansion, bathed in a soft mist with its tall pillars caught in a fleeting ray of sunshine, her heart lifted. Not only was this place going to be her new home, it was where she intended to better herself in ways that would never be possible in the East End.

Exhausted by the long climb of the staircase, Hilda stopped outside Mrs Burns' door. Balancing the tray in one hand, she gave a discreet rap. She had learned, to her cost, that she must never be later than a quarter to six. By this time Mrs Burns was always up, washed and dressed in her black satin and white frilled collar with the key belt tied at her waist. Hilda had reached this room five minutes late on her first morning and had been thoroughly scolded.

'Good morning, Mrs Burns,' Hilda said, keeping her eyes down as she placed the tray on the wooden table beside the bed.

Mrs Burns, sitting at her desk, didn't answer. Instead, as Hilda left, she muttered, 'Tell Mrs Harris I shall be down shortly.'

Hilda nodded and quickly left the suffocating atmosphere of the housekeeper's quarters. She had noticed that Mrs Burns had no photographs of loved ones or family. Only a small crucifix and framed religious prayer were placed on the wall. The room's drabness did not suit Hilda at all.

Running down the stairs, Hilda was met by Gracie who whispered, ''Ere, take this tray up to Violet, quick. The old dragon's breathin' fire this morning. The mistress wants dinner for twenty tonight. And Mrs 'Arris ain't been given no notice. I warn you, it's gonna be bedlam today.'

'Twenty?' asked Hilda, at once dismayed and excited by this news. How much extra work would be involved for her? Would there be fine ladies and gents attending that Hilda might catch a glimpse of?

But Hilda didn't have time to consider this longer, as Mrs Harris' loud voice echoed from the kitchen.

Gracie was gone in a flash. Hilda started up the stairs to Violet's room. She knew Violet would also be up, preparing herself before going to wake Lady Bertha. Hilda tapped on the door and opened it. The familiar smell of lavender wafted out. Hilda knew Violet filled her chest of drawers with linen pouches of lavender. She also placed them in her wardrobe to cover the strong odour of mothballs.

'Leave the tray there,' Violet said, pointing to the small table but glancing at the mantel clock. 'You're five minutes late, Hilda.'

'I'm sorry. There's a panic in the kitchen.'

'What about?'

'Mrs Harris has twenty to cook for tonight.'

'Lady Bertha's friends are up from town. I'm helping the mistress to decide on the menu this morning.'

This was said very formally and piqued Hilda's interest. Gracie had told Hilda that sparks often flew between Violet and Mrs Harris. The cook and lady's maid both laid equal claim to advising Lady Bertha, Gracie had reported. Each day, Mrs Harris would confer with the mistress on what was to be prepared and cooked. Every so often, Violet would tell the cook there had been a change made to the arrangements, which made Mrs Harris very irritable. Gracie had also revealed that Violet, a spinster in her late thirties, had served the mistress for only four years. This had come as a disappointment for Hilda; such a recent appointment meant Lady Bertha was hardly on the brink of wanting a replacement. Hilda had found Violet's fashionable and rather youthful appearance a surprise too. Violet's pure pale skin, small-featured face and wide hazel eyes were not displeasing. So the news from Gracie that there was some disagreement between Mrs Harris and Violet came as welcome to Hilda's ears.

'I'd like you to dust around the shelves in here today,' Violet said and Hilda groaned inwardly as she gazed around the room. Not that there was much to dust, but the chore was added to her already full schedule.

From the corner of her eye, Hilda noted the extent of her duties. Having returned with the family from Italy,

Violet had brought back some souvenirs: travel books and Venetian glass and miniatures of golden-domed churches. Hilda's eyes fell on Violet's bureau. It was cluttered with cards and sketches of foreign lands. The most attractive feature of Violet's room, Hilda decided, was the bed coverlet that Lady Bertha had presented to Violet. The greens, blues and yellows were quite dazzling.

'Thank you, Hilda, that will be all.'

Hilda's brow creased as she made her way downstairs. Her plans had been set around the position that was now occupied by Violet. Hilda had gone to sleep at night wondering how this could be changed.

'There must be a way,' Hilda muttered aloud, lost in thought as she rushed down the stairs. Suddenly, one of the doors leading to the main house that were used by the housemaids opened sharply.

Hilda stumbled back against the banister in fright. The surprise of the door opening and the tall, dark figure hidden in shadow made her think of the stories told to her by Gracie. Was this the deranged earl, or his silver-haired valet, Turner, who Hilda had never seen and Gracie was terrified of meeting?

Hilda let out a shriek as the shadow came towards her. She stepped back, trapped by the banister. Her breath came rapidly, her body trembled. She put out her hands in fear, glancing down at the dark stairwell beneath her.

Hilda froze. She hadn't believed Gracie's ghostly stories, or at least thought they were exaggerations. But what if they were true? Blinking rapidly, she felt the sweat on her spine. If only she had been paying attention as she came down the stairs!

'Step towards me or you will fall.'

Hilda could barely bring herself to look at him let alone move her legs. His presence seemed to surround her.

'Come, let me help you.' His fingers curled slowly around her wrists. 'Don't be afraid.'

Hilda could do nothing but allow him to pull her away from the stairwell. She would never forget her first sight of the man as he stepped into the light. Instead of the ghostly apparitions she feared, a real person stood there. She recognized him at once. Like the life-sized painting she had seen in October, his jet-black hair curled around his neck. His shoulders were broad under his crisp white shirt and his dark gaze was just as she remembered it.

'Oh!' was all she could say as her body now trembled, not in fear but with delight.

'That's better,' he told her, his eyes roaming over her with an appreciative gleam. 'You must be careful on the stairs.'

'Y . . . yes, my lord,' Hilda stammered.

'Are you new to Adelphi?'

'I came here in October, sir,' she replied as his fingers slipped from her wrists.

'What's your name?'

'H . . . Hilda, sir . . . I mean, Lord Guy.'

He smiled, his eyes seeming to drown her in their ebony gaze. 'No doubt we shall meet again.' Then, as swiftly as he had appeared, he disappeared again, speeding down the staircase, the sound of his light footsteps echoing back to her.

Chapter Thirteen

At the end of November a letter arrived from Will.

'My dearest girls,' he wrote in handwriting that was barely legible and on crumpled, brown-stained paper,

> I read your letters every day, Flora. They give me hope that I am not too far removed from sanity. Whilst this nightmare around me seems real, your words remind me of the world I came from and want with all my heart to return to. As I write, shrapnel bursts above us, flares light up the evening sky. I crouch by the gun wheel that rolled into the trench from the last bombardment. God only knows what happened to the troops who manned it. Thousands have perished in this God-forsaken land. We hardly have legroom in the mud and filth mixed in it. Our gumboots reach our thighs and clip to our belts, but even so, the mud fills them. We lost many men at Artois. The enemy is firing constantly, never letting us rest. Comrades fall silently around me, or sometimes with unbearable screams. The rats drive us mad. They chew into our haversacks and

scavenge the rotting corpses. They are afraid of nothing, not even the shelling, and flourish in abominable conditions. Perhaps my letter will never arrive in England. Perhaps you'll never hear of me again. I am already trapped in purgatory and await hell. Pray for me and my fellows, dear sisters. I rely on you, Flora, to intercede to the Blessed Virgin for my survival. With deepest and everlasting affection. From your miserable brother, Will.

Flora dropped the letter in her lap. She was sitting alone in the airey, beside the hearth. The fire that she had built that morning before work had kept the cold at bay. But inside her she felt chilled to the bone. Will's vivid description of his life in the trenches had brought tears to her eyes. A feeling of hopelessness overwhelmed her. Like all the men who had come to the surgery, his account of the war was unbearable. What good could come of all this killing? Flora could find no answer.

That night, she went on her knees and threaded her rosary between her fingers. She begged the Blessed Virgin Mary for protection for Will and his comrades.

Once again, it was all she could do for the dear boy who meant so much to her and Hilda.

The first week of December brought heavy rain and, each day, Flora mopped the floors of the surgery as patients arrived, many whom had suffered from the cold in November and now were laid low with bronchitis and flu. There were also more victims from the battlefront. They spoke of the Artois–Loos offensive that had failed in the autumn. Will was ever-present on Flora's mind. Each casualty gave an account of the mud-filled trenches and, as Will had written, the armies of rats spreading disease amongst the troops.

'Machine-gun fire felled us in our hundreds,' one soldier told Flora and the doctor. He was stick-thin and in distress with stomach pain. 'The snipers shot our wounded who were trying to get up and run but struggling to take off their equipment. I was grazed by a bullet, but managed to get back to our lines.' His haggard face fell. 'Though sometimes I wish I hadn't made it. I fell into the bog that contained the dead and dying. Bodies floated on the surface and piled up. I shall never forget them; those sightless eyes and bloated bodies.' He paused, wiping the moisture from his eyes with shaking hands. 'They . . . they fished me out and took me back to the field infirmary. I was sick and fevered. There's no lavs in the trenches, just pits that we dug and never filled in. They overflowed in the rain and the stench was unbearable. Nor did we have any clean water. We could only get supplies when we got back to the reserve lines.' The soldier groaned, putting his arms across his stomach and bending forward. 'The doctors told me I had dysentery and sent me home.'

'And not before time, young man,' said the doctor, as he dispensed a little white medicine into a small cup. 'This will help to ease the diarrhoea and subdue the pain.

But you must rest in bed. Drink as much clean water as you can. Take small quantities of barley water, milk or light soup. Have you someone at home to care for you?'

The soldier nodded. 'Me mother.'

Flora knew that, as with the victims of poisoned gas, there was little more they could do for those who had dysentery. Men who survived the first stages were often troubled by frequent attacks throughout their lives. Those who were too weak to fight for their health soon perished.

As the young man left, he was replaced by another: an older man in his thirties who had volunteered for Kitchener. 'I can't stop scratching,' he complained. 'And I got a fever that's left me as weak as a kitten.'

Flora helped the doctor to unravel the man's thick clothing. Over his chest, arms and legs were the red sores caused by lice. 'You have pyrexia or, as it's more commonly known, trench fever,' the doctor explained as he examined the patient. 'Your rashes and bites are caused by lice, though I see no evidence of the creatures on your body now.'

'The orderlies shaved me,' the man said, scratching his bald head. 'Then put this stuff all over me that felt as if it was burning my skin. We were given these blue sterilized suits to wear. I still can't stop scratching even though the lice are gone. They burrow into you, into your clothes and pants and then it feels as if they enter your insides. Some of them are as big as rice grains. We used to light candles and drop the wax on 'em. You heard 'em pop and the blood would spurt out of them. Yet you'd never be able to rid yourself of the buggers. I wake up fevered in the nights, still tearing at my skin and drawing blood.'

'My nurse will apply a suspension of zinc and iron oxide,' the doctor consoled him, nodding to Flora to administer the pink-coloured lotion from the trolley. 'This will reduce the inflammation of your sores and help you to resist scratching. The fever will come and go until you've completely recovered.'

'My wife is afraid I'll spread the disease to her and the kids,' the soldier said miserably.

'To address her worries,' the doctor advised, 'suggest that she use Naptha disinfectant in and around the house. Keeping the body and home clean is a deterrent to the spread of any disease.'

'Do you think the army will call me back up to the lines?' the man asked as he rose unsteadily.

'You're far from fit,' Dr Tapper replied. 'I shall vouch for your convalescence.'

When they were alone that evening, Flora told the doctor about Will's letter. And about how, when Will had volunteered, he had believed that the war would be over by Christmas last year.

'I'm very sorry, my dear,' he replied. 'But it seems the stories are one and the same. Your young friend, together with thousands of others, must have had had a very rude awakening.'

Flora knew the doctor was thinking of Wilfred. She wanted to ask him if he had any news of his son. Wilfred had been missing for six months. And now, after all she and the doctor had witnessed, Flora knew that with each passing day, as conditions in the trenches worsened, Wilfred's chances of survival were slim.

The following weekend, Flora went to see Mrs Bell.

'You're soaked through.' Mrs Bell tutted. 'Come into the warm.'

Mrs Bell took Flora's wet coat. The heat of the black-leaded range soon made the gabardine mac smell.

'Read this.' The cook slipped an envelope from her pocket.

Flora recognized Hilda's small, tight handwriting. But all that was written on the paper was a request for Mrs Bell to lend her a pound, if possible, well before Christmas.

'Not a thing about her new post, or any little details that might tickle me fancy,' Mrs Bell said crossly, as she poured tea and turned a sponge from a baking tin onto a plate.

'Why didn't Hilda ask me for the money?' Flora wondered.

'Don't know.' Mrs Bell sat down and cut the sponge in half. 'Well, perhaps I do. I'm afraid I got into the habit of helping Hilda out.'

'That was very kind of you.'

'I didn't think sending her a few shillings would do no harm.' The cook spread jam and cream thickly on both sides of the sponge then placed it in the middle of the table. 'Did you know she's paid less than she was here?'

Flora had been worried when Hilda had told her this, though Hilda hadn't seemed to mind at the time.

'Hilda's not one to save,' Mrs Bell continued, slicing the cake. 'She might go out to the village and throw money away on all sorts of distractions. Perhaps even at the local inn.'

'But Hilda don't drink.'

'I hope it stays that way.'

'She's only sixteen.'

'But looks older.' Mrs Bell frowned. 'Maybe she's not been paid yet.'

Flora was beginning to feel concerned. A pound was a good deal of money.

'I really don't know what to do for the best. The money don't trouble me. I always have a pound or two put by. It's what our Hilda wants it for that's worrying me. The lowers often take to tippling, my dear. A nasty habit to get into. But there's plentiful temptation for those who see it as their right to polish off the fine wines the family might leave, or sample the strong brew that can be bought in the villages on a day off.'

'I really don't think Hilda would do that.'

'You'd be shocked at the change in character that overcomes a girl when the work piled on her is never-ending. In the big houses, even the cook might reach for the sherry bottle at the end of her busy day.' Mrs Bell looked anxious, her hands tightly clenched together. 'And what of these village wenches that Hilda has to mix with? They wouldn't think twice about leading a young girl astray. The drinking that goes on in taverns amongst country folk – well, I've seen it all in my time, Flora. And money washes down the drain as fast as water.'

Flora could see that Mrs Bell was very upset. She didn't know how to advise her.

'Though I wouldn't rest if I didn't send her something.' Mrs Bell looked at Flora.

'Perhaps ten shillings,' Flora suggested. 'Half a pound should go a very long way.'

'Yes, you might be right.'

They ate their cake and drank their tea in silence. Flora wondered why Hilda hadn't written to her; it was almost two months since she'd left the East End.

By the time Flora left Hailing House, she had managed to bring a smile back to the cook's face. Mrs Bell thought a great deal of Hilda. It would be hard for her to refuse Hilda's request, even though there was no explanation to say why Hilda needed the money. More importantly, Hilda hadn't taken the trouble to write about her new life at Adelphi Hall. A few lines, thought Flora, a little put out, would have easily satisfied Mrs Bell.

Chapter Fourteen

It was Tuesday and Flora was clearing up. The morning had been very busy and now, at last, the waiting room was empty.

'What are your plans for Christmas?' the doctor asked, peering over his half-spectacles as Flora swept the floor. The patients had brought mud and dirt in from the streets on their damp shoes and clothes. Flora took particular care in the wet weather. It was in the damper conditions that diseases thrived. She knew the uncarpeted wooden floor would be just as dirty this evening, but still she left no corner untouched. The smell of disinfectant was all around as the doctor sat at his desk.

'I'm going to the midnight service with Mrs Bell. And Aggie too, if she's free.' Flora had tried not to think how much she would miss Hilda this year. Since they'd left the orphanage, their tradition was that after Mass she and Hilda would come back to the airey and Hilda would sleep the night on the big sofa. Christmas Day was very special for them. They made their own decorations and cooked a roast dinner. The chicken would be very small, but they always had plenty of vegetables. Will joined them, bringing freshly spiced buns and marshmallows from the bakery. They would eat them by the fire, toasted on long forks. But last year had been very different. Will had enlisted and she and Hilda had celebrated alone.

'Your friend won't be visiting from Surrey?' the doctor enquired.

'Hilda hasn't written,' Flora said a little dejectedly.

'Then perhaps you might think of joining me for lunch,' said Dr Tapper. 'Mrs Carver insists on leaving me much more than I can eat. And of course, without Wilfred . . .'

Flora realized that Christmas for the doctor held only memories of times past and he would be very alone this year. 'Thank you. That would be very nice,' Flora accepted, replacing the mop in her bucket.

She was still thinking about the doctor's kind offer when he continued. 'I'm sad to say that a death has been reported to me. Stephen Pollard, whose leg was amputated at hospital.'

She looked sadly at the doctor. 'What will become of his widow and children?'

'Mrs Pollard has been admitted to a sanatorium.' The doctor brushed back his thick grey hair with his hand. 'And the children sent to temporary care.' He stood up and braced his shoulders. 'Let us hope, she will recover soon.'

Flora knew the doctor was very upset. She was about to leave, when he said quickly, 'There is, on the other hand, good news from my colleague, Gordon Whitham.'

Flora recognized the name at once. 'The doctor you sent Sidney Cowper to?'

'Yes. It seems, so far, Sidney is improving.'

Flora felt excited. 'The new treatment has worked?'

'Not entirely. Many months of painful exercise must be endured for complete rehabilitation. I shall look forward to hearing again. But even this is welcome news.'

Flora knew the doctor was trying to keep cheerful. It was, after all, the Christmas season.

'Perhaps we will close the doors a little earlier today,' he said, with a smile.

Flora knew how much he cared for his patients. But he couldn't let the thought of the many unfortunates, like Mrs Pollard and her family, overwhelm him. The news of Sidney Cowper had been especially welcome today.

Flora decided she would go to the market and buy Christmas cards. She wanted to end 1915 by reminding Will and Hilda about the happy times they had shared. And tell them her prayers were with them, no matter how far away they were.

The traders of Cox Street market had made an effort at Christmas cheer despite the shadow of war, Flora noted happily. Wrapped up warmly in her coat, scarf and hat, she made her way through the crowds. Bunches of holly and mistletoe were nailed to the beams of the stalls. Some of the handmade paper-chains strung across their interiors had turned limp and bedraggled, but still looked seasonal. The fruit and vegetable stalls were doing a brisk business, despite the shortage of food supplies that Flora had heard everyone complaining about. She noticed how people were still buying in large quantities – vegetables, oranges and apples were arranged enticingly on the costermongers' stalls. The barrow boys selling hot chestnuts turned the crisp fruit on their braziers. She loved the smell of the roasting nuts; after browning on the tin plates, the chestnuts disappeared into boat-shaped newspaper bags, still steaming in the misty air. In the distance, she could hear a man singing, 'Pack Up Your Troubles In Your Old Kit Bag'. The song reminded her of Will.

Dotted about the market she saw street urchins: scrawny, red-nosed children holding their caps and begging for charity. One or two made an attempt to sing carols as she passed, holding out their filthy hands for offerings. Others rushed to grab overripe fruit or vegetables thrown in the gutters as waste.

An aroma of coffee wafted pleasantly in the air. Flora remembered the time when she and Hilda had witnessed the attack on Old Fritz, just after the *Lusitania* had sunk. His bric-a-brac stall had been turned over and his stock scattered far and wide. The old man had never returned to the market.

Flora wandered over to the bric-a-brac stall that was now standing where Fritz's stall had been. A tall, middle-aged woman was serving behind it. She had a long nose, small, shrewd eyes and hair stuffed under a shabby-looking felt hat. 'Fancy a nice trinket or two for the holiday, dear?' she asked, holding up a pretty brooch in the shape of a butterfly. 'This would suit you. Real silver and a sturdy clasp.'

'It's very nice, but I couldn't afford it,' Flora replied politely.

'What do yer want then?'

'I'm looking for some Christmas cards,' Flora replied. 'Some festive ones, with cheerful greetings.'

'You won't get many of those,' the woman said, dropping the brooch back in the box and pointing to the front of the stall. 'They're out of fashion. But I've got some nice ones there. I'll give you tuppence off if you buy six.'

Flora gave the cards a swift glance. They all had crude drawings of the kaiser, or Kitchener, or soldiers or sailors; the jokes written on them didn't seem very funny. 'They're not for me, thank you. My friend is a soldier and I'd prefer something happy to remind him of home.'

'Your sweetheart is he?' the woman asked, giving Flora a wink.

'No, a good friend.'

'Oh, is that what you girls call 'em nowadays!'

Flora hesitated. She wasn't sure she liked this woman. 'Do you know what happened to Old Fritz?'

The female trader narrowed her eyes until they almost disappeared under the bags of loose skin. 'He was kicked out of the market. Good riddance to him, too.'

'But he'd been here a long while. He was a nice old man.'

'Friend of his, are you?' the stallholder said accusingly.

'I was here the day he was attacked. He was treated very roughly.'

'That's because he was a dirty German. A spy, no doubt, for the other side.'

'What rubbish!' a deep voice said, causing Flora to look up into the solemn face of a young man wearing a peaked cap. He was tall and slim and dressed in army uniform. 'I knew the man,' he said, looking sternly at the stallholder. 'Like this young lady, I'm sorry to hear of such foul behaviour towards him.'

The woman's thin lips curled and twisted. 'A soldier like you should know better than to fraternize with the enemy. If you don't want the same treatment, you'd better keep that sort of opinion to yerself.' She went off to join another trader.

'Forgive me,' the young man said to Flora, his face pinched by anger. 'When I couldn't find Fritz, I rather feared something may have happened to him.'

'Did you know him well?' Flora asked.

'My mother is a customer of his. He sold very nice jewellery, not of the expensive kind, but quite charming pieces. I came here today to find a brooch or necklace she might like. A small gift for Mama as, since coming home on sick leave, she's looked after me rather well, despite my often miserable mood and complaints. But when I saw the space occupied by another stallholder, and overheard your conversation, I realized that the poor old man had been singled out along with others of German extraction living in Britain.'

'Then you know he couldn't defend himself,' Flora said passionately. 'The crowd tore down his stall and spoiled his stock. He had to escape before they turned on him.'

'It doesn't make sense, does it? A man can be good and decent, but his birthplace is against him.'

Flora saw his green eyes flash angrily in his weather-beaten face. The emotion drew in his gaunt features and although he could only have been in his mid-twenties, he looked older. But suddenly he smiled, and Flora saw that this smile changed everything.

'Please allow me to introduce myself.' He swept off his cap, and his teeth flashed under his parted lips. 'I'm Michael Appleby.' He seemed, as he spoke, to draw a halting breath, and an almost imperceptible wince indicated a moment of pain. Quickly returning his concentration to the moment, he laughed lightly. 'I still can't get used to this damned thing.' He nodded down at his walking cane. 'The ridiculous article is more likely to trip me up than support me. But sadly I find it necessary to walk even a short distance.'

Flora gestured to the benches under the canvas roof of the café. 'Would you like to rest for a moment?' Accustomed to helping the patients at the surgery, she reached out to help him.

'Heavens, there's a thing!' he exclaimed in surprise. 'I must look an old crock, to be given such kind consideration.'

'Oh, no!' Flora drew back her hand sharply. 'Of course you don't. It's just—'

'I'm only teasing,' he assured her. 'And yes, I would very much like to rest. Would you care to join me? Perhaps a cup of tea or coffee would revive us both in this miserable weather?'

Flora blushed deeply. 'I hadn't quite finished my shopping.'

'How thoughtless of me!' he exclaimed, looking disappointed. 'But drinking on one's own seems rather a sad thing to do.'

The light went out of his eyes and Flora hesitated. This was obviously a young man who had been wounded in battle. Surely she could spare a few minutes to console him! 'I'm not in a hurry,' she decided. 'Let's sit at the back of the café where the roof doesn't leak.'

'Wonderful!' The smile was back again and this time she saw what a perfect smile it was. Broad, full lips parted to reveal the whitest of teeth; the corners of his eyes creased into laughter lines and returned his youthful looks. 'Allow me to fetch the drinks. Something to warm you or perhaps lemonade?'

'Lemonade would do very nicely.'

Flora watched him limp towards the tea stall. The sun had made a brief appearance, warming the damp streets, and she hadn't even noticed.

'Well, not too much lemonade spilt,' Michael Appleby said, chuckling, as Flora took the tray from his firm grip.

His green eyes were very penetrating, she thought, and were enhanced by the dark shadows of exhaustion beneath. He removed his cap and ran his hand through his brown hair, cut unflatteringly short, service style. As he lowered his arm, Flora noted the pattern on the cuffs of his dark-green-grey uniform denoting his rank: lieutenant.

'Once again, I'm very pleased to meet you,' he said as he sat beside her on the bench. 'I'm sorry, I didn't catch your name.'

'It's Flora,' she told him softly.

'Flora? How splendid! Do you come to the market often, Flora?'

'I usually meet my friend Hilda here.' Flora found herself wishing she'd taken more trouble with her own appearance before coming to the market. She had hurriedly put on her old coat and grey cloche hat, with no thought as to whom she might meet. She realized that had never been bought anything by a young man before, except ice cream by Will. Nor given her name to a total stranger. But for some reason that Flora couldn't quite fathom, this didn't really seem to matter.

'So, Hilda didn't show up today?' He seemed interested, watching her intently as she pushed a loose strand of hair under her hat. She hoped he hadn't noticed the tear in the hat's seam.

'Hilda's gone away,' she explained as she sipped her lemonade, 'to work in service.' She couldn't resist adding proudly, 'For the Earl of Talbott.'

'Ah, the Calveys. A well-known military name.'

'Do you know of them?' she asked in surprise.

'The fourth earl fought in both Boer wars,' he told her, just as Mrs Bell had said. 'Lord William was a fighting legend. However, the earl's son showed no interest in his father's profession. Adelphi Hall is well known now for its many lavish parties.'

'Oh, dear!' Flora thought of what Mrs Bell had said about Hilda being faced with temptation.

The officer sat forward. 'Have I said something to upset you?'

'No, but . . .' Flora felt she couldn't confide in someone she had known only a short while. 'It's just that Surrey is so far from London. Hilda's only sixteen, you see. She's never been away from home before.'

'Did Hilda live here, in the East End, with her family?'

'We're both orphanage girls,' Flora said, a little hesitantly. 'Neither of us had been out of London before Hilda's interview at Adelphi. I went with her as her companion for the day.'

'And all was well?'

'Yes, Hilda had her heart set on Adelphi from the moment she saw it.'

'Mama once visited there,' he said with a thoughtful frown. 'Most impressive, she said. But I would think a very big wrench for two good friends. No doubt you've seen each other through thick and thin?'

Flora looked into his kind face. He seemed most understanding. 'We look on each other as family. Together with Will, of course.'

'Might this be the young man you were thinking of?' he asked, quickly adding, 'I'm afraid I couldn't help overhearing what you said to the trader.'

'Will was a volunteer for Kitchener last August. He was certain he'd be home by Christmas. Instead he's been fighting ever since.'

Michael Appleby's face became grim again. 'Your friend was not alone in thinking the war would be over by Christmas. Indeed, some in the government promised a swift end to the conflict. But how wrong they have been proved. Both the Western and Eastern Fronts are deplorable. We are gaining no measure against enemy lines.'

For a few minutes they fell silent. Then Flora asked, 'And you? Are you recovering well from your wound?'

He gave a tight shrug. 'I escaped with my life at the Dardanelles. But I have been dragging this dashed leg around with me for the past three months.'

'We've read how bad it is at Gallipoli.' Flora recalled the many articles the doctor had read aloud from the newspaper. She knew he was always hoping to find something that would give him a clue to Wilfred's disappearance.

'Many of my men were lost,' Michael Appleby said, dropping his chin. 'Anzacs, French and British, falling side by side against the Turks. Had a bullet not torn through the muscle in my leg and put me in the field hospital, I should be lying alongside of them.'

Flora knew that this young man was quite unlike any other she had ever met. He didn't sound bitter from his experiences, as were some of the veterans she'd nursed. But she understood the pain he must have suffered and, like Will, the nightmare he'd endured.

'What is the outlook for your injury?' she asked, hoping she didn't sound too bold.

'I've had several operations,' he replied, 'and am delaying more. The thought of returning to hospital and its rigours . . .' He shook his head, turning away.

'Perhaps you might speak to Dr Tapper,' she suggested impulsively. 'He's a wonderful doctor. In the three years I've worked for him, he's helped so many people.'

'You're a nurse?' He glanced at her sharply.

'No, just the doctor's assistant. He always does his very best for the wounded veterans.'

The lieutenant gave a soft sigh. 'I've seen a number of medical men, only to be disappointed.'

'You mustn't give up hope.'

He smiled, tilting his head. 'What splendid advice. I shall certainly try to take it.'

Was he teasing her? Flora blushed. She knew she had overstepped the mark. After all, they were perfect strangers.

The lieutenant moved his cane. Tapping it on the cobbles, he then stood up. 'Is this doctor far from here? If you would allow me to drive you home in my car, then perhaps you could point his surgery out to me. And then I should be able to call to see him at some future date.'

Flora told him where both she and the doctor lived. Holding out his arm for her to take, he invited her once more to be his passenger. 'I shall take great care of you,' he promised as she hesitated. 'Driving a car is the one thing I can still do quite easily.'

Flora had never travelled by motor car, though she had often admired the new form of motorized vehicles that were beginning to fill the London streets. Though she hadn't known Michael Appleby for more than an hour or so, she found herself accepting his offer.

Rising to her feet, she laid her hand lightly on his cuff.

'The car is just an old jalopy,' Michael Appleby explained as they left the market and walked to the next street. 'While I've been off sick, the mechanics have given me something to occupy my time.' They stopped beside a large dark-red vehicle at the side of the road. It had a black roof and two large brass headlamps. 'Well, here she is, let me help you up.'

Flora felt panic. What was she to say to this stranger smiling at her with his intense gaze? She didn't even know which door opened, or how you climbed into it.

'Take my hand, place your foot on the running board there and I'll do the rest.'

Flora did as she was told. Soon she was sitting comfortably in the front seat. Moments later, he had joined her.

'Fortunately, I can operate the clutch with my good leg,' he shouted above the racket of the engine. 'The accelerator needs only a small pressure. You see?'

Flora wanted to say she had no idea what he was showing her. But the noise of the engine was too loud for her to speak above and so she just nodded. He grinned and released the lever beside him. Flora heard a loud bang. It reminded her of the day that she and Hilda had travelled to Surrey and had heard a car on Tower Bridge make the same noise.

'Hold tight!'

Before Flora could even blink, they were moving forward, the horn sounding loudly as they joined the flow of horse-drawn traffic.

Chapter Fifteen

Flora stood outside Tap House in the darkening light. She listened to the clatter of Michael Appleby's car as it turned the corner and disappeared.

Would she ever see him again, she wondered? Flora shivered lightly. It was very cold now, though she hadn't noticed in the motor car. She had been too excited and delighted by the feeling of being swept along and the power that came from the throbbing engine.

From over the roofs of the houses came the distant sound of a barrel organ playing Christmas carols. Flora looked up at the sky. It was turning dark blue and stars studded the heavens. A very bright star twinkled above. Reluctantly, she made her way down the airey's steps. She had enjoyed the young man's company, and the journey in the noisy, pulsating vehicle had been an experience she would never forget.

Flora drew up the key behind the letterbox and unlocked her door. The fire that had burned so brightly this morning was now almost out. She had hung a few sprigs of holly from the shelves and handmade paper-chains over the hearth. Arranged on the mantel were three tiny plaster figures of Mary, Joseph and baby Jesus. The Nativity scene was accompanied by a candle that she would light on Christmas Eve before Midnight Mass.

Flora sat beside the glow of the ashes, reflecting on all that had happened at the market. Her concerns over Will and Hilda faded as she recalled her meeting with the young lieutenant. He had overheard her conversation with the stallholder and hadn't hesitated to speak out in defence of Old Fritz. She liked him for that. As a serving soldier, having lost many of his regiment in Gallipoli, he too could have condemned the old German, as many had.

Flora closed her eyes and leaned back in the chair. Perhaps today's encounter would fade like a dream, a happy one for her, but for him just a moment in time where he had met an orphanage girl at an East End market and bought her a lemonade in exchange for some well-meaning advice.

The next morning before surgery, Flora told Dr Tapper about her meeting at the market. If, against all odds, the soldier decided to consult him, then the doctor would be in full possession of the facts.

'Appleby?' The doctor repeated when she gave him the name. 'And Gallipoli, you say?'

'A bullet went through the lieutenant's leg. He lost some of his men and fears he won't be able to fight again.'

'I read only this morning that the War Office is expected to abandon Gallipoli,' the doctor related. 'A tragic waste of life all round. It's perhaps a good thing that he'll be prevented from returning.' He looked at Flora curiously. 'What makes you think I can help this young man where other doctors have failed?'

'You helped Sidney Cowper,' Flora said eagerly.

'Mr Cowper's wound was quite recent, with little surgery performed to complicate matters.' The doctor paused. 'Have you considered that another failure might not help this young man at all? In fact, it might depress him all the more. I'm sure you tried your best to help, but every wound is different, has its own specific problems and healing can never be guaranteed even by a qualified physician. And from what you've told me, I think Lieutenant Appleby understands his predicament very well and has been sensibly advised by his own doctors.' He patted her shoulder kindly. 'Now, let's turn our minds to those who really need our help. We have enough poor souls here, ready and willing, to keep us busy well into the evening.'

Flora began to arrange the trolley, setting out the bandages and ointments. She knew the doctor had gently reproached her for being too impulsive. But she remembered the expression on the young soldier's face as he tried to hide the discomfort he was having to endure. She didn't regret speaking out. All the same, she knew the doctor was probably right and it was unlikely she would ever see Michael Appleby again.

* * *

The following day, a letter finally arrived from Hilda:

Dearest Flora, you'll be happy to know that I'm in the pink! I haven't fallen into trouble or mischief as Mrs Bell vowed I would! Lady Bertha and Lord Guy entertain a great deal and we are kept hard at it. Me and Gracie went to the village on our afternoon off. As I haven't been paid yet, I was kindly lent a pound by Mrs Bell to enjoy meself. After eating the most delicious tea in the tearoom, we were accosted by two young recruits, waiting for posting. They tried to persuade us into the tavern. But you'll be very pleased to hear we declined! (Gracie liked hers, but mine had ears the size of saucers and was commonly spoken.) Adelphi brims with decorations, bought from Harrods to impress the guests arriving the weekend before Christmas. I wish you a very happy Christmas and hope to see you in the New Year. Fondest love from your prospering friend, Hilda. P.S. I think of Will often. Please tell Mrs Bell I hope to write in the New Year when I have less on me plate.

Flora smiled. The mystery of the pound was solved! That evening she decided to visit Mrs Bell. The cobbled streets of the island were lit prettily by the lights of the public houses; she could hear sounds of laughter inside. Even though the war had taken most of the young men, the older ones were trying to cheer themselves up.

When she arrived at Hailing House, the large building stood silhouetted against the night sky. A frost was beginning to creep over the ground, and the tall, thick chimneys belched smoke. Flora tapped lightly on the kitchen door.

'Flora!' Aggie screeched as she opened it. The scullery maid, who unlike tiny Gracie was broad beamed and pink cheeked, called excitedly over her shoulder, 'Mrs Bell, Flora's 'ere.'

Wishing Aggie a happy Christmas, Flora took off her coat, hat and scarf. 'How is your baby?' she asked as the maid led her through the porch and into the warm, steamy kitchen.

'Bouncing, 'e is.' Aggie grinned, showing her large, uneven teeth. 'Got another on the way an' all.'

Flora felt Hilda's absence at that moment as she would definitely have had something to say on the subject of Aggie's expanding family.

The kitchen shelves were decorated with sprigs of holly and the moist air smelled of spices and ale. Flora knew Mrs Bell had been baking Christmas pudding; generous helpings were given to the poor and destitute on Christmas week.

'Flora, come in, come in,' called Mrs Bell and hurrying to her she wrapped Flora against her large bosom. 'I wasn't expecting to see you until Christmas Eve and the midnight service.'

'I've something to show you.' Flora took her usual seat by the warm range.

Mrs Bell reached for the large kettle. 'I was going to make tea but would you prefer a ginger beer? After all, it's nearly Christmas.'

Flora nodded. 'A ginger beer would be lovely.'

'We'll have a nice bowl of pudding and custard to go with it, piping hot off the stove.'

Aggie hovered expectantly, her eyes wide in her round face.

Mrs Bell quickly prepared the drinks, allowing the fizzy liquid to bubble over the rims of the glasses. Then, removing the cloth that covered a large bowl, she served up two portions of Christmas pudding, pouring custard over them from a large china jug. Then glaring at the scullery maid, she demanded, 'What are you waiting for, Aggie? You ate your portion of pudding at tea time! Be off with you, girl, home to your babies! There's some treats in that package over there for your young 'uns. And think yourself lucky that I had a few bits left over.'

Aggie's smile returned. She hurriedly snatched up her thin coat and the grease-stained brown-paper parcel, dropping it in her battered straw basket. ''Appy Christmas, Flora. I'd better be going before my old man comes 'ome. He likes to have his dinner on the table the moment he walks in.'

When Aggie had gone, Flora gave Mrs Bell a card. She had made her own cards in the end, sewing a little lace on the paper edges and drawing a red-breasted robin inside. 'Just for you,' she had written. 'Wishing you a very merry Christmas, from Flora.'

'Oh, Flora! Fancy that. You're a very thoughtful girl. Thank you. Now here's mine to you.' Mrs Bell took an envelope from the mantel shelf.

Flora opened the card. On it was a picture of a Victorian lady dressed in a long red cape. She was gazing into a brightly lit butcher's window. Rows of feathered fowl hung upside down from large, wooden hooks. Inside the card Mrs Bell had written in rather lopsided writing, 'The best of the season's wishes, my dear.'

'Have you heard from Hilda?' Flora asked and on receiving a brisk shake of the head she took Hilda's letter from her pocket. 'There's something in here that will interest you.'

The cook put on her half-moon spectacles. She peered at the letter. After a few seconds, she grinned. 'Oh, bless me! The girl hadn't been paid and only wanted an afternoon out.' Mrs Bell tutted. 'Now I feel shamed for thinking she was up to mischief. And look, she behaved herself with the two recruits!'

Flora began to laugh. Mrs Bell did too as she read what Hilda had written of the saucer-eared soldier.

Mrs Bell took off her spectacles and sighed. 'She even thought to put in a P.S. that she was thinking of young Will and would write to me. Ah well, now me mind is at rest and I won't have to spend too long on me knees at Christmas, praying to the good Lord to keep her safe.' Mrs Bell returned the letter to Flora. 'Now let's eat our supper before it spoils.'

As usual, the food was delicious. After they'd finished, Mrs Bell raised her glass. 'Here's to Hilda and here's to us, Flora, and here's to all the young men who are fighting for king and country. God bless 'em all.' A tear sprang to her eye. She wiped the moisture away quickly with the corner of her apron.

Flora hoped Will would receive her card before Christmas. On it she had drawn a Christmas angel. Its wings were coloured in the palest pink, blue and yellow chalks. 'An angel to keep you safe.' She had written this in her best handwriting, along with a heartfelt message of deep affection.

'Aggie and me will see you for the midnight service,' Mrs Bell said when Flora was ready to leave. 'Though it won't seem right without our Hilda.'

Flora hugged Mrs Bell close. She knew the elderly lady had been very lonely, as Flora had, without Hilda. But Hilda's letter had arrived in time to make them all feel happier.

A few flakes of snow fell as Flora made her way home. She recalled how, as children, she and Hilda and Will had played in the snow. They had made snowballs and snowmen in the orphanage yard, their thin mittens freezing on their fingers.

Flora lifted her eyes to the shining star that she had first seen on the night she had met Lieutenant Appleby. The star was still there, shedding down its light on all the earth. She hoped that whatever happened to him, he would find peace in the future.

The next morning, the waiting room was crowded; coughs, colds and winter ailments abounded. Fevers, swollen glands and bronchitis caused Flora to constantly keep water boiled to mix with drops of eucalyptus oil. Several patients came to sit in her small room, to bend their heads over the steaming decongestant. A few words of comfort and sympathy, she felt, were as beneficial as the treatment.

On Sunday, Flora placed several more sprigs of holly on the shelves of her sitting room. Some she reserved for the waiting room upstairs when, on Christmas Eve, she would fill small tumblers with port. One for each patient before they left the surgery. Dr Tapper always celebrated Christmas this way, giving his patients an extra special glow. Flora smiled as she thought of the happy faces that would make their way home that day.

In the darkening afternoon, Flora walked to Island Gardens. Though it was bitterly cold, people were enjoying the last weekend before the holiday. A band was playing carols by the entrance to the underground tunnel which led under the river to Greenwich. The blue-and-red bonnets of the Salvation Army bobbed amongst the brass instruments. An audience stood watching and joining in. Flora knew that if Hilda was here with her, they would have stopped to sing, too.

Flora walked down to the fence that separated the park from the riverbank. The great River Thames looked an unfriendly grey in the dull afternoon light. Despite this, the South Bank of London was still visible. A few small boats and tugs ploughed their way through the uninviting water. The tide was out, leaving a thick, wet blanket of mud. There were no mudlarks today:

young boys who trawled the sticky brown surface for lumps of coal dropped from the barges, or pieces of soaked timber that could be dried out for kindling. Instead, the river curled towards the city and lapped eastward into the estuary that flowed towards Tilbury and Gravesend.

Flora turned to study the seasonal sights once more. The domed entrance to the Greenwich tunnel, the crowds enjoying the loud, cheerful carols: 'God Rest Ye Merry Gentleman', 'Adeste Fideles', 'O Come, O Come, Emmanuel', and the clear favourite, 'Silent Night'. Some families were accompanied by the disabled veterans of war. A young man in a Bath chair, another on crutches, one or two hobbling along with walking sticks. She thought of Michael Appleby. What would he be doing this Christmas? She hoped he wasn't suffering too much pain.

Flora sighed softly. Her thoughts finally turned to Hilda. They had come here to watch the big ships bring in their exotic cargoes: crates of sausage skins packed in brine, India chutney and bales of jute, animal skins from Africa and India, coffee beans, tea, spices, potteries, oils, perfumes, the list was endless. They had seen the river traffic in every season, dressed as she was now in warm winter clothing, and in summer, their skirts, white blouses and straw boaters. The sights, sounds and smells of the docks had always been exciting. They had felt part of the busy highway, imagining their lives unfolding in the heart of Britain's capital city.

Tugging her coat tightly around her, she made her way over to the carollers. The night air was filled with hot, happy breath and Flora joined in with the chorus of 'We Three Kings of Orient Are'. The words described a star of royal beauty bright; she gazed up to see her special star sparkling. It was just as magnificent, she imagined, on this Christmas of 1915, as it was all those years ago, when a tiny baby had been born in a stable at Bethlehem, in Judea.

Chapter Sixteen

'Hilda, you will be required to help John carry the dishes into the dining room, followed by Sophie and Amy, the two village girls,' Mrs Burns barked as she stood with Hilda in the corridor. 'You will wear your best black dress. Your hair will be plaited under your cap, your eyes kept down, averted from the guests, and every order given to you by Mr Leighton will be followed at once.'

Hilda nodded and her heart began to pound. It was Friday, the first night of the grand house-party. There had been chaos for the past six hours. Two of the village girls had failed to arrive. Their unskilled substitutes, Sophie and Amy, had been found by Mrs Burns at short notice. To add to the housekeeper's misery, yesterday as the many casks, boxes and trays of food and drink were being delivered Hilda had watched James drop a barrel on his ankle. Hilda thought the injury did not look serious, but Mr Leighton had been furious at the inconvenience of a limping footman.

Hilda stood, quaking in her shoes. Fear and excitement rushed through her veins. There were thirty visitors together with their staff to accommodate. The past week had been a whirlwind of activity. The rooms on the top floor had been opened, their bathrooms scrubbed, fires lit and their wardrobes and carpets, rugs, cushions and ornaments all cleaned. After this, she had laundered the bedclothes, taken down the curtains, brushed, ironed and re-hung them. Hilda had hardly been able to keep up with the gruelling schedule. Now, she couldn't believe her luck. She was going to see Lord Guy again!

'I expect no mistakes, Hilda. Make certain you pay attention to Mrs Harris and, for goodness' sake, don't drop anything.'

Hilda nodded eagerly. The memory of her meeting with the young lord on the servants' staircase made her shiver. Gracie had almost fainted when Hilda had told her what had happened. She said she had never known Lord Guy, or any of the family, to use that particular door.

'Are you paying attention, Hilda?' Mrs Burns' sharp tone brought Hilda back to the moment.

'Yes, Mrs Burns.'

'Go along to Mrs Harris. I've already told her you are to be helping in the dining room tonight.'

Hilda did as she was told. The thought of being part of the elaborate plans for the weekend made her go weak at the knees. She was still shaking as she hurried to the kitchen, where Mrs Harris, red-faced and sweating, stood at the range. She saw Hilda and shouted, 'I've just spoken with Lady Bertha and there's a change of plan. Oysters and caviar as first decided, but not the lobster with French dressing as I had in mind to serve. Instead, Violet has persuaded Lady Bertha to settle for common-place sirloin steak.' Mrs Harris sniffed with disdain. 'Fortunately, we still have the soup and foul on the menu, with poached salmon, cutlets of lamb and veal escalope to follow, all as I had originally suggested. My hot strawberry soufflé, peach melba and banana flambé have also been confirmed.' Mrs Harris tossed her head as though she had triumphed over the wishes of Violet. 'Now, find Gracie and we'll prepare the fish soup, pâté and glazes. Hurry, girl! Hurry!'

Hilda rushed through the passage to the scullery, where Gracie was preparing the vegetables. 'Gracie, we've to help Mrs Harris with the soup!'

The water was running from the single tap over the sink. Gracie's red hands were full of peeled potatoes. 'I can't. I've got the beans to do yet and the parsley and mint.'

'Leave them. Mrs Harris is in a real tizz.'

Gracie knew this was a danger sign and quickly wiped her hands on her dirty apron. She pushed her thin hair up under her cap, muttering under her breath. Together they ran back to the kitchen.

'The strainer, Gracie, at once!' Mrs Harris commanded.

Gracie took a large white cloth from the drawer. She pushed two ends into Hilda's hands and took the opposite corners. Once placed over the empty bowl on the table, the cook began to pour the thick liquid from the saucepan.

'Hold it still and pull tight,' Mrs Harris ordered. When the saucepan was empty, the cook seized a wooden spoon and began to mash what remained.

It was a long, hard process in the hot kitchen. Sweating, and still thinking about Lord Guy, Hilda held the cloth tightly. The steam and stink of mashed vegetables and fish made her stomach turn, but all this would be worth the effort for one more glance of his handsome face.

All about her, Hilda could hear the rush of feet, the boiling of pans on the range, the shouts of the kitchen staff as they followed their orders; in the distance, Mr Leighton, with one footman disabled, was roaring at Billy and Joseph, the two stable boys who had been brought in as reserves for the evening. Hilda felt the excitement grow inside her. She couldn't wait until tonight, when she would look into Lord Guy's dark gaze. He would recognize her and somehow let her know that she had been in his thoughts since the moment they first met.

'Mr Leighton will be lucky if he can turn them two sow's ears into silk purses by tonight.' Mrs Harris, referring to the stable boys, gave the mashed contents of the cloth one last pounding.

Hilda looked at Gracie through the clouds of steam and stifled a giggle. Gracie was as red as a beetroot, holding on to the cloth for dear life. A clatter came from the long passage and voices were raised. Hilda knew Mr Leighton was preparing the ancestral silverware, which he kept locked in the safe. Candelabras, jugs, plates and tureens had been placed out in his quarters for polishing; the dinner tonight was to be of the highest standard.

Hilda smiled to herself through the steam. Almost everything in her life was as she imagined it would be. The disputes between Mrs Harris and Violet were more frequent. Their clear dislike of one another was evident to one and all. The cook always had the upper hand; Hilda had been told that by Mrs Bell who knew only too well of rivalries below stairs. To add to this, Hilda had noticed that Violet had become ill-tempered and wore a sullen expression. Tonight, Hilda would look her very best. At least, as best as she could in this dour uniform. She would try to catch Lady Bertha's attention and Lord Guy would watch her every move, too. Even the beautiful women he entertained would pale in contrast to Hilda's youth and freshness.

Lord Guy had told her he would see her again, hadn't he? He had almost made a promise. Hilda knew she was attractive to men. John and James flirted with her. When she and Gracie went into the village, they had no shortage of admirers. Though Gracie always shrank from attention, Hilda loved it. She knew how to hold herself in an upright fashion, sway her hips and accentuate the curve of her breasts. Hadn't Lord Guy held on to her longer than was necessary on the staircase? In one glance he had taken in her beauty.

'Right, off to the scullery, you two, and bring me the vegetables,' Mrs Harris boomed, thrusting the filthy straining cloth into Gracie's hands.

Hilda and Gracie nodded and dashed out of the kitchen together. Hilda's plans were working out already. Christmas was going to be wonderful this year!

It was Monday of Christmas week. Flora's busy day was almost at an end. The strong smell of disinfectant was thick in the air. Flora had cleaned the grubby chairs and floorboards after the doctor had gone upstairs to his rooms.

Flora took off her apron and washed her hands. She was about to turn down the gas lights when a heavy knock came at the front door.

'Good evening, Flora.' The man was dressed in a long blue overcoat. His shoulders were broad, but hunched against the cold. He wore a large brimmed hat and was leaning heavily on a cane. He took off his hat.

'Michael!'

'I hope I'm not too late?'

'I . . . well, no . . .' she stammered. Realizing he was waiting for her to open the door, she stepped back.

'I've no excuse I'm afraid,' he began as he stepped forward. A gust of cold night air swept in with him. 'I gave what you said a great deal of thought. But—' He swayed, only just managing to steady himself. Flora caught his arm and guided him towards a chair. He sunk down with a sigh and grimaced. 'Thank you.'

'Are you in pain?' she asked softly.

'I try to tell myself I'm not,' he muttered, 'but my leg says otherwise.' He laughed emptily. 'You should throw me out! A complaint in the first moment of seeing you.'

She smiled. 'I'm glad you decided to come.'

'Are you?' He lowered his head. 'I don't deserve your consideration.' Raising his eyes, he added, 'Our chance meeting inspired me. Your words encouraged me. But at the last moment, I lost my nerve.'

'Dr Tapper is a very special doctor.'

His eyes held hers. 'I do believe you, Flora.'

She pushed back her tangled hair. What did she look like after the busy day? She felt his eyes on her. Did he really come here because of what she had said about the doctor?

'After our meeting at the market, I felt more alive than I have done in months. You gave me hope again. Hope that I'd almost lost.' He adjusted his position on the chair so that he didn't lean quite so heavily on his cane. 'I thought a great deal about what you said. About the doctor and your friends, Hilda and Will, and the orphanage. Your life must have presented you with many challenges. And yet you overcame them. I was humbled.' His voice grew rough and he glanced away. 'In battle a soldier is faced with his mortality. He sees life extinguished in a second. One day it might be his life that's taken.' Slowly, he returned his gaze to Flora. 'But death is not the worst. To become wounded is almost shaming. To abandon one's men . . .'

'But you didn't abandon them! You were wounded and could have died.'

'Sometimes, I wish—' He stopped as a shadow fell across them.

'Good evening.' Dr Tapper stood at the door.

'This is Lieutenant Appleby.' Flora wondered if the doctor had overheard their conversation. He had a very sympathetic expression on his face.

'I'm very pleased to meet you, sir.' The young man struggled to his feet and took the doctor's hand. 'I've heard a lot about you from Flora.'

'Have you indeed . . .'

'I hoped you would see me, but it's very late.'

Dr Tapper patted his pockets as Flora often saw him do. She knew he was considering Michael carefully. At last, he gave a short nod. 'You'd better come into my room.'

Flora watched the two men walk together across the floor, one elderly and bent, the other young and disabled. She knew that if anyone could perform miracles, it was Dr Tapper. But as the door closed and she went back to sit in her small room, the time passed very slowly.

Almost an hour had passed and Flora was restless. Was this good news or bad, she wondered? Was there hope for the young soldier or would it be as both Michael and the doctor had feared: another damning verdict to add to the others.

Just then the doctor's door opened. 'Flora, would you join us?' the doctor said, leading the way into his room. 'Please, stand over here by our patient.' Dr Tapper indicated the couch on which Michael lay, propped up by a pillow. He was wearing just his undergarments: a white flannel button-up vest and pants. His left leg was stretched out on the couch, his right one bent at the knee, his bare foot on the floor.

Flora had helped many patients undress in readiness for an examination. She had seen arms, legs, chests and even the more private parts of the male anatomy. But now a great heat washed up from her neck and filled her face.

'As I've explained, I don't wish to raise any hopes,' the doctor began to say. 'The treatment I'm about to propose can be uncomfortable in the extreme but has been proven to work in some cases, such as with our former patient Mr Cowper. With Lieutenant Appleby's wound, we must bear in mind that surgery has already been performed – twice. Post-operative procedures are controversial and yet I think nothing can be lost here. That is, other than the degree of pain it will involve.' He raised an eyebrow in Michael's direction.

'I'm willing to try,' Michael said at once.

The doctor patted his pockets, then bent over and placed his hand lightly on Michael's bandaged thigh. 'Your leg muscle has been weakened here and here. Though the original sites where the bullet entered and exited have partially healed, the nerves are damaged. It's stimulation of these nerves that we must attend to. I believe that with a regime of massage and exercise, we may be able to address the problem. In the years after the African wars, I had some experience as a young doctor of what was then quite controversial physiotherapeutic techniques.' He hesitated, raising his shoulders slightly. 'Time, effort and patience will be needed, I'm afraid.'

Flora couldn't help herself and looked into Michael's eyes. She felt as if she was drowning in their green depths. Had hope come back into them?

'For this to work I shall need your cooperation, Flora. Over a period of weeks and months, I hope to train you to use these methods. And between us we shall try our very best to effect a satisfactory result.'

Flora was surprised when the doctor urged her closer to their patient.

'There is no time like the present.' Dr Tapper took off his jacket and hung it on the peg. 'Watch carefully, Flora, as I position our patient comfortably and support his thigh with one hand – like so.' The doctor demonstrated. Flora heard Michael try to hide a groan.

'I'm very sorry,' the doctor said, pausing in his actions. 'If the degree of pain becomes too much, you must tell me.'

Michael nodded, waving aside his suggestion.

The doctor continued. 'Lifting the leg with my other hand, I raise it as far as possible towards the head, then once we have some natural movement, rotate the leg in hold, fix the knee, and lastly support the ankle. All this to be performed with the minimum of discomfort to Lieutenant Appleby. After a few weeks we shall introduce stretch exercises, followed by massage.' The doctor demonstrated several more times. Then turning to Flora, he said, 'Now I should like you to try.'

Flora felt very anxious as the doctor took her hands and showed her how to grasp and support the young officer's leg. She was keenly aware of Michael's gaze as her fingers played on his skin and moved a little tremblingly over his limb. Telling herself he was just another patient, she soon found she was performing the movements with ease and was able to follow the doctor's guidance.

It was only when Michael bravely stifled his gasps of pain that she fumbled. She didn't want to hurt him. But she knew she had to distance herself and act professionally. Just as she would with any other patient who came under the care of her employer.

Chapter Seventeen

It was the last night of the long weekend of Adelphi Hall's grand Christmas house-party. Hilda had never been more exhausted. But nor had she ever been more excited.

Each night, forming a line with the other maids, she had carried the many dishes from the kitchen to the dining-room sideboards. This had been done in the manner of 'service à la russe'. Mr Leighton, John the footman and Maxwell, Lord Guy's valet, had then taken each dish and served accordingly. Hilda had overheard cross words between Mr Leighton and Mrs Harris. The cook preferred the traditional French style of carving the meats on the table and allowing the dinner guests to help themselves. But Mr Leighton's word was law. Hilda had also learned from Gracie that it was Violet who had persuaded her mistress to go Russian. Not that it seemed to matter to the fashionable young women who sat at the dining table, Hilda noted with amusement. They discreetly pecked at the courses served to them, and hardly ate a bean! Dressed in their beautiful silk-satin crêpe gowns and bird-of-paradise plumage, the very epitome of fashion, they had no desire to fight with their tightly laced corsets. Instead, they ate sparingly, trying to fool everyone by exposing a few inches of tantalising white breast above their V-shaped necklines. Hilda loved the new fashions. They were so exotic!

Despite the war and all its troubles, Hilda thought how everyone was out to enjoy themselves. The guests talked, laughed, even proposed toasts that had nothing to do with Kitchener's men or the kaiser's onslaught across Europe. The raised glasses were offered to those closer to home: the titled and wealthy, the grand names of society, whom Hilda knew rolled off the tongue of every individual present as easily as cream over strawberries. By the time the last course was served, Hilda had lost count of the indiscretions below-table. Black-stockinged legs had touched gentlemen's calves or thighs, embroidered shoes had quite clearly nudged or entwined with highly polished leather.

Lady Bertha herself hadn't indulged in such behaviour, Hilda reflected. Her jet-black hair was fashioned glossily around her head; her dark, quickly moving eyes were swift to see whose glass needed replenishing. She held a fan of dyed ostrich feathers that, Hilda decided, befitted a much older woman. Gracie had told her that the mistress was in her fiftieth year. Hilda thought that if she were Lady Bertha's personal maid, she would have recommended a plain cream or fawn silk gown rather than the unflattering dull-blue chiffon that she wore. To Hilda's surprise, the sight of Lady Bertha's husband, James Forsythe, proved extremely disappointing. Although he looked much younger than his wife, the monocle balanced on his large nose and his weak chin were most unattractive! The small amount of hair he possessed was combed thinly over his head, like a pie top on a pudding.

Absorbing every small detail, Hilda had raised her eyes every now and then to study Lady Bertha and her guests. But it was not Lady Bertha or her guests who had occupied her thoughts since Friday night. It was the most outstanding man in the room, Lord Guy Calvey, who had set her pulse racing. She had felt very jealous as he laughed and teased his pretty companions. Hilda had deliberately paused closely to him, setting down the dish she was carrying with extreme care on the sideboard. Then just as carefully on her return across the floor, she had linked her gaze with his. Even now, she still couldn't believe their eyes had met—

''Ilda, where've you been?' Gracie yelled, bringing Hilda sharply back to the moment. Gracie was at the kitchen door, waiting for her. Hilda felt a little sorry for the scullery maid who had never been offered the opportunity to serve at table.

'You know where.' Hilda shrugged, a little out of breath. 'Mrs Harris asked me to run across to the greenhouse for more parsley.' She held out the jug that contained the herb. 'Peter's so slow, he took ages cutting me fresh sprigs.' Hilda knew this sounded a poor excuse, but Gracie seemed satisfied. The true reason for the delay was that Hilda had found a broken mirror just inside the greenhouse. Whilst she'd waited for the gardener to appear, she'd plucked a few strands of hair from under her cap and twirled them around her finger and across her forehead. Then she'd arranged her braided bun of thick brown hair to lie more loosely at the nape of her neck. The tea-time inspection that Mrs Burns had given the maids had required white caps to be positioned fully over the head. There was not to be one hair escaping. This was a very plain look and Hilda didn't hesitate to change it.

'Are all the guests sitting in the same seats?' Hilda enquired before Gracie could note the improvement of her appearance.

'The place names ain't been changed,' Gracie said suspiciously. 'Why are you askin'?'

Hilda shrugged. 'I wondered if Lord William would be present. It is the last night, after all.'

'Lord William?' Gracie repeated, scraping her hand across her nose. 'You'll never catch sight of 'im at one of these parties.'

'But it's Christmas.'

'That don't matter to 'im. He's just like a bloomin' ghost, haunting the house. Fact is, 'e might as well be one. If it wasn't for old Turner, his valet, looking after 'im, you'd never know there was a fourth earl moulderin' out his days at Adelphi.'

Hilda wasn't particularly interested in Lord William. An old man like him was welcome to his privacy as far as she was concerned. She'd only asked about the seating arrangements in order to divert Gracie's suspicions. The truth was she was eager to discover whether Lord Guy would be seated at the head of the table. From this vantage point, he had full view of her, and she had of him, when she brought in the trays.

'Mrs 'Arris says you're to follow Maxwell and John who'll be in charge of the soup and pâtés.' Gracie gave Hilda a little shove. 'They're in the kitchen now, waiting for you.'

Hilda felt excited and fearful all at once. She couldn't wait to be in the heady atmosphere of the dining room. It was like a theatre in which she also played a part. She was certain Lord Guy would be looking out for her. Hadn't he given her a secretive smile again last night? Teased her with his mysterious dark eyes and followed her movements across the floor? She knew she had caught his attention.

And she would make sure tonight would be no exception.

'Thank yer, ducks, and good health to yer,' said the old man, smacking his lips and downing the thimbleful in one.

It was Friday and Christmas Eve. Dr Tapper had provided Flora with a bottle of port to distribute amongst the patients; there had been many smiling faces at the surgery today, thought Flora happily. The last to leave was an elderly man and he chuckled wheezily as he accepted the tumbler that Flora offered him. 'Good luck to you, love, and the doctor. Here's to all our soldiers abroad.'

Flora smiled. She was thinking of one very special soldier.

'Got a sweetheart in the trenches, 'ave yer?'

'Someone very close,' she replied.

'Well, if yer let me have that last drop, I'll do them another honour.' The old man looked greedily at the remaining finger of port.

Before Flora could reply, she saw a tall figure standing in the doorway. Michael leaned his cane against the wall and shook the flakes of snow from his overcoat.

'Good evening to you, gov, I was just doing the honours,' the old man said, grabbing the tumbler in his gnarled hands. 'Here's to this young lady's beau and let's hope he comes home to claim her, all in one piece with no bits missing.' The liquid went down his throat in an instant. 'God bless yer both,' the departing patient wished them as he pulled up the collar of his threadbare jacket and left.

Michael raised an eyebrow. 'I hope I'm not too early.'

'No. Please come in.' Flora managed to conceal the delight that filled her as she beckoned him into the doctor's room. Not only had Michael agreed to the doctor's treatment, but over the last few days he had thrown himself wholeheartedly into the strict regime of exercises.

'Good evening, Michael,' Dr Tapper said, getting up from his desk. 'And how are you today?'

'Well, doctor, thank you.'

'Are we making progress do you think?'

Flora took Michael's coat and hat. He was dressed casually in a shirt and waistcoat and heavy winter trousers. She saw that, after five treatments so far, he still leaned on his cane.

'Perhaps some,' he nodded.

'But the pain is worse?' the doctor guessed, urging Michael towards the couch.

'On occasions, I'm afraid to say it is.'

'Quite to be expected, as we are challenging the body to repair itself,' the doctor told him. 'I've made up a pain relief preparation for you to use when needed. And today, perhaps we shall try not to test you so much. Just a half an hour, Flora. That should be sufficient.' The doctor made his way to the door, then stopped. He turned and frowned. 'I take it you are with your family this Christmas, Michael?'

'Actually, no, sir. Mama is holidaying in Scotland with friends.'

'In that case,' the doctor said pleasantly, 'I wonder if you'd care to join Flora and I tomorrow for dinner? That is, if you are not busy elsewhere?'

'Not at all,' Michael replied in surprise, 'but I couldn't impose.'

'Mrs Carver has stuffed the bird and prepared the vegetables. All that is to be done is to cook and enjoy them.' The doctor looked at Flora. 'We shall be delighted to have your company, won't we, Flora?'

Flora tried to gather herself. She had been very surprised at her employer's kind offer. 'Yes . . . yes, of course,' she agreed.

'Very well. Shall we say one o'clock?' The doctor raised his bushy eyebrows.

'On the dot.' Michael gave a wide grin.

Ten minutes later, Flora was trying to keep her attention on Michael's injured leg, as the doctor had taught her. She had accustomed herself to gripping his leg firmly and guiding it. But as her hand supported his thigh, she felt the muscles in his calf as they reacted to her touch.

'Flora, is something wrong?' he asked.

'No.'

'I feel sure there is.'

'I'm trying to concentrate.'

'Would you like to stop? Are you tired? Perhaps these treatments have been too wearing on you.'

'Of course they haven't.' Flora tried to look unruffled. But the thought of spending Christmas Day with Michael had come as quite a shock. 'I don't want to hurt you, that's all,' she said as she lifted his leg gently into position.

'Your touch is very light.' Suddenly, he reached out and took her wrist. 'Come sit by me and rest a moment.' He gestured to the chair beside the couch.

Flora took a seat and clutched her hands tightly in her lap.

'I hope the doctor's invitation hasn't upset you.' He stared at her with his deep gaze for what seemed like endless minutes. 'Is it perhaps the thought of your beau, Will, that's causing you to be sad?'

'Will isn't my beau.'

'I'm sorry, I couldn't help overhearing your conversation with the old man. You said he was someone very close.'

'As I've said before, Will is like family to me and Hilda. We are the only family each of us has. Growing up in an orphanage is very different to the life you've led. Friends are scarce. Everyone looks out for themselves. The nuns of St Boniface were kind, but children can be very cruel.'

'Yes, indeed.'

'But we three had each other.'

Michael nodded thoughtfully. 'Has the doctor any family?'

'Yes, a sister living in Bath. The doctor's wife, Edith, died. Their son, Wilfred, is a soldier.' Flora sighed softly. 'This year he was reported as missing in action.'

'I'm very sorry to hear that.'

Flora sat quietly. She saw Michael's face grow sombre. Should she have told him about Wilfred, bringing back unhappy thoughts of the war?

'Are you sure you're happy to have me join you tomorrow?' Michael glanced at her sharply.

She kept a straight face. 'No, I'm very put out, as it happens.'

They both burst into laughter. Flora found her heart racing. When Michael laughed like that, something inside her – an emotion she couldn't name – made her feel so happy.

Michael said, 'For me, this Christmas will be very special indeed.'

And Flora knew it would be for her, too.

Chapter Eighteen

Christmas Day dawned and Flora wasn't surprised to arrive upstairs at the surgery to find the door unlocked. Dr Tapper must have come down from his rooms to turn the lock in readiness for their arrival. The smell of roast chicken and stuffing was wafting down the staircase and into the hall. The fumes of strong disinfectant had for once receded into the background.

The long case clock in the hall said a quarter to one. Had Michael arrived yet, Flora wondered anxiously? She hurried up the stairs, glancing at the photograph of Edith Tapper and her son Wilfred. If only Wilfred was here today! She knew that Wilfred had never missed spending a Christmas with his father even though, before the war, he led a busy life as a solicitor in the city.

The door opened before she reached it. Dr Tapper stood in his best dark suit, a white shirt and winged collar, with a silver fob watch pinned to his floral waistcoat. Flora knew he only wore his fob and this waistcoat on special occasions; they had been gifts from his late wife. 'Welcome, Flora. You look most charming.'

Flora blushed. The doctor never usually commented on her appearance. But perhaps that was because she was always dressed in her uniform.

'You're first to arrive.'

Flora felt very nervous now. Did she look presentable enough for Christmas Day? She was wearing the blue suit that Hilda had given her. Although the colour was very summery, it was the best suit she had. Before church last night she had washed the disinfectant from her hair and bathed in the tin bath in order to look and smell her best on Christmas Day. After the late-night service had ended, she had hurried home to set her fringe in sugar water and pins before going to bed. This morning she had paid special attention to combing it out and twisting the curls into place. Then, forming two glossy wings on top of her head, she had pinned the remainder into a golden bun at the nape of her neck. Michael always looked well dressed and smart, despite having to use the cane. She didn't want to let herself or the doctor down. 'I came a little early to help you.'

Dr Tapper beamed her a smile. 'Everything is in hand. I hope you remembered me in your prayers at church last night?'

'Mrs Bell helped me to light candles for everyone.'

'Heaven's gates were very busy, no doubt. Now leave your coat on the stand and come and warm yourself.'

When Flora walked into the large and comfortable sitting room, she felt at home. She loved this traditional Victorian parlour, with its long sash windows, comfortable green leather sofa, thick rugs and a fire burning brightly in the grate. It was as if the doctor's wife was still present, keeping it ready for guests. Flora knew Mrs Carver kept it clean and tidy, but the heart in this home was still as Edith Tapper would have wanted.

Flora particularly liked the many books on the shelves. Some of them were heavy medical tomes with names in gilt lettering on their spines that she couldn't pronounce. Over the wooden mantel and black-leaded fireplace surrounded by floral tiles was a painting of a country cottage. The pretty thatched building was set in a garden amongst beds of roses. The doctor had told Flora that this was his wife's family's house in Yorkshire. Underneath this, he had arranged his Christmas cards, one of which was her handmade card of a small boy with a red woollen hat and scarf, riding on a sledge in the snow, accompanied by her own writing, 'Season's Greetings from Flora'. She would have liked to write something more intimate, but didn't think that it would be suitable.

'Sit by the fire and warm yourself.' The doctor went over to a highly polished wooden cabinet in the corner. Opening its doors, Flora was surprised to see a row of dainty glasses and several bottles. 'A small port, Flora?'

'Thank you.' Flora didn't much care for the smell of port when she poured it out for the patients on Christmas Eve. But she wanted to please the doctor and smiled as he handed her the glass.

'Your good health, Flora.'

'And yours, Dr Tapper.'

He stood with his back to the fire, swaying slightly on his heels as he savoured the port. Flora took a small sip and wrinkled her nose at the liquid which tasted like cough medicine.

Just then, there was a tap on the door. The doctor put down his glass. 'That must be Michael. Would you welcome our guest while I see to the food?' He walked away to the kitchen.

Left alone, Flora felt her stomach twist anxiously. Why was she feeling like this? Perhaps it was the effect of the port.

'Happy Christmas, Flora.' The wide smile that lit up Michael's face made her catch her breath as he stepped in. 'I've brought champagne. It's quite a good one.' He handed her a large bottle.

'Thank you and happy Christmas,' she replied, as she clutched the bottle tightly. She was sure that champagne was a very expensive gift and didn't want to drop it. From her pocket she managed to extract the card she had made for him. The picture on the front was one she had drawn from memory: a red motor car with black hood. She had made her own snowflakes too, from white pieces of paper glued with flour and water. Inside, she had written, 'Many good wishes for 1916, from Flora.'

'What a keen eye you have for sketching, Flora. Thank you.'

'You're welcome.' She felt embarrassed as he leaned his cane against the wall and slid the card into his overcoat pocket. Did he really like it, or was he being polite?

'The beast refused to start this morning of all mornings,' he said as he took off his overcoat and hung it on the hallstand. Loosening the button of his expensive-looking dinner jacket, Flora caught a glimpse of a waistcoat with black satin facings and a pristine white shirt beneath.

'Did you manage to start it again?'

'Yes, with a little persuasion. The engine can be temperamental in cold weather. I shall do something about it soon in the workshop at Mama's. The workshop, as I call it, is just an old shed, really, but sizeable enough for the car.'

Flora thought how different this young man was to anyone she had ever known. Not that she had known any men from his class. But she had seen plenty of striking men who drove through the park on a Sunday in their open-top motor cars. And many more in the city with their fashionable partners on their arms, walking with a swagger and not a little arrogance. Michael was not like them. He had a reserved way, a quiet strength, even with the walking cane that he so hated so much. But today he looked every inch the gentleman, not the wounded soldier who limped into the surgery and watched her as she worked, his green eyes studying her without flinching. Today, he was someone of standing, who wore his exquisite clothes with natural ease; a man of breeding.

'Flora! Michael! Are you both there?' the doctor called.

Flora led the way along the narrow hall. Now, anxious

thoughts were racing through her mind. A whole afternoon spread out before them. Suddenly, she feared the hours ahead that would make it quite clear how little experience she had in making intelligent conversation. What could she contribute to the wealth of knowledge of two learned men? She was just a doctor's assistant, an orphanage girl, who had been fooling herself that a young man of Michael's background could possibly have an interest in what she had to say.

'A most accomplished dinner, sir,' Michael said, as they sat by the fire after their meal, the doctor in his chair and Flora beside Michael on the sofa. Flora's earlier concerns had disappeared as the hours had slipped by without her noticing. The two men had drunk several glasses of champagne, though Flora had discreetly put her glass to one side. When she looked in the mirror, she saw that she had developed very pink cheeks and bright, twinkling eyes.

'Had you always had an eye for the army?' the doctor asked Michael, as he took the poker and stoked the fire; the flames leaped and sparkled above the coal. The air was full of the scent of cigars that the two men had just smoked.

'It was adventure, sir,' replied Michael without hesitation, 'though, poor Mama was disappointed when I joined the military at twenty. She had hopes of a professional career for me. But four walls and a desk were not my idea of adventure. Papa, though I never knew him well, held some influence over me as a child. He was such a colourful character, you see, and made quite a fortune when he was young, importing exotic goods from abroad. Our house was crammed with such things as ivory, tiger skins and hunting trophies from the Far East. But his Achilles heel was gambling, in particular the illegal card game of baccarat. Debt soon befell him. Mama insists it was the stress of this that prematurely stopped his heart.'

'A great pity,' the doctor sympathized. 'Tell me, would there be a connection in your family to the Applebys of Buckinghamshire?'

Michael smiled in surprise. 'Yes, indeed. My paternal grandfather was Professor Reginald Appleby of Buckinghamshire.'

'A well-respected medical man.' The doctor nodded.

'You've heard of him, sir?'

'I've read the papers he published. On the aetiology of tuberculosis, if my memory serves me correctly.'

'The study of infectious diseases was his field,' Michael agreed eagerly. 'Under grandfather's direction, Papa studied for medical school in his early days, but soon quit. Their relationship suffered after this I'm afraid, and although I never knew either of them well, I understand they were clearly very different men. I hope I've kept the best of them in mind whilst I've made my own direction in life.'

'It's clear you have a strong and independent spirit,' the doctor said insightfully, 'just as Flora has.' He turned to smile at her. 'Without Flora as my nurse these past three years, my practice would have been severely tested. I was most fortunate to have been offered the opportunity of employing her. And that she agreed to be my assistant.'

Flora felt her cheeks fill with hot colour. The doctor made it seem as though she were someone of importance in his life. He had never spoken like this before.

'Good fortune for me too, in meeting you both,' Michael replied, 'as I now look on my injury more positively. But I fear that I may burden you too much . . . or take up too much of your time.'

'Not at all.' The doctor opened his hands. 'I am grateful to be able to revive some techniques that I hope might help future patients. As for Flora, the experience she is having will set her in good stead for the future.' His expression became wistful. 'It almost pains me to admit that she would do very well in the hospitals, who are under great pressure for skilled nursing staff. I have even thought of advising her to become a qualified nurse but so far have been too selfish to suggest it.'

Startled, Flora looked at the doctor. What could he mean?

'In all but name, you are a very capable nurse,' he told her. 'Has it never crossed your mind to try for your certificate?'

Flora shook her head. She was very happy working for Dr Tapper.

'The time will come for you to spread your wings. After all, your friend Hilda has done so already.'

Flora looked into the doctor's kindly but slightly troubled face. She knew that she would never leave his side. But before she could reply, Michael spoke again.

'Who knows what might happen in 1916?' he said, with a rough edge to his voice. 'I heard only last week that the men who survived Gallipoli are to be deployed elsewhere.'

'To the Western Front?' the doctor enquired.

'Some are to go to the Anglo–French force at the Greek port of Salonika.' Michael blinked his dark lashes. 'It seems there is no rest from the advance of Axis troops.'

Flora saw the doctor nod thoughtfully. Very soon the talk turned to the events in Europe that had carved a deep gulf in the earth from Flanders to the French fortress town of Verdun, where the doctor suggested that Wilfred might have served before being reported as lost in battle.

'There is still a chance, sir, that he may be found.'

Flora decided to let the two men exchange confidences and slipped discreetly away to the kitchen. She knew that the doctor would be able to talk about Wilfred to someone who understood and would give him some consolation in the absence of his dear son.

In the kitchen, Flora found that Mrs Carver had baked a rich fruit cake. It was covered in snowy white icing and decorated with green marzipan leaves. Carving several thin slices, Flora set them on the tray and began to make a pot of hot coffee.

Whilst the water boiled, she thought of what Dr Tapper had said today. Could she really become a nurse, as he suggested? The thought of taking examinations and working in a hospital gave her a feeling of unease. She had found happiness at Tap House and couldn't imagine herself being anywhere else. So much had happened this year. The war had unnerved everyone. She didn't have the courage that Hilda had to change her life.

Flora gazed out of the kitchen window to the twilight of Christmas Day. This year had proved to be the very best Christmas of her life. The cold pale blue of the afternoon sky had faded to a darker hue. The rooftops were covered not in smoke and grime but a blanket of ice that shimmered like polished silver. The world seemed so very beautiful. Yet, across the English Channel, a war was raging. With Will so far away, caught up in the killing, how could she be happy?

But she was.

The cold crisp night was silent as Flora, wrapped up in her coat, scarf and hat, stood outside Tap House. She and Michael had taken their leave, though Flora thought that neither of them had wanted to end the day. They had spent the evening playing backgammon, the doctor's favourite parlour game. The fire had burned down until the embers glowed scarlet. Now it was ten o'clock and their breath was forming clouds of vapour in the frosty air.

'May I see you again?' Michael's face was in shadow under the light of the lamp. 'I mean of course not as a patient, but as a friend.'

Flora dug her hands deep in her pockets and folded her fingers tightly. What was she to say?

'Are you worried the doctor might not approve?' he asked.

'You are his patient, after all.'

'But what can be wrong in two friends meeting up? I would of course speak to the good doctor first.'

Flora knew she wanted to be with Michael again. But would that be right?

'I'm sure we would enjoy one another's company,' Michael urged. 'A drive to the country perhaps? A trip to the theatre? Or just tea in the West End at Lyons or a decent hotel? You see, I haven't been able to talk to anyone the way I've talked to you.' He added quickly, 'And of course the doctor. I understand now why you think of him as very special. But . . .' He shook his head, pausing a few seconds. 'Forgive me for doubting you,' he said in a gruff voice. 'Sometimes my frustration gets the better of me.'

There was an awkward silence as they stood in the street. Flora shivered.

He touched her arm. 'You're cold. I've kept you out here too long.'

'Thank you for such an enjoyable Christmas,' she said.

'Happy Christmas, my dear Flora. And please think over what I've asked of you.' Then he took a small box from his pocket. 'This is for you. A small token of my appreciation.'

'But I didn't buy – I have nothing for you—' Flora began but he put his finger to his lips.

'You gave me a card made by your own hand and I shall treasure it.'

Flora opened the box. Inside she saw a gleam of silver. 'Oh, how beautiful!'

'I hope you like it.'

Flora took out a dainty silver butterfly. It sparkled under the lamplight.

'I tried to find one similar to the one at the market.'

'That was very kind of you. But you shouldn't have done this.' Flora put the brooch back into the box. 'I can't accept such an expensive gift.'

'I want you to know how grateful I am.'

'I'm supposed to help all the doctor's patients.'

He closed her hands over the box. 'Am I just that to you, a patient? I hoped I was more.'

Flora didn't know what to say. She wanted this too, but she was afraid.

'Please take it. I know that when you wear it, you'll have thought of me as you put it on.' Then, before she could reply, he turned and was lost in the darkness. A few minutes later, the engine of his car rattled into life and the dark shape moved off and into the night.

Flora stood there for some time afterwards. The box felt very precious in her hands. Even though she was very cold she wanted to remember this moment. Christmas was almost over and she had something very special to remember 1915 by.

In the early hours of the morning, Flora lay in bed, thinking of the pretty brooch that Michael had given her. It was very like the one she had seen on the market stall, the day they had first met. How had he managed to find one to resemble it? The brooch and the shawl were together in the drawer. The shawl was a reminder that she once had someone who loved her as a mother might. The brooch was from a young man who could become a part of her life, if she let him.

It hadn't mattered to Michael that she was an orphanage girl. The empty space inside her that she had tried to fill had begun to warm with a very different kind of love indeed.

Chapter Nineteen

Hilda slowly buttoned her dress, the familiar emptiness filling her, as Lord Guy Calvey got up from their bed of straw. As usual, after the strong wine that he had urged her to drink, she felt muddled and ashamed. Hilda knew that what she had done was very wrong in God's eyes. But she hadn't been able to help herself. On New Year's Eve, he had sought her out on the servants' staircase and kissed her with such passion that she hadn't been able to refuse him. And now he had captivated her. She only lived to be with him again.

'You're to say nothing of our meetings,' he warned her as he attended to his open shirt and riding breeches. Brushing his long, black hair away from his face he turned to her and bent close. 'Our little game must be kept a secret. If my aunt knew I was favouring you, she would dismiss you at once. And neither of us would want that, would we?' He raised one black eyebrow as he tucked in the loose tails of his shirt and refastened the narrow strip of leather at his waist. Then, retrieving his jacket from amongst the straw, he hooked it with one finger and tossed it carelessly over his shoulder.

'Oh, my lord, I'd never breathe a word to anyone,' Hilda vowed, forgetting her modesty as she sprang to her feet, exposing the full swell of her naked breasts below her blouse. She hurried to him, trembling, aching for his arms to be around her and his passionate kisses to cover her mouth again. The first time he had brought her to the barn, he had been so impatient to possess her that he had bruised and hurt her. She had been frightened at this first encounter with a man. But Lord Guy Calvey was no ordinary man. He had become a god in her eyes. She hadn't even tried to fight him off. She hadn't wanted to. The wine he gave her had helped a little, flowing through her veins and helping her to relax.

They had come to this place seven times. He would meet her at the stables in the early hours of the morning when everyone slept. Swinging her up behind him on his horse, she'd fold her arms around his waist and feel the thrill of the gallop across the fields. The ride had been exciting enough, but when he'd lifted her down from the big, sweating brown horse, Hilda had almost fainted with desire. Each time she had let him remove her clothes as they lay on the bed of straw. The cattle moved and grunted below them. In the hayloft they were completely alone. He had found the secret places that made her his willing slave. She couldn't stop thinking about him, about what would happen the next time she saw him.

'Do we have to go now?' she pleaded as she clung to him. 'I'll do anything, anything you want. Only let's stay a few minutes longer.'

In reply, he took hold of her chin, clasping it so tightly that it hurt. One lock of black hair fell roguishly over his face as he stared into her eyes. She could feel his heart beating against her breast and smell his sweat-dampened shirt. 'Patience,' he whispered, his full mouth curling into a smile. 'You're my hungry little kitten, eager to discover how you can use your claws. And mark my words, Hilda, I will show you how to use them.'

'I'm yours, my lord,' Hilda croaked, her eyes bulging. 'To do with as you wish.'

'I expect nothing less,' he hissed, tightening his grip even more. 'I saw willingness in your eyes when I first looked at you on the stairs. And then when you so brazenly flirted with me in the dining room, I saw wantonness in your gaze. I knew it was a desire that matched my own for pleasures of the flesh.' He twisted her face to one side, as if scrutinizing her profile. For a moment, Hilda was terrified. His grip was so powerful. His fingers dug into her skin and his black eyes glittered coldly. 'But remember, you must keep our secret, if we are to continue meeting.'

'I . . . I promise I'll never tell a soul,' Hilda choked.

'The other maid in your room – does she see you slip away?'

'No,' Hilda spluttered. 'Gracie is too worn out to wake.'

He nodded approvingly but then frowned. 'Do you write to your family? A friend? A sweetheart?'

She tried to shake her head, but he held her fast in his grip. 'I ain't got a sweetheart, my lord. Or a family. I'm . . . I'm an orphanage girl,' Hilda blurted out. She was upset to think that he thought she had anyone else in her life but him. She had never been with another man before. But when she'd told him that, had he believed her?

'You have no one?' he demanded again. 'No one at all?'

Hilda gurgled, her eyes feeling as though they were popping out of her head under the pressure of his fingers. 'My mother died in the convent laundry and the nuns took me in.' Hilda gulped what air she could into her throat. She thought that with just a little more pressure, he might break the bones in her neck. His dark gaze felt as though it was burning her skin. She didn't know what she had said to make him act in this cruel way.

Then, slowly releasing her, he smiled. He was now back to the man she loved and didn't fear. He softly stroked her face where his fingers had gripped her so painfully. 'An orphanage girl. Well, well, Hilda! A side to you I'm ignorant of. How fascinating!'

Hilda was shaking so much, she couldn't reply.

'No family, no relatives, no friends.' Pursing his lips, he blew gently on her eyes, making her lashes flutter. 'So delicate,' he whispered, 'so fragile.'

Hilda was entranced by his flattery. She would give anything to make him love her as much as she loved him.

'Come now, it will be dawn soon,' he said abruptly, as he turned away and lowered himself down through the trap door of the hayloft.

Gathering her skirts, Hilda followed and soon found herself in the darkness. By the light of the moon, he mounted the horse and reached down for her hand. Hilda gave a soft moan as he swung her up behind him; her body ached from their lovemaking. But the pleasurable pain was a reminder of how close they were. Of the bond that had been formed between them. It was to be expected that she must keep their secret for a while. But when he fell in love with her, all that would change.

As she threaded her hands around his waist, thoughts of the future filled her mind. A future that was beyond all her expectations. The upper-class women he entertained would fall by the wayside. They might wear fashionable clothes and chatter like pretty birds in gilded cages. But they were vain and self-centred. Hilda vowed she would always put his desires before hers. She would never refuse him. He had called her his hungry little kitten. Hilda shivered in delight at the thought. She would be patient, and when he asked her more about herself she would impress on him that he was her world. She loved no one else. She was certain her love and loyalty was what he wanted.

Hilda closed her eyes. The wind caught her hair and tore at her clothes. Her heart was beating in time with the pounding strides of the horse. What would Flora and Mrs Bell say if they could see her now?

One day, she would be more than just a servant at Adelphi Hall.

Of this she was certain.

Under the high Edwardian ceiling of the hotel, which was decorated by many glittering glass chandeliers, Flora sat beside Michael listening to the three-piece band, consisting of piano, violin and cello. Flora's pale hand rested lightly beside the white bone-china teacup that was now empty. This West End hotel was the most elegant place she had ever visited. Although, last week, she had thought the same of the Piccadilly teashop where she and Michael had spent the whole afternoon, talking and enjoying the sumptuous pastries. But here, there was not only music to accompany their meal, but a dance floor on which some of the couples had decided to venture.

Flora had never seen so many luxurious afternoon gowns in one small space before: fur-trimmed waist-length jackets, satin-ribboned and silk-tasselled dresses, short kimono-style overgowns, batwing blouses, three-quarter-length tiered sleeves, black, blue, white and green silk-chiffon frocks and fashionable hairstyles, finger-waved styles with side-partings, as Flora had seen advertized in the department store windows. Some women had added slim fitting head-bands with tall ostrich feathers or a sparkling jewel. Others wore heavy pearl or diamond earrings that glistened and sparkled below their ears. One or two dancers had matched their headwear to their shoes and silk stockings that were now clearly revealed by the daring new calf-length hemlines.

She eventually managed to return her attention to the waiter who was hovering beside the table asking if there was anything else they desired.

Michael raised one eyebrow. 'More tea, Flora?'

'No, thank you.' Flora couldn't manage even a sip more! It had seemed bad manners to refuse the wide selection of daintily made crustless sandwiches and French pastries. The waiter had set them out on three-tier stands placed on the spotless white linen of the table in front of them and served them with silver tongs.

Their waiter, a young man dressed in a white shirt, black bow tie and black waistcoat, removed the teacups and smiled charmingly at Flora. 'There's nothing else I can bring you, madam?'

Flora blushed. 'No, thank you.'

When the waiter had gone she giggled. 'Madam, indeed!'

Michael laughed. His thick, brown hair was brushed carefully away from his face, which still bore a slight tan. His broad shoulders were hidden under a smart dark jacket and his tie was a subdued navy against his blue-striped shirt. A silver tie pin and cufflinks to match were his only accessories. 'I must admit the last cream scone almost did for me.'

As always, Flora felt her tummy tilt and twist when he looked into her eyes.

'I would like to ask you to dance,' he said, his voice strained. 'But I would embarrass you, I'm sure.'

Flora only knew the steps to the waltz, anyway. The dancers on the floor seemed very accomplished and she would be embarrassed if she couldn't dance as well as they could. 'You'll walk without your cane soon,' she assured him.

'Do you really believe that? After the tumble I took last week, I'm not so certain.'

'But you got up and tried again,' Flora reminded him. Since Christmas, after each treatment with the doctor, Michael had tried to walk unaided. One day, he had stumbled, unable to break his fall. Despite his great embarrassment, he hadn't allowed the doctor or Flora to help him. When he'd finally pulled himself up, his face had been full of defeat.

'Perhaps I'm a lost cause, Flora.' His hand covered hers lightly.

Her heart beat so rapidly, she could hardly breathe. 'Please don't talk like that.'

'I'm sorry.'

'I know how painful the exercises are for you,' she acknowledged. 'But when I met you, you couldn't walk even a few feet without your cane.'

'I know I must be patient.'

She smiled. 'Patience comes with practice.'

'You're very wise for one so young.' He hesitated, his fingers tightening over her hand. 'Flora, we have enjoyed these few weeks together so much. And come to know each other so well. If I should get back on my feet and was to return to the conflict, I would hope that perhaps you would correspond with me.' He added swiftly, 'Of course, I may presume too much, as you're already writing to Will.'

Flora looked into his searching green gaze. How could she give him any sort of promise? It was true, they had become very good friends. After Christmas, he had taken her for drives in the car and short strolls along the Embankment. In the blustery weather of January they had sheltered in bookshops and teashops and had always found something to talk about. But what could come of such a friendship, Flora wondered, if he should ever return to the battlefield? There would be days and nights of endless waiting and worry that he would never come home again.

'I know how much you want to rejoin your men,' she told him. 'But that hasn't happened yet.'

'If I'm to recover, as you believe I will, then it may happen.'

Flora shook her head. 'I can't give you an answer, Michael.'

'Because of Will?'

She hesitated, as her feelings for Michael were growing stronger. To think that what was happening to Will might also happen to him was almost more than she could bear. 'Must we talk about the war?'

He looked away and sighed. 'Not if you don't want to.'

Flora looked at the couples dancing. She wondered if the Suffragette in Hyde Park had been right when she had said there would be fewer wars if women had a say in the running of the country. Could any war bring happiness at the cost of so many human lives? She knew Michael believed in the cause, but did she? Enough to give her promise to write to him? Flora looked down at their entwined fingers. 'Ask me again before you leave,' she replied, and at once saw the hope return to his face. She added quickly, 'But the selfish part of me wants you to be here in London where you're safe.'

'Then let's enjoy the moment.'

The trio continued to play and the music drifted pleasurably around them. But all the talk of war had cast its shadow. Flora didn't want to think of a future where Michael became a soldier again. But neither did she wish to see him remain a cripple.

Chapter Twenty

February brought gales and, in the middle of the month, a letter from Will:

> Things are not good here, my dear. Our dug-outs are filled with stinking mud and whatever elements rush into them after a downpour. Sometimes the mules and horses that carry our supplies and artillery are bogged down in the mess. A shell bursts and their remains are scattered, along with the poor souls who guided them. Yesterday, a shell burst in front of us. It knocked me senseless, but I came round to discover I was stuck in a large hole, with corpses flung over me. Some of the dead I knew, or had known. I wanted to give up then. I was finished! Before long another shell burst and I looked up to see a German standing at the top of the crater. His rifle was directed towards me. I thought with some relief that my wish was granted. But then he toppled, and rolled down the incline towards the pile of bodies. I looked in his open eyes; no life was in them. It was his end that day, not mine.

And so here I am, writing to you. God only knows how I've lasted.

The letter was signed with his deepest affection. Flora brushed the tear from her eye and thought of her friend. He had been away for fourteen months. The young boy was now a man. He had experienced terrors of all kinds, and narrowly missed death. Flora folded the letter back into its envelope. Will's story was not unfamiliar to her. Each day, there were more wounded soldiers from the Front returning as well as merchant shipmen who had survived Germany's U-boat attacks.

The next morning, she found the doctor sitting quietly in his room. 'I've received news of Wilfred,' he told her. 'His remains have been found near Ypres.'

Flora sat down heavily on the chair. What could she say to comfort him?

It was some time before he spoke again. Clearing his throat, he continued. 'They say he is buried close to the firing line. His personal effects will be returned to me.' The doctor stood up, his shoulders bent forward. 'I shall write to my sister in Bath, Wilfred's aunt. They were close and no doubt she will help me to arrange a memorial service.'

Flora wanted to put her arms around him. But she knew he wouldn't want her pity. 'Is there anything I can do?'

'Nothing, my dear. You had better see to the patients.'

Flora wondered how it was possible for the doctor to continue as normal. He looked very tired; the grief in his face had made him seem a much older man.

'Perhaps I should send them away?' she ventured.

'It's quite all right,' he assured her, patting his pockets gently. 'I had prepared myself for the worst. Now, let us carry on.' He walked slowly to the door. Flora followed. It didn't help when she went into the waiting room to see, amongst the other patients, a young man leaning heavily on his crutch and another sitting on one of the chairs, shaking fiercely. The signs of shell shock were easy to recognize now. These men were suffering the after-effects of a prolonged violent experience, but at least had returned alive. Wilfred, even in death, was exiled. He lay, where so many hundreds of thousands of British men now lay, on foreign soil.

On Sunday, Flora went to see Mrs Bell to share the unhappy news with her. By the time she arrived at Hailing House, the rain was driving down, sweeping across the road in gusts and forming large puddles in the gutters.

'You'll catch your death coming out in all this,' said Mrs Bell as Flora shook the rain from her umbrella. 'I'll put your coat by the range. You'd better give me your boots too. And don't try to hide the newspaper you've put inside them.'

'I've been meaning to buy some new ones.'

'About time too. There's more holes than soles in these.' She held the wet newspaper up and wrinkled her nose. 'If I was your mother I'd scold you thoroughly for not taking proper care of yourself. But then as I'm not, and am only a bossy old lady, you'll no doubt think of me as just a wretched nuisance, like our Hilda did.'

'I'll never think that.' Flora smiled.

'Can't you afford a new pair of boots for yourself?'

'I'm saving up to visit Hilda.'

'In that case I'll see what I can find in the charity box.' Mrs Bell disappeared, but was back very soon, minus the newspaper and holding a pair of brown leather boots. 'Lady Hailing gave me plenty of cast-offs for the poor and needy in the soup kitchen. There's any amount to choose from so you won't be leaving anyone short. These look about your size.'

Flora took the boots. They weren't much to look at, but were of the strong brown leather variety with hard-wearing thick soles. 'Are you sure you can spare them?'

'They'll see you all right for now. Slip them on and I'll pour us a cup of Rosie. Then I can show you the letter I had from Hilda.'

'She wrote to you?' Flora asked as she sat down at the table and leaned over to lace up the comfortable boots.

'Yes, I'm relieved to say she did.'

Flora watched Mrs Bell pour the rich brown tea, followed by creamy milk and a teaspoon of sugar, and serve a generous slice of Bakewell tart. Then Mrs Bell sat down beside her and took the letter from her pocket. Placing her half-spectacles on her nose, she began to read:

Dear Mrs Bell, I was paid my wage at Christmas and should be returning your pound. But Mrs Burns has asked me to make a new dress. Good cloth is very expensive so I hope you can wait a little longer. You'll be pleased to know I am highly regarded here by someone special and hope to improve my position soon. Is Aggie still with you? We are to lose more staff. James and John, the footmen, may have to go. I shan't like that at all. Even more jobs will be put our way. I'm already rushed off me feet along with Gracie. But I take comfort from the fact I won't be a maid much longer. With my best wishes, yours, Hilda.

'So what do you make of that?' asked Mrs Bell, a frown on her forehead.

'She's told you a lot about what's going on,' said Flora, who was impressed at the length of the letter. 'And she hasn't forgotten your pound.'

'She could have bought material for ten dresses with that.'

'Hilda likes quality.'

'I would have thought she had plenty of quality in the clothes she took with her.'

'It could be a working dress.'

Mrs Bell tapped the paper. 'Someone special, eh? Could he be one of the footmen?' She screwed up her small eyes and studied the letter again. 'If so, the girl is sure to be dallied with! Footmen are usually too handsome for their own good.'

'Hilda might have impressed Lady Bertha,' suggested Flora, 'which would explain why she needed the pound for a dress.'

'You could be right,' agreed the cook doubtfully. 'But you know Hilda, always with an eye for the men.'

'But Hilda's ambition is to be a lady's maid,' Flora reminded the cook. 'That's why she went to Adelphi.'

Mrs Bell's face softened as she folded the letter away. 'I knew you'd put me mind at rest, Flora, love. So I might send her a little something.'

'Hilda's very lucky to have you.'

'Oh, what's a pound to me? When it might make all the difference to how Hilda's looked upon by the uppers.' Mrs Bell looked pleased and she nodded in satisfaction.

'I'm afraid I have some sad news,' Flora said, reluctant to spoil the cook's pleasant mood. 'It's been confirmed that Dr Tapper's son, Wilfred, is dead.'

'Oh, my dear!' Mrs Bell clapped her hands on her cheeks. 'When are they bringing him home?'

'Wilfred's remains are buried near the front line.'

'Oh, to think of it! The doctor's one and only child, gone for ever without a proper resting place. What will the doctor do now?'

'Lieutenant Appleby has driven him to Bath to see his sister.' Flora couldn't hide her blush at the mention of Michael.

Mrs Bell sat up. 'Lieutenant Appleby? Who might he be?'

Flora told Mrs Bell about Michael's injury and the treatment that had been prescribed by the doctor. 'Dr Tapper even asked him to dinner on Christmas Day.'

'My goodness, what for? Hasn't he got family of his own?'

'Mrs Appleby was wintering in Scotland and I think the doctor was thinking of Wilfred and saw in Michael something of his own son.'

Mrs Bell looked keenly at Flora. 'So you spent your Christmas in the company of this young man? You didn't say anything about it at the midnight service.'

'I didn't know if he would turn up.'

The cook replenished the teapot, crooking an eyebrow at Flora. 'How old is he, may I ask?'

'Twenty-four.'

'And you, barely sixteen. I hope you'll remember he's a soldier.'

'I can't forget that.'

'The government is very short of men,' Mrs Bell was swift to remind her. 'Haven't you seen the lines of recruits marching down the street in their civilian clothes to the recruiting depot at Bow? Should this young man recover, he'll not be long in England.'

'I know.'

'Just you take care, my love.' Mrs Bell lifted her hands and sighed. 'The war is a long way from ending. On both the Eastern and Western Fronts, the conflict shows no sign of stopping. You may be tempted to start a friendship that is very difficult – and painful – to stop.'

Flora thought about Mrs Bell's warning as she made her way home. Michael had asked her to write to him if he rejoined his regiment. It was only fair to give him her answer. After all, the time he was spending driving her out and about, and taking her to fashionable hotels for tea, he could be spending with someone else. A girl who would be happy to comply with his wishes.

At this thought, a violent emotion gripped her. Flora stopped still. Her legs had gone quite weak and her pulse raced. What was this she was feeling? At the thought of Michael with another girl, she felt very miserable. How painful jealousy was!

On Monday, the surgery seemed very empty without the doctor. Flora had to tell the patients he was away in Bath and unlikely to return that week. Most of them understood when they heard that Wilfred had perished and the doctor was making arrangements for a remembrance service.

'I suppose we'll have to walk all the way to Blackwall,' one patient complained. 'To see the miserable old goat who calls himself a doctor and charges a shillin' just for stepping over his doorstep, never mind the cost of the medicine.'

Flora reminded the irritable lady that Dr Tapper never charged his patients unless they could afford to pay. Many of them couldn't, but he continued to treat them anyway. She added that he gave his time and attention to anyone who was sick and always without complaint.

'Me rheumatics will have to wait I suppose,' conceded the lady, which brought a smile to Flora's face. She knew that there were very few men like Dr Tapper and most of their patients appreciated that.

On Tuesday, a tall figure wrapped in a heavy driving coat arrived at the surgery door. 'I delivered the doctor safely,' Michael told her as he stepped in. 'I'm to return for him on Sunday.'

Flora smiled, a little embarrassed as, after her talk with Mrs Bell, Michael had often been in her thoughts. 'Will there be a service for Wilfred in Bath?'

'Yes, it's where he spent a lot of time as a child, I was told. He was very close to his aunt.' Michael hesitated. 'Would you mind if we postpone my treatment today?'

'Are you in pain?' Flora asked anxiously.

'No, in fact, quite the opposite.'

'Perhaps an improvement is all the more reason to keep up your exercises,' Flora scolded gently.

He laughed. 'What a hard taskmaster you are!'

Flora felt guilty. She knew it was not up to her to tell Michael anything.

'Oh, please don't look so sad.' Michael reached out and touched her arm. 'I was only teasing. Let me reassure you that I shall come for my exercises later this week, but there is something I would like to ask you, Flora.'

Flora waited as he transferred his cane to the other hand. What was he about to say?

'Could we go somewhere a little more, well, homely,' he asked after an awkward hesitation.

Flora knew he meant the airey. She had never asked him in before. It would seem improper to invite him into her home, unaccompanied.

'I promise I won't take up too much of your time. It's just that here I'm reminded of this,' he nodded at his leg, 'and don't really feel at ease to talk.'

He had such a hang-dog expression on his face that she found herself unable to refuse. And few minutes later, after she had locked the surgery door, they were making their way down the steps to the airey.

Michael looked around approvingly. 'Your home is most charming.' He began to peel off his coat and driving gloves, though she hadn't offered to take them.

'Would you like some tea?' Flora felt obliged to ask. She was feeling very nervous. What could he want? Having given her the brooch, which must have been very expensive, did he expect something in return?

'That would be perfect. Thank you.'

Flora felt her hands trembling as she put out the china and warmed the teapot before stirring the freshly brewed leaves. Could he be about to ask more of her than she was prepared to give? The thought made her feel as miserable as the other thought of someone else being with him. She tried to slow her movements. Was she reading too much into this? But he had never spoken this way before.

'So this must be Will,' Michael said when she returned with the tray. He was standing at the mantel, studying the photograph of Will in uniform.

'It was taken before he left the East End.'

'A handsome young man.' He sat down in the chair beside the fire. 'How are things going for him?'

'Very badly, I'm afraid.'

'But he has survived so far.'

'Yes, though in his last letter he admitted to wishing he could join his dead comrades.'

'I've heard some men say this.' Michael's voice was a rough whisper. 'Men who've lost all hope.'

'War is so terrible,' Flora said as she poured the rich brown tea into the cups and added the milk. 'Why do we have to have them?'

He paused for a while before answering. 'Some would say war is in the nature of man. Others would argue that their baser nature could be transformed, if worked on, to another state altogether.'

She was amazed to hear him speak such words. 'But you are a soldier. And not a volunteer. You must believe in the conflict.'

'I believe it's my duty to fight for king and country.' His eyes slipped away to the fire. 'Though war has come to mean something very different to me now.'

They were silent for a moment until he asked curiously, 'Does Hilda write to Will as conscientiously as you?'

Flora shook her head. 'Hilda isn't one for letter writing. Although she loves to receive letters, almost as much as Will does.'

He looked at her for a long while. 'So you and Will have grown even closer? Forging a bond, I suspect, that is very strong.'

'Yes, a bond that is unbreakable even by war,' Flora agreed as she drank her tea, thinking of Will. Michael was right. She was the only one who Will could exchange such life and death confidences with. The war had come to mean something very different to him too, just as Michael had experienced.

'I want to ask you,' Michael said after a while, 'if you would like to come with me when I next visit Mama? She would be most pleased to meet you.'

Flora sat up in her chair. 'But . . . but why?'

He laughed, his face surprised. 'She would love to meet you. I've told her all about you.'

'You have?'

'Please say you'll come.'

'But . . . but what will I wear?' Flora burst out. She didn't have anything except her blue suit. And Michael had seen it on Christmas Day.

'You will look delightful in whatever you wear.'

In the warm glow of the fire, her heart beat very fast. She gazed into his eyes.

'Good, we're agreed then. We'll go at the end of the week after I've had my treatment.'

'But what about the surgery?' She was beginning to panic and said the first thing that came to mind. 'Perhaps someone might call who doesn't know the doctor's away— '

'Then we'll leave a note on the door to explain.'

Flora stared into his amused green eyes as he almost dared her to argue the point. But she couldn't. It was a perfectly sensible suggestion.

Chapter Twenty-One

Shire Street, filled with leafless March trees, was a long, slightly bumpy lane, set to the north of Poplar. Flora hadn't even known this road existed. It was pleasantly situated between two parks, and no house resembled the other. At one end, she noticed a crumbling Victorian villa standing next to a new development of houses. The builders were still demolishing the old buildings. Further up the lane, Michael slowed the car, stuck out his gloved hand to indicate a right turn and, before she knew it, Flora found herself in front of a large cream-coloured house. Its tall, lower windows were covered by faded, striped awnings and the long glass doors were thrown open onto the lawn. The uncut grass was bordered by what Flora guessed must be beds of last year's roses. A bicycle or two stood propped against the walls of the house; wooden flower troughs were propped lopsidedly on bricks and overflowed with straggly green and white ivy. A small patch of cropped grass stood to one side, with a number of croquet hoops driven into the ground. Facing this was a large, wooden hut. On the balcony of the hut were several wooden mallets, two wrought iron chairs with faded floral cushions and an artist's easel.

'You have a lot in common with Mama. She loves to draw and paint.' Michael brought the car to a shuddering halt. 'Once there's a glimmer of sunshine, she's off to the wood to paint.'

'But I only drew your car.'

'Mama liked it very much.'

'You showed it to her?'

Michael chuckled. 'Of course.' He looked at her. 'I'm very glad you wore your brooch today. It sits very well on your jacket.'

Flora reached up to touch her brooch. She still couldn't believe that Michael had given her such an exquisite gift. The butterfly consisted of small jewels that Michael had told her were marquisate. Every time the light caught them, they sparkled.

'The brooch doesn't come close to the beauty of its owner.' Michael looked at her as he said these words.

Flora blushed. Did he really mean what he said?

'I can see I'm embarrassing you. Let's go in, shall we?'

Flora loosened the scarf that she'd placed over her straw hat. She had tried to keep her hair in place as they had driven in the car with the hood down. Although it was a sunny March day, there was a stiff breeze. But the excitement was making her feel very warm indeed.

The drive from the island had been wonderful. Flora loved the feeling of the air rushing over her face. She'd decided to wear a plain dark-blue suit with a jacket that folded neatly around her waist. It was the suit she had worn to her interview with Dr Tapper when she'd left the orphanage. Fortunately, she had grown taller but not wider. With adjustments to the hem and the addition of her white button up blouse, together with the boots Mrs Bell had given her, she hoped to look presentable enough for her first meeting with Mrs Appleby. And of course there was the brooch, outstanding enough to distract anyone's eye away from her simple dress.

Flora wasn't quite sure what to expect by way of a greeting. Had Michael told his mother he was bringing an orphanage girl for tea? Did she even know of Flora's existence or of the role she played in her son's physical rehabilitation?

'Are you sure your mother won't mind me coming?' Flora asked again, as she peered through the windscreen to the wood at the rear of the house. 'If she's trying to work—'

'Don't worry, dear girl, Mama is used to all sorts of interruptions.'

This didn't reassure Flora at all. Was she to be regarded as an interruption? Although Michael had invited her for 'tea' perhaps this just meant a cup of tea? Flora began to feel that she had misunderstood what he had told her. Had she listened properly to his invitation?

'Michael, perhaps it's better if—' Flora began but Michael was already climbing out of the car.

'Come along, take my arm,' he told her as he opened her door. 'I can't wait to surprise Mama.'

Flora froze. 'So she doesn't know I'm coming?' Her voice felt very small. She wanted to climb back in the car.

'Of course she does!' Michael laughed, his shining green eyes framed by his ruffled brown hair. He looked so handsome in his driving suit, a checked two-piece with leather knee boots and shiny leather gloves to match.

Flora grabbed his arm and held on tight. He led her round the side of the house to the green croquet lawn in front of the wooden hut. 'Mama uses the hut as her studio.'

'Your mother must be a very gifted painter.'

'Yes, I've often thought so.'

Suddenly, there was a rustle in the thicket of trees ahead of them. From out of the bushes rushed two black dogs, leaping and barking as they flew towards them.

'Steady there!' Michael commanded, holding up his cane. One of them sped towards Flora. She had never had anything to do with animals and was a little frightened as the dog sniffed around her.

'This is Jack,' said Michael with a grin. 'And Ivy. Do you like dogs, Flora?'

She smiled, daring to pat Jack's soft head. As a warm, rough tongue slid over the bare wrist above her glove, she giggled. 'I think I do.'

He laughed again. 'They're quite harmless. All bluster and show. But you'll soon get to know them.'

Flora stroked the two dogs, laughing with Michael as the dogs panted and fell on their backs, vying for attention. She loved their gentle nature.

'Michael! I didn't hear that contraption of yours arrive!' A tall, slim woman, wearing a paint-smudged smock and a large floppy hat, rushed from the trees. 'But Jack and Ivy told me you'd arrived.' She threw her arms around Michael and kissed his cheek. Turning to Flora, she gave a wide, friendly smile. 'And you must be Flora? Welcome, my dear.' Mrs Appleby greeted her with a gentle embrace. 'I've heard so much about you.'

Flora blushed. 'And I've heard a lot about you too, Mrs Appleby.'

'You have?' There was a twinkle in the older woman's brown eyes as she glanced at her son. She quickly slipped her hand through Flora's arm. 'Please call me Lillian.'

'I hope we haven't interrupted your work?' Flora said softly as they strolled towards the wooden hut, leaving Michael with the dogs. Flora thought how handsome Lillian Appleby was. She had Michael's thick brown hair and olive skin and though the colour of her eyes was dark, they had the same warm expression.

'I welcome the company, Flora. Michael is only home by virtue of his . . .' she gave a little sigh, '. . . his injury. Before he met you, and of course the good doctor, the time passed very slowly for him. How grateful I am that he has found hope again. Lately, he seems to be moving much easier.'

'Dr Tapper thinks so too,' Flora said as they stepped up on the wooden veranda of the hut. 'He's hoping the improvement will continue.'

'That's wonderful news, Flora,' Lillian Appleby replied. 'Though as a mother, I fear the day when my son is well enough to go away again.' She looked into Flora's eyes. 'The future is so uncertain for our young men.'

Flora nodded. She understood how Michael's mother felt.

'But we mustn't talk of war just now. Let me take off this dirty smock and we'll go in for tea.' She went through the wooden door of the hut, leaving Flora alone. Michael made his way up the wooden steps surprisingly quickly to stand with her.

'Well, what do you think?' he asked inquisitively.

'About what?' Flora teased. She knew he was talking about his mother.

'Mama likes you, I can see that.'

'And I like her.'

He stood very close. She could feel his breath on her face and see the slight smile play on his lips. Was she imagining she could feel the beat of his heart as he pressed against her? His hand was on her waist, drawing her near. The March wind blew fragrances of an early spring around them; the dogs barked playfully on the lawn and Flora looked into his eyes.

'Michael, I . . .' she began but her words were lost as something inside her made her want to be close to him. Her mouth parted of its own accord and her eyes began to close.

But then a noise from inside the hut made them part.

Flora knew her cheeks were very red when Lillian Appleby stepped out.

Flora liked Lillian Appleby's house. Every nook and cranny was crammed with something interesting. Books and papers spilled along with tennis racquets, picnic baskets, boots and galoshes, wherever there was space to pile them. The chairs and sofas were covered in beautiful but elderly cushions, their silks and embroideries still fine, but faded. There were mementoes from many countries, which Michael had spoken of before: the tiger skin in the drawing room, the sculptured wooden furniture from the Far East with strange oriental markings, the head of a great antelope in the hall over a pair of mahogany doors that led through into the dining room. And bookcases stuffed with books, though all in a rather haphazard manner. Flora liked to see the dogs bound in, unchecked, through every room, their paws noisy on the bare boards.

'I've asked Jenny to set tea in the conservatory,' Lillian Appleby said, now dressed in an elegant floral frock, her slim figure seeming to glide through the house. She led them through a set of glass doors to a wide, airy room at the rear of the house, filled with potted palms and ferns. 'We might as well enjoy the sun while it's out. Flora, sit here by me.' Lillian indicated one of four cushioned white wicker chairs drawn up to a low table. Flora couldn't help but admire the sparkling white china teacups, large fruit cake and rack of small, triangular-shaped crustless sandwiches.

Flora sat down, aware of Michael's close presence beside her.

'Jenny, we'll have tea now, I think, or Flora, would you prefer coffee?'

'No, tea will be fine, thank you.' She smiled up at the pretty young girl with dark hair who, unlike any maid she had ever seen, was dressed in a plain white blouse and grey skirt. She wore no mob cap or apron and looked more like a visitor.

'Jenny is a neighbour's daughter,' explained Lillian when the girl had gone. 'She comes in once or twice a week to help in the house. I'm afraid the days of small households having the luxury of permanent staff are numbered. Young women these days prefer to work for the war effort. But there again, all our lives have been touched in some way.' Lillian glanced at her son, then crossed one leg over the other, arranging her long, flowing skirt over her knees. 'Michael has told me how your friend Will volunteered for France in August 1914. And later, how Hilda went into service at Lord Talbott's estate. You must miss your friends a great deal.'

Flora looked quickly at Michael. It seemed he really had told his mother all about her. 'Yes, I do miss them,' Flora admitted. 'Will is having a very hard time.'

'Do you know where he is?'

'No, but his letter came just after the German attack on Verdun.'

'Verdun? Such a nightmare.' Lillian looked up at Jenny as she brought in the tray. A large white china pot and a milk jug stood on it. 'Thank you, Jenny.' Lillian lifted the teapot. 'And Hilda? How is she faring? Michael tells me she hopes to be lady's maid to Bertie Forsythe.'

Flora frowned. Who was Bertie Forsythe?

'Lady Bertha is called Bertie by some,' Michael explained.

'Before Michael's dear father blotted our copybook,' said Lillian with a rueful smile as she poured the tea, 'we mixed in rather different circles. My husband took many trips abroad and always needed wealthy sponsors, hence the somewhat heady lifestyle we led. Michael's told you all about our family's chequered history, I think?'

Flora nodded hesitantly. She felt uncomfortable that Michael had shared with her what seemed to be such personal family details.

'Oh, please don't be embarrassed, my dear,' Lillian said with a chuckle. 'The world and his wife were once privy to my late husband's bankruptcy. Lady Bertha and I have known each other since my marriage to Michael's father, Julian, who was a favourite of Bertie's set.' Lillian raised her beautiful eyebrows and sighed. 'Julian was a charming adventurer and the life and soul of any party. Indeed, his passion for gaming took him into the most celebrated circles. Until finally, the money ran out. Or rather my grandfather's money, which had taken a lifetime to accumulate and took only a handful of years to fritter away.' She laughed lightly, surprising Flora. 'It's quite all right, Flora. Michael and I now look on our previous life with some amusement. Thank the good Lord we both survived. But no thanks at all to our dear departed.' She looked up and nodded to a painting hung on the chimney breast. The handsome subject was a man with light-brown hair and very green eyes. He wore a long Indian-looking robe of crimson and orange.

'My father,' said Michael with a twist of his lips. 'Mama painted him in one of his favourite get-ups, a gift from some Eastern maharaja.'

Lillian smiled. 'Michael has Julian's eyes and his courage.'

'A pity there is very little left of Father other than his trophies,' remarked Michael, as he drank his tea. 'A good name would have helped Mama in her hour of need.'

Flora heard a trace of bitterness in his voice; it was the first time he had spoken that way.

'And you, Flora,' Lillian said quickly. 'Tell us something about yourself.'

Flora glanced at Michael. Would he think any less of her if she talked about being an orphan? He smiled. She found the courage to answer. 'I was found as a baby outside the convent by one of the nuns on the first day of August 1899. I never knew who my mother or father were.'

'Did the nuns?' Lillian asked curiously.

Flora was taken aback. She had never been asked that question before. 'I was never told anything.' She hesitated. 'But after I left the orphanage I was given a shawl that Mother Superior said I was wrapped in when they found me.' Flora smiled. 'Someone had embroidered "W" and "S" in one corner.'

'Could this be a clue to your mother?' Michael asked, and his eyebrows rose. 'Are you sure the nuns didn't know more?'

'Mother Superior said that my teacher, Sister Patricia, might. But she's in France.'

'Oh, dear, that's very sad. But don't give up hope, Flora.'

Flora felt close to tears. How kind this lady was.

'Now, please let us all enjoy Jenny's tea.' Lillian unfolded her napkin.

Flora began to eat, but she wasn't really hungry and was glad when the meal was over.

'Shall we walk in the woods, Flora?' Lillian stood up. 'I am sure Michael has plenty to do in the workshop.'

Michael grinned. He knew he had been dismissed.

'What a pretty brooch you're wearing,' Lillian said with a teasing grin as they strolled arm in arm together through the trees, the dogs at their side.

Flora blushed. 'It's a gift from Michael.'

'He thinks a great deal of you, Flora. I hope that he has made it plain to you that he must go back to war if he recovers.'

'Oh, yes. From the very first moment we met, I knew that.'

Lillian patted her arm gently. 'He told me that you were asking after Fritz. And how upset you both were at the unforgiveable treatment meted out to him. He was such a pleasant old man and treated everyone with respect. I knew him for years and enjoyed buying my small pieces from him and discussing the ways of the world. It's very sad that the war has brought us all to this kind of reprehensible behaviour. Friends are very few and far between these days. But then of course, you understand that well.'

Flora nodded. 'I miss Hilda a great deal as we grew up together and always saw each other on our days off.'

'I do hope you will find her . . . settled,' Lillian said. 'Good friends in life are, without doubt, very rare. After our financial ruin, many of those I looked on as friends simply faded away.'

'That must have been very hard for you.'

'Yes, I discovered they were only fair-weather acquaintances. And I should never have known that, had not the worst happened.'

Flora wondered if Lady Bertha Forsythe was one of those so-called friends.

As they walked on, Lillian asked more about her work. Flora spoke of people like Stephen Pollard and Mr Riggs and poor little Polly and of the war veterans like Eric Soames and Sidney Cowper. Lillian listened very attentively, at last heaving a deep sigh.

'How fortunate it is that the world has people like Dr Tapper to look after it,' Lillian said as she came to a stop by the stream. She looked into Flora's eyes. 'And how very insignificant our daily woes are in the light of all this.'

'I often think the same when I read Will's letters.'

'Ah, yes, your dear friend Will. Has he no other relatives?'

Flora shook her head. 'Like me, he doesn't know who his parents are. Unlike Hilda, whose mother worked in the convent laundry. When Hilda was eight Rose Jones died and the nuns took Hilda in.'

'What marvellous work these nuns do.'

'Yes,' agreed Flora at once. 'We could have been sent to the workhouse.'

'A terrifying thought!'

Flora smiled. She knew that this kind lady didn't look down on her.

'It's wonderful to know that all three of you remain close.'

They stopped as the dogs ran barking and chasing into the trees. 'I wish Hilda was still safely in service with Lady Hailing,' Flora admitted.

'Lady Hailing – a wonderful woman and great philanthropist!' Lillian exclaimed. 'One cannot speak too highly of the family.' There was a long pause. 'Would you say Hilda is right for her new position with the Calveys?'

Flora hesitated as she thought about this. 'Mrs Bell, Lady Hailing's cook, has her doubts.'

'Does she indeed?' Lillian said as they turned towards home. 'And why is that, do you suppose?'

'Mrs Bell has always worked for Lady Hailing. She thinks Hilda would have fared better where she was. But that could be because Mrs Bell looks on Hilda as a daughter and worries about her dreadfully.'

Lillian looked thoughtful. 'You keep up a correspondence with Hilda, of course?'

Flora nodded. 'But she's a very poor hand with the pen. So I'm hoping to visit her next month.'

'Ah!' Lillian exclaimed as they came in sight of the house. 'And then you'll be able to see first-hand how things really are.'

Flora thought how very much she liked Lillian Appleby. There was nothing that Flora felt she couldn't discuss with her. However, she had reminded Flora that Michael would have to return to war if he recovered. It was the shadow lurking in both their minds.

Flora thought about the moment on the veranda when she and Michael had stood very close. She had felt a moment of great intimacy and all she had wanted was for Michael to kiss her. It was a very new feeling and had taken her by surprise. Could she be falling in love? If she was, her heart, as Mrs Bell would say, was ruling her head.

Chapter Twenty-Two

Hilda crouched low behind the prickly spring gorse, her heart thumping. She listened for the sounds of the pounding hooves and snorting of the horse as it charged after her. The cold March night was for the moment silent. This time, she had reached the trees to the south of the barn. She had never run this far before.

Perhaps Guy would find her in the forest. She hated the dark, eerie layers of branches, the carpet of noisy leaves and bracken that told of her every move. No, she wouldn't go in there. The open land was at least lit by the moonlight.

Hilda closed her eyes in distress. Would he ride up soon? The first time this had happened, she had been at her lowest ebb. Dizzy with the wine he made her drink and every bone in her body aching from the run. She had made her way across the dark field, towards the trees. Very soon he'd ridden after her, catching her easily on the big brown stallion. Its great sweating body had trembled as it reared up. Bursts of grey-white air streamed from its frothing nostrils. Guy had dismounted, laughing.

It was then she had first been frightened. Their game had lost its appeal. Guy appeared the same, with his beautiful face and body, but his eyes had glittered menacingly. She had tried to scramble away, but he'd caught her hair and dragged her to a wooded thicket. She had felt like some wounded creature, as the thorns had torn into her skin and red welts appeared over her arms and legs. Her beautiful dresses, the ones that Lady Hailing had given her, had been reduced to rags. To think of all she had done for him. The money she had borrowed from Mrs Bell to buy frivolous trinkets and perfumes to make herself more beautiful in his eyes. The lies she had told Gracie about where she had been at night. And eventually, the scorn in Gracie's eyes when the truth had finally come out.

Hilda listened . . .

All she could hear was the breath of a trapped animal. They were her own short, terrified gasps. She understood how a fox must feel at the point of capture. Or a deer, staring into the gaze of the hunter.

Hilda started in fright. The noise was familiar; a horse was thundering towards her. She fell backwards, the terror within her mounting. With her back to the rough bark of a tree she waited. Sweat poured from her, soaked her damp, torn dress, spread over her loose, full breasts and down her spine.

Suddenly, a shadow appeared. Clods of earth, leaves and bits of bracken fell into her hair. Long legs thrashed by her head, hooves flew past her cheeks. Hilda cowered, trying to protect her face.

'Come, come, Hilda, this is no time to pause,' called Guy from above her. 'Get on with you, girl, run faster. Our game must be made more exciting.'

She dared to glance up. Between the strands of his wet black hair, his eyes seemed to glow. 'I . . . I can't run no more, my lord,' she begged. 'Have pity.'

He stared at her, breathless and panting, his shirt open, exposing the black whorls of hair on his chest. The hair that Hilda had once run her fingers through in ecstasy. 'Run! This is your last chance!' he yelled at her.

Hilda dragged herself up. She knew that if she didn't obey him, his mood would worsen. At least if she ran until he brought her down, he would perhaps decide to end the chase.

Hilda began to run. Her scratched and bleeding bare feet were no match for the coarse forest floor. But still she tried. Through the pain she ran, her lungs almost bursting. The burs and twigs that caught in her hair fell across her face. Sharp, twisted branches slapped against her arms and legs. In the dawn light, Hilda saw only the dripping trees, their tiny buds yet to unfurl. The mist enfolded her as if taking her down to hell. Hilda listened to her own sobs of defeat. Her choked, cowardly gulps of fear.

At last she fell, headlong, sprawling and rolling down an incline. Over and over until she reached the narrow valley. Her head struck something hard, a stone perhaps.

When she looked up, dazed and terrified, there was silence. A warm trickle ran down her cheek. She lifted her fingers to touch the blood. A strange greyness came into her vision. She lifted her head, trying to adjust her eyes to the light.

The tall, sweat-soaked figure of her master loomed over her. Hilda gave out a pathetic moan, pleading for mercy. Her master kneeled beside her, touching her face tenderly, drawing aside her tangled hair.

'Your blood, Hilda – first blood.' He ran his thumb over the wound. 'You wanted to play, little kitten, you said you would do anything for me.' His eyes glittered. His mouth worked as the wet, shiny saliva formed over his lips. His hair, like hers, was limp and matted and clung to his face and neck. 'Do you still want to please me?'

'Y . . . yes, my lord,' she stammered.

He smiled, showing his white teeth, which reminded Hilda of the fox corpses she had seen, strung up by their legs, their mouths open. He took hold of the flimsy remains of her dress and tore it roughly from her. Hilda shuddered and trembled. He touched her naked breasts, looking at her with lust.

As he took her, Hilda told herself that she still loved him. She could forgive these silly games, because after the chase, he would make love to her. Even if he hurt her, she believed it was her fault; that she was not pleasing him as he wanted to be pleased.

If only she could convince him she loved him.

But then Hilda felt the brute force of his harsh demands. She allowed herself to be degraded. And as much as she pleaded with him, he seemed not to care and became this other person she didn't know.

It was almost Easter and Flora was happy to see the doctor looking better after spending the week with his sister. He had said very little about Wilfred's memorial service, but Flora knew that he had done all he could to say a last farewell to his son.

'I have told all the patients we've seen today that the surgery will be closed for Easter,' he said as they ended surgery on Thursday evening. 'I have an old friend coming to stay with me. We shall spend some time together in the city.' He smiled. 'We were young doctors together and we met up again in Bath. And I'm sure you, Flora, have plenty to keep you busy.'

Flora saw his eyes twinkle. She knew he approved of her friendship with Michael, and that he too had grown very fond of him and enjoyed their long discussions.

When Flora was at home that evening, she thought about Michael's offer to drive her to Surrey on Easter Monday. Perhaps she should accept. She was suddenly excited. She and Hilda had so much to discuss.

But when a letter came from Hilda on Saturday, Flora gave a low moan. 'I have been off-colour,' Hilda wrote. 'The reason being, we have lost more men to the services and I am wrung out with exhaustion. It wouldn't be any use you coming. When I am more myself, I will let you know. With affection, Hilda.'

When a knock came on the airey door, Flora was surprised to see Mrs Bell. 'Happy Easter, Flora. I've baked some Easter buns for you.' She took a brown paper bag from her basket. 'Thought you and the doctor might like them for Sunday.'

'Thank you.'

'You look a bit down, love.'

'I am. I was hoping to go and see Hilda on Monday. But she wrote she's not well enough to meet me.'

'What's wrong with her?'

'She says she's had a lot of work to do as more of the men have left.'

Mrs Bell rolled her eyes. 'Listen, Reg Miles, the costermonger who delivers to the house, is waiting. He's giving me a ride to the market. Would you like to come too? An afternoon at the market might cheer you up a bit.'

Flora smiled. 'I'd like that.'

'Go and put the buns away safely. I'll ask Reg to wait while you get ready. Better bring a coat in case it rains. And Hilda's letter. We can read it over a cup of Rosie.'

It took Flora only a few minutes to store the buns, after which she grabbed her coat and pushed Hilda's letter in her pocket.

Reg was waiting outside and helped Flora up beside Mrs Bell. 'Nice day for a bit of shopping,' he said from under his peaked cap. Flora had seen him at the market before; he was a tall, portly man with a florid complexion, who, even though he was not in his prime, worked very hard at his greengrocery business.

'Yes, even nicer, Reg, now you're taking us to the market.' Mrs Bell folded her arms over her plump chest, resting her basket on her stomach. She pushed her hair up under her small brown felt hat. 'Couldn't walk that far now. Not with me legs.'

Reg winked as he glanced at the cook sitting on the wooden seat.

Flora thought that Reg the costermonger seemed very friendly. She had never seen Mrs Bell like this before, with a blush on her cheeks that wasn't caused by her cooking.

'I did warn Hilda,' Mrs Bell said unsympathetically, as they sat together on the bench at the coffee stall, waiting for Reg who was delivering to his customers. As Mrs Bell hadn't brought her reading glasses, Flora had read Hilda's letter aloud. 'Cut-backs are common now. Lady Hailing has had to give up her chauffeur. All the big houses must comply; it's government regulations.'

'There was no mention of the special someone either,' said Flora with a frown.

'Don't dwell on it,' Mrs Bell advised. 'When Hilda has something to brag about, she soon lets you know. She'll be writing again only to tell you she's engaged to a wealthy prince or has finally become a lady's maid!'

They both smiled. 'Lieutenant Appleby had offered to drive me to Surrey.' Flora glanced at Mrs Bell.

'Lieutenant Appleby?' Mrs Bell quickly put down her mug.

Flora blushed.

'My, my! Are you walking out with this young man?'

'We're just good friends.'

'I can see that, my dear. And good luck to you, though I'm no judge of affairs of the heart. I never married. Never had the inclination. It's the Hailings who's been me family, as you know. But you're only young once and a drive in the country would do you no harm. Perhaps you should think about enjoying yourself for once. Let our Hilda get over her mood. We both do too much worrying over that girl.' She touched her elbow against Flora's arm. 'London can be very confining at this time of year. The lieutenant might drive you to the seaside, if you thought to suggest it.'

Flora was so surprised that her mouth fell open. She had expected another warning from Mrs Bell about becoming too fond of a soldier.

'Anyway, I can't sit here all day gossiping, as much as I'd like to. Lady Hailing and her daughters are visiting the house after Easter. Me and Aggie have all the fires to light and the rooms to air. Now, I'll go and find Reg.' She stood up. 'Do you want a ride back with us, ducks? It's no trouble at all.'

'No, thank you.' Flora smiled. 'I'm glad Reg is too old to enlist.'

Mrs Bell gave a chuckle. 'I'm glad too.' She added quickly, 'But only because he's fair with his prices.'

Flora watched her friend as she left. Mrs Bell even seemed to move with a more agile step, despite her bad legs. Her shoulders were pulled back under her coat and her hat sat squarely on her head. It came as a shock to Flora to realize that even Mrs Bell was losing her concerns over Hilda. Time had passed and the elderly lady had begun to take an interest in life. And Reg did seem a nice man, who looked as if he enjoyed his food.

Flora found herself walking slowly around the market. She was thinking of all that had happened since she, Hilda and Will had met that time in Hyde Park. None of them had realized then that the changes the war would bring would affect them in so many different ways.

She wanted to see Hilda more than ever now. If Michael offered again to take her to Surrey, she would accept.

It was the end of May and although she hadn't heard from Hilda, Flora was certain that her friend must be recovered by now. The spring breeze blew softly around her face as she sat in Michael's car, excited at the prospect of seeing Hilda.

Her new summer hat and soft chiffon scarf had been purchased from the market especially for the occasion. Her coat collar was trimmed with soft fur. It was also a second-hand purchase, but of excellent quality, a real treasure amongst the many items on the trader's stall. Pinned discreetly to her lapel was the brooch, catching the light as she moved.

She was proud to be sitting next to Michael, who was dressed in his tweed suit, sporty cap and driving gloves. After he had asked her if she would like to travel with the hood down, he had folded a blanket across her knees even though the weather was fine and sunny. She liked sitting in the open air, smelling the scents and being part of the passing world. He had offered her goggles for the journey. But Flora had laughed at this. The goggles, she thought but didn't say, made people look like fish, with big round eyes magnified by the glass lenses. She wanted to look her best when she arrived at Adelphi Hall.

'Fine weather all day is forecast,' shouted Michael above the clatter of the engine as they crossed Tower Bridge. He nodded as a motor car passed the other way. She had to hide her amusement when drivers acknowledged one another. This journey was very different to the simple one she and Hilda had made in Albert's cart.

Taking a contented breath, Flora looked down at the great River Thames. Though it was Sunday, the waterborne traffic was gliding elegantly on the current as the green-grey hue of the water turned to a silvery gold in the distance. She could see the gulls sweeping and circling, but their cries were lost in the noise of the engine.

Very soon, they reached the countryside which immediately filled Flora with delight. She recalled with pleasure the little villages that Albert had taken them through. Thatched cottages, winding lanes and fields of sheep and cows spread out on either side of the road as they sped along.

Flora began to wonder what Hilda would say when they arrived. Would she throw her arms around her and hug her? She was certain that Hilda would be pleased to see her. And what would she say when she saw Michael?

Their visit would be a surprise for Hilda!

Chapter Twenty-Three

'Hilda Jones?' The old man frowned, then shook his head in answer to Flora's enquiry. 'There's lots of wenches from the village here now. They all look the same to me. I has to have instructions, to let anyone in.'

'But it's to be a surprise visit,' Flora persisted as she looked out from the car.

'I have to be careful. You could be anyone: hawkers or pedlars or thieves even.'

Flora saw Michael remove his gloves and then his goggles. He took out his wallet and slid a note towards the gatekeeper. 'I can assure you we are quite trustworthy and have no intention of causing trouble. We simply want to see Miss Jones, who we understand has been out of sorts and could do with a visit to cheer her up.'

The gatekeeper snatched the money and pocketed it. 'It's plain you aren't rough sorts and so I'll make an exception this time. Take the road to the left and be sure you're out of the grounds before dark.'

Michael nodded and pushed a lever. The car moved forward slowly.

'I didn't think we'd have to pay to get in,' Flora said in dismay.

'It's the way of the world.' Michael shrugged. 'And only to be expected. It's what's known as the perks of the job. Which, after all, must be very boring for the poor old chap.'

'I'll pay you back.'

Michael looked offended as he turned to her. 'I have no intention of allowing you to do such a thing.'

Flora hadn't thought about the gatekeeper when she had made her plans to visit Hilda. She had decided on impulse, hoping that Mrs Burns would allow them to see Hilda as she had been unwell. Now she was wondering if she had acted wisely.

As they entered the dark shadows of the wood, Flora shivered. She remembered how Hilda didn't like this lane and had been disappointed she was not allowed to walk up the wide sandy drive. Michael turned the car to the left of the sign that indicated the tradesmen's entrance. 'Perhaps we should have brought something to deliver,' he teased. But when Adelphi Hall came into sight, he stopped the car abruptly, opened-mouthed at the first sight of the house. Its white pillars gleamed in the sunshine, the many windows shone and the gardens either side spread out to the velvet lawns. 'Quite spectacular!' Michael exclaimed.

'It is very beautiful.'

'And look there, by the entrance! A magnificent example of the latest Rolls-Royce limousine.'

Flora watched as a tall man wearing a hat climbed out of the shiny black vehicle and went up the steps to the house.

'One chauffeured passenger,' Michael mused. 'Perhaps it's the earl himself.'

'Mrs Bell told me that he went a little strange after his wife died,' Flora remarked as they watched the car drive away.

Michael raised his eyebrows. 'Stories abound of this great place. Whatever is true, I couldn't say.'

They stopped a few minutes longer to admire the scene, then Michael drove on. But as they neared the archway that led to the stable, Flora felt anxious. Was it sensible to visit without invitation?

But as they reached the stables and outhouses, Flora's excitement soon replaced her doubts. Hilda was part of this magnificent estate and was living the life that she had always dreamed of.

Flora couldn't wait to tell Hilda how proud she was of her.

'Oh, lor'! It's you, miss.'

Flora smiled at the scullery maid, who had been hurrying back from the greenhouse with a basket of sweet-smelling herbs over her arm. 'Hello, Gracie. How are you?'

'Thank you, miss, I'm all right.'

'This is my friend, Lieutenant Michael Appleby.'

Gracie did a small bob, her white face going pink as she looked at Michael.

'I'm pleased to meet you, Gracie.'

'Likewise, sir.'

Flora glanced at the house. 'We've come to visit Hilda.'

Gracie's skin soon returned to a pasty white. She looked almost frightened as she peered out from her washed-out eyes hidden by straggly wisps of thin hair which escaped from beneath her cap. 'Is Mrs Burns expecting yer, miss?'

Flora shook her head. 'I didn't write, as I wanted to surprise Hilda.'

'You know Mrs Burns don't like surprises.'

'I was hoping she could make an exception this time. I hear Hilda has been unwell. Or, at least, Hilda wrote that she was not feeling her old self.'

At this, Gracie's eyes widened and she swallowed. 'Did she tell you that? What else did she write?' Gracie closed her mouth and looked down. 'I'm sorry, it ain't my place to ask you that.'

'We don't plan to stay long, Gracie,' Michael said in a reassuring tone. 'Perhaps Hilda could meet us outside in the gardens somewhere? We shouldn't inconvenience Mrs Burns by coming inside, if that's the problem.'

Gracie clutched her basket tighter. Her lips trembled a little and her eyes flashed to the kitchen entrance that Flora recalled from her first visit. It was here that she had first seen Mrs Burns talking to Gracie. 'Oh, it ain't up to me, sir. You'll have to ask Mrs Burns. It's a blessing you've come, see? But, oh, dear, oh, dear, you'll set the cat among the pigeons and that's for sure.'

Flora was about to ask her what she meant when a figure came out of the kitchen door.

'Gracie, come here at once!' Mrs Burns called.

Gracie stepped back, almost tripping in her haste to leave. 'If I was you, I'd write to 'Ilda first and—'

'Gracie!'

Flora saw the girl jump and, clutching her basket, she ran to the house.

'What do you make of that?' Michael said as they watched Mrs Burns approach. 'The poor girl seemed frightened out of her wits.'

'Yes,' agreed Flora. 'I thought so too.'

The housekeeper strode towards them and stopped a few feet away. Her small, penetrating eyes and thin lips gave no indication of a smile. Her black dress, trimmed with small black beads and lace at the neck, looked exactly as it had before, starched and ironed to perfection. Her lace cap sat squarely on her head and rested on the tight bun of grey-black hair at the nape of her thin neck. 'Yes?' Mrs Burns ignored Michael, fixing her chilly stare on Flora. 'I have only a few minutes to spare.'

'I'm Flora Shine. Perhaps you remember me?' Flora declared. 'I've heard from Hilda that she's not very well.'

'As I warned you before, visits must be settled in advance.'

'Apologies,' Michael said. 'But in such circumstances, when one is concerned about a friend, I'm sure an exception can be made.'

For the first time, Flora thought that Mrs Burns looked unsettled. She stared at Michael, folding her hands tightly in front of her as though preparing to stop them by force if necessary from entering the house. Her mouth opened, her lips parted as if to speak, but Michael spoke again.

'Let me introduce myself,' he said slowly, with an authority that Flora had never heard before. 'Lieutenant Michael Appleby, presently recovering from injury and hoping to see our friend before I return to the conflict. I am certain that, in the light of these circumstances, you will do all you can to afford us a short while with Hilda.'

Flora had to stifle a giggle. The housekeeper's smooth hair looked as though it might bristle if she wasn't wearing a cap. Michael's unswerving gaze refused to leave her face, silently demanding that she comply with their wishes. Flora knew that Mrs Burns was only ever addressed this way by her superiors.

With a brisk flash of her eyes, Mrs Burns gathered herself, squared her shoulders and looked at Flora. 'I shall see what I can do.' This was a snub, Flora realized, and clearly not an invitation to follow her into the house, as she turned on her heel and strode away.

'Well, that seemed to do the trick,' Michael said with a rueful smile. 'Though I dislike having to pull rank, as it were.'

'Thank you, again.' Flora knew that Mrs Burns would have turned her away if she had been on her own.

'I hope you're not offended when I said Hilda was a friend?'

'No, of course not.'

'Rather odd, don't you think, not to comment on Hilda's state of health?' A frown pleated his forehead.

'Yes, I thought so too.' Flora pointed to the garden bench. 'Perhaps she'll send Hilda out to speak to us. I sat there last time and it's very pleasant.'

'Then it's a good idea to sit there again, don't you think?' Michael accompanied her to the wooden seat. 'Has Hilda ever complained of her treatment here?' Michael asked as they made themselves comfortable.

'No, she's always sounded happy enough. She even wrote that someone special was taking an interest in her.'

'Did she say who?'

'No. I thought perhaps it might be Lady Bertha but Mrs Bell said it could be one of the footmen.'

'Ah,' sighed Michael. 'Perhaps we'd better not speculate and let's hope that when you see Hilda your mind will be put at rest.'

As they sat in the sunshine, Flora saw the gardener working in the greenhouse. He was alone. The big, rambling building looked neglected; some of the large panes of glass had been broken and some were missing. The impressive fountain with its urn and lilies beneath was silent, a mossy green rim and empty pool replacing the sparkling water and dainty flowers. Weeds sprouted, unchecked, across the lawns and pathways, just as they had grown over the cobbles of the deserted stables where they had left the car.

Hilda had said that more men had been called up. The many duties, she wrote, had to be shouldered by the women. The grounds of Adelphi Hall were not looking their best, Flora decided, as she cast her gaze over the silent, untended gardens. Perhaps the work at Adelphi Hall really was too exhausting for Hilda, even though Mrs Bell had shrugged off the notion. She hoped Hilda would appear soon and put all her worries to rest.

Half an hour later, Gracie found them again. ''Ilda says to tell you she's sick and in bed and can't see you. She says 'er fever might be catching and she'll write soon when she's better. And not to come again until she's good and ready to see you.'

'What sort of fever is it?' asked Flora anxiously.

'The 'ot kind,' Gracie replied. 'She caught a cold and was burning up for nights on end. I know as I sleep next to her and could hear her tossing and turning, till one morning she couldn't get up. Now the doctor says she has to stay in bed till the fever's gone.'

'Couldn't I see her, just for a minute? Surely, Mrs Burns would let me.'

''Ilda wouldn't like that.'

'But Gracie,' protested Flora, 'you said it was a blessing we came.'

Gracie gave another nervous twitch. 'That was before 'Ilda stuck 'er 'ead under the bedclothes and told me to tell you to go away. She can be very stubborn, can 'Ilda. You must know that.'

'Yes, she can be, but—'

'I've got to go now.' Gracie glanced behind her. 'Mrs Burns don't want me lingering.'

Flora caught Gracie's wrist. 'Tell Hilda to write me as soon as she's well. And that – well, that I miss her.'

Just then, like an apparition, Mrs Burns appeared. 'Go along in,' she ordered the scullery maid.

When Gracie had gone, Mrs Burns tightened her hands in front of her once more. 'You've heard what Gracie has to say. I hope that next time, you will make arrangements in advance and save everyone time and trouble. Good afternoon.' She turned and strode back to the house.

Michael gave a snort of disgust. 'What an objectionable woman! I really do feel we should take this further. Let me go into the house and see what I can do.'

Flora shook her head miserably. 'Hilda doesn't want to see me, Michael.'

'So you do believe Gracie?'

'Yes. Hilda is very stubborn and can have her moments.'

Flora felt her feet dragging as they walked back to the car. She had wanted so much to see her friend. Hilda knew very well that Flora wouldn't care about catching germs. She was amongst diseases of all kinds at the surgery and didn't fear a fever in the least.

But Gracie had passed Hilda's message on. And now there seemed nothing else for it but to return to London.

* * *

Michael drove slowly along the winding path from Adelphi Hall until they came to the slight incline before the wood, where he stopped the car. 'Well, it seems our journey was fruitless,' he said, sighing, turning off the engine.

'Hilda must be in very poor spirits.'

'At least we were told the doctor has seen her.'

'Yes, Mrs Burns must have arranged it.'

Michael nodded slowly. 'You would have thought the woman would have said.'

Flora looked down at her lap. 'It's my fault. I should have written first and asked Hilda to get permission.'

Michael smiled. 'Come along, cheer up. We'll come another time. Meanwhile, shall we take one last look at Adelphi before we leave?'

Flora walked with him to the fence, where the sunlight was playing down on the vines and ivy that grew in abundance around the trees. Before them was the low sweep of land that led to the hall, with views across the countryside. She could see the house was still bathed in sunlight and the clouds parted in the late afternoon sky to reveal a flawless horizon.

'Do you know the Calveys have owned this estate for generations?' Michael said as he leaned his elbows on the wooden fence. 'The fourth earl, Lord William, so Mama told me, brought great dignity to his home that befitted his high rank and distinguished service in the army. But in later years, after the death of his young wife, Lady Amelia, he must have lost interest.'

'Gracie told me that Lord William is never seen now.'

'I can't think why,' Michael replied with a frown. 'He's not elderly, perhaps in his late fifties, and was such a leader of men that it is quite a mystery that he should allow Lady Bertha to run the estate with his son.'

Flora gazed back at the house. It looked so elegant in its beautiful surroundings. She couldn't imagine Lord William allowing the estate to deteriorate. But perhaps she had seen the first sign of it in the gardens today. 'Did the earl never re-marry?'

'Mama said the earl was unlucky in love and found no one to replace Lady Amelia.'

Flora shuddered. She thought what a lonely life the earl must lead.

'You're cold. We must go.'

Flora looked into Michael's eyes, so large and expressive, as green as the grass that rolled lushly down to Adelphi Hall. Something inside her gave a little twist. She wanted this moment to last, even though today had been a bitter disappointment. The feeling grew, a longing that they might remain close like this, just as they were that day in Lillian Appleby's garden. All else seemed to slip from her mind, even Hilda. Flora wanted to reach up and touch his face. To see what his skin felt like, to run her fingers over his hollowed cheeks and into the dark-brown hair that flicked softly over the collar of his coat. Without his driving cap and goggles, she could see how thickly his hair grew, and how his parting fell naturally in a wave to one side.

Flora wanted them to stay where they were, on the curve of the road, overlooking the house in all its glory, savouring a moment that might not come again in London. But then he gave a reluctant smile. 'Stay here whilst I put the hood up. It will take just a few minutes.'

She watched as he limped to the car, leaning his cane against the door and unhooking the clips that released the soft hood. Just then, Flora heard a noise in the distance. She turned to see a horse and its rider. They sped at a gallop out of the wood.

Towards her.

Chapter Twenty-Four

The rider brought the horse to a halt; the animal's eyes were white-rimmed and its mouth frothed as it chewed at the bit. Flora couldn't take her eyes from the young man seated high in the saddle. She recognized him at once. His long black hair framed his arrogant dark eyes; though he wasn't dressed formally as in the photograph that hung in Mr Leighton's office, and instead wore a white open-necked shirt and riding breeches, this was clearly Lord Guy Calvey.

She felt Michael shaking her arm. 'Flora, are you hurt?'

She managed to shake her head, though she was trembling

'That damned animal could have run her down!' Michael shouted angrily at the rider. 'What the devil do you think you're doing?'

'Michael, please don't upset yourself.' Flora could feel the dark gaze going over her. Her body felt cold and shaky under his piercing stare. She knew that Michael was unaware of who this was.

'You could have brought the horse up yards away,' Michael continued, his hand protectively outstretched across her.

Lord Guy cast him a disdainful glance. 'You, sir, are standing on my property. I am Lord Guy Calvey and take exception to trespassers.'

Flora glanced at Michael. He showed no sign of surprise or fear, though his face was full of anger. 'We have no intention of trespassing,' he replied coldly. 'Surely, you can see we mean no harm?'

'Who are you? What is your business here?' Lord Guy demanded. He returned his attention to Flora. 'Do I know you?' he added with a suspicious frown. 'I seem to know your face . . .'

'You know neither of us,' Michael returned immediately. 'I am Lieutenant Michael Appleby from London and we have come to visit Hilda Jones, a housemaid here. Unfortunately, we made no prior arrangement and were turned away.'

Flora saw the expression on the rider's face darken. For a few seconds, he sat quite still in the saddle, skilfully controlling the restless horse beneath him. His gaze travelled over Flora's hair and face so intimately that she felt she wanted to turn away.

'A mistake on your part, then, sir,' the rider muttered.

'It was a mistake I shan't make again.' Michael seized Flora's arm and guided her to the car.

After he had helped her in, Flora looked from the window. The dark, penetrating gaze was still on her, watching her as she waited for Michael to climb up beside her. Hilda had once told her that she thought Lord Guy Calvey was the most handsome man she had ever seen. But Flora could only see cruelty and arrogance in his expression. She shivered again. She wanted to look away, but couldn't. What was it she saw that frightened her so much?

'Devil take the man,' Michael cursed as he took hold of the steering wheel. 'He rode like a madman at you. I couldn't move fast enough to distract him. Damn this leg!' He hit his thigh with his clenched fist.

Flora saw how upset Michael was. She knew this was her fault.

When at last Michael drove them away, she glanced back. The silhouette on the horizon was still there, of the horse and rider carved black against the setting sun.

A lone figure watched from the house. Steadying the well-worn military binoculars, his lean hands grasped the instrument tightly. The bones in his be-ringed fingers were taught against his skin as he adjusted the sight to its keenest view. The sun caught his vision momentarily and he swore softly under his breath. He had seen everything; his gaze had been fixed to the rider and horse as they had travelled fast towards the girl. He had watched with bated breath as the horse had stopped only feet away, a muscled, sweating animal that towered above the delicate female form. She had shown great courage, standing her ground; a slip of a thing, with hair the colour of corn. Hair that brought back so many memories and gave him the disturbing feeling that he knew her. But how could he? He must be mistaken. Yet, even from this distance he had recognized something – something that he had not seen in many years and had never expected to see again.

He swallowed, lowering the binoculars to rub his eyes against the deceiving hallucination. It wasn't possible. Could not be possible. Heaven alone knew the secrets it kept for him, and it was a place far beyond this mortal coil. She was gone from his life and he had accepted this fate and now, after so many years, he was seeing only ghosts.

Once again, eager either to torture himself or correct his mistaken vision, he pressed the hard metal against his eyes. The driver of the car had come to stand beside her. A tall man with excellent gait had it not been for the cane and limited movement. A veteran perhaps, a soldier once? Yes, he had that air about him.

The sun had shifted behind the trees and was dipping. The girl moved with grace but, he thought, also with fear. No wonder, after the charge the horse had made. She was escorted to the motor car, helped into her seat and hidden from his vision.

A few moments later, the vehicle drove off, taking her with it. He watched, anger and bewilderment filling his chest until at last the vehicle vanished into the wood.

Horse and rider remained where they were. He had no need to look at them. He knew them well enough and had no interest in them. Though deep in himself, in the muscles of his stomach that now tightened with anxiety and longing, he feared for her.

Whoever she was, whoever she wasn't – and she couldn't be—

'Ahh!' he cried aloud, closing his eyes and turning, casting aside the instrument with unreasonable fury. He listened to himself and knew that the pain long hidden inside him had been refreshed.

By a stranger – a vision!

He pulled his shoulders back and walked to the dresser, where only one item stood on the gleaming mahogany surface. A rosewood-framed photograph that he lifted, running his fingers tenderly over the glass and bringing it slowly against his heart.

Hilda was propped up in bed by her thin pillows. Although she had told Gracie she didn't want any supper, now, at midnight, she felt very hungry. She had waited all evening for Gracie to finish her duties and come to bed. 'You could have brought me up some bread and cheese or one of Mrs Harris' pies,' Hilda complained.

Gracie looked worn out as she flopped down on the iron bed beside Hilda's. 'Don't start, 'Ilda. Me back is aching something rotten. And me feet have got blisters. I almost ain't got the will to live.' Without hurrying, she took off her dirty apron, unbuttoned her dress and unlaced her boots.

'Oh, and a shiner like this and a nearly broken arm is nothing to bother about, I suppose?' Hilda said unsympathetically as she touched the bruised skin around her right eye. It was still very swollen and when she had looked in the mirror that morning, she got a real fright. Her eye was lost under puffy folds of skin. The scratches on her face from the gorse into which she had fallen were still raw and painful to touch. But it was her arm that hurt the most. Her wrist had swollen up inside the sling to the size of a small balloon. The doctor had pronounced the arm as not broken but badly sprained, and said that it needed to mend. Mrs Burns had been very annoyed. Even though Hilda had insisted she could still use her left hand to perform her duties, Mrs Burns had banished her from the kitchen. Hilda knew that Mrs Burns didn't want the village girls to see her and gossip. The housekeeper had forbidden Hilda to show herself downstairs. 'I'll send Gracie up with your meals,' she had barked when the doctor had left. 'You are to stay here until you're presentable again. This is very careless of you.'

Hilda had looked down at the bedclothes, unable to meet the housekeeper's stare. The only excuse she had thought of was falling down the stairs. It was the only one that accounted for all of her injuries.

'You brought it on yourself, 'Ilda.' Gracie stripped down to her stays and knickers. 'You wouldn't listen to me when I said you was playing a dangerous game. Rules is rules. The lowers don't mix with the uppers. You should have stayed away from him. You shouldn't 'ave given him all those looks in the first place.' She splashed water from the bowl over her cheeks, then snatched off her mob cap. She slid the pins from her braids and let her thin brown hair loose. Lifting a brush from the small bedside table, she dragged it roughly over her head. 'And now you've got me involved, too. I felt dreadful lyin' to your friend.'

'The doctor said I had a fever.'

'Yes, but not from a cold.'

'A bad arm is much worse.' Hilda pulled the bedclothes up to her chin with her free hand. She lay back on the pillow and gave a self-pitying groan. 'It hurts.'

'Well, it would, wouldn't it?'

'I didn't want Flora to know I fell down the stairs.'

'You didn't, did you?' Gracie hurried, shivering, to her bed, removed her stays and quickly jumped under the thin cover. 'Even Mrs Burns knows that was a lie.'

'What makes you say that?' Hilda asked.

'Mrs Burns ain't daft.'

Hilda suspected the same. But she also knew Mrs Burns didn't want the truth to leak out. Mrs Burns' job was to protect the family from scandal. That was why she had insisted Hilda stay in her room and instructed Gracie to perform her chores.

'I like staying in bed,' Hilda exaggerated, intent on getting her point across. 'I was worn out with all the extra chores.'

'Huh!' Gracie's puff of indignant breath made the candle flicker on the table. 'And I'm the donkey well-laden again!'

'You didn't mind helping me before.' Hilda glanced reproachfully at Gracie with her one good eye. 'And anyway, my arm will soon be better and I'll be able to work.'

'And what's gonna happen then? Are you going back to your old ways, that's what I'd like to know. 'E 'urt you bad this time, but what about the next?'

'It's a game we play, Gracie, that's all. It got a bit out of hand.'

'You ain't supposed to play games with the uppers. 'Specially him.'

'Stop speaking about Lord Guy like that!'

'Blimey, just listen to you. He 'alf killed you, 'Ilda!'

'Gracie, you don't understand. He didn't mean it.' Hilda was shocked at the change in Gracie's attitude. Once upon a time, she would have done anything for Hilda just to keep her friendship. Now, she was getting on Hilda's nerves, always warning her that something terrible was going to happen if she didn't stop her night-time excursions. But Hilda was sure that her lover had changed his ways. After the horse had knocked her down, he had been so kind and considerate. He'd lifted her in his arms and soothed her, kissing her eye that was bleeding from the graze the horse's hoof had made. He had even wrapped her arm in a sling made from his torn shirt. He had lifted her carefully onto the horse and ridden slowly back, cradling her in his arms. Then he'd woken Mr Leighton and told the butler to help her. Hilda had felt elated, even in the pain she was in. Mr Leighton's face had been a picture of shocked indignation. But he'd done what his master had instructed: bathed her scratches and placed her arm in a fresh splint. The next day, Mrs Burns was told she'd had an accident on the stairs and a doctor must be called.

Hilda smiled to herself as she sat in bed. Now Mrs Burns and Mr Leighton both knew that Lord Guy had chosen her. She was special to him. They could do nothing but accept the situation. Hilda recalled her master's gentle kisses and his regretful whispers that their game had gone too far. From horror at his actions, she had begun to believe that in his own way he really did love her. That the man she had known, who had terrorized her, was in fact now a changed person. The man she had at first fallen in love with and so adored. Hilda was happy to be here in bed, knowing that he loved her. She only wished he had sent her a message, or somehow found a way to reassure her. But then, he couldn't trust anyone other than Mr Leighton.

'You don't need to worry, Gracie.' Hilda tried another tactic as she knew it was wiser, for the moment, to have Gracie on her side. 'Lord Guy would be relieved to know you're keeping the secret.'

Gracie gave a despairing sigh. 'You'll never learn, will you?'

'What have I got to learn?'

'That 'e's just using you, 'Ilda.' Gracie turned over, staring at her. 'Like what all the toffs do, if they can.'

'Guy's different. You should have seen him after the horse kicked me. He told me he would make amends. He could have just left me if he didn't care.'

'And let you tell the world?'

'I wouldn't!' Hilda turned and let out a yelp of pain. Her arm and her eye both hurt at the same time. It was Gracie's fault for upsetting her. 'I love him and he loves me. One day we'll be together.'

Gracie stared at her with tired eyes. Then, saying nothing, she blew out the candle.

Hilda lay in the darkness. She felt angry with Gracie, with Mrs Burns and with Mr Leighton. They were all against her. She even felt angry with Flora, who had come to see her with a man. Who this man could be, she didn't know. Gracie had just said that he was tall and had a posh voice. Well, that wasn't very helpful! Hilda decided it must be someone that the doctor knew. Or even Lady Hailing. Someone wealthy enough to own a car. Flora must have told everyone she was coming to Adelphi Hall.

At this, Hilda grew even angrier. Flora could have spoiled everything. She would have made a great fuss if she'd seen Hilda's black eye and bound arm. Insisted that something else be done for her injuries. In her heart, Hilda needed her friend's sympathy. She had always had it before. Mrs Bell's too. And now she missed their attention.

Hilda managed to find a comfortable position under the bedclothes. She felt ugly and sorry for herself. Guy was the only person who had shown her any sympathy. No wonder she loved him as much as she did.

Chapter Twenty-Five

'I'm going to ask you to walk without your cane this evening,' the doctor said as he completed his examination of Michael's leg. 'After all, there is definite improvement. The muscle is firming up and your cane could be redundant.'

Without speaking, Michael slid his legs from the couch and dressed with Flora's help.

She caught his grateful gaze, just for a moment, but today she felt there was something wrong. Before Christmas last year, he had hardly been able to bend his leg without agony. But that had all changed over the months of exercises. He was always eager to try to test himself, to do all the doctor asked of him. But tonight, the energy seemed to have deserted him. Since their return from Surrey two weeks ago, Flora had noticed how quiet he'd become.

'We'll try with the cane first,' Dr Tapper said when Michael was fully dressed. 'Walk a direct line to the window, then turn to your left and pause at my desk. Retrace your steps to the door and back to the window again.'

Michael took his cane from beside the couch. He stood still for a few seconds, staring at the window, then moved slowly towards it. Flora noticed how pronounced his limp was and it became worse when he left the desk and walked to the door.

'What is it?' the doctor asked in concern.

'Nothing. Perhaps just a little discomfort in the thigh.'

Flora couldn't understand what this could be. Over the weeks and months, the muscles had slowly healed and the nerve endings had ceased to radiate pain. After half an hour's massage, Michael was always eager to try to walk. It was the doctor who cautioned him not to hurry.

Michael limped on. Flora saw how slumped his normally straight shoulders were. How his leg dragged as he shuffled towards the window.

'Now, without the cane,' Dr Tapper said. But when Flora looked at him she knew he was thinking the same too. Had Michael relapsed in his recovery?

Michael leaned the cane against the wall. He turned, and his face was white and tense with small beads of sweat across his brow. He took three steps forward then reached out and gripped a chair. Shaking his head, he looked up. 'I'm afraid I'm making a hash of this.'

'Keep trying,' the doctor encouraged.

Michael took a handkerchief from his pocket and wiped his forehead. He tried to walk forward but stumbled. Then his tall, lean frame started to sway. Flora wanted to rush forward and help him. But the doctor glanced at her and shook his head. She knew he wanted Michael to recover on his own.

Another faltering step came, then another. After passing the desk, Michael stood still, once more stroking his handkerchief across his damp forehead. Shaking his head slightly and blinking his eyes, he took a long step, but then hesitated, almost overbalancing.

The doctor reached him before he collapsed completely. Flora ran over too, and between them they helped Michael back to the couch.

He sat silently, his head in his hands. 'I think I'm beaten,' he said wearily.

Dr Tapper looked at Flora. 'A cup of tea, my dear. Can you make a pot in my kitchen and bring it down? I don't think Michael will attempt the stairs today.' She read the message in the doctor's eyes. He was as bewildered as she was. Only a few weeks ago, Michael had seemed close to walking without a cane and eager to try. But the beaten man who now sat before them looked a shadow of his former self.

'I can find nothing wrong with him. His thigh bears the scars of his injury, but on examination shows no sign of deterioration,' Dr Tapper told Flora after Michael had left. 'Yet, as we saw, he was unable to walk more than a few feet without discomfort.'

Flora stared at the cups of cold tea that no one had drunk. Everything had been going so well until they had gone to Surrey.

The doctor looked at her keenly. 'What is it, Flora?'

'As we left Adelphi Hall, we stopped to look back at the house. A horse and rider galloped towards us. Michael was by the car, putting up the hood, but I was by the fence. I thought for a moment the horse wasn't going to stop.'

'And Michael tried to reach you?'

'Yes.'

'Tell me again exactly what happened,' the doctor said, at once alert and sitting forward.

Flora repeated in more detail all that had happened. As she spoke, he listened carefully and when she had finished, he sat back with a long sigh.

'This, I believe, is important.'

'Do you think Michael hurt himself as he rushed from the car?' she asked.

'No. But something happened that is far more worrying.' He was deep in thought for a few moments. 'As you know, Flora, many of the men we see in surgery suffer the effects of conflict when they return home. Our first casualty was Tom Howe, but we have seen many such cases since. Michael is different. He showed no signs of emotional trauma. In fact, he seemed to be extremely well adjusted, other than his concerns about surgery. He was eager to return to his regiment. However . . .'

Flora held her breath. She knew that what the doctor was about to say would be very important.

'Michael is a soldier, trained for battle. All his instincts would have been to defend you – and he failed.'

'But he didn't fail.'

'No, he did not,' the doctor agreed. 'In fact, he acted gallantly, attempting to prevent the horse from injuring you. But I believe that in this moment, in his inability to move swiftly and take action, a memory or memories were triggered of something that happened in Gallipoli. Something he buried deep inside and, until his meeting with Lord Guy Calvey, had stayed hidden.'

Flora felt her heart sink. If only they hadn't gone to Surrey! If only she had taken notice of Hilda's letter. Even Mrs Bell had suggested a trip to the seaside instead.

The tears were suddenly close.

Her feeling of dismay deepened the following Tuesday when Michael didn't arrive for his appointment. Nor did he come to the surgery the following week. By the time the month was out, there had been no message from Michael. Each day Flora took the shawl and butterfly brooch from the drawer and gazed at them. What had happened to her mother? And Michael? Would she ever see him again?

On a hot Sunday morning at the beginning of July, Dr Tapper knocked on Flora's door. He was dressed in his best black frock coat and held his Gladstone bag.

'Last night, I was visited by a patient,' he told her. 'The mother of a young man who has just returned from the fighting. He is suffering from shell shock and walks with a stick. I'll call on him today. Would you like to join me?'

Flora was dressed to attend Mass at St Edmund's, wearing Hilda's blue suit and a soft blue beret. She hoped to counteract the worries that had beset her since she had last seen Michael by an hour on her knees and a special novena said at Our Lady's altar. Even Mrs Bell, whom she had spoken to about Michael the previous week, had reminded her that heaven's gates sometimes needed battering.

But five minutes later, Flora was sitting in the trap instead. She could smell the salty tang of the river as the breeze blew off the incoming tide and gave relief to the still warmth of the summer's day. The pony's head bobbed up and down, reminding her of the last time she had accompanied the doctor, on their call to Mr Riggs. Over a year had passed since poor little Polly had died and the *Lusitania* had sunk. Her thoughts went back to that time, when Will had found himself a victim to life in the trenches and Hilda had uprooted her whole life at Hailing House. So much had happened in the two years of war. She thought of Michael and their first meeting at the market. A young man who, since then, had never been far from her thoughts.

The symptoms of shell shock were very clear on Archie Benson's gaunt face. His eyes held a fearful expression. His shaven head and big ears looked too large for his thin body. Flora noticed his walking stick which was positioned by his chair. Mrs Benson had rolled up one trouser leg, exposing the bandage on his calf muscle, in readiness for the doctor's examination.

'They brought him home on a merchant ship,' Mrs Benson told them as she sat on the narrow couch. The living room of her small Poplar terrace was neat and tidy, Flora thought, but it was filled with the invisible tension that came with ill health. 'I'm lucky, I know, to have one son survive,' Mrs Benson continued. 'My eldest, Stan, was killed at Flanders. Archie was caught in an explosion. A piece of metal went into his leg, but the surgeon got it out and it seems to be healing. But it's the memories of what happened that torment Archie. The nightmares he still has, of the men from his unit who were killed.'

Archie gave a gurgling sound.

'What is it, son?'

'Th . . . they was st . . . still alive, my mates . . . they was . . .'

'He saw them die, Dr Tapper. That's what he's trying to say.' Tears shone in Mrs Benson's eyes. 'I tried to stop him volunteering. He wasn't even eighteen. He was just a boy, doctor, just a boy!'

Suddenly, Archie began to shake. Uncontrollable jerks took hold of his body. The violent spasms seemed to catch him unawares, and he gave a strange grunt as he tried to get up.

Mrs Benson took her son's hand. 'It's all right, Archie. Sit down.'

The doctor leaned forward. 'As your mother has told you, you are not in any way threatened, there will be no more fighting and I'll give you some medicine to help calm you. Do you think you can tell me more about what happened on the day you were wounded?' The doctor spoke softly, his hand on Archie's arm.

As they listened to Archie's stumbling account, his breath almost a hiss as he told them of his friends who died beside him, Flora cleaned and redressed his calf wound. Mrs Benson was right, she thought with relief. The injury had healed very well and Flora guessed that eventually he would be able to walk unaided again. It was, she knew, the horrifying images still in his mind and that he now described that would not be swift to heal.

When the time had come for them to depart, Mrs Benson saw them to the door. 'What's your verdict, doctor?' she whispered. 'Will he get better?'

'Physically, yes, Mrs Benson,' the doctor answered a little vaguely. 'With the help of your good self and a nourishing diet. As for the mental trauma . . .' He considered his words, before finishing. 'I shall refer Archie to a specialist consultant. Would you be able to attend the hospital?'

'Yes, but they won't put him in an asylum, will they?'

'No. But he will need treatment. It will be a very slow process.' The doctor tipped his hat.

When Flora climbed up beside him in the trap, she glanced back at the house. 'Can Archie be helped?'

'Perhaps,' he replied as he gathered the reins. 'At least Archie will speak of his experiences. Unlike Michael, who has locked them away.'

Flora thought back to all the many hours she had spent with Michael. They had discussed their lives and talked easily together. But Michael had never spoken of his active service, or in any detail of the day he was wounded. Why had she never thought of this before?

The doctor raised a bushy grey brow. 'We're not far from Shire Street.'

Flora smiled. She wanted to see Michael more than she dared say.

Lillian Appleby gave them a warm welcome and led them through the house to the conservatory. As they passed the portrait of Julian Appleby dressed in his Eastern robes of crimson and orange, Flora remembered what Lillian had told her that day. Michael had inherited his father's green eyes and courage. Flora felt a pang of alarm. Perhaps Michael felt he had lost his courage and the meeting with Lord Guy Calvey had served to confirm this.

'I'm so pleased to meet you, Dr Tapper,' Lillian said as they sat on the comfortable wicker chairs in the sunny, glass-windowed room. 'Michael's told me so much about you.'

Flora looked into her face and saw beyond the warm smile. Lillian's dark eyes, framed by her rich brown hair drawn elegantly up behind her head, held an anxious expression. She was dressed as before in a long, sweeping dress, and sat with her hands folded in her lap. She returned Flora's gaze with a quick smile. 'Flora, it's been some while, hasn't it? I was hoping to see you again soon after our last meeting. But I know how busy you are.'

'We called as we have a patient in this area,' the doctor said quickly. 'Michael hasn't arrived for his weekly treatments. We hope all is well?'

'I am afraid to say that my son is not his usual self, Dr Tapper,' Lillian said uneasily. 'I'm most relieved you called.'

'Can I be of help?'

'Oh, I wish I could say.' Lillian raised her hand and dropped it heavily into her lap. 'I'm afraid I can't get a word out of him. He refuses to tell me what's wrong. Of course, Michael is always a dear, polite boy and we share a close relationship, as you know, Flora. But lately, I'm afraid, he prefers his own company and either takes out the car or reads in his room. I would say he has become . . . melancholy.' She looked at Flora with her big brown eyes open wide. 'He was so full of hope, so determined to return to good health.'

'He was most certainly recovering,' Dr Tapper agreed. 'Until a few weeks ago.'

'Michael told me he'd been disappointed at his last test. That he had been unable to walk without his cane.'

'Yes, an unexpected turn of events.'

'But why is this?' Lillian's pale face was full of concern.

'That's something we must discuss with your son. I believe that his physical injury has healed and he should be dispensing with the cane.'

Just then Flora heard a noise. They all looked round to see a tall figure appear at the door. Lillian smiled eagerly. 'Michael, where have you been? We have visitors, as you can see.'

'I walked down to the stream, Mama, for some air.' He smiled a tight, guarded smile as the dogs bounded in beside him. Flora reached out to stroke Ivy and Jack as they panted softly at her feet. Their soft black fur and warm bodies made her remember fondly the day she had first come here with Michael. Then he had been happy and smiling, eager for her to meet his mother. Now, the light had gone from his once clear green eyes, despite his best effort to smile. 'I'm very pleased to see you both,' he said, limping over, his cane tapping on the polished boards of the floor. He took a chair rather clumsily. 'I've been meaning to call at the surgery. But after the disappointing results of walking without my cane, I thought better of it. I fear I've failed you both.'

'Not at all,' the doctor was quick to assure him. 'But I should have liked you to continue with your treatment.'

'I thought perhaps a rest might help.'

Flora looked into his steady gaze. He seemed to be Michael, the man she had become so fond of. But he had changed and was keeping his distance from them as politely as he could.

'Yes,' the doctor agreed. 'When you feel rested, perhaps we can start again.'

'Yes, of course.'

'You must stop for some tea now that Michael is here.' Lillian turned to the doctor. 'Would you care to enjoy it in the garden, Dr Tapper? We can sit on the lawn and enjoy some sunshine. Are you interested in gardening at all?'

'My wife came from a country family in the north,' the doctor said, rising to his feet. 'I'm afraid we never had much more than a yard in London.' He smiled. 'I should enjoy your offer of tea very much.'

Flora watched him accompany Lillian out of the room.

'You must think me very rude,' Michael said quietly when they found themselves alone. 'I should have driven over to see you.'

'Michael, what's wrong?' She wanted to hold his hand, to comfort him. But she knew he wouldn't want that.

'I feel I've misled you, Flora. And God knows, that was not my intention.'

'But how have you misled me?'

'I believed I could recover and be as I was before.'

'But you will be.'

He laughed without humour. 'I think not.'

'I should never have let you drive me to Adelphi.'

At once, Michael rose to his feet. 'On the contrary. It was there that I realized my limitations. How wrong I was to ask a commitment of you.'

Flora felt sick with heartache. Was Michael telling her he didn't want to see her again?

'Let's join the others.' His polite smile returned as he extended his arm. Flora could do nothing but grasp it. They walked in silence to the garden and the croquet lawn and beyond Flora could see the wooden hut where they had once almost kissed.

Chapter Twenty-Six

Flora opened her eyes the next morning and thought of Michael. Their friendship was over. Whatever had happened at Adelphi Hall had changed his feelings towards her.

She got ready for work, but without enthusiasm. It was a day like any other, but her heart felt heavy, as though something inside her was missing. She knew the doctor had been upset at Michael's decision to stop the treatment. But on their way home in the trap, he said they had to abide by Michael's decision.

The day passed as usual with patients coming and going. The talk was of the war and how hard it was becoming to find cheap food now that British ships were being torpedoed by Germany's U-boats. Britain was cut off from its suppliers and to make things worse, the doctor told Flora that morning that the Irish troubles were worsening. Dublin was staging a full-scale rebellion against British rule. Many of the patients had relatives in Ireland. Flora knew it was only natural for the Irish community in the East End to feel sympathetic to their families. But it was hard to ignore the jibes against the British that were often voiced.

That night, Flora dreamed of the conflict and Will. Of the mud and dead troops in the trenches. Every now and then she called out his name. But her voice was so faint.

She woke up in the middle of the dream with a start. Her nightdress was wet with perspiration. After she had washed and dressed and eaten a small breakfast, she went up the airey's steps into the bright summer morning. The air was soft and still, but she couldn't shake off the bad feeling of her dream.

''Ere, nurse, 'ave you 'eard?' their first patient said. The woman carried a dirty, runny-nosed child in her arms. 'There's been thousands of our lads killed at the Somme. And every one of 'em a volunteer. Lots of 'em come from the London Regiment – gun fodder for the Hun. I reckon you'd best be prepared for all the poor injured sods coming back.'

Flora felt quite sick. The dream seemed very real. Will had been sprawled in mud. The blood had seeped through his jacket and was pouring into the black, slimy puddles. She had called out, trying to help him. But there had been no one to help. The noise of the bombs in her ears had been deafening. Will was not moving. Was he dead?

'You all right, love? You've gone as white as a sheet.'

'Yes, you can go through to the doctor now.' Flora led the way. But when the door had closed behind the woman, she sat down in her small room. The sweat was running down her spine. The dream of Will had been so very real.

It took all her willpower to return to the waiting room and try to sort out the patients.

'This is for you,' Mrs Bell said when Flora arrived at Hailing House on the first Sunday of August. 'I know it was your birthday last week, but I did send a card.' She gave Flora a small parcel, tied with string.

Flora undid the paper and took out a delicate chiffon scarf.

'Blue is your colour, my dear.'

Flora threaded her fingers over the soft material. 'It's beautiful, thank you,' Flora said gratefully.

'Did you celebrate on Tuesday?'

'No, we were too busy at the surgery.' Her seventeenth birthday had come and gone very quickly. She had received cards from Mrs Bell, the doctor and Mother Superior and the nuns of St Boniface. Each year, they remembered her birthday and usually Will did too. But this year there had been no cards from her friends, or even letters. There hadn't even been time during the day for Flora to think about being seventeen. There had been plenty of patients to see that day. There had been a sudden rise in temperature and people were suffering from the heat. The conditions in the dock factories had led to many casualties. Fainting and exhaustion was common as were prickly heat rashes and impetigo. Some factories were no more than huge tin sheds; in winter they were freezing and in summer, stifling.

'You deserve the best.' Mrs Bell kissed her cheek. 'Now, I've got a broth simmering, so when you've put on Aggie's apron, I'd like you to drop in a few more potatoes.' Mrs Bell returned to the hot stove and was soon dabbing her forehead with her handkerchief as she laboured over the heat.

Flora put aside her scarf and tied Aggie's apron around her waist. She dropped the chopped potatoes into the steaming saucepan and stirred vigorously. Now, in this time of crisis, when so many bereaved families needed feeding, she had offered to help Mrs Bell. So many had suffered after the Somme. There were many more killed than the authorities had at first recorded. At the soup kitchens, the women told their sad stories to Mrs Bell, who repeated them to Flora. Husbands, brothers, relatives, thousands upon thousands, so it was said, were lost in the first five minutes of battle. Flora had heard for herself the terrible tales from the wounded men. They were slowly beginning to arrive home; they hobbled, stumbled and were even carried to the surgery by relatives or friends. Dr Tapper did all he could, but the pitiful sights of wounded servicemen were endless.

Flora thought of Michael and sighed. If only she could talk to him . . .

'Lady Hailing will have to send us more help,' Mrs Bell complained, breaking into Flora's thoughts. 'Me and Aggie are working all hours. With daily soup kitchens there's no time to look after the house.'

'I'd help you more, but the doctor needs me.'

'Course he does, love. And it's domestic staff we need, not nurses. But, as you know, the young girls won't go for service. They prefer a factory job with good pay. This war's changed everything. Including the aristocracy. Many of the big houses are being used as hospitals now. Can't see how life for the uppers will ever be the same again.'

'Do you think Hilda will come home if Adelphi Hall is turned into a hospital?' Flora wondered aloud.

Mrs Bell shrugged as she shredded the beef through the mincer. 'Who knows! Pass me that cloth, love, I'm making a mess.'

Flora gave Mrs Bell the cloth. These days, Mrs Bell didn't mention Hilda or seem concerned about her. As Hilda never wrote, Flora guessed it was to be expected.

'I'm going to the market next Saturday with Reg,' Mrs Bell said. 'Would you like us to call for you?'

'No, I don't think so. Not while we're so busy.'

'Don't work too hard, love.'

'Since the doctor lost Wilfred he works very hard.'

'And no doubt you're always at his side.'

'I don't mind.'

Mrs Bell began to fry the minced meat. She thrust it around in the pan with onion and carrots. 'This will make a nice broth. I like a change from soup occasionally. Now, how is that soldier of yours?'

Flora felt her face flush. 'He doesn't come for treatment now.'

'Is he better, then?'

'No.'

'Well, the doctor can't cure everyone. Now, add the stock and vegetables, dear. Later I'll pop in a dumpling or three.'

As they worked, Mrs Bell forgot about Michael and began to repeat again what the 'lost souls', as she called them, had told her in the soup kitchen. 'The women are wives and mothers, nurses and breadwinners all rolled into one. Their heart-rending stories are endless! There's one poor wretch who has to look after her father, husband and brother. Now, if that's not a cross to carry, I don't know what is.'

Flora listened sympathetically. She knew that, in a strange way, the war had put an end to Mrs Bell's loneliness. The lost souls of the soup kitchen had become her family.

'Just you watch out for them Zeppelins,' Mrs Bell warned her as she left that evening. 'You never know when one's flying over.'

Flora looked up into the dusky August sky, which glowed in the east with a fiery scarlet sunset. Michael had once told her that although the Zeppelins were frightening, they were often blown off course by high winds. They were also difficult to control and their crews inexperienced. Many airships had crashed, he assured her, and others had been lost in uncharted territory. They had talked about so many things . . . shared so many confidences.

Flora tried to stop her thoughts from wandering. Her memories of Michael were happy but they always left her feeling blue.

It was after a particularly busy Thursday surgery that Flora found the doctor had fallen asleep at his desk. His head was bent low and the pen had dropped from his hand.

'Dr Tapper?'

He roused and blinked. 'Oh, it's you, Flora.'

'Shall I close the doors?'

'No, I have to call on Mrs Benson with Archie's medicine,' he said, standing up slowly and pushing his hand through his dishevelled grey hair.

'I'll take it,' Flora offered, as he looked very tired.

'Please make sure Mrs Benson is following the directions I left with her. This sedative is strong and must be used with care.'

Flora assured him she would and half an hour later she set out for Poplar. The evening had turned cooler and as she walked she heard a distant rumble of thunder. Dr Tapper had warned her that Archie was still waiting to be seen by the hospital doctors and until then he must take the potassium salt sedatives he had prescribed.

'Oh, thank goodness you've come,' Mrs Benson said when Flora arrived. 'My Archie is in a terrible state. That's why I couldn't come to the surgery. I daren't leave him.'

'What happened?' Flora couldn't see Archie sitting in his usual chair.

'There was a loud noise in the street. It was from one of them new-fangled motor cars. Archie went wild, shouting "bombs" and ran upstairs, shutting himself in his room.' She blinked and looked at Flora as if seeing her for the first time. 'But where's Dr Tapper?'

'He couldn't come tonight.'

'What are we going to do, then? Archie won't listen to me and I doubt he will take any notice of you. He seems to have gone crazy.'

'Has he had his medicine?'

'No, I ran out of it.' Mrs Benson's pale, thin face flushed and she looked away. 'I thought a bit extra at night would make him sleep.'

'The doctor writes the instructions on the packet. You must keep to the dose.'

'Yes, but I needed to sleep too.'

Flora took the small packet of salts from her bag. 'Go and mix the right amount with water and bring it up to Archie's room.'

Mrs Benson took the packet and rushed away to the kitchen.

Flora climbed the narrow staircase. The only light was from an oil lamp on a small table. She passed an empty bedroom and went to the next. Knocking softly on the closed door, she waited. When there was no reply she took the oil lamp and turned the handle. The room was in turmoil. Clothes and books were strewn everywhere. Behind the bed, a shaven head poked up. 'What do you want?' Archie whimpered. 'Have you found the bomb?'

'There isn't one, Archie.' Flora stepped inside.

'There is. They've hidden it.'

'Shall I look?' Flora knew she had to win his trust. 'I can see better than you by the light of the lamp.'

Flora heard Archie scramble under the bed. She lowered the lamp to the bedside table, then folded the clothes back into their drawers. After arranging the books back on the shelves, she looked under the bed.

'There's no bombs, Archie. It's safe to come out.'

'I don't want to die.'

'You won't die. Take my hand and I'll help you.'

Slowly, Archie crawled out. He was holding Flora's hand so tightly that she could feel his thin bones creak between her fingers.

Mrs Benson came into the room with Archie's medicine and he drank it noisily. 'My poor boy,' she sighed heavily, wiping her hand over her tired face. 'If only I was a bit younger and your father still alive.'

'When did you become a widow, Mrs Benson?' Flora asked in concern.

'When Archie was three. I've brought him up on me own and it's been hard. My husband was much older than me, near to twenty years. We never thought we could have children. Then, when I was forty, I discovered I was having a baby. It was a difficult birth and nearly killed us both. Archie only knew his dad for a short while and now I'm gone sixty, still trying to make ends meet and look after my son at the same time. I'm at the end of me tether.'

'You must try to rest,' Flora told her gently. 'Go downstairs and I'll see to Archie.'

After Mrs Benson had gone, Flora washed Archie with cold water from the china bowl standing on the marble-topped wash stand. She was relieved to discover that his wound had almost healed and did not need attention. Finally, she helped him to put on clean pyjamas.

'Are you feeling better now?' she asked as he sat on the bed.

'I ain't got the shakes.'

'And you look very nice after your wash.'

For the first time, Archie smiled. It was only a shaky grin, as the sedative began to take effect.

'Tomorrow, you must try to wash and dress yourself. I'll hang your clothes over the chair.' Flora took a white shirt and pair of trousers from the wardrobe. 'Do you think you can do that, Archie?'

Archie nodded, though his gaze seemed vacant.

'Now, here's your dressing gown. We'll go down to the kitchen for something to eat.' Flora fastened the dressing-gown cord around his thin waist.

As she did so, Flora was thinking, and not for the first time, that a return to normal life for Archie and his mother would be difficult. Caring for an invalid in Archie's condition would be exhausting. She hoped that with Archie taking the proper doses of his medicine, he would soon be able to help himself.

* * *

'Eat up,' Flora encouraged, when Archie was seated at the kitchen table. 'Your mother made you this broth.'

Flora was pleased to see that Archie gulped it down quickly and showed no loss of appetite. He had suffered under the heavy doses that Mrs Benson had mistakenly given him in her effort to get him to sleep. Then when the medicine had stopped abruptly, he had suffered a withdrawal. Now he seemed to be enjoying the nourishing liquid and the thick slices of bread that his mother had prepared. He also responded to Flora's questions with fairly normal answers. Flora was also very pleased to hear the soft snores of Mrs Benson from the front room.

'Is me mum all right?' Archie asked as he ate.

'Yes, but she is very tired and needs her rest.'

'She ain't gonna die?'

'No. But if you can do a little more to help yourself, she won't get so tired.'

'What about me shakes?'

'They will get better if you take your medicine regularly.' The doctor had assured Flora that the potassium bromide, if taken correctly, would keep Archie's hysteria at bay.

'Will the bombs come back?' Archie asked between mouthfuls.

'No. This is England, Archie, not France.'

'I forgot. Me ma told me that too.'

'Have you finished your supper?'

He nodded, giving her another shaky grin. He sat like a little boy at the table, his shoulder bones poking out from under his dressing gown and his dark eyes sunken in his thin face. Every now and then he would twitch or shake, making a soft noise as he did so.

'We'll go and sit down in the parlour. But be quiet so we don't wake your mother.' Flora didn't help him to walk this time. He pushed his chair back and Flora followed him into the parlour.

'You won't need that now.' Flora took away the stick by the hearth and stored it in the cupboard under the stairs.

As she did so, her thoughts went to Michael. Would he ever be able to walk without his cane? It was a question even the doctor couldn't answer.

Mrs Benson awoke at eleven o'clock. 'Why, bless me, you're up and about, Archie,' she said dreamily as she looked across at her son, who was sitting in his chair.

'I'm gonna dress meself tomorrow.'

'Archie's a little better,' Flora confirmed as she picked up her basket. She had swept the parlour floor and cleaned the surfaces of the kitchen with Sunlight soap, leaving the air smelling sweetly. 'His leg wound has healed. Archie won't need his stick now.'

Mrs Benson wiped her eyes with her handkerchief. 'You've been very kind.'

Flora nodded to the unlit candle in its holder. 'To help your son sleep soundly, mould a little warm candle wax into his ears before he goes to bed.'

'Thank you. I'll try to remember.'

The streets were very dark and gloomy as Flora left. The taverns had all turned out and Westferry Road was hidden in shadows. A solitary cart trundled past her, its Tilley lamps swinging from the tailgate. She was thinking about the Bensons when suddenly the sky lit up. Long beams of light pierced the darkness, as she had once seen before when the Zeppelins flew over the East End. A thunder in the distance caused Flora to stop still.

People opened their front doors and ran into the street. 'It must be the Zeppelins,' a man yelled. 'Our guns are trying to shoot them down.'

Flora watched the panic begin. People filled the street and looked up. She, too, searched the sky for the flying airships that she had never seen, but had heard some of the patients describe. She felt both frightened and excited at the same time. Another horse-drawn cart pulled up next to the first one. A man jumped off a bicycle and joined the crowd of onlookers.

The distant rumble of guns became sharper. Still nothing happened. No one seemed to know what to do or where to go.

Flora wondered if she should run. But where to? It might be dangerous. The Zeppelins carried bombs and dropped them indiscriminately. She could see nothing above, only the lights in the sky. They were beginning to make her feel dizzy.

Then suddenly it appeared. A cigar-shaped balloon so immense that its underbelly filled her whole vision. The vast, floating cylinder had tapered ends and fins attached to its sides. The Zeppelin seemed to glow in the search-lights. Then, without warning, a terrible bang, then another, caused Flora to run. She didn't know where she was going. She was running because there seemed nothing else to do. Her heart beat faster and faster. The strength washed out from her legs.

When she fell, she thought of all the soldiers in the mud-filled trenches. She understood the terror they must have felt as they tried to escape the poison gases. As she lay helplessly in the road, the Zeppelin came closer and trapped her in its great shadow.

Michael stood on the surgery steps, leaning heavily on his cane. He had tried downstairs at the airey first, but no lights were on. He had to warn Flora and the doctor: the Zeppelins had reached England. A policeman had told him that coastal alerts had warned the city police that the Zeppelins were flying above low cloud and headed for the East End.

Michael knocked on the surgery door again. A few minutes later, it opened.

'Michael, is that you?' Dr Tapper peered out into the darkness. He was still dressed, but he looked as though he had been sleeping.

'I'm sorry to disturb you at this late hour.'

'Is something wrong?'

'I couldn't get a reply from the airey.'

Dr Tapper pushed back his thick grey hair and stepped out. 'Flora went to visit a patient for me.'

'Should she be back by now?'

The doctor nodded slowly. He was looking tired and bewildered. 'Yes . . . yes, she should. Something must have happened to delay her.'

'I have it on good authority that the Zeppelins are flying over the East End. I was on my way back from the city and several roads were shut off. A policeman explained that the anti-aircraft were about to operate in—'

Just then, they heard gunfire. Then a loud bang, and another that shook the street. Michael took the doctor's arm, 'I advise you to take cover, sir.'

'But Flora—'

'Give me the patient's address and I'll find her.'

After memorizing it, Michael urged the doctor back inside. 'Extinguish your lamps,' he advised hurriedly. 'The airships will aim for the docks to release their bombs.'

The doctor nodded in silence. Michael knew he was worried, not for himself but for Flora.

Limping down the steps to the street, Michael cursed the injury that had caused him to become so ineffective. He was a soldier, a man of action. And look at him now. He could not challenge a child to a race. He couldn't bring himself to let go of this wretched implement that, if he had his way, he would break in half.

As he drove away, there was gunfire. The sound it made returned him to the battlefields of Gallipoli in spring of last year. The brave but small force of Anzac and

French troops, accompanied by the British, were caught under the heavy fire of the Ottoman forts. The Allied battleships and cruisers had disappeared from the blue horizon of the Sea of Marmara. The beach was scattered with bodies and men had fallen into the dunes cleverly laced with barbed wire. Michael saw the white sandy hill before him and signalled to the remainder of his men to follow. He blinked hard, trying to erase the memory. Still, it wouldn't leave him. He was no longer driving the car, but scrambling upward, the sound of enemy fire loud in his ears. He found a foothold in the cliff face and hauled himself up, the sand running through his fingers. His equipment and backpack felt a ton weight in the burning heat. He could hear the cries of dying men as they called out for help. He turned to the young infantry soldier at his side and waved him on. Then there was an explosion . . . a deafening crescendo, splitting his eardrums that hurled him to panic, towards the barren green flatness of the hilltop.

'What the bloody 'ell do you think yer up to?' a rough voice demanded.

Michael wiped the sweat from his eyes. Somehow he had brought the car to a halt. He was no longer in Gallipoli climbing the sandy hill, but back in the present. Two men were staring angrily in the car window. 'Look what yer done,' one of them shouted from under the brim of his cap. 'Yer drove right at us, yer silly bugger!'

Michael saw two carts and their shying horses, somehow entangled with the front of his car. Then there was an almighty bang. It seemed to rattle his bones and teeth. The men bolted at once. People who had been standing in the road began to run. The eerie glow of the street's gas lamps made them look like ghosts. Above, the Zeppelin hovered in the sky. Fear filled every pore in his body as he saw something on the ground. It was Flora.

He pulled himself out of the car, sliding from the seat onto the road. Pressing himself through a space between the two carts, he began to run towards her. His lungs filled with air and a rush of oxygen caused him to stumble. He bounced off a wall like a drunken man and sprawled headlong, saving himself as he caught hold of a window ledge. Then he found himself running again and the salt tar of the docks washed bitterly into his mouth.

At last, he reached her and threw himself over her with all the force he could muster.

Chapter Twenty-Seven

The noise was deafening.

'We're going to make a dash for it, Flora,' Michael said.

'I can't move.'

'Once you stand, you'll be able to run.'

'But the airship might follow us.'

'My car is not far away. We can drive away from it.'

Flora felt sick and weak. She had never seen anything so large and threatening in the sky. She had been stuck to the cobbles of the road, unable to move.

'Don't look up. Hold on to me.'

Flora feared she couldn't even take a breath, let alone run. But with Michael's help she managed to climb to her feet. They began to run towards the carts blocking the road. The vegetables squelched and burst beneath her feet, she could hear the horses whinnying. How had all this happened in just a few minutes? Michael wouldn't let her stop. He dragged her on, towards the carts and through the space between them.

'There's my car,' Michael urged. His voice was calm as he pulled her through.

When they reached the car he opened the door and helped her over the running board. 'We'll soon be away from here.'

Flora looked up at the sky and sat very still, fearing to move. From out of the window she could see the great swaying body above and the searchlights crossing it. A very loud noise shattered the silence. Flora closed her eyes and immediately thought of the Bensons.

'It's all right, Flora. The airship has passed over us.'

'Where are we?'

'Almost home.'

Flora realized she had been sitting with her hands over her ears and her eyes squeezed tight. She hadn't wanted to hear or see anything after that enormous noise. The clatter of the car engine was for once welcome.

'But how did you find me?'

'I called at the surgery to alert you and the doctor to the incoming Zeppelin. Dr Tapper gave me Mrs Benson's address and on the way there I found you. Look, the doctor is waiting on the surgery steps.'

Michael brought the car to a shuddering halt. Flora jumped out of the car and ran to the doctor.

'There, there, my dear,' he said, patting her back gently. 'You're quite safe now. Thank heaven that Michael found you.'

Flora began to explain all that had happened with Archie and Mrs Benson and how she had come to find herself walking home so late. 'The airship suddenly appeared,' she recalled, shuddering. 'I began to run, just like everyone else.' Flora held back the tears stinging in her eyes. She would never forget how terrifying the first sight of the Zeppelin had been. 'Then there was a terrible bang. I fell . . .' She looked up at Michael. Had she really seen him running?

'It appears you are walking unaided, young man,' the doctor observed.

'I saw Flora on the ground and forgot my leg,' Michael said as though he couldn't believe it himself.

Flora stared at the tall, upright young man who had risked his life for her. He looked so very different without his cane.

Flora saw it all again. She was at the Bensons' and Archie was in his bedroom, hiding behind his bed. Mrs Benson was exhausted by the long hours of caring for her son. Then she was transported to Westferry Road and was gazing breathlessly up at the sky. The Zeppelin hovered above and people had come out of their houses to look at it. The noise of the explosion had sent them all running. And she had run too, only to fall and lie frozen with fear under the airship.

'Flora?'

She opened her eyes, realizing she had been dreaming. She was laying on the doctor's sofa with a blanket over her. The drapes were open and the dim light of dawn was flowing in through the window. Michael stood beside her. He had washed the dirt from his face and combed his hair back into place. He was smiling, although his green eyes were full of concern.

'Did I fall asleep?'

'Yes. How are you feeling?'

She sat up and lowered her feet to the floor. 'I was dreaming about what happened.' She blinked. 'Is it true you can walk without your cane?'

He sat down beside her. 'Yes, it's true.'

'Are you sure?'

He laughed. 'Perfectly. Perhaps the remainder of a limp, but the doctor assures me that the recovery will now continue.'

'I'm very happy for you, Michael.' Flora remembered how he had held her as they lay on the road. How he had told her they would run for the car. She wanted to throw her arms around him but instead she sat quietly, listening.

He took her hand. 'And there's more good news. Whilst you slept I drove Dr Tapper to the Bensons. He was concerned that Archie had been upset by the noise of the Zeppelin bombs. When we arrived and knocked, there was no reply. Thinking something must be wrong, Dr Tapper pulled the key from the letterbox. We let ourselves in and were met with darkness. Then we heard someone snoring. Mrs Benson was asleep in her chair. It took several minutes before we could rouse her. The candle-wax earplugs had given her a grand night's sleep.'

'And Archie?'

'Together with his medicine and the earplugs, Archie didn't wake. Mrs Benson was surprised when we told her that a Zeppelin had flown over only half a mile away.'

'Was there much damage?'

'Some houses have come down in Westferry Road and Deptford Dry Dock. The station at Norway Street was bombed and also Greenwich.'

'The airship was a frightening sight,' Flora recalled, remembering the moment when it had appeared. 'I thought of the soldiers trying to run from the clouds of poison gas. I realized how impossible it would be to escape.' She looked into his eyes. 'Until I saw you . . .'

Michael squeezed her hand. 'And I realized how much you meant to me.'

Flora took a breath. Did he mean it?

'Ah, you're awake, Flora. Time for breakfast,' the doctor said as he brought in a tray and set it before them. Flora looked at the buttered crumpets, jelly jam and pot of hot tea. She still couldn't believe everything that had happened.

'I am as surprised as you are,' Michael said when the doctor enquired again what had happened to his leg. 'I . . . I was driving, just driving,' he recalled, his brows knitting together in deep concentration. 'The street was in front of me, the cobbles, the walls of the houses, the roofs and the windows. I was thinking of Flora and how I could most swiftly find her. Then I heard our guns fire. Suddenly, I was detached from myself and somehow in Gallipoli. The beaches were littered with the dead and the heat was unbearable. Already the flies from the many corpses flew around us. The stench of death was in the air, in our very breath. I urged my men forward, though only one young soldier was beside me. A boy, running terrified at what he had seen and the prospect that he too would almost certainly fall under gunfire. We made for the hill, attempted to climb its sandy face. We reached the top, though God knows how – and then, as I climbed over, there was an explosion.' He raised his eyes slowly and they were full of pain. 'When I came to, I was alone. I lay stunned, hearing a faint cry for help. I pulled myself to the edge and looked down. He was there, calling out for my help.' Michael's voice faltered and he gave a deep, shuddering sigh. 'His leg had been blown away. Every movement he made must have been agony.'

They sat in silence and Flora knew that Michael was reliving that moment. A moment he had kept hidden, perhaps even from himself. He shuddered again as a long sigh escaped his lips. 'I grasped his wrist and pulled, dragging him up and almost to the ledge. Then the sniper's bullet found my own leg.' Once again, there was silence until he continued. 'I felt him slipping. I couldn't hold him. Eventually, I let go.' He swallowed, the muscles of his face tightening.

'It was not your fault,' the doctor assured him. 'You did all you could for the boy.'

'It wasn't enough.'

'No man can do more than his best.'

Once again, Michael stared down at his leg. Then looking at Flora, he said quietly, 'I knew I mustn't fail this time. It was as though I had been given a second chance.'

Flora felt a warmth fill her. The emotion spread into her heart and it was then that she knew she truly loved him.

The doctor gave a little cough and nodded. Then he continued to pour the tea.

Chapter Twenty-Eight

Hilda was sitting on the window seat, gazing out at the view. She was bored beyond words and yearned to go out and enjoy the golden September day. The leaves were beginning to turn brown and the smell of woodsmoke was in the air. The strong aroma reminded her of the island and its thousands of chimneys that burned through the whole year. Her life there seemed very far away now.

Hilda leaned forward to get a better look at the gravel drive leading from the house and up to the archway of trees. The front doors of Adelphi Hall were directly below the window, three floors down. She made sure she didn't knock her arm. Though it was now free of the sling, the doctor had warned her to be careful. The small fracture of her wrist had not been discovered at first, not until it was too late and the bones had begun to heal in the wrong way. Her wrist had stayed swollen for weeks. Putting any pressure on it still caused her great distress and Mrs Burns, fearing that she would only stir up more trouble, had virtually locked her away. If it wasn't for the fact that she had dared to creep out when everyone was asleep, she would have gone mad. She knew Mrs Burns would have been furious if she'd discovered her wandering in the grounds. But luckily, they had met no one, though Gracie, who had accompanied her under protest, had refused to go anywhere near the stables.

'I'll only come if you behave yerself,' Gracie had warned her, making Hilda promise to venture no further than the kitchen garden. 'Cavorting about in the night is how you ended up like you are. Anyway, you won't be bumping into '*im,*' she added with a toss of her mousy head. ''E's orf to Venice with that Lady Gabriella and hasn't spared a thought for you, nor will he. Next thing we know, it'll be marriage bells, mark my words.'

Hilda had been furious. Lord Guy would never marry the stick-thin, po-faced Lady Gabriella Beresford, who had made cow's eyes at him at the Christmas party. The intimate expression in Lord Guy's gaze had been for Hilda alone. She shivered inside when she thought of how he had torn away her clothes and explored her body in the soft straw of the barn. He had spoken with scorn of the women who fawned over him, assuring Hilda that they were of no interest. The memory of her willing surrender and acts of passion made even Hilda blush. She couldn't imagine the vain, self-obsessed, doll-faced Lady Gabriella unlacing her corsets and throwing both caution and her knickers to the wind. It was Gracie who was trying to poison her thoughts . . .

Hilda sighed softly as she gazed out on the beautiful countryside. These were the fields and woods in which she and her master had played their games. It was entirely her fault that she had disappointed him. Inexperience and fear had held her back. She hadn't realized that his boisterous nature meant he might sometimes go a little too far. But next time she would indulge him in all his wishes without protest. He would love her for this. Four months of boredom with Lady Gabriella would send him eagerly back to her arms.

With her finger, Hilda drew a heart in the dirt on the window she had yet to clean. Now, at least, Mrs Burns was allowing her to perform small duties, well away from the rest of the household. She had been banished to the top floor, with strict instructions to clean there between midday and two o'clock while Lord William was resting. Mrs Burns had sent Gracie, too, who was now the eyes and ears of the housekeeper. Gracie couldn't be trusted to be Hilda's confidante any longer. When Lord Guy returned, their meetings would have to be secret. Hilda felt a tremble of the old excitement when she thought of her lover. He would seek her out, she was convinced of that. A love like theirs couldn't end. And with time, she knew she would change him. She understood him and forgave his dark moods.

''Ilda?'

The sound of Gracie's squeaky voice made her jump but Hilda deliberately ignored her.

'Didn't you 'ear me? What are you doing just sitting there?'

'My arm is aching,' Hilda threw over her shoulder.

'If you start complaining, Mrs Burns won't like it.'

Hilda turned and narrowed her brown eyes at Gracie, who stood with her red raw hands on her hips and a lock of thin, mousey-brown hair falling out of her cap. Hilda thought resentfully how once Gracie had been only too willing to be her friend. She had been grateful for Hilda's attention and had even told her that she would shoulder any duty that Hilda didn't care for. Now, the tables seemed to have turned, Hilda thought crossly. She was beginning to detest Gracie's bossy ways.

'Look 'ere, 'Ilda,' Gracie continued in her irritating sing-song voice, 'you'd best get that window cleaned. We're for it if Lord William or Turner decides to appear. They could be round this way any minute, so quiet you'd never 'ear 'em.' Gracie's eyes went wide and fearful. 'This floor gives me the collywobbles, it truly does.'

Hilda managed to hide her amusement and dabbed her cloth disinterestedly at the glass. Gracie was a fool if she believed the stories that had been passed down to the lowers. Fairytales they were, so Hilda believed. The first day she'd worked here she had searched every dark corner and listened for footsteps behind her. But there had only been silence on the upper floor, which smelled musty and forgotten. Sometimes it was so quiet you could hear a pin drop. If Lord William or his silver-haired valet walked these corridors, then Hilda certainly hadn't seen them.

'Five minutes,' Gracie snapped. 'By the time I come back, I want that window finished.'

Hilda seethed in silence as she watched Gracie walk away. Gracie was just a dim-witted skivvy whose newly found air of importance made Hilda's fingers itch to go round Gracie's scrawny neck and squeeze tight. How dare a servant tell her what to do! But as much as Hilda would like to put the scullery maid in her rightful place, a tongue-lashing would serve no purpose. Gracie was the only channel of information that Hilda had. Despite Gracie's uppity ways, there was little that happened in the household, both upstairs and down, that Gracie didn't know about. Hilda knew she must bite her tongue and suffer Gracie's annoying attitude if she wanted to know what was going on in the outside world. Hilda's most immediate concern was finding out when Lord Guy would return to Adelphi Hall.

Hilda closed her eyes and thought longingly of the last time they were together. After the horse had reared and knocked her down, Lord Guy had lifted her into his arms and kissed her bloody eye. Then he had made a sling for her arm from his shirt. She thought of the feel of his naked, sweat-covered shoulders as she clung to them. Of the slender trail of jet-black hair that snaked down his chest and disappeared beneath the buckle at his waist. Tears filled Hilda's eyes. She missed him so much. And hated, with every ounce of her strength, the spoiled and ugly Lady Gabriella Beresford.

The weeks had passed quickly since the night of the Zeppelin attack and Flora counted herself lucky to be alive. She had read in the newspapers that the airship had claimed nine lives and injured many more during its flight over London. Had Michael not come to her rescue, she might well have died under the collapsed buildings of Westferry Road.

As Lady Hailing had given Mrs Bell another maid to help in the kitchen, Flora was now free to see Michael each Sunday. The crisp autumn days were turning to winter and Michael often drove them into the country. Flora liked best their strolls along the Embankment, pausing to eat roasted chestnuts or drink hot coffee. She always felt proud to be on the arm of the handsome young man who strode beside her with barely a limp. But she never failed to keep in mind that as soon as he passed the army medical, they would have to part.

One late November evening after they had enjoyed tea at Lyons, Michael suggested they make their way to the river. The lights of the city twinkled as they walked arm in arm while all around them was an air of excitement. The stores were showing signs of Christmas, despite the shadow of war. Barrow boys and coffee stalls were not to be outdone and strung sprigs of holly on their stands. Michael gave a shilling to a beggar who was singing 'God Rest Ye Merry Gentlemen' and offered to sing another carol of their choice. Flora knew that people were trying to look on the bright side even though most families were suffering the loss of a loved one, or life-changing injuries. But still, the season of goodwill was upon London and the Embankment, when they reached it, was layered in a fine river mist, sending people's breaths curling up into the cold winter's air.

'Christmas is almost upon us,' Michael said, as they stood at the river wall. 'But I fear the holiday might come too late for us to be together. I shall soon be deemed fit to return to service.'

Flora had hoped and prayed that he would still be at home for the 25th of December. But each day now, men were being called up; many to replace the thousands of troops lost at the Somme and Verdun and all along both the Eastern and Western Fronts.

Michael lifted his fingers to the wisps of silvery blonde hair that escaped over her ears, tucking them gently inside her small fur hat. Then gently touching the brooch pinned to the lapel of her coat, he murmured, 'Your butterfly brooch is a reminder of life for us after the war, Flora. That is what you want, my dearest?'

She nodded, a sharp pain close to her heart from the thought they might soon be separated. 'When I wear it, I shall always think of you,' she assured him. 'If only the war were to end now.'

'Who knows when it will be over?' Michael replied. 'Or how long it will be before we see each other again?' He took her in his arms, careless of the glances of the passers-by. 'There are no guarantees of a future, my darling, but I promise you that wherever I am in this world, I will always let you know I'm thinking of you.'

'And I shall be thinking of you.'

'Are you sure this is what you want?' he asked her one last time. 'Am I right to ask it of you? You already have Will—'

She reached up to lay her fingers on his lips. 'I have both of you, safe in my heart and my prayers.'

Before he could reply, a small figure appeared beside them. Michael quickly let her go.

'Matches for yer, sir?' the match-girl asked, a tangle of brown ringlets falling over her dirty face. Flora saw she was shivering under her thin, grubby coat and she could hardly hold still the battered tray in front of her.

'Find me a nice bundle, will you?' Michael said kindly as he pressed a large coin into her palm.

''Alf a crown! Oh, sir – m'lord – your majesty, fank you!' The match-girl quickly pocketed her treasure. 'I'd give yer heather as well, but I ain't got none. Still, keep the matches in yer wallet and I promise they'll bring yer good luck.'

'I'll keep you to that, young lady.' Michael chuckled as he accepted the roughly cut wooden sticks tied with frayed string.

They watched her scurry off into the mist, a small, bedraggled figure with wild brown ringlets bouncing on her shoulders. Flora thought of Hilda. Had it not been for the nuns of St Boniface, she and Hilda could easily have been beggars too.

'My lucky talisman,' Michael said as he tucked the matches in his pocket. 'Now I have something for you.'

He slipped his hand under his red silk cravat and took out a small box. 'I hope you like this, Flora.'

The box felt as soft as velvet between her fingers. She opened the lid carefully. A flash of light dazzled her before she realized what she was holding. 'A ring?' she gasped. 'Michael, are you sure this is for me?'

'Who else would it be for?'

'It's so very beautiful.'

'Three small diamonds,' he explained, indicating each nugget, 'fashioned into a cluster to sit on your delicate finger.'

Flora had never held a diamond before. She had never even seen one! The gems on the jeweller's stall at the market were mostly glass and paste. She couldn't take her eyes from the ring's exquisite beauty.

'I love you with all my heart, dearest.'

She gazed up at him, the words trembling on her lips. 'And I love you.'

'Then that's all that matters.' His lips touched hers in a kiss that was full of everything she loved: the mist on the river, the salt in its water and the scents of the winter air. A kiss that was full of promise and of the life that one day, they might share.

He kissed her again, but this time she felt the passion of his longing. 'If you accept this, then I know you are to be mine,' he whispered, lifting her hand to slip on the ring. She spread out her fingers. 'But you are very young yet. And you may change your mind before I can return to marry you.'

'No, I'll never do that.'

The diamonds glimmered and above their heads Flora caught sight of the star. Their star. The star that would shine on her husband-to-be and bring him home safely to her arms.

Chapter Twenty-Nine

It was Saturday, the day before Christmas Eve, and the surgery had been full of the walking wounded, the young and the elderly and the disabled veterans of war. Flora had offered each adult a glass of port and mince pie and all had accepted, enjoying a little warmth on a grey winter's day that held little other seasonal cheer. The complaints of the patients rang in her ears; there were few who regarded the election of a new prime minister as compensation for the failure to return the men who had been too long at war.

'All washouts!' exclaimed one older be-whiskered patient, whose painful gout had been temporarily forgotten after downing a port. 'Asquith was conspired against and ousted by Lloyd George's puppets. The king got involved too. All with promises to end the conflict and still there ain't no sign of peace!'

'Aye,' agreed a young veteran, his hairless scalp displaying the scars of hurriedly performed stitching, 'they're all useless. The politicians blow 'ot and cold just to win themselves votes. I'd like to see all these stuffed suits at

Whitehall kitted out with a private's tunic. Stand where a soldier stands, made to jump over the top and run like stink towards certain death. Oh, yes, I'd like that—' The man began to cough heavily, waving aside the help offered as he stumbled towards the door, never finishing his sentence.

There was silence amongst the last few patients who sat in their seats, nodding their agreement, and despite Flora's attempts to lighten the air, there wasn't a smile to be seen. Flora found herself grateful that the week had come to an end. With the last of the port drunk and the mince pies eaten, she knew that for the people of the East End, this Christmas would be the hardest and leanest of the war so far.

As she washed and dried her hands in her small room, she looked at the empty space on her left finger. Her ring was too precious to wear to work. She kept it safely with her shawl and the butterfly brooch in the drawer downstairs.

She had wanted to say so many things to Michael, but there was no time. Now all she had was memories of their last, brief goodbye.

'Time to close the doors,' Dr Tapper said, startling her. She hadn't heard the last patient leave, so deep was she in thoughts of Michael. Now as she regarded her employer, she could see the relief in his face too. 'I fear that Christmas 1916 will leave us all a little underwhelmed,' he said, echoing her thoughts. 'Too many grieving and too many hungry. What interest has the ordinary man in Lloyd

George's new-style cabinet? Or a reshuffled coalition that plays on tactics involving the king? The people need reassurance, not division.' He shook his head, then looked at her wearily. 'Forgive me, my dear, you have your own loss to contend with this year, without my grumbling.'

Flora smiled. 'Would you like to eat with me on Christmas Day, Dr Tapper?'

'I would like that very much.' A twinkle returned to his eyes.

That night, Flora sat by the fire and considered her plans for Christmas. She had been to the market and bought a small chicken, some fresh vegetables and a little fruit. She counted herself lucky to have purchased a scrawny bird, the last hanging on a hook, from the butcher's stall. She'd paid twice the price, and had to haggle at the fruit and vegetable stall. The cabbages and apples were the smallest she had ever seen.

'You should have come early,' the stall-holder admonished her. 'What we had weren't much, thanks to our ships being sunk and merchant men going down like swatted flies. We're at war and have to tighten our belts but I'll bet you the buggers up at Whitehall will still 'old out their palms for our taxes to keep their fat arses on parliament's seats.'

Flora understood these complaints and listened patiently. She knew everyone was letting off steam, frustrated by the interminable war.

The warmth from the fire glowed on her cheeks. A fire that would be welcomed by many in homes that were suffering from the bitter cold and a scarcity of food and fuel. Once again, Flora thought how fortunate she was to be earning a wage and enjoying a roof over her head. She gazed up at the photographs of Will and Michael. They stood side by side, decorated with a sprig of holly. Next to these was a card from Hilda that had come last week. It showed a winter's scene in the countryside. Inside, a short message read:

> To Flora, from your very best friend, Hilda, who misses you. I hope you have a happy Christmas and miss me too. I am recovered now and things are changing here. We are told that after Christmas, the east wing of the house is to be set aside for the returning injured troops of the conflict. Mrs Burns is not at all pleased as she insists she has enough to do already. And Mrs Harris will have much more to complain about if she is asked to cook for the army! As for me, I ain't a bit put out as it will be a treat to see a few handsome new faces. Please write with news and don't be too long.

Flora was surprised by this turn of events. How would her friend fare in the changing circumstances that had befallen Adelphi Hall? Would Hilda be expected to help the wounded soldiers? Flora couldn't hide her smile as she thought of Hilda's weak stomach.

Her gaze travelled up to the photograph of Michael. She thought of their last brief embrace on the day they had told Lillian they were engaged.

Lillian had held her close. 'I couldn't be happier, my dear Flora,' she had whispered. They had all sat in the conservatory and spoken of the time when peace would reign. But as Michael had kissed her goodbye, they had needed no words.

The truth was, no one could predict the events that would take place in the cold months ahead.

Chapter Thirty

The New Year began with freezing temperatures and a spread of bronchitis that kept Flora busy at the surgery. During the day, she made sure the air smelled sweetly of ginger and eucalyptus and the peppery balsams that helped to ease the many chest complaints. At night, when she scrubbed the place clean, these were replaced by the eye-watering odours of Naptha and Jeyes disinfectant.

In the middle of January, a West Ham munitions factory blew up. Flora was to think again of the Zeppelin attack of August.

'Must be spies!' the traders at the market said. 'The explosion was ear-splitting, you could hear it for miles around. Let's hope they don't come round 'ere.'

'We'll give 'em what for if they do,' others threatened.

'That's the trouble. Yer can't see 'em,' one costermonger shouted above the rest. 'Yer can't 'ear 'em. The kaiser's men are everywhere and nowhere. They even dress up to look like us. Before we all know it, the buggers will take over the country.'

Flora hated these rumours that stirred everyone up. There was no proof that the explosion wasn't accidental. This was the same talk of sabotage and German spies that had ended Old Fritz's livelihood.

On a bitterly cold morning in February, even the doctor voiced an opinion. 'One hundred and thirty-four neutral vessels, including America's, have been sunk in the last three weeks,' he informed Flora as he read the newspaper. 'I shall not be surprised if America's entry into the war is approved by Woodrow Wilson's congress. The National Guard and navy militia have been ordered into service. Even the United States cannot ignore such open hostility.' The doctor slipped off his reading glasses and rubbed his eyes. 'The rest of the world is watching and the president cannot be seen to be weak. Though if America does declare war, then I fear the neutral countries will be forced to take sides.' He glanced at Flora. 'And of course, Greece has always maintained her neutrality.'

Flora thought of Michael and knew the doctor was thinking of him too. Michael had told them he expected to return to his regiment in Greece. 'But we mustn't jump to conclusions,' the doctor added cautiously. 'It's true King Constantine openly favours Germany, but his prime minister supports the Allies. We have to hope that an agreement will be reached between them to avoid a coup and, naturally, in our favour.'

The newspapers were full of rumours once more. Each day the doctor read out the latest developments to Flora.

With America poised to join the conflict, threats and boasts abounded.

'Our boys have won at Gaza,' one patient announced on a foggy March morning. He flourished a newspaper at the huddled figures in the waiting room. 'We outmanoeuvred the Turks and sent 'em off with their tails between their legs. The British could do with more good news like this for our forgotten troops at Salonika.'

'Salonika?' Flora repeated, remembering that Michael had told her that some of his regiment had been sent there from Gallipoli. 'Why are they called forgotten troops?'

''Cause the British and French can't make up their minds what to do there,' replied the man. 'The Greeks are split down the middle, see? Some are loyal to the king and the Central Powers. Others to us. Why? You got someone there?'

'He might be.'

'The Greeks have got to make their minds up, 'stead of sitting on the fence,' the man argued, scratching his dirty whiskers. 'If they go against the Central Powers then our lads'll be right alongside 'em.'

Flora felt her heart sink. Was Michael to be drawn into this fresh conflict?

'Oh, put that rubbish away,' commanded another man. 'If it ain't the Greeks, then it's the Irish, or the Ruskies.'

'You should keep your ear to the ground, chum,' retorted another patient. 'This Lenin fella is getting all cosy with the Germans. It's said the Russians are freezing to death and want to get out of the war. But where would that leave the Allies on the Eastern Front?'

'We're already at death's door,' a young mother complained as she cradled her baby in her arms. 'With no bread, or coal or wood, how are we expected to survive? My baby's only six months old and he's got a chest like a foghorn. His nose and eyes are running muck, which ain't surprising when you look at the dump we live in. Two rooms and walls alive with roaches. Nutty slack that don't burn and just smokes the place out. With an empty larder, five kids and an old man on the stones, I'm expected to perform miracles. So don't talk to me about foreigners. The war started with 'em in the first place, so they should finish it and leave us alone.'

The rest of the shivering, hungry, waiting patients nodded their agreement. But the man with the newspaper stubbornly shook his head. 'You don't understand, love. The British nation and its Allies fight for democracy.'

'At the cost of how many lives?' an elderly man croaked. 'I had two sons before Kitchener took 'em to their deaths. And I'm supposed to believe in freedom of speech? You must be jokin', mate.'

Flora sighed and went about her duties. People were cold, hungry and sick, which often led to them expressing bitter, unreasonable views. It was only when a casualty of battle limped in to join them that the self-pitying faces took stock and kept their tongues in check.

The days passed slowly and Flora saw no sign of spirits lifting. To make matters worse, a heavy snowfall had frozen the country. She had made her way to the market through streets banked with mucky snow drifts and dangerously iced cobbles. And when she'd arrived there, the stalls had little stock and the home-grown vegetables were browned with frost.

As she sat alone in the airey with the luxury of a small fire, she thought about the freezing Russians, the troops in the flooded trenches of the Front and Michael, from whom she had not yet heard. And felt guilty that she was comfortable and safe from danger when he wasn't.

Then one early April day, the sun suddenly broke through the clouds. 'America joins us! Now we'll show 'em!' the newspapers vendors shouted on every corner. 'The doughboys will soon be in Flanders alongside our troops and giving Fritz the pasting of his life.'

The news soon reached the surgery and Flora listened to the excited cheers of the waiting patients. From the depths of despair last week they were now jubilant, anticipating a swift victory.

But the doctor made only one comment.

'America is flexing its muscles, doing as Britain did over two-and-a-half years ago, when thousands of our young men volunteered to fight for king and country.

'And never returned home again.'

One evening after work, Flora found a letter on the mat. It was addressed to 'Miss Flora Shine' and was written in a hand she didn't recognize.

Flora took off her cap, let loose her hair and sat by the unlit fire. Slowly unpeeling the sealed edge of the envelope, she took out the letter. It was written neatly on a sheet of plain white paper. The address in the top left-hand corner stated clearly, the Bristol Infirmary for War-Wounded.

'Dear Miss Shine,' the writer began, 'I am a nurse working at the infirmary and care for the wounded veterans of war. One of our patients is Private William Boniface from the London Regiment.'

Flora's heart almost stopped. Will was alive! Alive! Could she believe it? After all the months of silence, the news had come that not only was he alive, but in Bristol, England. Then slowly her eyes refocused and her heart steadied as she read on:

> William received injuries in France last year and was taken first to a dressing station and after, to the casualty main clearing station and finally to a base hospital. His injuries were assessed and in December it was decided to return him by hospital ship to England. I am aware he regards you as closest to him and you may wonder why we have not contacted you before. It is enough perhaps to say that the nature of William's complicated injuries have meant he has been treated at several hospitals across the country. Our infirmary has been his last port of call and we are considering his discharge to convalesce. It is with this in mind that I hope you will write back, perhaps with the suggestion of a visit to

William. I can offer you transport from London to Bristol with the help of the Red Cross. My sincere regards and in anticipation of your reply, Nurse Sara Parkin.

Flora read the letter again. She wanted to feel joy that Will had survived and was about to be discharged from the infirmary to convalesce. But her instincts told her that there was much more to this letter than Nurse Sara Parkin had decided to write.

'Of course you must go,' the doctor said after reading the letter the next day. 'Whatever Will's injuries, I'm sure he will want to see you.'

'Nurse Parkin didn't say.'

'We can only conclude that Will is struggling with his recovery.'

Flora had been thinking of the possibility that Will may have lost a limb. Or had he been caught in the clouds of poison gas? How would she react when she saw him? She must try to think of him as a patient, as she did at the surgery. 'I'll write back to Nurse Parkin and accept.'

'Would you like company, my dear?' Dr Tapper leaned forward as he sat at his desk. 'I am sure one or two days away from our patients won't hurt.'

Flora wanted to say that she would like nothing more than to have him at her side. But she also knew their patients came first.

'We could travel to Bristol on Saturday morning and return on Sunday,' he suggested with a light shrug. 'I've great regard for Will, as you know. He is a most personable young man. But without doubt, he will have suffered and I should like to be there to help you both.'

Flora felt close to tears. 'Thank you.'

'We shall pull together for Will's sake.'

That night, Flora wrote to Nurse Parkin. She told her that both she and Dr Tapper would visit and would be most grateful of the offer of transport.

It was a bright May morning when Flora and Dr Tapper stood together in the courtyard of the London Hospital, awaiting their transport. The weather had turned warm at last and Flora had dressed in Hilda's blue suit and had bought a small blue hat from the market. She hoped that the colour was bright and cheerful and would please Will, who must have spent many months in the drab environments of the hospitals.

Nurse Parkin had replied with information on where to meet the ambulance and a warning that the vehicle might stop on several occasions to fill its tank with fuel. 'The Red Cross ambulance that is to take you is spartan,' Nurse Parkin wrote, 'but is reliable and will be quicker than a horse-drawn vehicle.'

The hospital grounds were very busy. Flora saw many disabled veterans climbing from ambulances or being stretchered on to others. Flora thought that the ambulance that arrived to take them to Bristol did indeed look old and battered.

But their driver was young and energetic. She wore a tunic of dark grey, a belted jacket and calf-length skirt with sturdy laced-up shoes. Her small cap bore the emblem of the Red Cross and she smiled warmly as she held out her hand. Flora took it and felt her firm handshake.

'I'm Sally Vine,' she said cheerfully. 'Sorry about the stretchers piled inside but yesterday I delivered to Brighton and didn't get home till late. Still, I think we'll squeeze you in,' she explained as they walked round the high-sided van which displayed a large red cross on a white background.

They all peered into the rear of the vehicle. A strong smell of fuel and disinfectant curled unpleasantly in the air. There were stretchers on one side and a large white box above them, labelled FIRST AID. On the other side, behind the driver's seat, were four wooden flaps that folded down to make seats.

'This ambulance is a converted lorry and used to transport the wounded troops from London to military or private hospitals,' Sally said apologetically. 'I'm afraid so many men are returning from war now that the ordinary hospitals are unable to take them. Hence the importance of vehicles like this. No matter where the patients are sent, we deliver them.' She paused. 'Is it family you are travelling to see?'

'We're visiting my friend, Will,' Flora replied.

'Have you gone before?'

'No. A nurse wrote to say he'll be discharged soon.'

Sally gave an understanding nod. 'I see. Well, we'd better get on with it. Now I'll just let the tailboard down and you can sit.' She unlatched a chain on either side of the back and lowered the tailboard.

'We don't want you sliding about,' Sally said with a grin as she pulled down the wooden flaps for them to sit on. 'You must excuse our Heath Robinson standards of travel.'

Flora smiled. This was luxury compared to Albert's cart.

Minutes later, Flora was sitting behind the driver with Dr Tapper beside her. The clattering vehicle bumped and rocked along the roads of the East End, whilst Sally talked over her shoulder. Flora was not surprised to hear that their driver was a member of the suffrage movement.

'Have you ever thought of joining us?' she asked Flora.

'No, not really.'

'I'm sure we'll have the vote soon. We are doing so much to help the war effort that we must be recognized as equal to men. Things are changing for women, you know.'

'Did you drive before the war?' Flora asked.

'My brother has a car and he taught me to drive. But now he's at the Front.'

'Oh, so was Will, the friend I'm going to visit.'

A big bump in the road caused Sally to slow down the ambulance. 'Sorry about that. Was he badly wounded?'

'The nurse didn't say. Only that they are sending him to convalesce.'

Sally turned briefly. 'I hope not to somewhere in the wilds.'

'She didn't say where.'

'If you have somewhere in mind, then my advice is to speak up before they take action. Tell them where you want him to go.'

At once, Flora thought of Adelphi Hall. 'But would they listen to me?'

'Do you have connections to this place?' Sally enquired.

'It's a country house called Adelphi Hall. Hilda, our friend, is a maid there. Part of it has been turned into a hospital for the war-wounded.'

'Sometimes it helps to have a name.' Sally slowed the ambulance for a line of black and white cows being herded across the country road. 'Most big houses have been requisitioned by the government,' she agreed as they moved on again. 'It's worth making yourself and your opinions known. Remember the motto of the Suffragettes: "Deeds not words". Perhaps start with this nurse who wrote to you.'

Flora decided she would do just that. How wonderful it would be if Will could be close to Hilda. Flora hoped the doctor would wake so she could tell him about Sally's advice. But he was still fast asleep.

Flora listened to Sally as she talked about the suffrage movement. Though Flora admired these women, she was not a militant. She wouldn't chain herself to a railing or go on hunger strike in prison. Although, now Sally had given her this advice, she knew she had to speak up for Will.

'Just look at what women are doing for the country,' Sally shouted over her shoulder. 'We perform most jobs that men do. I worked with the Red Cross at the field hospitals in France for six months. Nothing prepares you for what you see there. Man or woman, you just have to get on with it.'

Flora's tummy jolted. Here she was, making plans for the future, when she hadn't even seen Will yet. How was she going to feel when she saw him? Whatever injuries he had, she mustn't let her feelings show.

When the ambulance stopped to take on fuel, Dr Tapper woke up. 'Are we there?' he asked, sitting up on the uncomfortable wooden seat.

'No, but Sally has given me an idea.' Flora couldn't wait to tell him. 'It would be wonderful if Will was sent to Adelphi Hall.'

Dr Tapper raised his bushy eyebrows. 'The authorities will have their own ideas on that.'

'Yes, but so have I.'

A gentle smile touched his lips. He patted her hand. 'There's no doubt about it: when you make up your mind on something, Flora, you have a certain look about you.'

She blushed, but she was also excited. Somehow she would make Nurse Parkin see the sense in her idea.

By the time they set off again the weather was on the turn. From a bright, clear day, heavy clouds now filled the sky. Flora watched Sally with admiration as she battled the ambulance through the pouring rain. All the while, another part of Flora's mind was working. Sally had asked her if she knew of a contact at Adelphi Hall. She didn't, but perhaps Hilda did.

'Dratted weather,' Sally mumbled as she peered at the drenched windscreen and hard-working single wiper. Her only protection against the storm was a large tin plate over her head and a flimsy canvas flap.

Meeting this independent and courageous young woman had been a blessing. Flora knew that if she wanted Will to go to Adelphi Hall then it would be up to her to set the plan in motion.

Chapter Thirty-One

After almost a day's travel they finally arrived at the infirmary. The rain had stopped at last and the air was still damp under overcast skies.

'Well, good luck,' Sally said as they climbed from the ambulance. 'Don't forget what I told you, Flora.'

'I won't.' Flora watched her go. She had felt inspired in Sally's company. But when she turned to discover a long line of wooden huts silhouetted in the hospital's grounds, her heart sank. There were dozens of patients being wheeled in Bath chairs and just as many on crutches. The smell in the air was sickly. 'These huts look like garden sheds,' Flora said dejectedly. 'Do you think Will is in one of them?'

'It's the work that's carried on inside them that's important,' the doctor reminded her as they went up the steps to the main infirmary. 'I'm sure Will has had the very best of care.'

The high-ceilinged hospital was also full of milling people. Flora took the doctor's arm. 'Nurse Parkin said she would meet us here, if we ask for her at reception.'

They pushed their way through to a long queue. Two women in business-like suits worked furiously amongst the many papers and files that spilled across a piece of flat wood that looked suspiciously like an old door resting on plinths.

'We'd like to see Nurse Sara Parkin,' Flora said when it came to their turn.

'Is she expecting you?'

Flora nodded. 'Yes, we've travelled from London to visit one of her patients.'

'Do you know the number of his unit?'

'Do you mean one of those huts outside?'

The receptionist, who looked to Flora to be in her fifties and had a pinched, tired face, nodded. 'The units are very spacious and clean. Now, you've come a long way and must be in need of refreshment. If you go to the canteen, three huts down, I'll send for Nurse Parkin and tell her you're there.'

'Thank you.'

Flora tried to prepare herself as they made their way outside. In just a short while, she would be with Will again.

Flora and the doctor sat at the canteen table. The busy, stale-smelling room was crowded with people who had come from far and wide. Everyone had the same anxious look on their faces. The hut's windows were streaming with condensation. The rows of wooden benches and tables were stacked with dirty enamel dishes. Flora had managed to eat a little broth, and the doctor, a slice of apple pie.

'Miss Shine?'

Flora looked up. A slender young woman, about Flora's height and wearing a dark-blue uniform, stood at the table. Her short, neat brown hair was tucked under a white cap.

'Are you Nurse Sara Parkin?'

'I am.'

'This is Dr Tapper.' They all shook hands.

'Shall we sit together for a moment?' Nurse Parkin said in quiet voice. 'You must be eager to see Will, but I would like to speak to you first.' She folded her slim hands together and leaned them on the table. 'May I call you Flora?'

'Yes, of course.'

'Will has spoken at length of his life at the orphanage. And how your letters have been a lifeline for him during the fighting. If it wasn't for you, he might never have had the will to live.'

'Does he know we're visiting today?'

Nurse Parkin nodded. 'Yes. But I would ask you to keep in mind that Will is still very ill.'

'Will he get better?' Flora couldn't wait any longer to know.

'A shell burst close to him and he was left unconscious. To compound his injuries, it was some time before the stretcher-bearers found him. There is a lack of sterile dressings at the Front and infections are always likely.

Even the smallest cut can become a threat. He was in immediate danger from blood loss and severe shock.' Nurse Parkin hesitated. 'I'm afraid the surgeons had no choice other than to amputate his arm.'

Flora tried to breathe. Her head was spinning. She knew she was about to faint. The last thing she remembered was Dr Tapper holding her.

'Sip the water slowly.'

Flora looked up into Nurse Parkin's concerned face. 'I'm sorry.'

'It happens to the best of us,' said the young nurse, 'especially when it's close to home. We can stand up to a lot but when it's personal . . .' She put down the mug. 'I'm very sorry to be the bearer of such bad news. Perhaps I should have said more in my letter, but I was concerned you might not come.'

'I would never let Will down,' Flora insisted. The waves of dizziness were leaving her.

'You may be surprised to hear that many men are abandoned because of their injuries. Sadly, their relatives or friends cannot face long months or even years of rehabilitation. Some simply haven't the accommodation or courage to take in a disabled or a disfigured man.'

Flora made herself swallow. 'Is Will disfigured?'

'His head was injured in the explosion and his hair is just beginning to grow back. It will be some while before he regains his confidence.'

'How much is left of his limb?' the doctor asked.

'The top of his upper arm. In time, if he heals, he could be fitted with an artificial appliance.'

They all sat silently, until Flora finally spoke: 'I would like Will to be sent to Adelphi Hall in Surrey. The house belongs to Lord William Calvey and has recently been converted to a hospital.' She went on to explain about Hilda and how being close to her might help Will's recovery.

Nurse Parkin raised her eyebrows. 'I don't have any say in the placements, I'm afraid.'

'Who does?' Remembering Sally's advice, Flora wasn't going to give up.

'The matron and others.'

'Will you ask her?'

Nurse Parkin took in a slow breath. 'Well, it does make sense. But, as I say, it's not up to me.'

'Please try.'

The young woman smiled. 'You can be very persuasivc, Flora.'

'I would do anything for Will.'

'Yes, I can see that. Now, are you ready to see your friend?'

Dr Tapper rose and put his hand under Flora's arm. 'We're quite ready.'

Flora knew that no matter what had happened to Will, it was now that he needed her, more than ever.

Chapter Thirty-Two

Hilda stopped what she was doing and put down the basket that was full of soiled, heavy vegetables. Each day, she had to dig up a variety for Mrs Harris, who was now twice as busy as ever preparing meals for the convalescing soldiers and nursing staff.

She could hear voices coming from the stables on the other side of the thick yew hedge. Stepping towards the half gate, she peered carefully over it. Khaki uniforms abounded, as did the browny-pink uniforms, white shoes and head caps of the nurses who were helping the wounded men across the lawns and into the house. They looked as though they had occupied Adelphi Hall for fifty years, rather than five months.

Hilda cast her gaze to Lady Bertha. She was still a striking figure with her black hair drawn severely back from her face, wearing a military-style dark-grey tunic top and serge skirt. She was talking to a tall officer, waving her arms about as if to direct the men. Hilda had overheard a conversation between Mrs Burns and Mrs Harris about the wounded soldiers coming to the hall.

'Well, her ladyship couldn't stop 'em from coming,' Mrs Harris had argued, 'so she joined 'em instead. Whoever would have guessed she'd let the army have her precious dining room. Mr Leighton nearly quit his job when she instructed him to put beds in there. But in the end he had to do as she wanted.'

'The circumstances are unique,' Mrs Burns had replied haughtily. 'We must all do our bit. And her ladyship is doing hers.'

Hilda remembered the conversation vividly. Just after that she had been detailed by Mrs Burns to help Peter the gardener and the young boys from the village. 'There are many mouths to feed now,' Mrs Burns had barked at her. 'And it's about time you started to earn your keep again.'

Hilda had wanted to wipe the smile off the housekeeper's face. Nothing could have given Mrs Burns more pleasure than to see Hilda digging in the allotments, her nails always black with filthy earth and her face blotchy and red from outdoor duties. But Hilda had been forced to accept her fate. She clung to the hope that one day Lord Guy would rescue her.

Hilda listened carefully as she hid behind the yew hedge. At least she was free to roam the gardens now. She wasn't imprisoned in the house. How Gracie could put up with making all those wounded men's beds, full of lumpy mattresses and soiled sheets. Hilda felt sick at the thought. Trolleys and water jugs filled every hallway. The smell of sickness and disinfectant was everywhere.

'Hey, you!'

Hilda wheeled round. She lost her balance and fell against the hedge.

A firm hand caught her wrist. 'Who are you spying on, boy?'

Her heart pumped frantically as she found herself in the presence of Lord Guy. She couldn't believe it was him. Was she dreaming?

'N . . . no one, my lord,' she mumbled. 'I j . . . just heard voices.' She could hardly speak for the excitement and fear trapped in her chest.

'Hilda, is that you?'

'Y . . . yes, my lord.'

'What the devil are you dressed up like that for?' He released her wrist and stood back to cast his eyes over her. Hilda trembled. Here he was, the man of her dreams. Looking at her with those hooded black eyes, their expression causing a thrust of desire inside her that had her gawping at him wordlessly.

'I . . . I'm helping the gardener, my lord.'

'Mrs Burns has no use for you in the kitchen?'

Hilda blushed fiercely and bowed her head. She wanted to tell him how badly she had been treated since the accident. How Mrs Burns had more or less held her captive, away from the other staff. How she'd been made to work alone, or with Gracie, a lowly scullery maid, who had nearly driven her mad, telling her what to do and how to do it. And how her heart had nearly broken in two as she had watched him escort Lady Gabriella last year. Driving out in the carriage or in the big new motor car, or riding together across the fields.

'Well, in an odd way, the boy's garb is quite appealing,' he drawled, appraising her again.

Hilda looked up, her eyes suddenly bright. 'Thank you.'

'But too cumbersome for a warm day like this.' He stood, hands on hips, his hair shorter than when she had last seen it at Christmas, on the day of the last family dinner in the dining room. She had not been asked to serve the twelve-course meal with the other staff. Mrs Burns still kept her in check, in the kitchen or scullery. But she had caught sight of the family as she stoked the fire, before being shouted at by Mr Leighton and made to run full pelt back to the kitchen. Now she could only stare at her one true love. He was so unbearably handsome in his casual dark trousers and jacket, with a blue silk cravat at his neck. His rakish black hair shone, and his inky eyes stared at her with almost an open invitation.

Hilda drew in her breath. It had been so long since he'd touched her. Over a year since they had played that fateful game of chase. If only she had not hurt herself! If only she had played their game as he had told her to, and run faster, longer . . .

'I see that you are now fully recovered.' His eyes lowered to her arm, then her full breasts that were hidden under the coarse grey blouse, and down to her legs encased in rough trousers and working boots. Hilda felt elated. He had been thinking of her, there was no doubt of that!

'Yes, my lord.' A shiver of delight went through her. He was here at last to rescue her. It had taken over twelve months for him to return to her. And now he had found her. But, oh, why was she dressed in such an ugly fashion? Humiliation filled her cheeks, making them rosy. Her full lips trembled as he came closer.

'So my little kitten has become a fully grown cat. A tiger perhaps, a lioness?'

Hilda nearly died on the spot as he removed her cloth cap and her hair tumbled down to her shoulders. Her legs wanted to give way with sheer delight. He always used to call her his little kitten. He remembered! Oh, he remembered!

'Such beautiful hair,' he muttered, pushing his fingers into it. Suddenly, his hands were on her shirt. His fingers moved carefully over the cloth and loosened its buttons. Then they entered the gap that remained and slid slowly over her breasts. Dipping past her underwear they stroked her bare nipple. It immediately peaked, yearning to be touched.

Hilda closed her eyes. She didn't know how she found the strength to stand up. Her legs felt full of air. She could barely swallow. His touch sent her to paradise. She had almost given up that he would come to her again. Almost . . .

'You are beautiful. Ripe and ready to be played with.' His breath was on her face. It smelled of pleasure, of lust, of desire.

She opened her eyes, catching her breath noisily. 'Oh, my lord . . .'

'Still as accommodating, still as playful, still wanting?'

All she could do was nod. He could do whatever he wanted with her. She wouldn't complain. Not ever. She would run across the fields until she was dying of exhaustion. She would go wherever he told her. She would never again act the silly, naïve . . .

'Now, we shall see if this is genuine,' he muttered, squeezing her nipple until it hurt and she cried out. 'Ah, it seems you really are ready.'

His fingers tugged impatiently at the belt at her waist. His strength and power overwhelmed her. In just a few seconds his hand was pressing down, inside her underwear and playing over her stomach until they stopped above her most sensitive part.

Hilda gasped and sobbed all in one breath.

A smile formed on his lips. Those lips she loved so much, missed so much. They were close, oh, so close.

'You don't disappoint, Hilda. Take down your trousers.'

Hilda was terrified. There were people beyond the hedge. Both patients and staff. What if Mrs Burns or Mr Leighton was to see her! 'Oh, my lord, not here, please!' she begged.

His smile fell away. 'Do you dare disobey me?'

'Oh, no, no, my lord. But—'

'Then do as I say.'

Hilda looked around. She could hear movement and voices, but she couldn't see anyone. With luck, Peter would be in the greenhouse with the boys. As for the kitchen staff . . .

Her fingers were trembling so violently that the rough material of her trousers caught at her hips. Her boots were laced and the ends of her trousers pleated into her socks. He laughed at her embarrassment and slid his hand into her open fly.

Hilda almost swooned. She could see herself standing there, her trousers at half mast around her knees. She didn't care. Exquisite pleasure drove through her as his fingers entered her. Her body was throbbing and her breath on fire. She cried aloud, only just remembering to stop herself, as she gulped for air.

'Cry, my little cat. Cry loudly. We could be caught. Just think of it! We are on the very point of discovery.'

Hilda was lost in the turmoil of her body: her delight, her fear, her sensual pleasure. Within seconds he too had opened his fly and was inside her. Groaning and muttering, he took her roughly.

Hilda had by now forgotten who she was or where she was. She only knew that she had never experienced feelings like these before. Her body was a stranger to her. Her need for him was not ordinary. She had risked discovery. And she hadn't cared.

When he had finished, he stepped back. Casually, he thrust a hand through his hair.

Hilda quickly pulled up her trousers. She looked around. It seemed that no one had observed them.

Lord Guy took hold of her chin. 'You still want to play, little cat?'

Hilda was shaking too much to think of an answer. She wanted him to tell her he loved her. That after all this time, he had returned to her. That for all the months she had been in exile, her trust in him was to be rewarded.

But he only laughed. It was a sound that both terrified and excited her. And in just a few strides he had vanished.

Gone, as though he had never been there.

Flora glanced at the men who lay on beds or sat in chairs, many swathed in bandages. The more mobile used crutches to make their way over the bare boards. A handful of men wore slippers and sleeveless hospital gowns. Many had limbs missing and some even two.

'Will is here by the windows. He likes to see out to the lawns.'

Flora saw a slight figure sitting in a Bath chair. The man had very short fair hair with one side shaved, revealing an ugly lump. The loose sleeve of his jacket was pinned up to the shoulder. Flora's heart raced as he turned slowly towards them.

It was Will. But a different Will altogether to the one she had last seen that day in Hyde Park, in the summer of 1914. His thick blond curls had vanished and his blue eyes were hidden by swollen pouches of skin.

'Will!' Flora hurried past Nurse Parkin.

'Flora?' It was Will's voice, but a very different rasp to the youthful sound she remembered.

'Oh, Will, it's been so long.' She stepped forward. 'Can I hold you?'

'Yes, but be careful.'

She put her arms around him slowly. He felt as thin as a child.

'Hello, Will,' Doctor Tapper said quietly. 'It's been some time since we last met.'

Will smiled weakly. 'Yes, before I joined up.'

Flora knew this was a very changed Will to the one she remembered.

'Will's injuries are still extremely sensitive,' Nurse Parkin warned them. 'Please sit down and make yourselves comfortable. Are you staying overnight at the hospital?'

'If there is accommodation,' Dr Tapper said as he sat on a wooden chair beside Will's bed.

'There is a shelter to the north of the hospital. Very basic, I'm afraid, set up by volunteers. But it's somewhere to spend the night. Now I must leave you with Will.'

'How are you faring?' the doctor asked when Nurse Parkin had gone.

'I'm alive,' Will replied gruffly. 'As you can see, I shall never be able to work as a baker. Or do things that normal people do.'

Flora stretched out her hand and took his fingers. 'You've been so brave.'

'I don't know about that.'

'Why didn't you write to me?'

'Can't you see?' He looked at his loose sleeve.

'I meant before that happened.' She felt embarrassed at her clumsy question.

'There was nothing I could write about except death and the dying.' He spoke in sharp, bitter bursts, trying to get his breath.

'I wouldn't have minded what you said.'

'You don't understand what life was like in the trenches.'

'No, that's true, we don't.' She squeezed his fingers and smiled as he returned the pressure. 'Oh, Will, I can't believe you're back. One day you'll be well again.'

'I don't think so,' he said quietly. 'No one will want a cripple. Where shall I work? What will I do? I'll become a beggar in the streets.'

'You mustn't say that. And anyway, I wouldn't let you.'

'Although it seems unlikely now,' the doctor added firmly, 'you will start to make a new life.'

'I doubt that.'

Flora swallowed her tears. 'Keep strong, Will.'

'Hold me again, won't you?'

She put her arms around him as he wept on her shoulder.

It was some time before they broke apart. 'Dry your eyes now.' She gave him her hanky.

'You used to tell me that in the orphanage.'

'And it worked. You soon pulled your socks up. Sometimes you could be very lazy.' Flora was trying to say things that sounded normal.

Will smiled. 'Nurse Parkin is trying to teach me to write with my left hand.'

'She is very nice.'

'Yes, but bossy.'

Dr Tapper laughed and glanced at Flora. 'All nurses are bossy, Will.'

Flora blushed. The time went by quickly as Will told them about his life at the Front. He had been living in a rat-infested swamp and had contracted dysentery. 'And now I can't even go to the toilet by myself. It's humiliating.'

'But it will get better,' Flora promised him.

Will began to look very tired. His head drooped to one side.

'We must go,' Flora said, leaning forward.

'I am rather tired. Will you come tomorrow?'

'Yes. In the morning before we leave.'

She embraced him tenderly. The stub of his arm jerked inside the loose sleeve.

'Good night, sleep well, Will,' the doctor said.

Flora kissed his cheek. 'Good night and God bless, my dear friend. Please remember you will always have me and Hilda. You'll never have to go back to the Front. And in a short while, life will be worth living again.'

Flora hid the catch in her voice. She tried to smile, but as Dr Tapper led her away, she knew she would give way to tears later.

Chapter Thirty-Three

'There are two more passengers travelling back with us today,' Sally told them early the next morning outside the hospital. 'We leave at eleven on the dot.'

'Thank you.' Flora was eager to see Will, but Sally took her arm.

'Did you sleep well?'

Flora nodded although the truth was that she had spent a restless night thinking of Will. Trying to sleep on the makeshift bed provided by the hospital's charity workers had been impossible. One hut had housed men and the other women and children. All night there had been loud snores and children crying. But it was Will who had occupied her thoughts, and what was to become of him.

'It was adequate,' the doctor answered Sally's enquiry, gruffly.

'Did you ask about Will and Adelphi Hall?' Sally looked expectantly at Flora.

'Yes, but I was told that matron deals with all that.'

'Don't let them put you off,' insisted Sally as she slid

on her driver's cap. 'Make a nuisance of yourself, if you have to. It's the only way.'

Flora knew that causing trouble would be the Suffragettes' way. But it wasn't in Flora's nature to create a disturbance. However, that might change if she couldn't get what she wanted for Will.

'Will is looking forward to seeing you this morning,' Nurse Parkin said as she greeted them at the unit. 'Your presence yesterday really lifted his mood.'

'Did you speak to the matron?' Flora asked at once.

'Yes, yes,' Nurse Parkin said hesitantly. 'And normally, our patients are discharged with family in mind. But in Will's case—'

'Nurse Parkin, me and Hilda *are* Will's family,' Flora insisted.

The young woman nodded. 'I'll ask if she will speak to you.'

'Oh, Will, you look better this morning,' Flora said when they arrived at the bedside. He was sitting on an ordinary chair and dressed in a white open-necked shirt and trousers. 'Look, your hair is beginning to grow.'

'Nurse Parkin combed it over my lump.'

'You look more like your old self,' the doctor agreed as they sat down.

'I don't feel myself. Not at all.'

'Many young men have similar wounds,' the doctor replied. 'When you are completely healed, you can be fitted with a false arm. Great headway has been made with recent discoveries for the war-wounded.'

'Yes, but that costs money. And I haven't a penny to my name.'

'We'll worry about that when the time comes,' Flora broke in. 'For now, we just want to see you improve. And the next time we visit, I hope to see you walking.'

There were tears in his blue eyes. 'Are you leaving?'

'We must, I'm afraid. The ambulance is waiting.'

'Now I'll be alone again.'

'I'll see you soon, I promise.' She reached out for his hand. 'I've asked to speak to the matron. I want you to be sent to Adelphi Hall where Hilda in service. It's been turned into a hospital for the war-wounded.'

'But will they listen to you? Some men are sent far away.'

'I won't allow that to happen to you.'

Will managed a tired smiled. 'Your old bossy self is coming out.'

Flora smiled. She knew they were both remembering the times in their childhood at the orphanage. She had always protected Will. Hilda had never needed protection.

Suddenly, a figure stopped at the bedside. The matron wore a wide white cap of starched linen and a dark-blue uniform, with sensible lace-up shoes. She looked stern, with her hair hidden away and her hands folded together in front of her. 'I should like to speak to you, Miss Shine, before you leave. I'll meet you outside.'

Flora hugged Will gently. He clung to her with his good arm, like a child. All the times they had shared together, both good and bad, swirled in Flora's mind.

'Have courage, my dear Will. And I promise to do all I can to have you close.'

Will nodded, holding back his tears.

The doctor took her arm to lead her away. It was a very sad moment and Flora knew that Dr Tapper was thinking of Wilfred.

'You must realize,' said the matron in an authoritative manner, 'that William's papers record him as an orphan with no family.'

'Your information is wrong,' Flora said firmly. Her cheeks glowed red. 'Me and Hilda are his nearest and dearest, as I've told you. We might not be blood relatives but we are as close as brother and sisters can be.'

'I can see that you are very eager to have your way, Miss Shine, but rules are rules. Those men with mothers, fathers and wives must have priority in the placements.'

'I think Will deserves priority,' argued Flora. 'He has, after all, lost an arm for his country.'

'And so have many other men who have fought in this war.'

Flora looked into the woman's florid, unsympathetic face. 'If you want Will to recover, he needs me and Hilda to be with him.'

'We want all of our patients to recover. William is no exception.'

'Would you send him to Adelphi Hall if someone in a high place ordered it?' Flora demanded, unable to hide her anger.

'Quite irrelevant, Miss Shine!'

'I'm sure you would.' Flora was thinking of what Sally had said about contacts.

'I think we have said all there is to be said on the matter. Now, I have other matters to see to. Good day, Miss Shine.'

As the matron walked off, Flora felt very angry. Mostly, with a faceless power that was blind to people's individual circumstances. She could understand why women became Suffragettes. If voting in parliament gave the female sex more power to have their say about things, then she applauded the suffrage movement.

She found the ambulance waiting with the doctor inside.

'Not good news?' he asked as she sat beside him.

'The matron refuses to help.'

Sally jumped in the driving seat. 'Any luck with Boadicea?' she asked over her shoulder, adding with a chuckle, 'I saw you talking to the matron.'

'She was very unhelpful.'

Sally pursed her lips. 'Don't give up, Flora.'

'I won't.'

'That's the spirit.' Sally revved up the engine. 'And remember, things are changing in this modern world. Our movement is making everyone sit up and think. You should come along to one of our meetings. I think you would like what you hear.' She put on her driving gloves and turned to welcome the two extra passengers as they boarded the ambulance.

Flora was glad she had met Sally. She didn't think she would go as far as becoming a supporter of the women's movement. But Sally's pep talk had made her even more determined to fight on Will's behalf.

The moment they arrived home, Flora knew what she had to do. She wrote immediately to Hilda, explaining about Will. Then she wrote another letter to Lillian Appleby, asking to meet her as soon as possible.

At the beginning of June, Flora caught the bus to Shire Street. At Lillian's request, she was going to call on her, as Lillian also had news for Flora. The plan Flora had formed for Will was going round in her head. And she was eager to discuss it with Lillian.

The June breeze caught her hair as she left the bus and made her way to Shire Street. The lane was full of budding trees and pretty, well-tended gardens. When Flora saw Lillian's house, her heart beat fast. The warm sunshine flowed over its creamy-coloured walls and lit up the tall glass windows. The faded, striped awnings were not yet opened but the troughs beneath were filled with young spring plants. The patch of cropped grass outside Lillian's studio was green and smooth and an easel and elderly, wrought-iron chairs were pulled up on the porch.

Flora stood still. She wanted to remember Michael's tall figure. The moment they had stood there and almost kissed.

'Flora!' The voice was Lillian's.

Jack and Ivy ran to greet her. She bent down as they came to sit at her feet, looking up with dark, glossy eyes. As she kissed the tops of their silky heads, she remembered Michael asking her if she liked dogs. He had laughed when she'd replied that she thought she did. Tears were close as she leaned her face into their soft fur.

'Oh, Flora, how good to see you.' Lillian embraced her.

'I hope you don't me inviting myself?'

'You know this house is always open to you, Flora. We don't see enough of each other as it is. Besides, I have some very good news for you.'

'Is it Michael?' Flora asked eagerly.

'Yes. Come along to the conservatory.'

This house hasn't changed, Flora thought fondly as she walked through the porch and cluttered entrance hall with its many coats hanging on pegs and boots stacked untidily under a wooden bench. The large painting on the wall of Julian Appleby in his Eastern clothes of crimson and orange still dominated the comfortable home that reminded Flora so keenly of Michael. Time hadn't changed anything here, and Flora was grateful for it.

'Jenny, bring in the tea,' Lillian called as they took their seats in the bright and airy conservatory. Plants of all kinds spilled from the many pots and the cushioned wicker chairs where Michael had sat with them were just as Flora remembered. Lillian, too, hadn't changed. Her thick, luxurious hair, as before, was pinned up at the back of her head. Her elegant flowing gown made her look even more stately.

Lillian's eyes went to the ring on Flora's left finger. 'When you both came to tell me of your engagement before Michael left,' she said softly, 'I couldn't have been happier. But it's no easy life, Flora, to be committed to a soldier at war. I was worried about you. Most women would think twice about such a responsibility, especially as Michael was wounded once and could be again.' Lillian smiled slowly. 'But you are not most women. I knew that the instant I met you.'

Flora felt she could tell everything to this kind woman. 'It's about Will that I've come. I went to visit him at the Bristol Infirmary.' Flora swallowed. 'He's lost an arm.'

'I am so sorry, Flora. Your dear friend Will has been through such terrible experiences at the Front.'

Flora began to tell Lillian of her request to send Will to Adelphi Hall, and how it had fallen on deaf ears. 'We were driven to Bristol by a young girl who is a Suffragette,' Flora explained. 'She advised me to follow the motto of the suffrage movement: "Deeds not words". So I tried my very best, but the matron refused to help as I'm not family, even though I told her about Hilda and me. So I wondered, if it is at all possible—'

'I shall help you, Flora,' Lillian said at once. 'I owe you so much. You saved my son's sanity. I do know some people I can ask who might be able to make a difference.'

Flora felt as though she could clap her hands. 'If you could. I'm sure Will would recover if he was close to Hilda. And I would travel up at weekends.'

Lillian nodded. 'I shall drive you there myself.'

This wonderful woman reminded Flora so much of Michael. She turned the gold band on her finger that she had worn especially for her visit today. The small diamonds felt like little glass eggs. Pinned on her green bolero was her butterfly brooch. All these, the house and Lillian brought her closer to Michael. 'And you have news of Michael?' Flora couldn't wait to ask.

'Yes.' Lillian took out two envelopes from her pocket. 'I received these last week. As you know, the army is very hush-hush about their movements in wartime. Michael asked a friend of his, an officer taking leave, to deliver these to me.'

'Does he say where he is?' Flora asked eagerly.

'Yes, but this information is for our eyes only. Your letter is of course private, my dear, and so please wait, if you can bear it, until you are alone to open it. Meanwhile let me tell you the news that I gleaned from mine.'

Flora's fingers trembled as she held the buff-coloured letter. Her name was printed on the front and addressed care of Lillian Appleby. She wanted to tear it open and read the precious words inside.

'As Michael suspected, he was sent to Salonika.' Jenny came with the tea and Lillian paused. 'Thank you, Jenny, that will be all for now.' The young girl nodded, smiling at Flora, as she left a tray of china on the low table. When she had gone, Lillian began again. 'Do you know anything about the Macedonian Front, Flora?'

'Only that our soldiers at Salonika are called "forgotten troops".' She recalled the patients talking about the confusion in Greece.

'In 1915, the Allies tried to help Serbia. But Germany, Austria-Hungary and Bulgaria won. However, their victory was complicated by the reluctance of Greece to join the war on either side.'

'Have they decided now?' Flora asked, butterflies in her tummy as she thought of Michael and the part he would have to play in a war that seemed so far away.

'King Constantine favours the Central Powers, but others in government side with the Allies.' Lillian took a breath. 'But almost as we speak, there is movement to exile the king and reunify the country under the guidance of Prime Minister Venizélos.'

'Is he on our side?'

'Michael thinks so. But the situation is delicate. The Ottoman powers are weak, but they are not finished. A wild animal is at its most dangerous when it is wounded.'

'Will Michael be safe?' It was the only question Flora wanted to ask.

'As safe as can be expected in such a volatile situation.'

Flora looked at the letter in her hands. She couldn't wait to open it.

'And so, Flora, we know that Michael was safe and well up until the time he gave these letters to his friend.'

There was a note of finality in Lillian's voice. Flora knew that they both would treasure these letters.

'Please enjoy a cup of tea and some of Jenny's pastries.'

Later, they spoke of Will again and Lillian's hope to call in a favour in order to help Will. She didn't say who, but Flora trusted Lillian to do exactly as she said.

'Thank you for helping Will,' Flora said when it was time to go.

'You are to be my daughter-in-law, Flora. But at this very minute, you are more like my own daughter. Michael and I love you very much.'

Flora held back a sob. It was the most wonderful thing in the world to be loved. She wondered if her own mother had loved her like this.

On the journey home, Flora held Michael's letter close. After she had read it that evening in the peace and quiet of the airey, she would place it with her shawl, her ring and the butterfly brooch. Together with these, she would never forget the affection she had been shown by Lillian today.

Chapter Thirty-Four

Lillian Appleby sat down to write. She drew out the pure white sheets of notepaper from her drawer and settled herself comfortably at her desk. Collecting her thoughts for a moment, she paused. Not only did she have a loving son, for whom she would do anything, but now a daughter too. Flora was as close to her as any daughter could be.

Lillian felt blessed. Julian had always wanted a large family. Unfortunately, fate hadn't granted them their wish. But, perhaps, on reflection, that was not a bad thing. Bankruptcy and scandal had not come easily to Lillian. And Julian, an inveterate gambler, had never taken care to provide for such an emergency. She glanced around her comfortable home. Comfortable, yes, luxurious, no. At least not by her late husband's extravagant standards. But this was hers. Hers and Michael's. A shelter in the storm after they had fallen from grace.

A few thoughts of regret skimmed through her mind. Regret for her son, who had to bear the sins of his father, and had borne them without complaint. At least Michael's schooling had been locked in trust by Grandfather Reggie.

'Ah, you found your way in the world,' she murmured softly as she thought of her young son. Though Michael had never warmed to following in his esteemed grandfather's medical footsteps. Instead, he had excelled at military school. How she admired him for his spirit and courage.

Julian would have been proud of his son. Yes, Michael had his father's courage but this was combined with unselfishness and loyalty.

'You must watch over him, Julian,' she whispered to the painting a few feet away. She looked into the smiling face of her late husband and both affection and an ache of his absence filled her. 'Do what you failed to do in this life.'

Lillian picked up her pen. In elegant, flowing handwriting, she addressed her letter to Lady Bertha Forsythe, Adelphi Hall, Surrey.

'Dear Bertie, though it is many years since we met, I was happy to hear that you have now generously created a sanctuary at Adelphi for our injured veterans of war. How I admire you!'

The hour passed swiftly. She wrote of her own situation and of Michael, engaged to a young woman of the island. Lillian included everything she knew of Flora, Hilda and Will and of their life at St Boniface's Orphanage.

Her request was stated clearly. She asked Bertie to exert her influence and bring William Boniface to

Adelphi Hall, in order to be near his friend Hilda Jones, who was in service there.

Lillian put down her pen. She considered her choice of words.

'Bertie, you owe me this,' she said aloud, frowning at the memory of Julian's passion for indulgently wild parties. Then, gazing up at the image of her husband, her eyes moistened. 'I may have forgiven you, Julian. But I haven't forgotten. Now it's time for you to do your part.'

Lillian lifted her hand and blew a gentle kiss from her fingers.

And it seemed, just fleetingly, that Julian acknowledged her.

Flora was thinking about Michael's letter as she stood in the kitchen of Hailing House. Mrs Bell was nearby shouting at the scullery maids. Flora's mind often drifted to his words, which had been full of love and of hope, too. Just a few lines, as he had been in a hurry to give the letters to his friend. But they had given her new life through the past few weeks. Whenever she had a moment, she thought of his promise to return. Of his hopes and dreams for the life they would lead together.

'Hold this steady for me, Flora!' Mrs Bell was pressing a large china bowl into her hands. 'You're all over the place this morning, my girl!'

Flora almost stood to attention. 'Sorry.' She grasped the bowl tightly.

Mrs Bell poured the mixture of whipped eggs, flour and salt into the bowl. 'Are you thinking of your young man, by any chance?'

Flora blushed. 'He wrote me a letter. It was given to Lillian – Mrs Appleby, Michael's mother.'

'And what did he have to say?' Mrs Bell licked the pancake mixture from her finger.

'Oh, not much.'

Mrs Bell let out a knowing chuckle. 'Whatever it was, he's put a twinkle in your eye.' She let out a slow breath. 'Now, what's this about Will going to Adelphi?'

'Michael's mother has received an invitation to visit Lady Bertha.'

'And you're going along too?'

'I hope to see Hilda.' Although she had written in advance, as usual Hilda had not replied.

Mrs Bell gave the mixture another whisk. 'Remember what happened last time? Hilda was none too pleased that you turned up.'

'But how could she not want to see me after all this time?' Flora insisted.

'I hope you're right, ducks. Now slice the bread, will you? And make them generous portions as I've baked more than enough to go round.'

Flora did as she was told, enjoying the rich smell of hot dough as she carved the bread. There was to be a Saturday soup kitchen at the house. The demand was so great for charity that Lady Hailing had taken on two more scullery maids besides Aggie to help with the catering.

Just then, the scullery maids burst in with Aggie. They all looked flustered. Aggie was puffing and her cap was tilted on her head. They all wore aprons spattered with the green-grey stains of the vegetable broth Mrs Bell had just cooked.

'Well, get yourselves trays and clear up the mess before you take this lot in!' Mrs Bell cried, hands on hips, shooing them back to the dining room.

'Do you want me to take a message to Hilda?' Flora asked as she got ready to leave.

'What message would that be?' The elderly lady was silent, then muttered, 'But you can take her sewing bag if you like. I put a few pennies inside it.'

Flora looked into Mrs Bell's plump, wholesome face. For a moment, their eyes met. Flora knew that she still cared deeply for Hilda.

The cook gave a rueful smile. 'And tell her I send me love.'

Flora felt happy as she leaped up the stairs to Hilda's old room. Mrs Bell hadn't forgotten Hilda after all.

The landings and corridors all smelled musty and were freezing cold even in the middle of June. When she opened the door to Hilda's room, she gave a soft sigh. Memories of the days when Hilda had first started at Hailing House flooded back. They had been happy in their new lives away from the orphanage. Hilda had been given a room of her own, even though it was in the attic. She had made it warm and homely with the help of Mrs Bell. Now the little room felt abandoned. The smell of the cook's polish had faded and a coat of dust lay over the furniture.

Hilda's sewing bag was on the bed. Flora held it close. Hilda didn't appear to be returning to Hailing House. This might be the last time that Flora would come in here.

Early on a warm Friday morning in July, Flora waited eagerly for Lillian to arrive in Michael's car. When she heard the noise of the rattling engine outside, she hurried up the airey's steps.

'All set?' asked Lillian from the driving seat. The hood was down and she was wearing a wide-brimmed hat and goggles.

Flora climbed into the passenger seat. She was careful to button up her coat and wind her scarf around her head.

'I'm glad to see you've dressed sensibly,' said Lillian approvingly.

Flora saw that her companion had chosen to wear hardy tweeds, leather driving gloves and long boots.

'This automobile has a mind of its own,' Lillian said as they leap-frogged forward. 'Now hold tight!'

Every so often the car would make a loud bang. When that happened, pedestrians stopped to stare at them. It wasn't very often that a woman was seen to be in command of a motor vehicle.

As they crossed the bridge, Lillian squeezed the rubber hooter. A bicyclist jumped down from his bike and glared at them. Lillian only laughed. 'This automobile is not at all like the van I drive for the voluntary service.'

'So you are a volunteer driver?' Flora held on tightly as they bounced along.

'After Michael left I decided to do my bit to help the war effort. I offered my services to a volunteer organization for women. Some are from the suffrage movement, just like the girl you told me about who drove you to Bristol. In my opinion, women make very good drivers. Perhaps one day I can teach you, Flora.'

'I'd like that.'

Flora smiled as Lillian expertly drove them through the streets. Lillian was like Sally: strong and independent. Flora was sure that if anyone could persuade Lady Bertha to take Will at Adelphi Hall, it was Lillian.

'It's very beautiful, isn't it?'

Flora and Lillian paused on a mossy, green bank overlooking Adelphi Hall. The house stood in all its glory amidst the green parklands. Its marble columns gleamed in the sunshine and Flora remembered how disappointed Hilda had been when they were instructed to take the tradesmen's route. Now, Lillian pointed the car towards the long winding path that led to the main entrance. But instead of the stately black car that had been parked there previously, army vehicles and ambulances were lined up outside.

'It looks very different to when I last visited over twenty years ago,' Lillian said wistfully as they climbed back into their rattling seats. Lillian hadn't turned off the engine for fear that it might not start again.

'Did you ever meet the earl?' Flora asked curiously.

'On one occasion, yes.'

'What was he like?'

Lillian smiled thoughtfully. 'In his youth, he stood out among men.'

'Hilda says he's never seen now.'

'He and his sister, Bertie, never really got on. She resented the fact that she could never inherit Adelphi. Lord William's first wife, Lady Amelia, tried to draw the family together. But after she died in childbirth, Bertie took advantage of her brother's grief. She filled the house with her fun-loving friends and spoiled Guy. Lord William went back into the army and became a very remote figure to his son and heir.'

'Why did the earl never remarry?' Flora asked.

Lillian sighed gently. 'The story is that he was entranced by a beautiful servant girl. Some say they were lovers and a child was conceived. Bertie discovered their secret and, fearing her brother would make this girl his wife, so making their offspring a rival to Guy, she had them, well, disposed of.'

'Do you mean she—'

Lillian nodded. 'So the story goes.'

'But could Lady Bertha really do such a thing to her own brother?'

Lillian shrugged. 'Who knows?'

Flora was shocked as they drove down the wide path to Adelphi Hall. Could this story be true? If so, then no wonder the poor earl shut himself away from such a cruel world!

Lillian parked the car behind one of the ambulances and they climbed out. Flora gave a soft gasp. Adelphi Hall was even more beautiful, more breathtaking, up close. Even its new role as a hospital couldn't diminish Adelphi Hall's grace and splendour.

Lillian took Flora's arm. 'I promise I will do my best for Will.'

Flora smiled. 'Thank you.'

Just then they heard a loud voice. The orders barked out were from a dark-haired, middle-aged woman addressing two stretcher-bearers. She wore a tunic, belted at the waist, with epaulettes on her shoulders and brass buttons down her jacket.

Lillian nudged Flora, and whispered, 'That's Bertie!'

Flora's mouth fell open.

Chapter Thirty-Five

'I'm sure you will want to join your friend.' Lady Bertha Forsythe looked down her long, aristocratic nose at Flora. 'Tell Mrs Burns to feed you. I shall send someone for you later.'

Lillian gave Flora a warm smile. 'I shan't be long, Flora.'

'Nonsense, Lillian,' interrupted Lady Bertha sharply. 'The girl will find plenty to occupy her below stairs. You and I have twenty years to catch up on. After lunch, I should like you to meet Guy. He was just a boy when you saw him last. And there is someone else too: his fiancée, Lady Gabriella.'

Flora returned Lillian's intimate smile. She knew that Michael's mother intended to do everything in her power to convince Lady Bertha to take Will.

As she walked round to the stables, Flora thought about Lady Bertha Forsythe. The question in her mind was, could this lady be capable of treachery and perhaps murder?

A cold chill went down Flora's spine as she recalled Mrs Bell's warning to Hilda. Now, Lillian had added much more. The stories were not proven to be true. But perhaps they weren't false either.

Flora glanced through the tall windows. She saw the tops of iron bedsteads, and a strong smell of disinfectant poured out of an open window. Adelphi Hall was now a place of rest and healing.

But perhaps that had not always been so.

From the attics of the house a tall figure surveyed the vehicles beneath. He was accustomed to the noise and activity now. And although he kept hidden from view, the arrival of the medical staff and wounded soldiers gave Lord William Calvey the greatest pleasure to watch. The house, at last, had regained its dignity. There was purpose to its life. No longer were there fanciful carriages containing their equally fanciful passengers pulling up, to be lavished and spoiled by Bertha and Guy. The war had achieved much more for Adelphi Hall than he could have done himself. Yes, he had been weak and a fool. He had allowed Bertha to usurp him, to destroy the foundations of his world. But nature had taken recourse and now his great house was living again as it truly should.

Then suddenly his blue eyes widened. A vehicle approached. Did he recognize it? Didn't he know it? A woman climbed out, tall and elegant, from the driver's position. His eyes were playing on her, studying her, but he could not tell from this position, four floors up, who she was. Then, with a dainty step, a young woman joined her from the passenger seat.

The earl took a sharp breath. His stomach tightened, gripped in a vice. Her figure was slim, her fair hair bounced in waves over her shoulders, and the way she moved . . .

He blinked hard, recalling the day he had raised his binoculars and seen her before. She'd been accompanied by a man, a young, upright fellow who had used a cane, and had tried to hurry to her as that fool of a son of his had almost ridden into her.

Yes, he'd only glimpsed her then.

But now he could see her clearly. The shape of her head, her curls, her soft, gentle movement, and he felt himself falling against the window, his heart clamouring to be out of his chest, his throat dry as he ached to call her back.

He pressed his face against the glass. His lips moved tremblingly as he followed her every movement as far as he could.

And when she had disappeared, he stayed there, wondering if he was dreaming, whispering in a halting breath, 'Constance . . . Constance . . .'

'We'd better look sharp,' Mrs Harris shouted across the kitchen. 'Lord Guy and Lady Gabriella are dining with Lady Bertha and her husband this evening.'

'Dinner for six served to the family this evening,' agreed Mrs Burns as she supervized the kitchen staff, sending the maids in all directions. 'Not in the dining room of course, but on the second floor. Now, Mrs Harris, what have we to prepare?'

'We've poultry, game and roast woodcock, Mrs Burns. Creamed spinach, braised celery and creamed potatoes, though I'll find something special to end with. Perhaps some jellies in those moulds we used before the war. Something big and colourful to take the eye. You can only do so much though, with catering for the sick too. It'll have to be tarts, blancmange and fruit from the greenhouse, so we'll need fresh supplies from the kitchen garden.'

'Her ladyship has another guest for high tea, an old friend from London, don't forget.'

'I forget nothing, Mrs Burns, don't worry on that score. Now perhaps you'd alert Mr Leighton to the drinks we'll serve with the meal?'

'I have it all in hand,' Mrs Burns said tersely, glancing sharply at the figure entering the rear door of the kitchen. 'Ah, and about time too.' She narrowed her gaze at Hilda, who stood waiting for orders as the maids and footmen flew in and out of the kitchen, barely giving her a glance. She usually felt out of place in the kitchen in her trousers and shirt, but what she'd overheard distressed her more deeply at that moment. Lady Gabriella! The name she dreaded to hear. How could Lord Guy turn his attention to such an ugly woman? Hilda had watched their cars arrive yesterday. Lady Gabriella and her maid, both spilling jewels and high fashion, even in wartime. With a troop of servants following like a circus parade.

'Are you listening to me, girl?' Mrs Burns demanded.

'Yes, Mrs Burns.'

'Here is your list. See Peter, and make certain you bring Mrs Harris all she needs.'

'Yes, Mrs Burns.'

'I expect you to continue with your duties today.' Mrs Burns drew herself up. 'I understand her ladyship has kindly permitted you a visitor?'

'Yes, my friend, Flora.' It was clear to Hilda that Mrs Burns disapproved. But at the same time, she could not ignore Lady Bertha's command that she was to be allowed two hours off in Flora's company.

'Very inconvenient, when we have guests.'

'Sorry, Mrs Burns.'

'Remember, Mrs Harris' list comes first. Now off you go.'

Hilda left the hot kitchen, pleased to be outside in the sunshine. Though not pleased to be considered unworthy to serve at table, as she had done before her accident.

Hilda made her way towards the greenhouses, thinking of her lover. If only he were that: her lover, and hers alone. Why did he come for her so infrequently now? And when he did, there was hardly a word passed between them. He took her roughly when and wherever he wanted. Though never when Lady Gabriella was visiting. The times they were together were growing fewer and fewer. She ached for him. She longed for him. What had happened to their love?

'Hilda!' A soft voice came across the lawn. She turned and saw Flora. Hilda's eyes filled with tears.

'Flora!'

They embraced and Hilda smelled Flora's fragrance, sniffed the scent in her hair and saw the blush on her cheeks. She was suddenly envious. Flora was a reminder of how she once looked, of freedom and of the island.

'It's been such a long time. Are you better now?'

'Yes.'

'I've missed you.' Flora gazed down at Hilda's trousers. 'Hilda, what are you wearing?'

'Sometimes I'm asked to collect the vegetables. Not always, of course, only when staff are short.' Hilda lied, knowing that Flora thought she was still a housemaid.

'Why haven't you written?'

'I don't get much time.'

'But Hilda—'

'You can come with me, if you like.'

Flora threaded her arm through Hilda's. 'I've got so much to tell you. Something about Will.'

'Will? Is he all right?' Hilda felt guilty. She hadn't written to Will either.

'He might be coming to Adelphi.'

Hilda stopped still. 'Will? Coming here?'

'Hilda, I'm sorry to tell you that he's lost an arm.'

The news was so shocking, so sudden, that Hilda burst into tears. Flora put her arms around her sobbing friend. 'I should have said in my letter.'

'Why didn't you?'

'I wanted the whole thing to be a surprise.'

'Losing an arm *is* a surprise,' Hilda sobbed.

Flora gave her a handkerchief. 'Michael's mother knows Lady Bertha and is going to ask if Will can come here to convalesce.'

Hilda blew her nose. 'You'd better tell me all about it, while I get what Mrs Harris wants.'

'I'll help you.' Once again, Flora drew close.

Hilda only wanted to weep, though she held her tears in check. Time had passed her by. Her friend had blossomed while she was left behind. She felt abandoned by Lord Guy and bullied by Mrs Burns. Even Gracie had been made up to a housemaid. It just wasn't fair.

Miserably, Hilda led the way to the greenhouse, hoping Peter and the boys were working in the fields. She didn't want them to give away her secret that she was just a glorified skivvy.

'I'll use my influence to have him brought here from Bristol at once.' Lady Bertha stood with Lillian Appleby under the vaulted ceiling of the vast interior gallery of Adelphi Hall. Beneath them the staircase wound down to the reception hall, which was filled with noisy strangers. Bertha missed the old days: the parties and excitement, the splendid gowns and perfumes of her friends and the gilt-framed paintings on the walls, now removed and packed away with all of Adelphi Hall's treasures. Only the golden lion emblazoned on the Calvey coat-of-arms remained on display. A proud relic of the past; a past that, it seemed, had now returned to haunt her.

Trying to hide her fear, Bertha's agile mind raced. This boy that Lillian spoke of, could he be the one – could he? He was the right age, almost twenty. A Boniface brat. Bertha's mind slipped back two decades to her brother's refusal to give up the servant girl. William was a fool. A wealthy fool, but a sentimental one. He'd had a perfectly acceptable wife in Amelia, who gave him an heir before she died. Why endanger Guy's inheritance by wedding a simple-minded peasant? If only William had seen sense. There would have been no need for the measures she had to take . . .

'Thank you, Bertie. Will is an orphan and has had a bad deal in life.'

'And he knows one of our housemaids?'

'Yes, Hilda Jones. Together with Flora, the three of them were Boniface children.'

'Remind me again of what you wrote? The girl who accompanied you today is your son's fiancée?'

Lillian Appleby looked into her eyes without blinking. 'Flora is very lovely, don't you think?'

Bertha did not think so at all. Had Lillian taken leave of her senses? To condone a union between her only son and an orphanage brat was complete madness! 'Then congratulations are in order to you and your son,' Bertha replied tightly.

'Time drags, of course, as we wait for Michael to return from the war. You must be relieved that Guy is well out of it. How is he these days?'

Bertha shrugged indifferently. 'He has his moments. The last time he had an episode was in spring of last year.

He was out hunting when an attack overcame him. Fortunately, his horse brought him back safely.' Bertha omitted to mention that her nephew's quarry had not been animal but human. The girl hadn't perished but was found to be injured. Guy had drunk far too much wine and, as usual, gone to extremes. If only he could learn to be more discreet.

'And your brother, the earl, what of him?' Lillian enquired.

'Much the same!' Bertha snapped. Talk of William always made her nervous. He was a threat, always had been. But a weak one. Choosing to remove himself from the family gave her the upper hand. Let him sit and dream of his glorious past, his lost love and their bastard son. They were nothing more than relics of the past. A past that Bertha was determined to keep hidden. When this boy arrived at Adelphi, in the guise of concern for his welfare, she would speak to him and decide what she must do.

'Adelphi hasn't changed,' Lillian was saying as she gazed down into the busy hall. 'Still as beautiful as ever, despite the hospital disruption.'

'We suffer in silence,' Bertha murmured piously, 'for Britain's sake.'

'How noble,' Lillian responded softly.

Bertha glanced out of the corner of her eye. Was she being mocked? Reluctantly giving Lillian Appleby the benefit of the doubt, she gestured ahead. 'Shall we go? I've asked Guy and Gabriella to meet us in the library for tea.'

'Is Gabriella staying the weekend?' Lillian asked as they turned to walk along the richly carpeted hall.

'Yes, we are to announce their engagement to friends.'

'Then I mustn't keep you long.'

'Oh, perhaps you should stay?' Bertha said without enthusiasm. Lillian's company was tiresome. Now that the favour of the boy was done, there was little else to be said. But she supposed she must go through the motions.

'I must take Flora back soon.' Lillian Appleby smiled. A sweet, tolerant smile that made Bertha feel undermined. She had never really liked Julian's wife, but had tolerated her when their lives in the city had coincided. It was Julian who had brought them together and Julian who had separated them. Julian, with his devilish charm and good looks and his lean, energetic body that never tired between the sheets . . .

Bertha wondered smugly if Lillian had ever guessed they were lovers.

Chapter Thirty-Six

Flora, Hilda and Gracie sat on the benches in the pretty folly by the kitchen gardens. Flora had not been invited into the house, nor did she wish to go. The few hours with Hilda in the open air had been most enjoyable. Now, they were ending the afternoon with Gracie who had brought a tray spilling over with succulent slices of Mrs Harris' freshly cooked gammon. To accompany this were fresh cheeses, sweet salads, warmly baked bread and ripe red strawberries.

'Mrs Harris has gone to a lot of trouble,' Flora said to Gracie as they drank the pressed apple juice from thick glass tumblers. 'Please tell her how much I enjoyed it.'

'I'll tell 'er,' Gracie said as she stuffed the last strawberry into her mouth. 'But she probably won't hear. Too busy sweating over the stove for tonight.'

'What about tonight?' Hilda asked, looking bored.

'Ain't you 'eard?' Gracie's pale face flushed.

'No.' Hilda sat up.

'Don't matter. It ain't nothing.'

Hilda looked thunderous. Gracie prepared to leave, and Hilda pulled her down again.

'You'd better tell me, Gracie,' Hilda said threateningly. 'Or I'll go to Mrs Harris meself and find out.'

'Ouch. You're 'urting me arm.'

'Well then?'

'Everyone knows. I thought you did,' Gracie said. 'It's the master and Lady Gabriella. They're . . . they're—'

'What are they?' Hilda's brown eyes were fixed on Gracie's face.

'They are engaged.'

Flora saw Hilda blink and shake her head as if she hadn't heard.

'Engaged?' Hilda repeated, her bottom lip trembling. She stared at Gracie.

'I ain't tellin' fibs,' replied Gracie, nervously licking her lips. She pushed the wisps of mousey fringe under her cap. 'They're to be wed.'

'That's very good news, isn't it?' Flora broke the strained silence. 'A marriage at Adelphi. How lovely that will be.'

'She's plain and dowdy and just horrible!' Hilda spat.

'She has a mare's girth,' Gracie pointed out, 'just right for child-bearing.'

Flora stared at her friend. They had enjoyed such a lovely afternoon. And Hilda had been touched when Flora had gone back to the car for her sewing bag, delivered with Mrs Bell's message. They had discussed Will and, despite Hilda still pleading a weak stomach for hospitals, she had promised to visit Will frequently, if she was allowed.

But now, Hilda's change in mood was evident. What did this engagement mean to her?

'I've got to go.' Gracie piled the dishes on the tray. 'It's been nice seeing yer, Flora.'

'You too, Gracie.'

'And if you can knock some sense into 'er 'ead, please do!' Gracie nodded at Hilda and quickly left.

'What did she mean?' Flora asked when they were alone.

'Search me.' Hilda looked under her brown lashes.

'Hilda, what's wrong?'

Hilda sniffed, wiping the end of her nose with the back of her hand. 'Oh, Flora, how could he do such a thing to me?'

'Who?' Flora said, handing Hilda a handkerchief.

'I can't say.' Hilda dabbed her eyes. 'You'd tell me I was mad. Or worse, just bad.'

'I'd never do that.'

'Flora, I love him,' Hilda spluttered.

'Who?' Flora asked again.

'Lord Guy, of course.'

'But you can't love a lord. He's marrying Lady Gabriella.'

'He doesn't want to, I'm sure,' Hilda argued. 'He's only marrying her because his aunt says he must, for the money. It's like that with rich people. If there's no money in the family, you have to marry into it.'

'But Adelphi is very wealthy,' Flora said in surprise.

'Gracie told me it's the old earl who holds the purse strings and he won't let 'em go to his family. Not till he dies, anyway.'

Flora sighed heavily. 'Hilda, even if Lord Guy wasn't marrying Lady Gabriella, he couldn't marry you. What makes you think he would?'

'Don't you remember I wrote and told you about a special person?'

Flora blinked. 'I thought you meant Lady Bertha. And Mrs Bell thought it was a footman.'

'It was Lord Guy. Oh, Flora, I'm so unhappy. I ain't ever been as unhappy as this before.'

'But he can't love a servant, Hilda. It just wouldn't be right.'

Hilda jumped up, her cheeks bright with anger. 'Well, he loves me! I know he does.'

'Hilda, you'll look back on this one day and smile.'

'No I won't. Not ever.'

'This is just a girlish crush.' Flora reached out.

'You don't understand,' Hilda replied, roughly pushing her away.

'What don't I understand?'

'I'm going to have his baby!' Hilda screamed, her eyes bright with defiant tears. 'That's what you don't understand!'

Dusk was settling amongst the trees and over the hills as Lillian drove them back to London. Flora sat in shocked silence.

'Flora, what's wrong?' Lillian asked.

'I don't know if I should say.'

'It will be kept in strict confidence,' Lillian assured her.

'It's Hilda . . . she thinks she's expecting.'

Lillian turned and gasped softly. 'Is she certain?'

'Yes.'

'Has she seen a doctor?'

'No. But she *is* feeling sick and has missed her monthly.'

Lillian looked thoughtful. 'Please don't be upset when I ask if Hilda knows who the baby's father is.'

Flora hesitated. Should she tell Lillian what she knew? Lillian was, after all, Lady Bertha's friend. 'Hilda says she has been seeing Lord Guy.'

'But Lord Guy is marrying Lady Gabriella!' Lillian exclaimed.

'Yes, but Hilda still loves him.'

Lillian was silent, staring at the road ahead. 'What is she going to do?'

Flora shook her head. 'Hilda doesn't seem to know.'

'She will lose her position at Adelphi.' Lillian turned the wheel sharply. 'The family will pull together and deny the affair. This is how it works in high places.'

'But he should be made to admit what he's done.'

'That will never happen,' Lillian replied tightly. 'Bertie said that Guy's last seizure was in spring of last year. Isn't that when Hilda was ill?'

'She told me today she wasn't ill, but had broken her arm.' Flora drew the blanket over her knees as it was growing cold. 'It was after this that he was kind to her.'

'A guilty conscience on his part?' Lillian drove a little faster.

'It could be, although Hilda doesn't think of it like that.'

'I wish I had known this afternoon. I could have challenged Bertie over the affair,' Lillian said fiercely.

'But you said the family would close ranks and deny it. And anyway, if you had, Lady Bertha might refuse to take Will.'

Lillian was silent as she gripped the wheel. Flora knew they were both aware that it would be Hilda who bore the consequences alone. Oh, if only Hilda hadn't allowed that evil man his way. But even now, Hilda believed he was in love with her.

Flora wanted to ask Lillian to slow the car down. The hedgerows and bushes were flying by. She knew Lillian was very angry.

For Flora, the time passed slowly as she waited to hear news of Will. As she was so concerned for Hilda, she had taken Dr Tapper into her confidence and asked him if he could think of a solution. But though they talked at length about Hilda's plight, there seemed no answer. Everyone knew that if a girl got into trouble in service, she was usually sent as far away from the family as possible.

'But where will she go?' Flora had continually worried. 'What will happen to her child?'

'Perhaps Lady Hailing will have her back,' the doctor suggested as they spoke a few words together in the middle of a busy surgery. 'But as for the infant . . .'

'Will it be taken away from her?'

The doctor glanced sternly at her but said nothing. He couldn't predict the future. And what a future it would be for Hilda, with no home and disgraced. Lord Guy would never admit his part in it and Hilda would be left to fend for herself.

The tears came close as she thought of Hilda and of all her dreams of becoming a lady's maid. If only Hilda hadn't given her heart to someone like Lord Guy.

But Hilda still believed he loved her, and would make her his wife when she told him about the baby.

If only that were so.

Chapter Thirty-Seven

At the end of July, Lillian arrived with news. 'Will is safely at Adelphi,' she said as she joined Flora and the doctor in the surgery. The day had been very busy, but now the waiting room was empty.

'How is he? Do you know?' Flora asked anxiously.

'I received a telegram from Bertie this morning. She said that she would make sure Will had the best of attention from the top doctors.'

'Did she talk about Hilda?'

Lillian took Flora's arm, her elegant figure and gentle manner reminding Flora of Michael. 'I am afraid, my dear, that if Bertie knows of Hilda's condition, she will not admit to it. The housekeeper will be given the task of sending Hilda away. And then—'

'How can she?' Tears burned in Flora's eyes. 'Why doesn't she make Lord Guy face up to what he's done?'

'You know the answer to that, Flora. He is to marry Lady Gabriella and there can be no scandal.'

Flora bit down on her lip in an effort not to weep. It was so unfair. One law for the rich and another for the poor.

'Come along, Flora,' the doctor said quietly as he got up from his desk. 'You aren't responsible for Hilda now. Nor can you do any more for Will. Your two friends chose their paths in life and will have to act accordingly.'

This did not make Flora feel any better as she said goodbye to Lillian and left for the airey that night. She sat quietly with her treasures: her precious shawl and Michael's letter, the butterfly brooch and her engagement ring. She thought of Michael and prayed for his safety.

Dr Tapper had given Flora the day off. It was August the 1st and Flora's eighteenth birthday. She had put on Hilda's blue suit and was going to Mass. She would ask the priest for prayers to be said for her friends. It was all she could do to help them.

When a tap came at the door, she was surprised to find a young boy there. He was dressed shabbily in a well-worn shirt and short trousers, but he had a clean face.

'Are yer Flora Shine?'

'Yes.'

'Sister Superior sent me. You got to come now.'

Flora frowned. 'To the orphanage?'

'Yer.'

'Do you know why?'

'No, but do I get a sixpence for running the message?'

Flora nodded and went back inside. When she came out, he grabbed the money and ran up the steps.

'Wait for me, I'll come with you,' shouted Flora, but all she saw was the back of his grubby boots.

As it was Wednesday, she caught the bus. Flora wondered what Sister Superior could want. Perhaps it was something to do with her birthday. Was there something else Sister Superior wanted to give her now she had reached eighteen?

Victoria Park was bathed in sunlight. It was a very hot day. She walked past the rows of identical houses and saw the convent's tall bell tower. As usual, her heart beat faster at the sight of the place she had known as her only home. She walked briskly towards the red-brick building with its stained-glass windows.

The heavy iron gate creaked as she opened it. At the big double doors with the shining crucifix, she took a breath. As she stood waiting, she wondered if now was the time to ask Sister Superior about Hilda's baby. After all, Hilda had grown up here. St Boniface's was far better than the workhouse or an institution. Perhaps the nuns could even find work for Hilda, just as they had for Hilda's mother. It would be history repeating itself, but at least Hilda wouldn't be forced into something dreadful. Like a life on the streets.

Flora's mouth dropped open as she sat in the convent visitors' room. She couldn't believe the sight before her eyes. Was it a holy apparition? Had Our Lady come down to answer her prayers?

'God's blessing on you, Flora.' Sister Patricia, reed-thin and slightly stooped, stood in front of her. Her hands were clasped around her rosary as she made the sign of the cross. Sliding the rosary under the folds of her habit, she stepped forward.

Flora stood up. She wanted to run forward and embrace her old teacher. But she knew that nuns didn't invite familiarity. Instead, Flora's eyes filled with bright, happy tears.

'What a beautiful young woman you have become.'

'I didn't think I would ever see you again,' Flora mumbled, as she cleared her throat.

'Nor I, you.' Sister Patricia's slender face and high cheekbones under the paper-thin skin made her look almost angelic. Her bright blue eyes were as radiant as ever. The white wimple followed the lines of her fragile bone structure and the black habit covered her entire body down to the floor. Flora thought how timeless she looked.

They sat down on the wooden chairs at the polished table. Flora had expected to see Sister Superior. And now, she was gazing into the face of the person who had taught her all she knew and encouraged her to help in the convent's infirmary. Also, the one person who could tell her about her past.

'Are you happy, Flora?' the nun asked quietly, sitting upright, her hands folded in her lap.

'Yes, sister. Very.'

'Mother Superior has told me that Dr Tapper is very pleased with you. And I'm glad to hear that you settled into life at his surgery. During the four years I have spent at the Motherhouse in France, I've prayed for you.'

Flora felt honoured. Sister Patricia had always taken an interest in her and now Flora knew this interest had continued after she'd left the orphanage. 'Thank you, sister. And I've prayed for you too.'

A soft smile touched the nun's lips. 'Then your prayers helped to bring me safely back to England with the help of our French brothers.' She hesitated, lowering her eyes. 'Many of my dear sisters were not so fortunate when the Motherhouse was . . . taken.' She gave a soft breath, then added calmly, 'Mother Superior tells me that Will Boniface is fighting at the Front and Hilda Jones is in service to the Talbott Estate.'

Flora nodded eagerly. She wanted to ask about the shawl, but knew there would be a right time. 'Yes, but Will was wounded and brought back to Bristol Infirmary. He lost an arm in the fighting.'

'I am very sorry to hear that.'

'But now he is at Adelphi Hall,' Flora rushed on, 'where Hilda can visit him every day.'

'Adelphi!' Sister Patricia exclaimed. 'He is at *Adelphi Hall*?'

'Yes, sister. You see, part of the house is used as a hospital for the war-wounded and—'

'My child,' Sister Patricia interrupted sharply. 'This is not good news.'

'But Sister Patricia—'

Once again, the nun interrupted her. 'Before you say anything more, I have something important to tell you.' She took a quick breath and looked steadily into Flora's eyes.

'Is it about my mother?'

'I opened the convent door to your mother. She stood there, as you did today, a child in her arms. She was desperate and terrified. After she told me her story, I took the infant, wrapped in the shawl. I gave her my promise that I would do all in my power to see that the child was kept safe.'

Flora felt as though the years were falling away. As though, finally, she was coming to know who she really was. 'B . . . but why . . .? Why was I not safe?'

Sister Patricia answered softly. 'That child was not you, Flora. It was Will, your half-brother. The year was December 1897. His father was the fourth Earl of Calvey. And his mother, a nurse to the young Lord Guy Calvey, was your mother.'

Chapter Thirty-Eight

Flora stared into the nun's blue eyes. 'Will – *our* Will – is the son of the old earl? Is my half-brother?' she said incredulously.

Sister Patricia nodded. 'Your mother, Constance, and the earl fell in love. But this love between a nurse and her high-born employer could never be. So the earl took your mother to safety, to a trusted farmer and his wife. There she gave birth to her first child, William. But the earl, a distinguished soldier, had to return to his regiment. While he was away, Lady Bertha Forsythe took steps to dispose of your mother and the baby. Fortunately, Constance escaped before the deed could be done. She fled to London and arrived here, at the orphanage.'

Flora shook her head in bewilderment. Could this be true? Was this incredible story her story too? 'But, if Will was that child,' she asked, 'who am I?'

The nun replied slowly. 'Your mother was in terror of her son being found by Lady Bertha. And so I took the boy in and arranged with the priest to find shelter for

Constance. Over the next year and a half, I heard no more. But then on August the 1st 1899, a man arrived, with you in his arms, the child of his marriage to Constance Shine.'

Flora's mind was whirling. 'Who was he?'

'Your father, a tavern keeper, protected your mother. He told me they were very happy for the short time they were together. They had been blessed with you, a daughter, but Constance was suffering from consumption. Your father had contracted the disease from her and the poor man himself was sick, close to death. Unable to safeguard your future, he brought you here to be reunited with your half-brother.'

'What was my father's name?'

'He was John Devonish, a good Catholic, and a kind and gentle man. I cannot say if your mother loved him as much as he loved her. But he told me they both loved and treasured you.'

Flora closed her eyes and opened them. Was Sister Patricia about to disappear like a vision? Could all this be true? Her father was a tavern keeper called John Devonish and will was her half-brother. He had taken her to the orphanage for safety.

Then, as what she had been told fell into place, Flora gave a soft gasp. 'But Will! Will is at Adelphi!'

'And the very last place he should be,' agreed the nun.

'It was me who wanted him there.' Flora felt sick. 'What am I to do?'

Sister Patricia opened her thin, pale hands. 'Should

the family discover his true identity, his life may be in danger.'

Flora's mind went to Constance and the terror she must have felt as she fled Adelphi Hall. 'If the earl really loved my mother, he would have married her.'

'Perhaps he was going to. Who is to know what really happened between them? But you must warn Will, at the very least, Flora. He must leave Adelphi.'

Flora sat silently. Thoughts were tumbling around in her mind. How could she help Will?

Hilda was deeply distressed. She had been feeling very sick. She knew the baby was making her feel ill.

'What's up?' Gracie asked as she walked into the greenhouse.

'Nothing.'

'Mrs 'Arris wants more spuds.'

'I dug up two full baskets this morning.'

'Well, it wasn't enough.'

Hilda's back ached from the digging and her hands were rough from the long hours of hard toil in the gardens. Peter never seemed to be around to help her and the two young boys were now in the fields bringing in the crops. Hilda hated country life. She hated the fresh air that burned her lungs on cold mornings and the heat that made her shirt rough and wet with perspiration. She wanted to return to the house where she belonged.

'Come on, I'll 'elp you.' Gracie grabbed a basket from

the work bench. 'Mrs 'Arris is chasing her tail. We'll get it in the neck if she don't get what she wants.'

They walked together from the greenhouse to the vegetable plots. The green leaves of the rhubarb, carrots and potatoes were like an emerald sea. The smell of the herbs melted into the evening air and caused Hilda's stomach to heave.

'I've got to go to the house, to see my friend, Will,' Hilda said as she dug the fork into the soft soil and pulled up the vegetables. 'He's lost an arm at the Front.'

'And 'e's 'ere at Adelphi?' Gracie asked in surprise as she shook off the clumps of soil.

'Flora wrote to say he had arrived from Bristol.' Hilda wiped the sweat from her forehead with the back of her dirty hand. 'At least I'll see inside Adelphi again.'

Gracie dropped the potatoes into the basket. 'It's not the same place no more.'

'No, but it won't always be a hospital.'

'Who knows what'll 'appen when Lady Gabriella moves in.'

'What?' Hilda put down the fork.

'Well, it'll all change after they're married. We'll 'ave to get ready for her family and friends staying. And Mrs Burns is preparing the nursery again.' Gracie brushed the dirt from her apron and looked at Hilda who was staring at her with startled brown eyes. 'I mean, there'll be babies on the way. That's what this marriage is all about. Making sure there's more heirs.'

'But he's already got—' Hilda stopped on the point of revealing her secret.

'What?' Gracie narrowed her eyes. 'Are you ill again?'

Hilda felt dizzy as well as sick. Lord Guy and Lady Gabriella. It just couldn't be. Her hand went to her stomach, to the flat surface under her trousers that would soon be rounded with her lover's baby.

'Listen, if I were you, I'd sit down. You don't look too good to me.' Gracie lifted the bags full of potatoes. 'Feels like a ton weight, these do. But never you mind 'elping me. You look as though you'll blow over in a puff of wind.' She went to walk away, then stopped. ''Ilda, are you sure you're all right?'

Hilda was very far from all right. If only she could tell her master about the child they had conceived. He needn't marry anyone but her. Oh, where was he? She had waited for him, in the garden, at the stables and in the fields. But he never rode out to find her.

After Gracie had gone, she made her way to the greenhouse. Here she stood under the sweltering panes of dirty glass. She longed to look beautiful once again. Hilda hurried to the pump outside. She swept off her cap and splashed cold water over her face. There was no soap for her hands but she scrubbed them as best as she could. When she was done, she went to one of the small sheds that Peter kept for his tools. On a lower shelf, she had hidden her uniform and a clean white apron. If ever Lord Guy had come to the gardens, she had planned to change quickly. Even her housemaid's uniform was better than these filthy trousers and shirt.

In a few minutes, Hilda was dressed. She brushed her

hair until all the tangles were gone and gazed into the broken oblong of glass that she used as a mirror.

Hilda smiled. She was pleased with what she saw. Her complexion was healthy. Her cheeks were rosy. Her brown eyes sparkled.

She was born to be a lady. And vowed never to wear those trousers again!

From a safe distance behind a curtained screen, Lady Bertha Forsythe watched the new patient and his visitor. She recognized the girl, Hilda Jones, at once. The maid who had caught Guy's attention, which had led to such inconvenient disruption below stairs. Fortunately, Mrs Burns had resolved the problem. Nevertheless, Bertha felt that the servant, who apparently knew the injured man, could not be trusted. She was pretty in a common way and far too forward for Bertha's liking. Easy prey for Guy. And now that her nephew was betrothed to Gabriella, an incident of that sort must not happen again.

Bertha studied the sick boy who sat in the Bath chair. She had not expected to see such an instant resemblance, and it had shocked her. She had spoken to him, enquiring after his health. She had gazed into his eyes and seen his mother's looking back at her. The clear, brilliant blue under the pouches of swollen skin had made her recoil. It had taken all her courage to face him – and smile. Of course, she had to smile, to show concern, and to confirm the information that she had been given by Lillian Appleby.

A bastard child. An orphanage boy, carrying the name

of his institution. Twenty years of age this coming December. Short, blond hair that was slowly growing back into curls over the unsightly bulge on his head. *Her* blonde curls, her smile. And her son.

How could this travesty have come about? Bertha had been assured that her brother's lover was dead, and her child dead with her. What trickery had returned him to the place where he was conceived? And William, her brother, a recluse at Adelphi Hall and far removed from life, but nevertheless this boy's father!

Bertha shivered. A cold, fearful sweat prickled her skin. An heir to Adelphi – her Adelphi. An illegitimate heir, but a threat. After Amelia had died, she had nurtured Guy as her own. He had been a weak, self-indulgent and greedy child. Perfect for her purposes. She had given him freedom, satisfied his lust for life and women that knew no bounds. She had made Guy dependent on her. Adelphi Hall was hers and always had been.

Bertha's eyes sparkled. Why couldn't William have taken Constance Shine to bed and be done with it? She was just a servant! The day William had told Bertha that he intended to marry the trollop and give their bastard child a legitimate claim to Adelphi Hall had been the day when Bertha's world had almost collapsed.

'Damn the man,' Bertha said under her breath. 'Damn Constance Shine and her brat for ever.'

'Lady Bertha?'

She jumped. Turning quickly, she found one of the white-coated doctors beside her. 'Yes? What is it?'

'There are many more casualties arriving from Ypres.'

'We can't take them all. You have almost all of the second floor now. And Lord William will *not* be moved from his quarters.'

'I was hoping we might stretch to temporary accommodation. Perhaps the servants' quarters?'

Bertha gave a stifled laugh. 'And where would the servants be sent?'

The doctor, young and wearing thick-rimmed spectacles, gave a light shrug. 'Not all their accommodation, of course. Just a few rooms on the lower floor.'

'You will have to speak to Mr Leighton and Mrs Burns about that.'

'Thank you, Lady Bertha.' He turned to go.

'One minute!'

He swivelled on his heel, looking alarmed.

'The boy, the patient from Bristol . . .'

The doctor nodded. 'Here at your request, Lady Bertha. I'm afraid the long journey has exhausted him.'

'He looks a weakling to me,' Bertha agreed. 'What is your opinion of his condition?'

The young man was thoughtful. After a moment, he said, 'The blood loss from his injury has not yet been resolved. And who can tell if the arm will heal?'

'Will he survive?'

'I shouldn't like to give an opinion.'

Bertha nodded, her face drawn and tight. 'That is all.'

When she was alone, she peered back through the screen. William Boniface was weak . . . weak . . . his recovery uncertain. And by the looks of it, as his head flopped back on the pillow as the girl talked to him, his strength was ebbing away.

She must act quickly before his death could not be explained by natural causes.

Chapter Thirty-Nine

It was late afternoon. The rain beat down on the roof of Michael's car and Flora gripped the seat. Lillian was driving fast through the slippery streets of London. Once again, Lillian had come to Flora's aid. After Flora had left the orphanage, she had caught the bus to Poplar and run to Lillian's house. Lillian, she knew, was the only person she could turn to for help.

And now, they were speeding to Adelphi Hall once again in Michael's car. The skies were black with storm clouds and lightening cut the dark sky in half. Rain splashed noisily on the windscreen making it difficult to see.

'Tell me again all that you know from Sister Patricia,' Lillian said, her eyes narrowed towards the rain-soaked road ahead of them.

At Lillian's house, Flora had hurriedly explained her story, and now she did so again.

'And it was only Sister Patricia who knew of your past?' Lillian asked.

'She said she had planned to tell me and Will when we were older. But then she was trapped in France.'

'Your mother must have loved the earl very much.'

'But did she love my father, John Devonish?'

Lillian smiled softly. 'There are many kinds of love, Flora.'

'I hope she found happiness before she died.' A little tear came to Flora's eye. She wiped it away quickly.

'And now Will is returned to Adelphi. What hand of fate has brought him there?' Lillian wondered aloud as she drove into the countryside.

'I thought it was for the best,' Flora said miserably.

'And it would have been,' Lillian said, reaching over to squeeze her hand. 'I only hope we aren't too late.'

Flora couldn't stop thinking about Sister Patricia's warning. Lady Bertha had tried to kill her mother. Would she try to kill again?

Flora closed her eyes, unable to believe this was happening.

There was just one night nurse to supervise the ward.

Bertha had issued orders for the new casualties from Ypres to be put in some of the servants' quarters. She knew the hospital staff would be busy.

Most of the patients were sleeping. She moved cautiously forward in the shadows, watching the nurse go to each bed. She swallowed nervously. This was her opportunity. She would put an end to any threat to Guy. Her nephew was her guarantee to a glorious future. Once the war was over, the house would be returned to her. Gabriella and Guy would do as she told them. There would be parties, hunts, balls and entertainments as befitted such a great estate. She would wear fine clothes and reclaim her true position as mistress of Adelphi Hall.

And William would die, old and shrivelled away in his attics.

Her confidence returned as she moved forward, slipping silently behind the curtain. She waited for the nurse to leave the room, then stepped out.

Bertha crept noiselessly towards the boy's bed. He was unable to defend himself. He was weak and she was strong. She would do as she had planned.

She took a pillow from an empty bed, grateful for the darkness. There was little light from the trembling glow of the oil lantern.

The boy murmured in his sleep. William Boniface struggled to breathe. His mouth was open as he tried to draw air.

Bertha stood at the bedside, watching. For a moment, she saw Constance Shine, the servant who had stolen her brother's heart. The girl who had given life to this bastard child and would have made herself mistress of Adelphi Hall.

Bertha lifted the pillow and placed it over the boy's face.

'What's wrong with the engine?' Flora asked as they stood in the rain in the quiet village street. The engine had spluttered then silently come to a halt.

'I think it must just be wet.' Lillian pulled her coat around her. The rain trickled down from her elegant head of hair which was pulled into a pleat at the back of her head. 'We'll have to find someone to help us.'

Flora shivered. She too was soaked through. They had turned the starting handle at the front of the car and all it did was rattle. She stood in a puddle, her boots letting in the water. There had been no time before they left to dress for wet weather. She was wearing her skirt, blouse and jacket and Lillian had found one of Michael's old raincoats in the back of the car. It was far too big, but now it served to protect her from the downpour.

'Let's ask at the post office.' Lillian nodded to the small shop on the other side of the road. It was in the middle of a row of village shops: a haberdashery, a grocer's, a café and a tobacconist. They hurried across the shimmering street and breathlessly arrived in the tiny shop.

'Our car has broken down,' Lillian said to the person behind the counter. The middle-aged man, with dark hair and a parting down the middle, frowned out of the window. 'Is there someone who can help us?'

'There's no one who knows about them things, ma'am. We only got horses here. There's a smithy down the road, though I don't think he'd be much help.'

'Doesn't anyone know about automobiles?' Lillian pleaded.

'A bit new-fangled for the sticks, ma'am. You from the city?'

Flora and Lillian both nodded. Flora felt the rain dripping down her neck. She was making a puddle on the floor of the shop.

'How far you going?'

'We're on our way to Adelphi Hall.'

'The Earl of Talbott's Estate?'

'Yes. We must hurry.' Lillian opened her purse. 'I shall pay handsomely for any help you can provide.'

The man's eyes widened as he saw the notes in Lillian's hand. 'Tell you what, the landlord at the White Buck keeps a trap for customers.' He lifted a wooden flap that divided the counter from the shop. 'I'll lock up here and take you over.' He unhooked his coat from a peg.

'Do you mean we should hire his trap?' Lillian asked in astonishment.

The post office keeper raised his shoulders. 'Tis the only way you'll get out of this village before dusk falls, ma'am.'

'Are you sure there's no other way?'

'I wouldn't recommend Shanks's pony in this weather.' The man pulled on his coat and, opening the post office door, gestured to them. 'This way, ladies.'

A gust of rain blew in and covered them.

Flora looked at Lillian. There seemed nothing else to do but follow.

It was dark by the time Flora and Lillian, together with a hired driver, set out from the village. Although they sat under the shelter of the trap's roof, they were cold and huddled close for warmth. The road ahead was strewn with branches and twigs from the dripping trees. The rain still poured down, little pellets of silver in the light of the Tilley lamps attached to the trap.

'How does he know where to go in such darkness?' Flora worried as they jogged up and down over the bumpy roads.

'The landlord said his driver knew the way. We shall just have to trust he'll get us there.'

'You paid them generously,' Flora said gratefully.

'I do miss Michael's car.' Lillian smiled in the darkness. 'How quickly we've become used to motor vehicles and the like. It seems very old-fashioned to travel like this.'

'Especially when we are in a rush.' Flora felt the rain soaking up her legs. She missed Michael's car too. This was no way to travel in an emergency.

'Lillian, will we get there in time?' Flora fretted. So many things were going through her mind. Why had she ever thought of that plan to have Will sent to Adelphi Hall? His life was in danger. At this very moment, something dreadful could be happening.

'I hope so, Flora. We are doing all we can.'

'I should never have got this far without you.' Flora looked at the woman beside her and saw Michael's profile. How she missed him. How very much she needed him now.

The trap bounced and shook and the driver yelled and whipped the little pony. The rain lashed down, they were wet through, but Flora knew that none of this mattered. They had to get to Will in time.

In time for what? a frightened little voice asked inside her.

Chapter Forty

Old sins cast long, long shadows, the tall, stooped man decided as he watched the watcher. Sins that he had committed, of negligence and of cowardice. He would have fought Bertha had he been as strong in his personal life as he had been on the battlefield.

In his heart, he had always suspected that Bertha had been responsible for Constance and their son's disappearance. On his return from his tour of duty, he had searched everywhere, followed every trail, from the empty farmer's house where he had left them in safety, throughout all of Surrey. He found nothing. For years, he had looked and never given up hope but eventually a deep loneliness had engulfed him. First robbed of Amelia, then Constance and his child.

He had finally shut himself away from a cruel world that refused to give him love.

Lord William Calvey drew in a sharp breath as he thought of the day in spring of last year, when his life had begun to change. The young woman on the prow of the hill. Constance's double. Her hair, her face, her movements; even through binoculars he had known that in some way she was connected to Constance. The fog of grief and loneliness had, by some miracle, turned to curiosity, and to hope. He had sent Turner, his valet, to listen to the servants, to discover who she was. He had learned about Hilda Jones and her connection to the girl. And recently, to the young man, Will, who had fought for Kitchener's men at the Western Front.

The young soldier, whose life hovered in the balance.

William Boniface, his son.

He reached out to steady himself. The pain in his chest was much worse today. But he couldn't rest, knowing the boy was here. He had stolen downstairs and, in the absence of staff, had stood at his son's bedside, reaching out to touch his face lightly. He had Constance's beauty. Her hair, her innocence. And he was in mortal danger once more.

Lord William Calvey gripped the finial of the banister, gritting his teeth against the overpowering assault on his heart. He was no longer the youthful warrior, a leader of men. He was old and weary and the tired muscle inside ached to stop beating. But he had a duty to fulfil before he left this earth. The duty he had neglected two decades ago. He must go on.

The long, elegant sweep of Adelphi Hall's stairs was behind him, above the coat of arms that symbolized his family's proud history. He must perform this last duty of his life with valour and courage.

Standing by his son's sleeping form was his sister, his nemesis. She was about to snuff out the life that he himself had created.

His blood rushed to his temples; his lungs were crushed by an iron band as he watched her lower the pillow.

Lord William Calvey, fourth Earl of Talbott, staggered forward. He reached out, arms outstretched, as she placed the pillow over his son's face.

'We have come to see Will Boniface,' Lillian said, as they stood on the flagstones of Adelphi Hall's entrance hall. 'I am a friend of Lady Bertha—'

'I'm afraid you are too late,' the doctor interrupted, looking harassed, his spectacles slightly lop-sided on his large nose. 'I am sorry to deliver the sad news. But the death was quite unexpected. The body has just been taken away by ambulance.'

'No!' Flora gasped.

'I'm so sorry.'

'But when? How?' Lillian said as she held Flora's arm.

'Earlier in the evening. The accident was discovered when the nurse returned from her rounds.'

Flora stood, the rain dripping through her hair and onto floor. Michael's coat was wet through around her shoulders. 'But this can't be,' she murmured as tears welled over her lashes and down her cheeks. Will couldn't be dead. He just couldn't.

'What happened?' Lillian held Flora's arm tightly.

'The night nurse was absent, but for only a short while as she checked the other wards. We have just had an intake of men from Ypres and have been exceptionally busy. Lady Bertha agreed to open the servants' quarters to accommodate them. We have been stretched to our limit both there and in the house.'

'Not a reason, doctor,' argued Lillian in an icy tone, 'to neglect your patients.'

The doctor went red and removed his spectacles. Wiping them nervously with a small piece of cloth, he snapped, 'We do the very best we can.'

'Excuse me.' A soft voice interrupted.

They all turned to see an elderly man wearing a dark uniform. He stood at the foot of the stairs, slightly out of breath. His white hair grew in a silky cap over his head. He was no taller than Flora and looked directly into her eyes as though he knew her. 'Doctor, this must be a great shock for our visitors. I shall escort them upstairs to his lordship's quarters and offer them some refreshment, if you have no objection.'

Flora didn't want any refreshment. She only wanted to see Will, and to understand more about why he had died. But the doctor had said he'd been taken away by ambulance. How could that have happened? If only the car hadn't broken down and they had arrived sooner!

'I am Lord William Calvey's valet, Turner,' said the elderly man, as finally they reached the top of the house.

The long winding stairs had seemed to go on for ever. He took them through a set of great double doors onto a landing that stretched ahead into a dark space. 'These are known as the attics, but are Lord Calvey's personal rooms,' he explained.

Flora sniffed back her sobs. She still couldn't believe they had been too late to help Will. What had happened? Why didn't the doctor tell them more?

'Please follow me into the library.'

Lillian urged Flora to follow. They were both silent, but clung together, their wet clothes seeming of no importance now.

A fire burned in the big grate of the library. The huge stone hearth was engraved with the same coat-of-arms that hung above the entrance hall. Above it was a very large painting of a young soldier on horseback. He wore a scarlet tunic and on the jacket were pinned many medals. The room was lined with shelves of books and lit by gaslight. The windows had thick, purple drapes that Flora thought must have, in their day, been very luxurious.

'Allow me to take your wet clothes. I shall dry them whilst I make tea.'

Flora took off Michael's coat and Lillian her jacket. Flora had no interest in the beautiful room, nor did she feel like sitting by the fire. She wanted to go back to the doctor and ask him about Will. Was he afraid to speak up because of Lady Bertha? Flora was certain that because of her, Will was dead.

Turner gestured to the two large armchairs by the fire. 'Please make yourselves comfortable while I bring the tea.'

After he had gone, Flora sat down. A deep sob came up from her chest. 'Poor Will. What can have happened, Lillian?'

'I am so sorry, my dear.'

'Was it Lady Bertha?' Flora was angry now. 'I can't bear to think of her—'

'Don't torture yourself.'

'But I have to know what happened.'

'As soon as we are dry and rested, we shall find out more.'

'I want to see my brother. I haven't said goodbye.'

Lillian nodded, her face pale in the glow of the fire. 'I shall make certain we have all the facts. And that you are taken to see Will.'

Just then, the valet returned. He lowered a silver tray with a silver teapot, jug, cups and saucers to the large polished table.

'We're grateful for this,' said Lillian, as Turner poured the tea. 'But really, there is no time to waste.' She gazed up at the valet. 'Miss Shine must be acquainted with the facts of her brother's death.'

'I have a great deal to tell you,' the valet replied, 'after which, I am sure all your concerns will have been addressed.'

'I only want to know how my Will died,' Flora said resolutely.

He nodded, his silver hair reflected brightly in the firelight. 'Of course. And you will be relieved to know that William is very much alive.'

Flora jumped up, her tears forgotten. 'Will is alive?'

'He is at this moment resting in the servants' quarters and is with your friend, Hilda Jones. He will remain safely in her company until you are finished here and go to meet him.'

'But the doctor said—'

'He was referring to Lady Bertha and assumed you had come to see her.'

'It's Bertie who is dead?' Lillian said in a shocked voice.

'I am afraid Lady Bertha was found unconscious. We must assume that her ladyship perished whilst trying to assist Lord William who collapsed at Will's bedside. No doubt she had courageously tried to break her brother's fall, but Lord William's considerable weight must have been too much for her. She struck her head and did not recover.'

'And it was Lady Bertha who was taken away in the ambulance?'

Turner nodded. 'A tragic accident.'

Flora blinked hard, gazing at the elderly valet. The doctor had been trying to explain away the circumstances of Lady Bertha's death, not Will's. He was alive!

Chapter Forty-One

'Will is Lord William's and my mother's son,' Flora repeated, nodding her head at this confirmation of Sister Patricia's story.

Turner gave another of his quiet smiles as the fire flickered around them. 'In 1895, when Lord Guy was just six years old, your mother, Constance, was employed as his nurse. Lord William and your mother fell in love. William – your half-brother – was born before his lordship was recalled to his regiment. A loyal retainer on the estate took charge of your mother and the baby, but,' Turner hesitated, 'their whereabouts were discovered.'

'I was told my mother fled to London. She was in fear of her life.'

The valet agreed. 'I am afraid she had good reason. Even though, on Lord William's return, Lady Bertha insisted that Constance left of her own accord.'

'Did Lord William search for her?' Flora asked.

Turner cleared his throat. 'He never stopped searching. Months passed, then years. Then one day, a young woman visited Adelphi. Lord William gazed from that very window and saw you standing on the hill overlooking the house. A young man was with you—'

'Michael!' Flora exclaimed. 'I was with Michael. But how did Lord William know who I was?'

'He didn't,' Turner replied with a shrug, 'but you are, Miss Shine, the very picture of your mother. Lord William sent me to Mrs Burns to discover who you were. My investigations led me to Hilda Jones, whom you had come to visit. I learned of the good sisters of St Boniface and of their orphanage. Lord William despatched me to London and I discovered more of Hilda, and of a young man named William Boniface who had been brought to the orphanage in the year of 1897. The same year that Constance Shine and her son William had disappeared. Quite recently, my master insisted on travelling to the convent himself to learn more.'

Flora held back the tears. Had this all really happened? 'Then Lord William knows my mother is dead.'

Turner said nothing, but nodded.

'Is he very ill?'

'I'm afraid so.'

'Can I see him?'

'He is expecting you.'

Lillian embraced her. 'Have courage, my dear.'

Flora swallowed and followed Turner from the library.

Flora felt the softness of the rug beneath her feet. A figure lay in the imposing bed, dwarfed by the heavy, dark furniture of the room. A white armoire was the only relief to the heavy flock wallpaper patterned with birds, trees and winding leaves. Flora felt that she would like to throw the windows open and let in the air.

Turner gestured to a big chair padded with cushions beside the bed. The dark colours of the room seemed enhanced by the pale light of the single glass chandelier that looked slightly out of place overhead, but reflected a clear light on the bearded face of Lord William Calvey. He looked up, his eyes watery and searching, as if unable to focus.

'Is that you, Turner?' He stretched out a shaking hand.

'Yes, my lord. Miss Shine is here.'

Flora sat down on the chair. Turner nodded, then made his way out of the room and softly closed the door behind him.

'Miss Shine.' Lord William's voice was weak and raspy.

Flora leaned forward. 'It's Flora,' she told him.

'Let me see you.'

Flora stood up and leaned over the bed. An aged hand came up to her face. She felt his touch, tender and inquisitive. A tear squeezed from the corner of his pale eye.

'Thank you.'

The hand flopped down on the embroidered cover. Flora took it. Her fingers slipped gently around his. 'I'm very sorry you're ill.'

A faint smile touched his lips under the grey beard. 'And I am sorry I have left our meeting too late. But

William is safe now. Bertha is gone and I have sent Guy and Gabriella to the Italian house—' He tried to draw in breath.

'Please save your strength.' Flora could see he was very ill. A soft rattle came from the back of his throat.

'Listen.' His words were growing fainter. 'William will be well provided for. I have seen to that.'

'Did you love my mother?' Flora's tears were very close now. It was the only question she needed to ask.

'Life meant nothing to me without her,' he whispered. 'I loved her beyond words. But I let Bertha convince me that Constance had chosen to leave Adelphi—' He coughed and gripped her hand. 'But I still searched for her and the baby. Until . . .' He raised his head with an effort. 'Look, there is your mother.'

Flora's gaze followed his pale eyes to a photograph of a beautiful young woman with curling blonde hair and pale skin. The ornate frame and its subject stood beside the bed on a mahogany chest of drawers.

'My mother?' she repeated.

'Yes. You see how you are so alike?' His head fell back again. 'Soon I shall see her.'

'Lord William, I—'

His bony fingers tightened around her hand. 'You and William – look after one another. Make good lives for yourselves. Tell him he is the son I always hoped for. And that I loved him. Pray God, he will forgive me . . .'

Flora watched helplessly as he gasped a painful breath. Slowly, his head fell a little to the side on the pillow. In the silence of the room, she sat still, grasping the still-warm hand of Lord William Calvey, fourth Earl of Talbott, and master of Adelphi Hall. The man who Flora believed had truly loved her mother.

Epilogue

16 months later
21 December 1918

Flora took Michael's arm as they stood at the graveside.

Discreetly, her husband changed his weight from one foot to the other. Flora hoped he was not in discomfort. His old thigh injury, the cause of his discharge three months before the war had ended in November, was never likely to leave him. He had survived the fighting with honours. And they had both had to accept his limitations with good grace. What was an occasionally painful limb in comparison to the fatalities many of his comrades had suffered during the Macedonian campaign?

'Do you think my mother and father are together?' Flora asked her husband. Even though Michael carried an umbrella, she was grateful for the warmth of her fashionable fur hat protecting her soft blonde waves from the icy flakes of snow. Huddling close to him, she gave a wistful sigh. 'Do you think, Michael, that life goes on for ever?'

'I believe our energies are eternal,' he replied with conviction. 'I saw many things at war. I learned about human character in times of great hardship. I was privileged to be with men who stood at death's door. And though they were afraid, a force beyond this life saw them through the experience. It is remarkable to know that hope is the very fabric of our souls.'

Flora smiled in gratitude as she gazed down at the handsome grey marble headstone feathered with snow. The inscription read, 'Constance Shine and John Devonish, beloved parents of Flora and mother of William, forever loved and sadly missed.'

'I know so little about them.'

'You know they gave you life and loved you. Can any of us ask for more?'

Flora shivered lightly, lowering the spray of winter flowers to the carpet of snow at her feet. She took comfort from the fact that, in a few months, they would return to find the crocuses and daffodils there, and winter but a distant memory.

'Come along, or the party will start without us.'

Flora said a silent farewell over the tribute she had created for her parents. It was a place to remember them, to honour the past. She hoped they would have liked that.

Michael guided her over the fresh scattering of lacy flakes, to the gravel path and waiting automobile.

Flora watched her husband open the car door. He looked so very handsome in his homburg hat trimmed with navy-blue silk, a shade lighter than his heavy deep-blue overcoat and black astrakhan collar. They had both worn dark colours since the armistice a month ago, as a sign of respect for the millions of lives that had been lost in the Great War. But it had seemed even more appropriate this morning, as they drove here first, before Christmas began, to honour her departed loved ones.

'Christmas will bring very mixed feelings for people this year,' Michael said as he drove them out of the icy white cemetery.

'Yes, so many families will be in mourning.'

'Yet, we must also give thanks for what we have.' Michael took his eyes briefly from the road. 'After all, we have something very special to celebrate.'

'Let's not tell anyone till after Christmas,' Flora implored. She wanted to keep their secret until the New Year. Somehow it seemed more fitting.

'As you wish,' he agreed reluctantly, 'but it won't be easy.'

Now she looked at his deeply tanned face, marked by the fine-lined scars of combat. His green eyes gazed back at her and softened as he spoke: 'How fortunate we are, Flora, to have our life together.'

'And such a wonderful life! Who could have guessed before the war began that Will was to discover his father. And that, despite losing his arm, he would return to his trade and make such a success of it.'

Very soon the bakery came into sight. Michael stopped the car and helped her out. Flora stared at the snow-capped peaked roof of the Poplar factory. How proud she was of Will and the success he had made of his business. The bakery's tall chimneys belched smoke over the great white-and-black sign that proudly announced, 'Boniface Bakeries. Fine breads, confectioneries and speciality tarts.'

'I am certain Will is set to rival even J Lyons and Company!' exclaimed Michael, with a wry smile. 'I wonder what delicacies your brother will have prepared for the Christmas party?'

'It has to be mince pies and Christmas puddings, perhaps his individual fruit pies – those that boast his secret recipe,' Flora said hopefully, recalling her recent craving for spices. 'But, Michael, you must help me to resist. My skirts are already far too small.'

'Isn't it said that an expectant mother must eat for two?' Michael's green eyes twinkled.

Flora felt a thrill of excitement. Even now, she found it difficult to believe that she was expecting. Or that her name was no longer Miss Flora Shine, but Mrs Michael Appleby. It was only twelve weeks ago that the priest had married them at St Edmund's. She had asked for a simple service, with Dr Tapper agreeing to give her away while Lillian arranged a modest wedding breakfast at Shire Street. Will and Hilda had taken their first day off from the factory since its opening at the start of the year. Will had baked them a three-tiered wedding cake and Flora had kept the two small figures, the bride and groom created in pink and white icing, to place with her treasures: her shawl and her butterfly brooch, and the framed photograph of her mother, which had once graced the bedside of Lord William Calvey. Treasures that one day she would pass to her children as they learned the story of their heritage.

Michael gazed up into the grey afternoon sky, which showed no sign of the midnight-blue universe behind. 'I wonder if we shall see our star this Christmas?'

'I'm certain we will.' Flora slipped her arm even more tightly through his. 'I looked out for it last Christmas. I saw it and asked it to keep you safe.'

'And so it did.'

'Do you remember the match-girl?'

He smiled. 'I kept her talisman close. Though I must admit –' he paused, raising a dark eyebrow uncertainly – 'there were times in battle, very cruel times, when I was tempted to strike one and light a cigarette.' His eyes flickered faintly, dark and hard, until suddenly he seemed to see her again and his lips lifted in a quick smile. 'But my talisman was too precious to use. Instead, I thought of you. And of England. And of when we would be together again. Like this. As husband and wife.'

Flora wanted to tell him that she too had experienced those hours of deep despair. Even now, if she allowed it, a little voice inside her echoed, 'Will this bliss last?'

'Michael, sometimes I feel a little afraid. Is the war really over?'

'Of course it is, my love. The world would be mad to create another,' he assured her, gently touching her face.

'And the baby – our baby, will it be safe?'

A frown etched his forehead. His eyes looked troubled. 'What makes you ask this, Flora?'

She gave a helpless shrug. 'I remember the patients who came to Dr Tapper, the men with shell shock and dying from the poisonous gas fumes. The crippled and the maimed. I can't believe we've been so lucky to escape with a future before us.'

'Yes. I, too, feel privileged.'

After the four years of turmoil that left the world changed for ever, Flora still found it difficult not to feel guilty. All those injured men and their sad families. It was not easy to accept that peace had at last come and she and Michael were so happy.

They walked hand in hand together to the factory gates. Lord William would have been very proud of Will had he lived to see this, Flora thought with pride. Will had built a thriving business in only a year. With Hilda's help, her two friends had established a life for themselves that they could only once have dreamed of. As always, as Flora thought of Hilda, she felt protective. Hilda had been through so much and her secrets were safe with Flora. But, as if Hilda preferred to lock her past away, she never spoke of Adelphi Hall now. Or the child she had miscarried. Flora knew in her heart that Hilda would find it hard to trust again. Even so, Flora held fast to the hope that her dear friend would find love again one day.

'Hmm,' murmured Michael, distracting Flora from her thoughts, 'I can smell something good. Coconut, almond, ginger and spices—'

'Currants and sultanas,' agreed Flora, lifting her face to smell the sweet essences of the bakery. 'And jams and chocolate and perhaps just a hint of treacle.'

They laughed together and walked a little more briskly to the large factory doors. Suddenly, they flew open and Flora waved excitedly to a small, smartly dressed young woman who waited to greet them. Hilda wore a camel-coloured wool suit and grey leather boots. Her face was powdered and rouged expertly and her lips plum-red. She carried herself like the lady she had become. The wealthy young woman that Will and the bakery had made her.

Soon Flora was holding Hilda close. The unmistakeable scent of a Selfridge perfume mingled in the air around them.

'Happy Christmas, you two.' Hilda tossed back her luxurious brown waves.

Flora linked her arm through Hilda's and Michael held open the doors as they made their way through the factory. Flora had visited here many times. But today the walls were decorated with garlands of holly. Each garland was brightened by scarlet berries and words, printed in gold, that read, HAPPY CHRISTMAS FROM BONIFACE BAKERIES.

Hilda grinned. 'After the party, you must come and see the new ovens we've bought.'

'They've arrived in time for Christmas?'

'Yes, but Will still grumbles. He don't favour this automated lark.'

'Do they work?'

'Not half! The rate they cook, we'll make more profit in a day than we did in one week.'

'Hilda, you sound very business-like.'

Hilda preened, her brown eyes sparkling. 'Here, want to know a secret?'

Flora and Michael nodded.

'We've bought the old flour mill up Aldgate. It was going for a song and is big enough to supply all London's teashops and High Street bakeries.'

'Oh, Hilda, well done!'

'Clever girl,' Michael said genuinely. 'Congratulations.'

Hilda nodded, giving a little curtsey. 'I'd like Mrs Burns to see me now. Though Gracie said she don't know where Mrs Burns and Mr Leighton have gone. Even though I didn't care for them, it must've been rotten getting the chop after so many years.'

It was the first time that Hilda had spoken of Adelphi Hall in many months. Flora saw the wistful shine in her friend's eyes.

'Do you hear from Gracie often?'

'Once in a while.' Hilda gave a dismissive shrug. 'The hospital management kept her and Peter on. But they have their own staff and there ain't no call for servants. Nor ever will be now. The old earl saw to that.'

'It was for the best, Hilda, that he bequeathed Adelphi to the nation's war-wounded. There are still so many in need of care.'

Flora had never told Hilda that Turner had written to

her to say that Lord Guy, after hearing of his aunt's death, had been committed to an institution in Italy. There had been talk of violent behaviour, and Lady Gabriella had returned to England. James Forsythe, Turner had added as a postscript, had been the last to leave Adelphi Hall.

'Well, then. We'd better get a move on,' Hilda said briskly and turned on her heel.

Flora glanced at Michael. They both knew that Hilda would never forget her past.

At the end of the long corridor, Hilda pushed open another set of doors. A chorus of voices rose in the air.

'Happy Christmas!' the three hundred and twenty bakery staff cheered. Amongst them were the faces of friends and family. People they knew and loved, who had struggled through a turbulent era and had come to celebrate Will and Hilda's good fortune.

Flora's eyes filled with happy tears. Here were hers and Michael's nearest and dearest. Those who had survived the long years of war to make new lives for themselves. Mrs Bell, who was now Mrs Reg Miles, and had retired from Hailing House to live with Reg near Covent Garden. Dr Tapper, who had just returned from a well-deserved six-month stay with his sister in Bath. And her mother-in-law, Flora thought with pride, Lillian Appleby, dressed elegantly in a long, pale-green coat with a fox-fur collar, and to whom she owed so much.

There were newer faces, too. Ones she had come to love and trust. Nurse Sara Parkin, who had moved to East London to be close to Will. Their romance, Flora knew, would almost certainly end in marriage. Sally Vine, still a loyal worker for the suffrage movement. A close friend now, who eagerly awaited the post-Christmas election and the government's approval of the right for women to vote.

But in the midst of all of them stood Will. Her friend, her brother, her kindred spirit. His chef's toque hat stood high above other heads, a pleated white symbol of his expertise and skill. His spotless double-breasted white jacket, a knotted white necktie and spotless white knee-length apron. A few blond curls peeped out from under his hat, hair that had grown quickly during his recovery and hid the ugly lump by his ear. And most impressive of all was the false leather arm, fitted with a metal claw. Flora had been amazed to discover that, with this, he could perform any duty he chose to undertake.

Flora clutched Hilda's hand. They walked slowly forward into Will's embrace. The bakery staff gathered round and raised their glasses of sparkling champagne.

Flora cast her glance to Michael. Their eyes met.

'Together again for Christmas,' she acknowledged softly.

'Together again for Christmas,' every voice in the room repeated, resounding clearly with gratitude and joy.